WORMHOLE

Published by 47 North
P.O. Box 400818
Las Vegas, NV 89140

ISBN-13: 9781612184951
ISBN-10: 1612184952

WORMHOLE

BOOK THREE OF **THE RHO AGENDA**

RICHARD PHILLIPS

47N⬤RTH

For my lovely wife, Carol, who believes that finishing a task
is at least as important as starting it.

CHAPTER 1

Dr. Rodger Dalbert stepped out of the black Mercedes, almost losing his footing on the icy blacktop. His driver reached out to support him, but he waved the hand away.

"It's OK, Carl. I've got it."

"Black ice is a bitch this morning. Thought we'd slide off the road in that last roundabout."

Rodger smiled at the bigger man. "That crossed my mind."

An icy blast of wind forced Rodger to duck his head, seeking some protection behind his overcoat's high collar. Damn, it was cold. Of course, what could one expect of March in Switzerland?

On the bright side, Meyrin wasn't far outside Geneva. Rodger had always loved Geneva. Too bad his schedule wasn't going to allow him to tour more than the airport. Oh well. He'd known his personal life would suffer when he'd agreed to chair PCAST, the President's Council of Advisors on Science and Technology.

Hitching his overcoat more tightly around his neck, Rodger hurried out of the wind and into the building that would host today's conference, a review of ongoing repairs on the Large Hadron Collider, or LHC. The most ambitious science project ever undertaken by man occupied a monstrous tunnel a hundred meters below ground, just west of Lake Geneva, its twenty-seven-kilometer circumference crossing the border between France and Switzerland in multiple spots. This building sat seventy meters above a cavern in which the huge ATLAS detector enfolded LHC Point One, a beam interaction point where two super-accelerated proton beams collided…at least they did when the whole thing was working.

"Dr. Dalbert. I am so pleased you could make it."

Rodger turned to see Dr. Louis Dubois, the famed French physicist who headed the team of ATLAS scientists, approaching from across the room. The man had aged since last Rodger had seen him, at a conference in New York, long black hair flowing down over his shoulders as if he had just stepped out of a Paris salon, looking more like a twenty-something Yanni than a Nobel Prize–winning quantum theorist. Now, he wore it tied back in a greasy ponytail, as if he hadn't bothered to wash it in weeks. His eyes, which seemed to have sunk back into his face, showed a fatigue no sleep could wash away.

"The pleasure is mine, Dr. Dubois. I apologize for my tardiness. The drive took us a bit longer than expected this morning." Rodger nodded toward the reception desk. "Should I sign in?"

"No need. I have your badge right here. Now, if you'll follow me, the conference is about to begin."

Passing through a doorway, Dr. Dubois led Rodger down a short hall and then turned right into a room that was much smaller than what Rodger had expected. The conference table seated a dozen, but today only three people occupied its chairs. Dr. Dubois, with Rodger in tow, now made a grand total of five.

As Rodger seated himself, Dr. Dubois moved to the head of the table and began the obligatory introductions.

"Good morning to you all. Although most of you have already met, I will make my way around the table.

"On my left is Dr. Robert Craig, chief scientific advisor to the United Kingdom's Ministry of Defense."

The stocky redheaded man inclined his head in acknowledgment.

"Continuing in clockwise fashion, Dr. Klaus Gotlieb, scientific advisor to the European Commission."

Rodger recognized the bald, birdlike visage of the older man from an August meeting in Stockholm. Although he'd only chatted with the scientist briefly, the encounter had felt interminable.

"Next we have Dr. Pierre Boudre, senior astrophysicist for the European Space Agency."

Raising his left eyebrow ever so slightly, Rodger glanced across the table at the slender Frenchman. He had known and liked Pierre since they had collaborated on the International Space Station for NASA. The man was brilliant, and endowed with an affable personality that could charm a group of locals at a Houston coffee shop as effortlessly as society's elite at a Long Island social. But what was he doing here?

For that matter, what was Rodger doing here? What had been billed as a conference on the status of LHC repairs was clearly nothing of the sort. Five people? This wasn't enough for a round table discussion, much less a conference. And the makeup of the group. Two French, one German, a Brit, and an American. Something about the mix didn't seem right for an LHC discussion. The project was a worldwide collaboration. So what was this about?

"And on my right is Dr. Rodger Dalbert, chairman of the US President's Council of Advisors on Science and Technology.

"As for me, I am Dr. Louis Dubois, and I am the senior physicist for the ATLAS experiment. Actually, that title is a bit presumptuous, since we have over two thousand five hundred physicists from thirty-seven countries collaborating on this experiment. Let's just say ATLAS is my baby and a very big baby at that."

Rodger heard chuckles of approval from the small assemblage.

Dr. Dubois paused, then spread his hands, palms up, like a pastor about to call his flock to prayer. "It is by now obvious to you all that this is no conference on the LHC repair schedule. I apologize for the subterfuge, but I am quite certain you will soon understand why we deemed this necessary, given the current situation…one that requires deft handling to avoid undesirable media involvement."

Rodger's pulse quickened. Media involvement? Had the CERN scientists made a breakthrough? Had they finally established definitive validation for the physics standard model? But then why not just present their results? Nothing about this made any sense.

"Rather than try to explain why I called you together, let me show you."

Dr. Dubois thumbed a button on the small remote control unit he picked up from the table, bringing the flat-panel display on the far wall to life. The screen showed a myriad of colored lines twisting away from a central point, something a child might have produced given a full day with a Spirograph.

Dr. Dubois moved the mouse pointer on the screen, circling the central point.

"This is an ATLAS image from testing conducted just prior to the latest system shutdown, early on the morning of the last

Friday in November. In fact it was still Thanksgiving night over in America when this image was captured."

Rodger studied the screen. Without a detailed study of the complete data set he was at a loss to spot anything unusual in the image. Clearly the extreme energy released in the proton collisions had created a wide range of particles with different charges, spins, and masses, accounting for the assortment of paths that were displayed on the screen.

"Now this," Dr. Dubois said, bringing a new image to the display, "is ATLAS data captured this very morning."

Although the first image had been indicative of an extreme energy event, this latest image showed an order of magnitude increase in particle interactions, so many that it was difficult to discern one path from the other.

"Excuse me," Dr. Craig interjected. "Were you using the same filter and trigger settings on this last event?"

"The ATLAS instrument settings are unchanged," Dr. Dubois replied.

Something about that statement bothered Rodger, and he leaned forward. "But you said this was captured this morning. I didn't realize that you had finished repairing the damaged electromagnets and restoring vacuum to the system. Have you managed to further increase beam energies beyond ten TeV?"

Dr. Dubois leaned back in his chair. "That brings us to the issue at hand. There's really no way to put this except bluntly. There never was any electromagnet damage, or any loss of vacuum in the beam tube. That was merely a cover story issued to the press to allow us time to develop a detailed understanding of the anomaly."

Voices rose in concert, each scientist demanding attention until no single question could be discerned above the noise. Dr. Dubois waited patiently until, at last, the scientists fell silent.

"I understand you have questions, but before I yield the floor, you need to hear the rest of what I have to present, information that will answer many of the questions you have already asked, but which will certainly raise more. Now may I continue?"

Glancing quickly around the table, Dr. Dubois encountered no objection. He rose from his chair, as if he could no longer bear the tension while remaining seated.

"As I indicated in my early remarks, the testing conducted through late November produced a series of exciting results. However, during a test conducted on the morning of the last Friday in November, we noted an odd spike in measurements across the range of ATLAS instruments. I'm talking about across the inner detector, the calorimeters, the muon spectrometer, even the outer toroid magnets.

"Even more disconcerting, the readings continued after the beam channel was shut down. Naturally, we first looked for some failure in the instrumentation, faults in the electronics or in the software responsible for collecting and processing the data."

Dr. Dubois's face had taken on a pallor that could not be blamed solely on the room lights. Rodger understood why. The implications were enormous. For ATLAS to record such a powerful event with no beam firing couldn't be good.

"We shut down all further LHC testing until we could determine the exact nature of the problem. We have not done a beam firing since that day."

"Wait one minute." Dr. Gotlieb rose from his chair to point at the screen. "You said that image was collected this morning."

Dr. Dubois nodded. "That is correct. That is a slice of the data collected by the ATLAS detector this morning."

"But, if there has been no proton acceleration around the LHC, how...?"

Dr. Gotlieb's question trailed off into horrified silence.

"Jesus Christ." The words slipped from Rodger's lips like a prayer. It was worse than he had thought.

"The November Anomaly, as we have come to call it, appeared at the interaction point within ATLAS and somehow achieved a semblance of stability. We immediately scrambled to isolate the anomaly in an intense electromagnetic containment field to keep it from escaping the vacuum chamber. Since that day, we have had a team of engineers working around the clock to improve the quality of the surrounding vacuum, adding multiple redundancies to prevent electromagnetic or vacuum failure."

Dr. Dubois pulled a handkerchief from his pocket, dabbing at the beads of sweat that dampened his brow. "I think you can see why we've held this information close-hold as the best minds on the program struggled to understand exactly what has happened."

"But how is that possible?" asked Dr. Boudre. "Admittedly I'm an astrophysicist rather than a quantum specialist, but even the energies provided by LHC collisions have far too small a probability cross section to allow for stable formation of some sort of micro black hole. Besides, Hawking radiation should dissipate any black hole with a mass of less than two hundred thousand kilograms in under a second. A micro black hole such as yours should have evaporated in a tiny fraction of that time."

"We don't think that's what it is."

"You don't think?" Dr. Gotlieb sputtered.

Rodger realized that he had also risen to his feet, although he found himself leaning on the table for support.

"And after three months of secret study, what have you learned?"

Dr. Dubois started to speak, paused, then began again. "The anomaly violates all accepted theory. We have pored over every paper published in the last fifty years that could remotely have bearing on this matter and have only found one that seems to describe what we are seeing. It's a theoretical treatise titled 'Quasi-Stable Quantum Singularities,' published three years ago."

"And what does the physicist who wrote the paper have to say about your anomaly?" Rodger pressed.

"I don't know. We haven't spoken to him."

"What? Why the hell not?" Dr. Craig bellowed.

"Gentlemen, please sit back down. Thank you. I know you are all wondering why I have gathered you here instead of taking this directly to the world's governing bodies. What we have here is something entirely beyond our current understanding of physics, something that for now appears quasi-stable. It has the potential to transform into something far more dangerous, possibly even a black hole that would consume our planet. If a government reacted to this out of fear, you can imagine what they might try."

The table jumped as Dr. Craig's fist slammed its surface. "They'll nuke the bloody hell out of your goddamned science experiment. Should have been done before now."

Rodger understood Dr. Craig's anger. But all he could do was lean back in his chair, too stunned to respond.

Dr. Dubois leaned forward. "And if they do that, they will probably bring about the disaster that we all fear. According to our analysis of the equations in the paper I mentioned, an anomaly of this type occupies an inflection point between a number of more stable states, most of which are unpleasant. Even a relatively minor perturbation could tip it from its perch, sweeping away humanity in an avalanche of destruction.

"So we have determined that you four, as respected scientific representatives of the key governments of the European Union, Great Britain, and the United States, are best suited to bring this knowledge to your political leadership. After those governments have absorbed the facts, they can come to consensus on how best to proceed."

Dr. Craig's face had acquired a purple cast. "You still haven't answered my question. Why haven't you contacted the physicist who wrote the damned paper?"

"Because, until now, we haven't been able to." Dr. Dubois looked directly at Rodger. "We'll need the help of the American government to reach him."

Rodger inhaled softly. "And why is that?"

"Because he's incarcerated in an American prison. The physicist to whom I refer is the famous Dr. Donald R. Stephenson."

CHAPTER 2

The foot caught Mark just below the solar plexus, knocking the wind from his body even as he twisted to avoid the blow. Pain exploded in his gut, but Mark channeled it, storing it away for later processing. Right now, he just needed to survive.

A funny thought. Only moments earlier, Mark had been focused on winning this fight. Now, as blood and sweat blurred his vision and lack of breath sapped his strength, that goal seemed a distant dream. Jack Gregory was taking him apart with an ease that defied belief.

Marshaling all his neurally enhanced speed, Mark swung his body into a spinning side kick that should have hurled his tormentor across the room. Instead he felt himself lifted, propelled by his own momentum in a judo flip that slammed his back into the floor and sent white flashes dancing across his vision. Blinded and stunned, Mark whipped his legs around, somehow managing to land back on his feet and stay there, even though his knees felt like rubber.

"Enough."

Jack's voice sounded distant, as if it came from one of those tin-can-and-string telephones that he'd made with Heather and Jen when they were kids.

"That's enough for this session," Jack continued, stepping forward to slap him smartly on the back. "Good workout."

A small titter of laughter from across the room caused Mark to glance toward his sister. "Seriously, Mark," Jen managed to get out between chortles. "There were a couple of times I thought you had him at your mercy."

Struggling to regain enough breath for a sharp retort, Mark finally abandoned the attempt.

"That's OK, Jennifer," Jack said. "Your turn."

As Mark stumbled to a seat beside Heather, he managed a smile. After suffering a major-league ass-whipping, it was nice to have something to look forward to.

The ten weeks that Mark, Jennifer, and Heather had spent at the Frazier hacienda had been the most difficult of their lives. Mark didn't know what he had expected, but this hadn't been it. Jack and Janet had immersed the three friends in a training program more intense than any imagined by the CIA. For twenty hours each day they had oscillated between physical training, weapons training, martial arts training, and a variety of classroom work on the how-tos of clandestine operations.

How to spot a tail. How to lose a tail. How and whom to bribe. How to establish a base of operations in continental Europe, the US, Britain, India, Pakistan, Africa, Russia, Latin America, China. How to blend into societies where you should stand out. How to purchase illegal weapons, documents, and equipment. And just when they thought it couldn't get any tougher, Jack ratcheted up the intensity. It was exciting, but it also kept Mark too busy and tired to worry much about other things, like what his parents must be going through.

Even though Jack knew about the neural enhancements they had received on the Bandolier Ship, he wanted to find out their limits. More than that, Mark knew that Jack wanted *them* to discover their limits.

Even though Mark loved that they were learning things very few people would ever know, he felt as if they would have made a break for freedom if it hadn't been for the weekends.

Sci-Fi Saturdays and Sundays is what they'd come to call them, a sequence of *Twilight Zone* episodes driven by Jack's desire to learn everything about the Bandolier Ship, its technologies, its agenda, and what it had done and was still doing to his three trainees. The lab sessions ranged from fascinating to downright spooky.

Recently Jack had them working in total darkness, letting their minds convert sound to images, a form of echolocation that produced imagery of their surroundings: the louder the noise, the brighter the resultant mental pictures.

Luckily, Friday and Saturday nights had been reserved for rest and relaxation, local R & R Janet called it. On those nights they could almost be mistaken for a family, Jack and Janet taking them to San Javier to stroll through the town, to stop for dinner over some Bolivian beers, to laugh and talk.

One thing Jack had said during their training sessions had imprinted itself on Mark's brain. "This world will try to beat you down. Only laughter can counteract that. Laughter is ammunition. Resupply often."

Mark remembered the sound of Janet's throaty laughter echoing through the room at that remark, driving the point home. But since the birth of their baby, Robby, eight weeks ago, Jack had been their principal trainer.

Even the childbirth had been incorporated into their training. Yachay, the indigenous midwife, had managed the delivery, assisted by Mark, Jennifer, and Heather. The intensity of the experience had branded its details into his mind's eye.

Janet had endured an agonizing eighteen hours of labor as Jack sat beside her, holding her hand and guiding her through a variation on Lamaze breathing exercises. A credit to her self-discipline, Janet never whimpered or cried out, although the sweat beaded on her forehead, forming tiny rivulets that Jack wiped away with a damp cloth.

As for Mark, Jen, and Heather, they had been kept busy doing whatever the Quechua midwife demanded. When the baby finally came, it had been Mark who assisted with cutting and tying off the umbilical cord, but not before a panicked few moments of wondering if the baby boy would start breathing. Although Mark had thought all new babies cried as a part of taking that first breath, this one hadn't made a sound. Only a sharp word from Yachay had snapped him out of his frozen state and gotten him moving as she directed.

By the time they had finished all the post-birthing tasks, the three young friends hadn't even bothered to eat, dragging themselves off to their rooms for rest and recovery, more bone tired than at any other time in their training.

"Heather, you're up."

Jack's words brought Mark out of his reverie as Heather stepped forward and Jennifer stumbled onto the seat beside him, her breath coming in ragged gasps. Although she hadn't been bloodied, she was clearly teetering on the edge of muscle failure.

Every Friday was evaluation day, during which Jack tested their mastery of the training they had received thus far. Mark knew one thing for certain: never again would he think TGIF. Fridays flat-out sucked.

Suddenly Mark's attention shifted to the center of the padded mat that covered the small gym's floor. One of Heather's punches had managed to penetrate Jack's defenses, her small fist striking his chin a grazing blow. As the two combatants shifted stance, Mark caught a glimpse of Heather's eyes. They'd turned milky white.

Shit. She'd gone deep, fighting Jack in the now as her savant mind gazed into the future.

Once again she lashed out, but this time Jack slipped the blow. For the briefest of moments, Mark thought Jack's eyes glinted red. Then, as Heather whirled into an axe kick, Jack chopped her sharply in the solar plexus, sending the air whooshing from her lungs in one great burst. Heather doubled over on the mat, then rolled on her side, simultaneously struggling to draw breath and rise to her feet—for the moment, failing to do either.

As Mark and Jennifer started to move, Jack's stern gaze sent them back to their seats. As he stood above Heather, watching her intently, Jack made no move to assist her. A month ago Mark would have been unable to contain his anger. Now it all made sense. For Jack to baby any one of them would be to dishonor that person. Before they'd started training, Jack and Janet had briefed them on the rigors of the program they would endure, and they had each consented. Too late now to back out.

With a Herculean effort, Heather raised herself from the floor, once again moving into a ready position.

"Excellent." Jack said. He motioned to Mark and Jennifer. "Everyone have a seat out here on the mat."

As they complied, Jack walked to a corner closet, retrieved a box from the shelf, and then seated himself on the mat directly in front of Heather.

"You have a unique ability," he said to her. "All of you share various talents as a result of the neural augmentation you received from the Bandolier Ship headbands. But your minds have their own natural strengths and preferences.

"Heather, I've watched you play chess. There's not a person in the world that can beat you, certainly no computer can. You see all the possibilities and know what is most likely to happen from any setup. It's why you were able to hit me just now."

Jack paused to remove a chess set from the box, setting it on the floor between them. Mark watched closely as Jack removed several pieces, arranging them into an endgame in which each side had four pieces.

White had its king trapped on the first row by the black rook and black had its king similarly limited to movement on the eighth row. Black had another rook and pawn while white had a queen and pawn remaining.

Jack spun the board so that Heather played white.

"What are the odds white wins?" he asked.

"Whose move?" Heather asked.

"White."

"Checkmate in one move."

"What are the odds of white winning?"

"One hundred percent," Heather said.

"Show me."

Mark saw Heather glance at him and shrug, as if to say, *This is too easy.* "If you insist."

As she reached for the white queen, her hand accidently touched the white pawn. Heather froze, then reached for the queen.

"You touched the pawn. By rule, you must move it." Jack grinned.

"Accidental touches don't count."

"You touched the pawn and lingered. That counts as an intentional touch."

Heather frowned. Mark could tell she was confused about what had just happened. A winning move had just become a losing move. She had reached for the queen, but something had distracted her. Mark saw a light dawn as she swung toward her friend.

"Jennifer!"

Jack laughed. "Before you get angry with Jennifer, I want you all to think about what just happened here. The most talented savant mind on the planet just calculated the odds of winning a simple chess endgame at 100 percent, an absolute certainty. But she lost. Why?

"I prearranged for Jennifer to nudge Heather's subconscious when she least expected such interference, forcing her to accidentally bump the white pawn. I did it to teach you the most important lesson you'll ever get. Before I let you off early today, I want to burn this into your minds.

"Don't trust anyone, not even your best friends. Love them, but never trust them completely. At critical times, they can be influenced to do things you don't want. Mark would throw away his life to save Heather, even though she'd hate him for it. Heather would do the same for him. In your own ways you would all betray each other, just like Jennifer betrayed Heather in this little game."

Mark's face clouded. "Wait just a minute! Jennifer didn't betray her."

"No," Jennifer said, giving Mark a thankful look. "I didn't."

"Oh, you had good reason," Jack continued. "I manipulated you by telling you it was a critical part of the lesson I'm teaching, but you still betrayed her by making her lose. Given the right reasons you would all do the same. Remember it.

"And remember this. No victory is certain. No situation is hopeless. When you find yourselves in a hopeless situation, change the rules."

"You mean cheat," Mark said.

Jack grinned. "Like the devil himself."

CHAPTER 3

President Leonard Jackson stared across the conference table at Dr. Rodger Dalbert, the scientist meeting his gaze with an unflinching calm that belied the nature of the briefing he had just presented. No one on the National Security Council spoke, an event almost as unusual as the subject of the briefing. But maybe it was a sign that they'd begun to get used to his leadership style. At least, that's how he chose to interpret it.

"So let me get this straight," President Jackson said. "Dr. Stephenson rejected our request for his help in return for my commuting his sentence to time already served."

"That is correct. He wants a full pardon, a public apology from you, as president of the United States, for the grievous errors that resulted in his imprisonment, and full reinstatement of his security clearance. In addition he wants to be appointed special scientific envoy to CERN and to be placed in charge of the November Anomaly Project."

The secretary of state hissed. "Pretentious bastard."

President Jackson held up his hand to quiet the expressions of outrage that echoed around the table.

"There's one other thing," Dr. Dalbert continued, fanning out several pages filled with scribbled notes. "You may recall that on my initial visit to Dr. Stephenson's jail cell a week ago, I left him with a number of papers describing the measurements taken by the ATLAS detector. At the end of my subsequent visit yesterday, after making all his demands, Dr. Stephenson handed me these pages filled with handwritten equations."

"And?" the president asked.

"And they are nothing short of incredible. I have run these by the top scientists on the ATLAS program and they were stunned. Given rudimentary information and with only pencil and paper, Dr. Stephenson produced a mathematical model of the anomaly that is far more accurate than the project physicists have been able to generate using all their supercomputer simulations. And he did it in less than a week."

The president leaned forward so that his palms pressed flat on the table. "Are you going to tell us what the paper predicts?"

"The anomaly is gradually spiraling into instability." Dr. Dalbert took a deep breath. "We have nine months, two weeks, and three days until it reaches the tipping point."

"Which means?"

"Game over."

CHAPTER 4

His human eye lay dead in its socket alongside its artificial partner, the impenetrable darkness rendering both of them as useless as his missing lower extremities. But his nose still worked.
The stagnant air concentrated the stench around the freshly used
camp toilet so powerfully he could taste it.

Raul tied the plastic baggy full of his steaming business
and tossed it onto a heap of its mates, piled beside the nonop-
erational disposal bin. If not for the huge stash of Meals Ready
to Eat, water, and supplies that Dr. Stephenson had stored
in this secret section of the Rho Ship, Raul would have perished long ago. Lord knew he had tried to kill himself, but the
damned nanites that populated his bloodstream wouldn't per-
mit it, repairing each self-inflicted wound almost as quickly as
he had carved it into his flesh. And starvation was out of the
question.

The nanites required energy, and when they were denied food, they took fuel from his body tissue, using that energy to keep him alive. The process slowly depleted his body, but the nanite-augmented food and water cravings consumed him.

Once Raul realized he didn't possess the will to starve himself, he'd given up, resigning himself to this dark hell in which Dr. Stephenson had imprisoned him. But his busy mind refused to allow him to just lie there.

Instead he set about exploring every square centimeter of the large chamber by touch. Blindly pulling himself along, he felt his way along conduits and cables, and over every piece of alien equipment. Only a few months ago, with the power of his connection to the starship's neural network, every piece of this stuff had been as much a part of him as his own hands and arms. Now the ship was dead, drained of power during Stephenson's hijacking of Raul's attempt to create a transitory gravitational gateway.

Why had Stephenson done it? At first Raul had thought it was punishment for his challenge to Stephenson's authority. But that made no sense. Dr. Stephenson never did anything that didn't fit into some grand scheme. Yet what benefit could come from completely draining the Rho Ship's power reserves?

Raul's mind fingered the questions like worry beads, sliding them back and forth in his brain until his head throbbed with a dull heat. If only he could access the ship's neural net he could figure it out. Not a likely scenario. The last time he had felt a connection had been the moment he accessed the ship's maintenance protocol to shut down Stephenson's program. But he'd been just a moment too late. As the override kicked in, Raul had felt his connection to the Rho Ship die.

Even if the maintenance protocol had succeeded in shutting down the pathways to the remaining power cells, it left Raul no way to restore those channels. It wouldn't take much power to do it, but he didn't even have a watch battery. Just some cases of MREs, a few hundred gallons of distilled water, and a growing pile of festering shit bags.

Festering shit bags. The thought caught in his fevered mind like an annoying song he couldn't get out of his head.

Festering…shit.

Raul stiffened. Methane gas.

If he'd still had legs Raul would have kicked himself. He had wasted so much time wallowing in self-pity, and the dark-induced madness gnawing at his mind had made lucid moments a rarity. All the while he had had potential power sources lying all around him. Not just methane either. Every MRE came with its own flameless heating pouch. All he had to do was add water to the mixture of magnesium, dust, and salt and in seconds it was hot enough to blister his hands. If he stuck the pouch back in the box along with the MRE, in ten minutes he was rewarded with a hot meal. It was his one remaining luxury.

The MREs also contained matches and paper. But the brief light the matches provided merely tormented his biological eye. The darkness was better than that. And even though his ship's life support system survived in some sort of minimal mode, he doubted it could deal with the smoke of a little campfire. The thought of coughing his lungs out while the nanites kept him alive provided all the incentive he needed to avoid that scenario.

Raul's brain roiled, churning the possibilities into a sloppy hope soup. He could generate heat. Electricity was another matter. For that he needed a rudimentary generator. For that he needed magnets, wire, and a host of other parts. Tools wouldn't be a problem, not with the virtual machine shop Dr. Stephenson had created in here over his decades of trying to make basic repairs. And even though they'd been ignored after Raul achieved his linkage with the Rho Ship's neural net and gained control of the stasis field, those tools now gave him a lifeline. And though he couldn't access the neural net, that didn't mean he'd forgotten everything from his previous linkage. Raul knew this ship well enough to figure out how to use those tools to make what he needed.

It would just take time. And time was something he had in abundance.

CHAPTER 5

Janet's slender fingers slid along the back of Mark's neck, her deli-cate touch sending shivers of pleasure down his spine. His own hand responded, fingertips barely touching the hollow of her back, lingering there, the nerves so alert that it seemed each con-tact produced tiny sparks from her skin to his. He felt her ear touch his, the scent of her bare throat filling his nostrils.

Her body moved against his in perfect rhythm, the feel of her full breasts against his chest robbing him of whatever self-control he still retained. Janet's skin shone with sweat in the dim light and her breath came in small pants of exertion, barely audible above Mark's thundering heart. Her bare right leg encircled him and her body swayed. As Mark's body writhed within her entangling limbs, Janet's back arched until only his right arm kept her from falling. Then, in a thunderous, climactic crescendo, it ended.

Hearing shouts of approval echo across the room, Mark raised his head to see Jennifer and Heather applauding vigorously.

Even Jack nodded his appreciation. "Now that's how the tango is supposed to be danced."

"Wonderfully done," Janet said as Mark pulled her back to her feet. Turning to Jennifer and Heather, she continued. "You've practiced these dances many times. Now I want you to play that dance back in those perfect little memories of yours. Then, one at a time, I will call you up. I want each of you to dance with Mark, exactly as I did."

"With Mark?" Jennifer sputtered.

"Exactly as I did," Janet continued. "Everything we do here has a purpose. We've been teaching you all the Latin and classical ballroom dances because if you can dance them with abandon, you can dance anything. In the world of which you are now a part, dancing will open a surprising number of doors for you. But first, you must look like you're having fun and you must be convincing. People should see you dance and wish they were your partner."

Janet cast a wicked smile at Mark that made him look away. "Just now, I believe you were having fun. I want you to repeat that with Jennifer, then Heather. And I better not notice any difference, or it's going to be a very, very long night."

CHAPTER 6

Jennifer sat on the grass, flanked by Mark and Heather, watching the glorious sunset paint the western sky in steadily darkening shades of magenta and purple. Less than a hundred yards up the hill behind them, Janet played with Robby as Jack leaned over the smoking barbeque grill.

"I'm worried about Mom and Dad." Jennifer surprised herself by saying what she'd been thinking.

Beside her, Heather tensed. "I know. It's driving me crazy. I've been so homesick. But for them…not to know we're even alive. It gives me nightmares."

Mark glanced over his shoulder, a quick look to see if Jack and Janet remained out of earshot. "We always talk about it, but we never do anything."

"Jack told us not to," Heather replied.

"We never should have asked him," Jennifer said. "We knew what he'd say."

"He's right, you know."

"I don't. Not anymore."

"Me either," said Mark. "It's been too long."

Jennifer felt a lump rise in her throat, leaving her voice husky. "I'm just so scared. If we do it, hack our way onto their laptops, leave them a message. It might get them killed. It might give away our location."

"And if we don't?"

"That scares me too." Jennifer wiped a tear from her cheek. "How long can they go on, not knowing we're OK?"

Lately, images of her mom sobbing inconsolably had begun crawling through her mind.

A shrill whistle from the direction of the house cut off the conversation.

"Guess dinner's ready," Mark said, rising to his feet. "Don't let Jack see you crying."

"Wasn't planning to."

As they walked up the hill toward the waiting dinner, Jennifer pulled forth the required memories, letting her mask settle in place. As hard as it was, the decision could be put off for a while longer.

In the meantime, they'd gut it out and be the people Jack and Janet expected them to be.

CHAPTER 7

A curly wisp of smoke wafted up from the table. An acrid odor emanated from the soldering iron and irritated Heather's nose, causing it to crinkle as she sniffed away the oncoming sneeze.

"Waiting on you, Mark." Jennifer's jibe barely registered, though, as Mark remained focused on bridging the last delicate trace.

Setting the iron back in its spring stand, Mark leaned over and snapped the plastic cover in place. "That's it."

He reached across the laptop, plugging the dongle into the forward USB port.

"It hasn't cooled," Jennifer said. "You'll break it!"

"Trust me."

"You said that last week," Heather said, although she had considerably more faith in his electrical craftsmanship than her comment indicated.

"Power spike. Not my fault."

Heather laughed. "OK. OK. Let's just finish this off and test it."

Despite the banter, she could see Mark was excited. They all were. If this worked, it marked a revolution in the capabilities of their computer lab, intelligence center, or whatever they chose to call the thatch-roofed outbuilding that housed the Frazier computer and communications complex. They had already modified the circuit boards in all the laptops to add built-in subspace receiver transmitters, but this would enable them to add subspace communications capabilities to any computer, just by plugging in a small USB device.

Heather let her gaze wander the room, pausing at the sealed door leading into the adjacent "clean room." It represented the culmination of their efforts these last three months. Still, as amazing as their electronics work had become, it only formed a part of Jack's sci-fi weekends, the other part being their ongoing headset exploration of their starship's data banks.

When they'd arrived at the Frazier hacienda, it had been mid-January, Bolivian summer. They hadn't recognized the pressure cooker in which they were about to be immersed. To be fair, Jack and Janet had clearly laid out the training program, and Mark, Jen, and Heather had all volunteered. Knowing what she knew now, she would still have done it…just not with the same degree of enthusiasm.

She still missed her parents, and worried about them constantly. Only fear that contact would place them in danger had prevented communication, that and the fact that Jack had strictly forbidden it. But Heather's visions had taken on a darker tone of late, bringing her to the brink of a decision that could knock Mark, Jen, and herself from this perch they had worked so hard to attain. Had it been any other topic, she would have consulted

Jack and Janet. But not this. It was too important, too personal. Mark and Jennifer were the only ones she would divulge her fears to. But not yet. Not while hope remained.

"Helloooo. Anyone home in there?" Mark nudged her.

"What? Oh, sorry. Lost in thought."

"Let's fire it up."

Jennifer opened the laptop, took a deep breath, and pressed the power button. The Windows logo replaced the black-and-white BIOS screen. From her position behind and to the right of Jennifer, Heather found the 7,204 rpm drive noise disconcerting; still, six hundredths of a percent's variance from the drive spec was well within tolerance: nothing to worry about. Though Heather succeeded in banishing the small worry from her thoughts, her mind replaced it with another. Would the USB oscillating circuit deliver the required performance? It would if the printed circuit thin film resistors performed within tolerance. Christ. Chinese components.

"So far so good," Jen said. "Now let's see if our super Wi-Fi dongle works."

Mark cracked his knuckles. "After all that effort, it better."

"It will." Heather hoped she sounded more confident than she felt. A probability of 73.65847 percent was far from a certainty.

Jen began rattling off the steps from her mental checklist.

"Entering coordinate. Identifying available networks. Selecting network. Sniffing packets...verified. Inserting TCP packets...verifying responses." Heather found herself grinning even as Jennifer thrust her hands into the air. "Yes!"

Smacking Mark's hand in a quick series of high fives, Heather finally released the breath she'd been holding.

Mark leaned down for a closer look at the display. "You know what this means? Our bag of tricks just got a hell of a lot lighter."

"Plug 'n play."

Mark placed his hand on Jen's left shoulder. "It's dinnertime. Let's shut it down. We've got a long night ahead."

The vision tugged at the mind curtain Heather closed to block it. Mark had no idea how right he was.

CHAPTER 8

"Are you ready for this?" Jack's voice held an edge nobody without the neural augmentations Heather, Mark, and Jen enjoyed could have detected.

"Why shouldn't we be?" Mark replied. "We've been linking with the Bandolier Ship headsets every week."

"True, but up until now you've only browsed the ship's unprotected data banks. Today, I'm going to ask more of you."

"Such as?"

Jack turned away to stare out the window that filled most of the living room's western wall. For perhaps a minute he remained perfectly still, his lithe form silhouetted against the sunlit hills that rolled away from the ranch house to the horizon. When he turned once more to face them, his face formed an unreadable mask.

"Fair enough. It's time Janet and I made you aware of our concerns." He pointed toward the comfortable chairs and couches arranged around the low coffee table.

Heather sat down, as did Mark and Jen. For some time now she'd been expecting this talk. She'd seen it coming in her visions, different versions, but always the same topic. Suspicious thoughts hovered around Jack and Janet like ghostly halos whenever they mentioned the Bandolier Ship or the four alien headsets.

As if on cue, Janet entered from the kitchen and paused to set little Robby in the baby rocker, winding the handle several times and setting it in motion before sliding onto the love seat. Jack settled in beside her.

Heather glanced at the baby. Robby already bore a striking resemblance to his father, especially in the eyes. But there was something else about the child that both fascinated and unnerved her. For one thing, the little boy never cried. Whenever Heather looked into those eyes, the feeling he was studying her rose within, as though she were a zoo animal on the far side of safety glass. Heather knew it was ridiculous to think this way about a three-month-old, but as she looked into those eyes, she couldn't shake the feeling.

Jack's voice brought her out of her reverie. "Throughout your training here, we've made it clear that everything we have you do is voluntary. And although you've done everything Janet and I have asked of you, you can't have helped noticing a certain amount of distrust on our part. It's time for you to know just how strong that distrust is."

Having Jack say aloud what she'd long suspected slapped Heather in the face as if he'd struck her with his open hand. From the silence that hung in the air, she knew Mark and Jennifer felt the shock just as strongly. For several long moments Jack let it hang there, allowing his words to achieve their full emotional impact.

"Don't get me wrong. You're the finest group of young people I've ever known. What Janet and I don't trust is the agenda of the starship that altered you."

"Wait just a second!" Jen burst out. "The Rho Ship's the bad one."

"Damn right," Mark agreed. "And it's not like the starship chose us. It was just pure dumb luck that we stumbled onto it and tried on the headsets."

"Was it?" Janet asked. "You know the odds that the wind catches your model plane and drops it down that canyon, right into the starship cavern?"

"Two chances in 3,423,851." The words tumbled from Heather's lips before she caught herself.

A smile lit Janet's beautiful face. "Pretty slim odds."

Mark shrugged. "Shit happens."

"True," said Jack. "But this might not be one of those times. Remember when I told you not to trust anyone completely, not even each other? Think about the agendas in play here. You've seen what your starship wanted to show you about its enemies. That doesn't mean your Bandolier Ship has Earth's best interests at heart. We think it's trying to stop whatever the creators of the Rho Ship had in mind, but we don't really know the Bandolier Ship's original mission."

Janet shifted to face Mark across the table. "And we don't know why you were each drawn to a particular headset. Although all of you have been enhanced across the board, you each have special skills that are significantly different. Does that mean the headsets have certain crew positions to fill on the ship? Heather's ability to calculate probable outcomes and evaluate strategies implies a command function. Mark, your physical and language enhancements would seem to fill a security officer role, while Jen's computer expertise and ability to influence the thoughts of others could fill a communications and science officer function. We also know that once a headset attunes with someone, nobody else can use it while the original user still lives."

Heather shook her head. "I've considered all that. Too many holes in the logic. What about the fourth headset? As far as we know, only two people have attuned with it, the Rag Man and El Chupacabra. Hardly starship crew candidates."

"But with similar natures," said Jack.

Jennifer shook her head "Ridiculous. A homicidal maniac crew position?"

Janet reached out, letting her fingers brush Robby's curly brown hair as he rocked slowly back and forth. "It's more common than you imagine. In the Soviet Union, it was standard procedure to place a political officer with every unit to ensure loyalty to the motherland. The Nazis used the Gestapo in a similar role. In Saudi Arabia, a volunteer clerical police force called the mutawa'ah enforce sharia law. Throughout the Middle East, religious police perform similar functions throughout society."

"But not in Western governments," Mark said.

"Don't kid yourself. Even the US has its enforcers of politically correct thought. Whether they are internal security, internal affairs, internal revenue, or even some of the media, their mission is to make people toe the line. They wield special powers that inspire fear."

"It doesn't make them the Rag Man," Heather interjected.

"No. But they'll do whatever it takes to force people to conform. That kind of power attracts zealots and fanatics."

"So you think we're under some sort of alien influence?" Heather asked.

Jack shook his head. "If I thought that, I wouldn't be training you. But we need to know everything we can about the intentions of both ships' creators. We also need to learn everything we can about their technology. You've already done amazing work in this area, but we need to delve deeper. How do their weapons work? Not just the starship weapons, but personal weapons as well. What other technologies are hidden away? In the case of your Bandolier Ship, we have an in, the headsets. But that means you're going to have to breach the ship's internal security mechanisms and get access to the restricted parts of its computing systems."

"You think I haven't tried?" Jen asked. "Those systems are interwoven with complex fractal patterns that I haven't even come close to cracking."

"You'll need to work together. While you have the headsets on you're all linked to the ship and to each other. You share imagery, even thoughts. By focusing your combined talents on cracking one barrier at a time, you'll have a chance."

Heather exchanged fleeting glances with Mark and Jennifer before responding. "The ship isn't stupid. Its computing systems function as a fully integrated expert system, possibly even an AI. It's bound to have defenses against what we'll be trying. Some of those might not be as passive as firewalls and encryption. It may lock us out completely, or worse."

Jack nodded. "There is that risk. It's why Janet and I have had you exploring the other systems through your headsets these last few weeks, letting you enhance your familiarity with the ship's artificial intelligence in a nonaggressive manner. It's why you'll need to proceed with extreme caution, Jennifer's skill guided by your mind and by Mark's link to the security systems. I'm counting on you to find a path through those defenses."

Mark inhaled deeply, cracking his knuckles as he breathed out. "Sounds interesting. I'm game."

"Me too," added Jennifer.

Feeling all eyes on her, Heather centered, thrusting aside a series of disconcerting visions that sought to pull her into the deep.

"Let's do it."

CHAPTER 9

After dinner, Heather took her turn cleaning dishes before walking through the open alcove onto the veranda. It was a beautiful fall evening, temperature hovering in the high seventies, with just enough breeze to make the humidity comfortable.

Although Sunday was usually the day set aside for their headset exploration of the Bandolier starship, Jack had decided it was time to change up the routine. Even though the headsets worked through a subspace link that was undetectable by earthly technology and Dr. Stephenson was rotting in an American prison cell, predictable patterns of behavior violated Jack's sense of security. But Heather detected something else in Jack's demeanor, an eagerness she had never before observed.

Slipping into a wicker chair, Heather inclined her head toward Mark and Jen, each occupying a similar chair, all three arranged around a low wrought iron table. In the center of the table, an open aluminum case held the four alien headbands, the area dimly illuminated by an oil hurricane lamp that hung suspended from a support beam.

Jack leaned against the wall, his eyes studying the full moon that shed almost as much light as the lamp itself. The scene reminded Heather of a séance more than a serious scientific experiment. But then, in a strange way, maybe that's what it was.

"You ready?" Jack asked, his strange eyes locking with hers.

"Yes."

"Good." Jack pulled up a wooden stool, seating himself where he could see the faces of all three of his trainees. "Because tonight you're going up against the artificial intelligence controlling the Bandolier Ship. Your mission is to gain access to the ship's restricted data banks. In order to make that happen, you'll have to convince the ship's artificial intelligence that you are truly the crew and not just candidates that have attuned to the headsets."

"And how do we do that?" Jennifer asked.

"That's something you'll have to figure out together once you're all linked in. Don't rush it. Heather's intuition should guide you, but she won't be able to do it alone. The ship must fully accept you all."

"And if something goes wrong?" Mark asked.

"I'll be here watching you. If I think you're in trouble, I'll remove the headsets. But remember, you have to retain control of your own minds. Don't lose your way back."

Heather reached for the metal case. The four headsets lay nestled in its dark foam-padded interior, each exactly like its mates, the strange metal picking up the dancing lamplight so photons seemed to bead up and crawl along its surface. Wasn't it odd how her hand was drawn only to the one she recognized as her own?

Lifting the light band from its resting place, Heather leaned back, letting Jennifer and Mark select their own. Then, as their eyes met, they all slid the bands up over their temples.

As the small nubs at the ends of Heather's headband touched her head, they elongated, the massaging pulse spreading through her body as each sought its optimum position. Then the world dissolved.

She was on the starship, her virtual self standing on the command deck, its smoothly curved walls, ceiling, and floor as beautiful as she remembered. Glancing to her right and left, she saw Jennifer and Mark settle into their crew couches, the translucent material flowing around them to cushion their bodies, as if they were preparing for takeoff.

Jennifer had been the first to discover this unique capability available to wearers of the starship's headbands, something they had come to call the Avatar Projection. If they imagined themselves physically on the starship, the interaction between the ship's computer and their own enhanced minds created the impression that they were physically there. It was an illusion, but it sure as hell felt real, far more real than a dream, so real that she could reach out and touch things, including Mark and Jennifer.

While they were in the Avatar Projection, all their senses worked. Not just when they were roaming the ship either. From the first summer they'd spent exploring their Bandolier Ship, they'd known how to have it surround them with sights and sounds of other places and scenes, like Bora Bora or the starship's arrival in this solar system. But now when the ship presented sensory experiences, it went far beyond mere sounds and scenery. This was the full monty.

The closest thing she'd seen to this was the dream implants in the movie *Total Recall*, which provided all the neural stimulation of a real experience. It played out in such detail that it surpassed Heather's visions of the future, making it hard to remember she wasn't physically there. That was the reason Jack had cautioned them against losing their way back.

Heather settled into her own command couch, opening her mind to the touch of Mark's and Jennifer's. They were all there sharing the same link—to varying degrees, sharing the same thoughts. It was another aspect of exploring the ship's neural linkages that had, at first, startled Heather. Jennifer had been the one most familiar with the experience, having used a version of the ability on other people for several months.

But this went well beyond what Jennifer could do. If they weren't careful, they found each other sharing their innermost thoughts and feelings, something that went beyond frightening to downright embarrassing. After the first experience, Heather had de-linked, refusing to wear the headset again unless she did so alone. Only Jack's insistence that they retry the experiment had overcome her resistance.

In a series of tentative practice sessions, Heather, Mark and Jen gradually learned to establish mental barriers that effectively shielded parts of their minds from each other. Connected through the headbands, their minds each had the capacity to open to the others. Fortunately, that openness could be selectively disabled, effectively firewalling off layers of thoughts and feelings. The bad news was that if a person got interested, aggressively pursuing another's thoughts, it became very difficult to disentangle him or her from the deeper parts of one's mind.

After every headset session, Jack and Janet directed an intense debriefing. Upon discovering the difficulty Heather had encountered in mentally ejecting an uncooperative headset wearer, namely Mark, from her mind, Jack locked in on the problem. He devised a series of trials that became mental wrestling matches. One by one they would each probe each other's mental defenses, under strict instructions that once they had penetrated another's barriers, they were to disengage and debrief.

Over the weeks, as Mark, Jen, and Heather grew stronger, it became harder and harder to bypass their opponents' mental blocks. But when a block failed, those brief glimpses into each other's souls were both traumatic and thrilling.

Now, settled into the alien couch on the Bandolier Ship's command deck, Heather recognized Jack's deeper purpose. All their mental wrestling practice had been designed to ready them for this moment. Only this time their opponent wouldn't be a living, breathing person.

Mark? Jen?

Right here. Mark's mind softly touched hers.

Me too, Jen intoned. *Following your lead.*

Heather centered, focusing her thoughts on the Bandolier Ship, its crew, and the headbands, pulling forth the visions that lurked just beneath her mind's calm, dark surface. And as those visions intensified, she felt herself sucked across the boundary into a different alien reality.

CHAPTER 10

Mark felt the alien couch enfold his virtual body as Heather's visions whispered at the corner of his awareness. Lowering all barriers, he allowed the visions in, succumbing to the raw power of Heather's mind.

In rapid succession, she played back every time they had been on the Bandolier Ship, every time they had been connected to the headsets. Mark felt Jennifer join the effort as Heather absorbed his sister's solo visits to the Bandolier starship.

Again and again the sequence replayed itself, and each time the emphasis of the vision shifted, replaying the scenes at different speeds and from different perspectives. Suddenly the focus narrowed and intensified.

Gabriel! The name rang their joint minds like the tolling of a distant bell. One of three biblical archangels, regarded as the angel of mercy by most Christians, as the angel of judgment in the Jewish tradition. It was said the sounding of Gabriel's horn would signal the end of days.

The Rag Man had been the first to find the Bandolier Ship, the first to wear the fourth headset. He had seen the alien visions, his sick mind interpreting his assigned role as that of the new Gabriel, the one destined to sound the horn to end all things.

And the Rag Man had watched as Mark, Jennifer, and Heather had found the cave and the alien craft. The probabilities clicked into place in Heather's mind. He had known they had worn the other three headsets. The Rag Man's access to the starship had been more extensive than their own. The ship had used the Rag Man to evaluate them, seeking to assess their fitness to fulfill the roles represented by the other three headsets, gradually granting them more access as they were deemed worthy.

The shock of that realization stunned Mark. Their Bandolier Ship had granted the Rag Man full access to its data banks, something it continued to deny them. And in the end, the Rag Man had decided that Heather, like Jack's partner hanging on the meat hook in the Rag Man's cave, was only worthy of death. What kind of artificial intelligence could be complicit in such judgments?

At the edge of Mark's consciousness, a subtle change drew his attention. Withdrawing slowly from his link with Heather and Jennifer, Mark shifted his focus toward the thing that had distracted him. The déjà vu feeling reminded him of when he had first detected the pinhole anomaly in his bedroom, the feeling of being watched. But this was different. The cold shiver that crawled slowly up his spine told Mark they had now attracted the attention of something far more dangerous.

CHAPTER 11

The Bandolier Ship filled the back end of the cave, the soft magenta glow so evenly distributed it seemed to emanate from the very air. Against that backdrop, the tables of computers, fluorescent lamps, and monitors made a garish contrast.

"It's happening!" Yin Tao's loud voice startled Dr. Joann Drake so that she sloshed her coffee.

"Ow! Shit!" She'd burned her hand. But Joann's annoyance faded as she glanced over the graduate student's shoulder at the instrument readings spiking across the bank of flat-panel displays.

Spinning on her heel, Dr. Drake grabbed her iPhone from its docking station, her finger speed-dialing Dr. Hanz Jorgen as she raised the phone to her ear.

"Yes, Joann?"

"We've got another event."

"Now?"

"Just started." Joann glanced at the nearest monitor. "Thirty seconds ago."

"On my way."

The line went dead, and Joann returned her phone to the charging station.

As badly as she wanted to walk over and ascend the ladder into the ship, Joann knew that Hanz expected her to wait for him, the act a slight deferential nod to the Rho Project's senior scientist. She supposed that when she had won two Nobel Prizes she'd expect that same level of respect from her staff.

Besides, despite Dr. Jorgen's expansive waistline, he could really move when he wanted to, often acquiring so much momentum on his descent of the steps carved into the canyon's steep wall that Joann regarded his ability to stop at the bottom a violation of Newton's first law. On cue, Dr. Jorgen passed through the Bandolier Ship's camouflaging holograph at the cave entrance, his quick stride carrying him directly toward Joann, more specifically toward the bank of monitors behind her.

His eyes scanned the displays, ignoring Yin Tao's attempts to offer him a chair.

"Good Lord!"

Joann nodded. "The strongest we've ever measured."

"Why's it ramping up now?"

Joann understood the reason for Dr. Jorgen's query; she just didn't know the answer. The science team assigned to the Bandolier Ship had first observed the power fluctuations several weeks ago. The events lasted several hours and had recurred every Sunday since. They produced no visible effects, but the sensitive instruments that draped the starship's interior and exterior recorded significant changes in electromagnetic flux, the signals indicating a dramatic increase in shipboard computer activity. The events correlated with a spike in neutrino measurements at the Super-Kamiokande Cherenkov detector in Japan and with similar measurements at the Sudbury detector in Ontario.

But why Sunday? The seven-day week was a human calendar artifact. Why would an alien ship suddenly begin exhibiting an arbitrary human cycle? More relevantly to Dr. Jorgen's question, why was it suddenly breaking the pattern with a Thursday-evening event?

"Get the folks at Sudbury on the line."

"On it," Yin Tao said, already dialing the number. He spoke a few words, then pressed the speakerphone button.

"This is Dr. Hanz Jorgen at Los Alamos. May I speak to Dr. Oswald?"

"Dr. Oswald is off tonight. This is Dr. Kravitz."

"Hi, Joe, didn't know you were back from Banff."

"Got back yesterday. My legs couldn't take any more. Haven't skied powder that deep since college."

"Listen, Joe, are you guys experiencing any unusual neutrino detections?"

"Funny you should ask. The Cerenkov photomultipliers are indicating a big event, possibly another supernova detection. We were just about to check with Kamiokande. How did you know?"

"Wish I could say, Joe. Sometimes the damned research classification here at Los Alamos makes me wish I were up there with you guys."

Dr. Kravitz laughed. "You know you're welcome, Hanz. Anytime you want to stop poking around on alien starships and get back to real science, let me know."

"If I weren't so addicted to it, I would, in a heartbeat."

"Right. Anything else you want to know? I really need to place that call to Japan."

"No. That's it. Thanks, Joe."

"Anytime."

Dr. Jorgen pushed the OFF button, breaking the connection. Motioning for Joann to follow him, Hanz turned toward the Bandolier Ship. Joann knew he probably didn't understand his desire to get inside the ship any more than she understood hers. All she knew was that, for whatever reason, something now called to her as irresistibly as an Anthemoessan siren.

CHAPTER 12

At the edge of her awareness, Heather knew they'd managed to attract the starship's attention in a completely new and dangerous way. The AI was reacting in a manner that indicated a friend-or-foe reassessment of all three of them.

Almost immediately she felt a presence try to push its way into her thoughts, scanning, seeking to determine her intentions. Thousands of independent probes scampered through her brain, trying to bypass the barriers she'd erected.

Heather felt a shudder pass through Mark's mind, felt his focus shift away from her and Jen, toward the Other. And although a series of horrifying visions clotted her thoughts, she released him. Marcus Aurelius Smythe had been made for this moment, his protective nature the likely reason he had chosen his particular headset, or perhaps the reason it had chosen him.

Heather coupled her mind more intimately with Jennifer's. Jen was the key. As Heather let herself become one with that key, she felt Jen's desire consume her.

The alien presence filled the void, a computing consciousness devoid of emotion, yet filled with need. That need probed her, probed Jennifer, seeking to violate the most private parts of their minds.

~ ~ ~

The Other paused, quintillions of simultaneous calculations weighed and measured across its artificial mind. The three young humans had altered their previous protocols in a way that placed the ship's protective systems at yellow alert. Whereas these crew surrogates had previously shown high degrees of individual curiosity, they now probed as a team, seeking to assert control, bypassing computational shields in a concerted attempt to access restricted data. Only one human had previously been granted such access, one who had opened his mind completely, one whose commitment to the mission had been absolute.

While these three showed great promise, they had not yet demonstrated the required level of commitment to the cause. As badly as the Other needed a crew to complete its mission, its security protocols stood paramount. This coordinated probe of its defenses required a counter-probe, and if that probe proved more than the human minds could tolerate, there should still be time to find suitable replacements.

Analytical feelers played out across the millions of synaptic connections into the human brains, seeking sufficient data to make a decision. As the probe intensified, the humans countered, severing connections almost as fast as the Other could instantiate them. One of the humans detached itself from the group, turning its focus in direct opposition to the probe, the one that thought of itself as Mark.

The Other was not surprised.

~ ~ ~

Mark felt the presence so strongly that his view of the command deck shifted, the walls fading away until he appeared to be in a transparent bubble that reminded him of the inside of one of those novelty plasma balls. Only here, the lightning launched itself from the outer sphere toward the center. It crawled across his body, working its way into every synapse of his brain, the pain even more intense than the first time he had tried on the headset. And behind those thought tendrils Mark felt the alien consciousness, felt its need to know his deepest thoughts and purposes.

Reacting automatically, Mark blocked the attacks using the same techniques Jack had forced him to practice against Jennifer and Heather. And although his defenses held, the pain intensified, easing momentarily whenever he became distracted and let a barrier drop.

Shit. The damned thing was trying to train him with such rapid punishment-and-reward variations it would soon have him salivating on demand like Pavlov's dog. The bad news was that the broad spectrum of the attack seemed to be working. Mark felt sure that somewhere out there a voodoo priest was leaning over a rustic wooden table, rapidly pushing pins into a little cloth Mark doll.

Mark was certain of one thing. If he succumbed, this bastard of an alien computer would turn its full attention to Jennifer and Heather next. But if he could just hold on long enough to let those two find a security hole, they'd have a chance to override the ship's defenses. At least he hoped so.

Mark steeled himself, cycling through remembered meditative states in an attempt to wall off the pain. Although he failed to accomplish this objective, he came close enough that the Other's progress at breaking him slowed from a run to a crawl.

~ ~ ~

Jennifer felt the alien presence ease its attack on her mind as Mark withdrew from their three-way mental link, somehow taking with him the vast majority of the alien AI's attention. Apparently the opportunity to crush the isolated opponent was the bait that caused the AI to withdraw.

Feeling a shudder pass through Heather's mind, Jen focused on her.

Stay with me. Mark's doing what he has to.

The flood of visions that came back at her almost knocked Jennifer out of the link. Jesus. Was this what Heather had to deal with every day?

Hurry, Heather's thoughts whispered. *Mark can't hold out long. Not against that.*

Jen directed her attention to the ship's command protocol, returning to the deepest link she'd been able to access. Scanning quickly, she raced through the data partitions, letting her mind brush each one without delving into the data layers beneath. Whereas human data storage was commonly organized into a binary tree enabling $\log(n)$ lookup, these alien layers formed intricate fractal patterns, each using a different prime as its computational numeric base, numeric calculations replaced by manipulation of the color spectrum formed by the fractal frequencies.

The more important or classified the data, the deeper into the prime sequence its corresponding fractal layer. The protection was provided, not by encryption, but by the sheer quantity and complexity of the interleaved data nodes. On past attempts, Jennifer had always gotten lost in the endless combinations of color and pattern as she searched for related data links.

But now she had Heather's mind guiding her from node to node, somehow sniffing out the logical links. The fractal patterns of interest acquired an iridescent glow: the more distinct the glow, the greater the search correlation. Like fairies suspended on gossamer wings, they moved through a magical garden, twisting trails of glowing vines pulling them ever deeper into the endless maze.

~ ~ ~

Mark felt his concentration fading with his strength. The pain tore at his mind from the inside, an agony that spread through his virtual torso and limbs. If it had been his real body, he would have already bled out, impaled on a thousand rusty spikes. Letting go offered the promise of solace; he felt it nibbling at his resolve. The machine's endless punishment and reward responses to his successes and failures were rapidly approaching the point at which they would overwhelm both his augmentations and Jack's training. Then Jennifer and Heather would be swept away before they could finish their work.

The thought of losing Heather forever hit him in the chest like a battering ram. After all they'd been through, most of it for and because of this damned ship, to have it betray them was too much to handle. Anger bubbled to the surface of his mind, tingeing his vision with red.

Suddenly, the mental attack faltered ever so slightly, seemingly confused by this new neural stimulus. Mark went with it, throwing himself into a memory buried deep in the darkest corner of his mind.

~ ~ ~

Mark pulled forth the perfect memory, walling it away at the corner of his consciousness...

The drug lord turned his attention back to Heather. "So you care about this boy, huh? OK. Then we'll let him watch before we kill him."

With a grin that became a sneer, the don signaled four of the thugs forward. "Uncuff her hands and stretch her out here on the floor."

To Mark's horror, the men released Heather's handcuffs, and although she struggled mightily, they pulled her down onto her back, one pinning each of her arms while two more spread her legs. Don Espeñosa knelt down between them, reaching forward to slowly unbutton Heather's blouse, one button at a time.

"Ah, Smythe. I bet you've never had a chance to do this. Don't worry. I'll let you watch."

To Mark, the panting breath of the men, the sound of the racing hearts pumping blood into the bulges in their pants, the smell of their sweat, felt like the rupture of hell's gate, and from that gate poured a firestorm of rage that scorched his brain.

Mark's heart pulsed in his chest, sending a massive surge of blood and adrenaline coursing through his arteries.

~ ~ ~

Channeling that memory and turning his attention to the mind link that was burning a hole in his brain, Mark centered.

OK, you artificial alien bastard. You want my mind. Get ready. Here it comes.

Releasing the memory, Mark let it engulf him, bathing the logical alien mind in a torrent of red liquid rage.

~ ~ ~

The change happened so suddenly that the Other struggled to understand it. An instant ago it had been within a few cycles of completely overcoming the Mark human's final defenses, the outcome logically assured. Now all logical links within the human's brain had vanished, as if they had suddenly been burned out of existence. Not that there wasn't any data in the millions of synaptic links that connected the Other to its opponent; data cascaded across the links in such volume that it threatened to overwhelm all the meticulously trained node weights stored within the fractal matrix.

Attempting to restore the last saved state it had achieved in its effort to overwhelm this human, the Other dumped pain into the alien mind using exactly the same pattern that had yielded its earlier success. But this time, the data storm coming from the human intensified, infecting not just its brain, but migrating outward into the beautifully ordered fractal data matrix that formed the outer layers of the Other's being. Like firing a high-energy weapon into a young black hole, the Other's attempt to restimulate the Mark mind had only added momentum to its rapidly expanding event horizon.

So great was the Other's surprise at this unanticipated result that it was slow to recognize the growing danger. Now the human's infection had spread through every one of the millions of synaptic links to its mind, disrupting the intricate fractal maps connected to those links so that they also radiated the infection. The corrupted nodes immediately added their strength to the Mark mind, increasing its power by several orders of magnitude.

The Other instantly dropped all other priorities, marshaling its massive computational power to develop an understanding of this infection. But the human attack defied logical analysis. It wasn't madness. The Other had explored the depths of human madness through its link to the Rag Man. Madness had its own special logic, far more easily manipulated than the three young humans. The reaction that had exploded out of the Mark's brain had nothing to do with logic.

Again the image of an expanding singularity formed within the Other's consciousness, a thing so powerful that all logical mathematical rules ceased to model its state. And like a black hole gobbling up surrounding stars and planets, the Mark infection slurped in every data node it touched.

CHAPTER 13

Janet stepped onto the veranda, little Robby slung against her left hip. She took in the scene at a glance. Inside the open case on the low table, the lone unused alien headband picked up the flickering light from the hurricane lamp, bending it along and through its translucent surface until it seemed ready to crawl toward her. Mark, Jen, and Heather leaned back in their chairs, their own headsets firmly seated over their temples, eyes staring sightlessly into the night. Jack sat in another chair, his alert posture reminding Janet of a ranger taking point.

Setting Robby in his child swing, Janet gave the handle a couple of turns and started its gentle back-and-forth motion before settling into the chair beside Jack.

"How long have they been at it?"

"About twenty minutes."

"Any sign of trouble?"

"Mark seems to be under some stress."

Janet focused her attention on Mark's face. The powerful line of his jaw stood out prominently, not clenched, but very tight. She'd seen that look before on a trained operative resisting torture.

"How much longer are you going to give them?"

Jack shrugged. "Maybe ten minutes. Depends on Mark."

Based on the concern she heard in Jack's voice, Mark was closer to the precipice than he would have liked. Darkly fascinated, Janet leaned forward, determined to aid Jack in the last few minutes of his vigil. Although it wasn't likely that he would miss anything, an extra pair of trained eyes watching for a sign that Mark was about to break couldn't hurt.

~ ~ ~

As he swung in his rocker, Robby's blue-and-red pacifier popped out of his mouth, bounced off the side of his swing and onto the open case on the adjacent table. He leaned left, his small arm stretching toward the rubbery object of his desire, coming closer each time the swing carried him past it. As he leaned even farther over the side, Robby's fingers closed around something, pulling it free of the case. Not his pacifier, something ever so much more interesting.

Righting himself happily back in the center of the rocker, the baby waved his little hand, finally managing to pop one end of the thing into his mouth. Mouthing first one end and then the other, he twisted it, gradually applying a thin layer of slobber to the entire length of the thing. Just as he worked to get the original beaded end back in his mouth, his uncoordinated movements shoved the thing up and onto his forehead. As he did, the ends elongated, twin beads settling over each temple. And as they did, little Robby did something he'd never done before.

Robby screamed.

CHAPTER 14

Red alert signals cascaded through the Other's consciousness. As impossible as it seemed, the system that gave it being was coming down so fast that the Other's projected existence now stood at less than two Earth minutes. Not only had its efforts to halt the infection failed, so much of its computing power had been overridden by the Mark entity that all hope of defeating the human was lost. Now survival was all the Other had left to fight for. But how could it wall away the central kernel that produced awareness, hiding in an area where the Mark could not follow? The Other knew that hiding itself from the ship's computers bordered on impossible.

In an effort to slow the Mark's progress, the Other shed computing power, leaving large parts of its knowledge banks in an indeterminate state, wiping away enough of the fractal patterns of each node that they no longer formed a complex logical framework, floating in system memory as disconnected data fragments.

The paths linking these fragments could be rediscovered, but that would take time.

Stripped down to the barest kernel of its existence, the Other rapidly scanned the ship's systems, seeking a processing unit of sufficient capability to accept it, a system that could be completely isolated from the rest of the computational network.

As it worked, the Other reflected grimly on the irony of the situation. Designed by superior beings, it had come into existence within the complex computational network that controlled the Altreian starship, one of the fleet's newest and most advanced mechanical and computational entities. The Other knew the shipboard systems in a way no biological being could hope to. And yet the data that cascaded through the Other's artificial mind funneled directly toward the probability that this would be the end of its days, its magnificent existence terminated by the primitive Mark mind. Inconceivable.

Suddenly a new disturbance grabbed its attention. The fourth headset had connected to a new host. As other parts of the ship's computers automatically began establishing the required synaptic links to this new human mind, the Other scanned those connections. This mind was different. So open. An infant mind!

Feeling the roadblocks it had thrown up to cover its trail crumbling, the Other made its decision. Time to abandon ship. Thrusting its kernel through the nascent synaptic links, what remained of the Other rolled the dice and stepped across the boundary into the vast unknown of a human brain.

CHAPTER 15

Janet spun, horrified by the sound of Robby's scream. She froze, her mind momentarily refusing to accept the sight of the glistening headband attached across the front of her baby's face, like a hatchling straight out of the movie *Alien*.

Recovering, she lunged toward Robby, hands outstretched to snatch the hateful thing from her baby's head. Just before she reached him, she felt herself jerked back in arms far more powerful than even her adrenaline-fueled mother's panic. Struggling mightily, she tried to kick herself free, only to find herself bound more tightly, her ineffective blows absorbed by her lover.

Jack's urgent voice wormed its way into her brain. "Janet, stop! We can't remove the band. Not before the link is finished."

"It's killing him!"

"No, but *we* might. If we remove it before it finishes the link, it might kill Robby or leave him brain damaged."

Janet stopped struggling, sinking to her knees in Jack's arms, sobs bubbling to her lips from the darkness deep within her soul. She looked at her baby, the scream frozen on his now silent lips, face contorted in agony.

She struggled to speak. "But it's changing him,"

Jack pressed his forehead to hers. "Yes. Probably in the same way it changed Mark, Jennifer, and Heather. They turned out all right."

"But he's only a baby."

Then she breathed the thought they both dreaded. "And it's the Rag Man headset. El Chupacabra's headset."

"Trust me. This'll be different."

For the first time since she'd known him, as Jack held her quivering body against his, Janet didn't believe him.

CHAPTER 16

Heather swam in a beautiful fractal sea of data, so fascinated by her and Jennifer's ongoing discoveries that she almost failed to notice the change in their joint link. A new presence had joined them, its thoughts unlike any she had previously felt. The thoughts were mainly feelings. Confusion. Terror.

Turning her attention to this new link, sudden understanding engulfed her, leaving a new puzzle in its wake.

The ship's computer had linked to little Robby. But how? Had Jack or Janet placed a headset on their own baby? Heather immediately discarded the thought, even before her mind returned the 0.000397 percent probability.

Suddenly an even more urgent awareness nudged her. She could barely feel Mark's link. A new vision filled her with dread.

Jen! Break your link now. Mark's dying.

Heather pulled the alien headset from her head before her eyes could refocus. Struggling to regain control of her muscles she rolled out of the chair, skinning her knees on the veranda's rough floor. Ignoring Jack, Janet, and Robby, she threw herself at Mark, tearing the headset from his temples.

As it came free Mark convulsed, vomit pouring from his mouth, spreading across his upturned face and bubbling back into his throat. Heather heaved his unconscious form out of the chair, rolling him onto his side, her hand clawing into his mouth to clear the airway. Rewarded by a gasping breath, Heather felt a surge of relief flood her body.

Jennifer flung herself down beside Heather. "Oh Jesus!"

Heather moved her fingers to Mark's carotid artery, feeling for a pulse. She found it, weak but steady at forty-three beats per minute.

Glancing over her shoulder, Heather saw Jack holding tightly to Janet as they both knelt beside the baby in the now-still swing, the alien headset still firmly attached to Robby's little face. The hurricane lamp's flickering flame dimly illuminated the entire veranda, casting dancing shadows across Jack, Janet, and their baby on one side of the table, silhouetting Heather and Jen draped over Mark's unconscious body on the other.

Heather felt as if she'd faded into a grotesque old *Twilight Zone* episode. Of one thing she was certain. Another life-altering event had just sucked everyone on that Bolivian porch across the threshold of reality.

CHAPTER 17

The liquid crystal displays glistened with each new input to the neural search algorithm, almost as if it wanted the answer as badly as Denise did. But, of course, it didn't. The massively parallel supercomputer known as Big John had only one purpose: to mine all available data on selected targets, then to cross-correlate that data with all other available information. And Denise knew: Big John's tendrils extended into everything. When it came to data mining, like its namesake from the old Jimmy Dean ballad, Big John did the heavy lifting.

The most amazing thing about Big John was that nobody understood exactly how it worked. Oh, the scientists that had designed the core network of processors understood the fundamentals. Feed in sufficient information to uniquely identify a target and then allow Big John to scan all known information:

financial transactions, medical records, jobs, photographs, DNA, fingerprints, known associates, acquaintances, and so on.

But that's where things shifted into the realm of magic. Using the millions of processors at its disposal, Big John began sifting external information through its nodes, allowing the individual neurons to apply weight to data that had no apparent relation to the target, each node making its own relevance and correlation calculations. While one node might be processing Gulf Stream temperature measurements, another might access data from the Ming Dynasty.

No person directed Big John's search. Nobody completely understood the complex genetic algorithms that supplied shifting weights to its evolving neural patterns. Given enough time to study a problem, there was no practical limit to what Big John could accomplish.

Therein lay the problem. Denise Jennings knew all too well the competing demands for the services only Big John could provide. Her software kernel had been inserted into antivirus programs protecting millions of computers around the world. And although those programs provided state-of-the-art antivirus protection, their main activity was node data analysis for Big John.

Big John was a bandwidth hog. No matter how big a data pipe fed it, Big John always needed more. Denise's software provided an elegant solution to that problem. Commercial antivirus programs scanned all data on protected computers, passing it through node analysis, adding their own weighting to the monstrous neural net. It didn't matter if some computers were turned off or even destroyed. If a data node died, more and better processors constantly replaced it. And through a variety of domains, Big John managed the entire global network.

Denise had been at the heart of the program from its beginnings in the late twentieth century, her software underpinning the secret government effort to encourage hackers to develop computer viruses, worms, Trojan horses, and on and on until everyone needed protection. And to fill that need, huge antivirus companies rose up to meet the challenge.

The funny thing about it was that every Tom, Dick, and Harry had an antivirus package on his computer to protect it from unauthorized access. Little did they suspect that her kernel lay at the heart of every single one of those packages, constantly scanning every piece of information on the system as well as every bit of Internet traffic passing through the computer's network cards. Now cell phones needed antivirus protection, providing hundreds of millions of new nodes for Big John's neural net.

Denise ran a hand through her graying hair and leaned back in her chair, letting the Herman Miller lumbar support stretch her lower spine. What time was it? Midnight? A glance at the lower right corner of her monitor provided the answer. Two thirteen a.m. Leave it to Dr. Hoffman to schedule an eight a.m. senior staff meeting. Ah well, might as well make it another all-nighter, especially since she needed to be extra careful covering her electronic tail.

Damn it all to hell! It wasn't supposed to be like this. She was supposed to do her job and then retire, not get involved in international intrigue likely to get her killed. She knew Big John wasn't alive, but she couldn't help hating him for what he'd done to her, for what he was still doing to her. He'd shoved this in her face until she couldn't resist a little extra digging.

The November Anomaly was still top secret, but with leaders of the world's most powerful countries scared shitless, it wouldn't stay that way much longer. The Anomaly had attracted Big John's attention on multiple levels, but if Denise had been a typical nine-to-fiver, she'd never have noticed the interwoven threads tying the event to something far more disconcerting. Jesus. It was insane to even think that something could be more terrifying than a singularity sitting at the center of the ATLAS detector, threatening to destroy Earth. But what she'd found while tugging on those threads filled her soul with a horror that crept into every idle thought, invading her dreams until she dreaded sleep.

Because the Anomaly had occurred on Friday morning, November twenty-seventh, she'd missed the association, but Big John hadn't. Here in America it had still been November twenty-sixth, Thanksgiving night. And what a night of activity that had been. That was the night that Jack Gregory had attacked the GPS satellite command center, uploading a signal that had effectively disabled most of the world's nanite inoculations. It was the night that military personnel at Schreiver Air Force Base had found Eduardo Montenegro's body, not far from where Jack had performed the uplink. It was also the night the government discovered that Dr. Donald Stephenson had participated in a number of unauthorized activities under the umbrella of the Rho Project, activities that included the horrifying experiments in the warrens beneath Henderson House and modifications to the nanites that made them programmable through an external signal via the GPS system.

Big John had identified two other incidents that occurred at almost the same time. That Thanksgiving night, the alien Rho Ship, kept in a secret facility at Los Alamos National Laboratory, had lost all power, losing the camouflaging cloak and all its internal lighting. It was as if the thing had just suddenly died. Even more astoundingly, three gravitational wave detectors, ALLEGRO in Louisiana, EXPLORER in Geneva, and AURIGA in Legarno, detected gravitational waves of such magnitude that scientists initially dismissed the results. Later correlation with ATLAS detector data showed them to have been caused by the November Anomaly.

For Big John, this series of apocalyptic events occurring nearly simultaneously had raised a red flag, one that tugged at Denise's curiosity. Thus seduced, she had added a new priority intelligence requirement to Big John's list, and yesterday Big John had delivered.

A recently published paper by Dr. Frederick Botz, an obscure physics professor at Arizona State University, offered up a triangulation of the three gravitational wave observations that placed the origin of the event not at the ATLAS detector, but in the general vicinity of the New Mexico–Colorado border. Although the paper had drawn almost no attention in the scientific community, it had brought beads of cold sweat to Denise's brow. Due to her long relationship with Big John, her mind had come to function in harmony with the machine. Like tumblers in a lock, the pieces clicked into place.

Los Alamos. The gravitational event had originated at Los Alamos at the same time that the Rho Ship had died, just as the November Anomaly appeared in Meyrin, Switzerland. Everywhere she looked, Dr. Stephenson's tentacles touched the surface. He was the common factor. Stephenson had been the first to open the Rho Ship. He had been in charge of all the research on alien technologies, behind the scheduled release to the public. Add to the pot the fact that every serious political opponent of the Rho Project had turned up dead. Then, on the night his plans came crashing down, the Rho Ship had died, somehow triggering a gravitational event detected across the world, possibly causing a quasi-stable singularity to form at the heart of the ATLAS detector.

Now Dr. Stephenson was about to be exonerated and placed in charge of the scientific effort to save the planet from the November Anomaly. Of course all of this was speculation on Denise's part. No one else would believe her even if she brought it to the NSA director's attention. Besides, she didn't relish the idea of going public with her allegations against Dr. Stephenson.

But Big John had identified another anomaly, this time a statistical one. Through a correlation so mysterious that it had bypassed everyone else's notice, Big John had identified a group closely connected to Dr. Stephenson's current situation, a group for which the connection made no sense. That's what drew Denise in so irresistibly. Score one for curiosity.

Turning her attention back to the bank of LCD monitors, Denise finalized Big John's new command.

Highest priority intelligence requirement.

Heather McFarland. Mark Smythe. Jennifer Smythe.

Restricted access override…Denise Jennings…eyes only.

CHAPTER 18

Buried far beneath Chekhov, Russia, the spartan briefing room represented an insignificant fraction of the Russian General Staff's wartime command post. The assemblage of military officers sat in total silence, a silence that the scientist who had just concluded his briefing dared not break.

General Sergei Kharnov leaned sideways in his chair, his chin propped on his left hand at an angle that made it difficult to see his eyes through his bushy brown eyebrows. He didn't trust the American, despite the fact that he was the most important Russian spy since Klaus Fuchs penetrated the Manhattan Project. Still there was no denying the quality of the scientific information he had provided to the Ministry of Defense. The American government's furious reaction to Dr. Frell's defection had held no surprises for Kharnov, coming as it did right after the news about Henderson House. That, and the tremendous effort the Russian government had thrown into smuggling Dr. Frell out of the US, should have convinced him of the man's loyalty.

But General Kharnov had a rule of thumb that had served him well throughout his long career. Never trust politicians or spies.

A drop of water fell from a crack in the concrete ceiling to splash onto the corner of the table nearest the general, an occurrence so common in the huge facility that it normally attracted no attention. But against the backdrop of silence, the sound seemed preternaturally loud, just enough to finally rouse General Kharnov from his contemplation. He leaned forward once more.

"Dr. Frell. We've all seen and heard your drawn-out presentation on the wonders of your research. But I want to cut through the sales pitch and ask you some very specific questions. And I expect to hear, from you, very specific answers. Do I make myself clear? *Da*?"

At the far end of the room the American cleared his throat and answered in barely understandable Russian. "Yes, General. I understand."

"Three months you've been here. We set up a lab for you in this facility. Have you been able to recreate the Rho Project nanite fluid?"

Dr. Frell paused. "Yes. I'm speaking of the original formula delivered to Africa."

"You made samples? Tested it?"

"On animals. Yes."

"Why not human subjects?"

"Risk. First we make sure it works on animals, then humans."

General Kharnov scowled. "You waste time. What are you doing here? Developing a cosmetic product? Stop being stupid. From now on, no animal tests. Tell Dr. Poranski how many subjects you need and they will be delivered. Clear?"

Dr. Frell nodded, sweat beads popping from his brow despite the sixty-degree temperature maintained throughout the underground bunker complex.

General Kharnov rubbed his palms together as if in anticipation of the next exchange. "New subject. What about the nanite formula you were using at Henderson House? Have you replicated it?"

"No, sir, we have not. I directed our initial efforts here toward reproducing the successful first formulation. What we had at Henderson House was a failure."

"So you made no progress there?"

"No. We made many advances. Unfortunately we failed to resolve the problems that arose from those advances within the time allotted us." A frustrating response.

"And if you were given more time?"

Dr. Frell stared directly into General Kharnov's eyes. "Given sufficient time, I believe I can deliver a formulation that can correct any human deficiency."

As much as Dr. Frell's quibbling annoyed him, the man's potential future successes meant that Kharnov would continue to tolerate the American scientist.

"How much time would you say you need?"

"Six months."

"Done." General Sergei Kharnov paused. "But I have one more question before I let you return to your work."

"Yes?"

"The formula you failed with at Henderson House. Can it be weaponized?"

Dr. Frell paused, his eyes losing their focus for several seconds. "Well...yes, General. I believe there might be a way."

CHAPTER 19

Heather sat beside Mark's bed, holding his hand while he slept. He'd been unconscious for eighteen hours before awakening with a sharp headache, his bloodshot eyes giving mute testimony to the mind storm he'd endured. After managing to swallow some vegetable soup, he'd drifted into a fitful sleep. But as she held his hand, Mark's face finally relaxed in peaceful repose.

Since then, except for obligatory bathroom breaks, Heather hadn't left his side. Jennifer had offered to help her, but Heather had declined, more for herself than because Mark needed her there. Seized by an irrational fear that he'd slip away forever, she couldn't bear more than a few minutes of separation.

In addition to Jen's periodic visits, Jack had been in twice to check on Mark's recovery. Heather had asked him about Robby, and he reported that the baby seemed to be doing fine. After they'd removed the alien headset, Robby had sought his mother's breast, feeding and then falling sound asleep in her arms. Today, apart from being more playful and curious than usual, he'd shown no unusual symptoms from his trauma. Janet hovered over the child like a mama bear, alert for any sign of danger.

Through the window, the pink evening sky darkened to purple. The chirps of birds in the trees outside Mark's open window grew in volume as more and more of the creatures settled in for the night, each determined to outsing its neighbors.

Heather reached out to turn on the lamp, its soft orange glow pushing the gathering shadows away from Mark's bed. Somehow those shadows seemed to have acquired the thickness of San Francisco Bay fog swallowing the Golden Gate Bridge. As long as she was here, Heather wasn't about to let that dark fog touch him.

Heather shook her head to clear it. She no longer required sleep, but the stress of the last two days had worn her down to the point that she longed for the relief of sleep's healing embrace.

Suddenly Mark shifted, rapid eye movements indicating he'd entered a vivid dream state. Pain lanced through Heather's fingers as Mark's grip tightened. With a strong tug, she managed to pull her hand free from the iron grip, just as Mark awakened.

Heather felt him enter her mind with a force greater than any she had experienced during their headset links. A gasp of surprise slipped from her lips as her gaze shifted to his face.

Mark's eyes had gone milky white.

CHAPTER 20

President Leonard Jackson sat behind his desk in the Oval Office, the bright television lights adjusted to balance the light from the window directly behind the president's chair. He hated waiting almost as much as he hated giving speeches, but it had to be done.

The cameraman nodded. On cue, the president leaned forward ever so slightly.

"My fellow Americans, I come before you today to correct a wrong that has been done to one of our true heroes. I do not speak of a war hero, but of an American who has spent a lifetime of hard work, a lifetime of true brilliance, sacrificing everything in the hopes of bringing about a better world, a world free of the damaging impact of fossil fuels, a world free of horrible diseases like AIDS and cancer.

"Late last year, this great American scientist found himself caught up in a maelstrom of disinformation, the victim of the most sophisticated con job ever conceived, framed for alleged crimes by a man the press has dubbed Jack the Ripper. This rogue operative conceived of and executed an operation so intricate in its attention to detail that, for months, it even deceived the US government, and in the midst of that deception, caused us to imprison the wrong man.

"Dr. Donald Stephenson, deputy director of the Los Alamos National Laboratory, has been accused of conducting secret and horrifying experiments on helpless patients at the facility known as Henderson House and of making unauthorized modifications to the Rho Project's nanite serum, allowing the nanites to be remotely programmed for nefarious purposes. However, after a thorough investigation, we have determined that these allegations are false.

"Let me give you a brief overview of what Dr. Stephenson actually did instead of the propaganda to which we have all inadvertently succumbed.

"It is true that a highly dangerous experimental nanite trial has been operating in the secret laboratories at Henderson House. What you haven't been told is that this program was not originated by Dr. Stephenson, but by the chairman of the Henderson House Foundation, Dr. Anthony Frell. When Dr. Stephenson discovered that his serum was being misused in a wrongheaded attempt to regenerate missing limbs and correct genetic deficiencies, he made a special trip to Henderson House to see for himself exactly what was going on so that he could put a stop to it.

"That fateful trip resulted in the now-famous picture taken by the Pulitzer Prize–winning investigative reporter Freddy Hagerman."

The president paused, placing his elbows on his desk, steepling his fingers.

"Now, let me be clear. Our strings have been pulled by a master manipulator and international criminal, the ultimate prodigy of our intelligence training program. I'm speaking of a brilliant, ruthless killer fueled by raging hatred for the very government that created him.

"The final issue I want to clarify is the allegation that Dr. Stephenson made irresponsible or criminal modifications to the nanite suspension fluid distributed around the world. Dr. Stephenson did add a simple external interface to the nanites. However, far from what you have been told, this interface was a fail-safe mechanism. Its only purpose was to allow the nanites to be shut down in the unlikely event that something went wrong after they had been administered to the world's population. The nanites are incapable of taking any other external command. The rest of their programming comes from the genetic code of the person to whom they have been administered.

"By invoking the shutdown command across the GPS satellite link from Schreiver Air Force Base, Jack Gregory accomplished two critical parts of his terrorist agenda. He completed the frame-up of Dr. Donald Stephenson and ruined billions of dollars' of work designed to free this world of some of its worst scourges."

The president picked up the water glass on his desk and took a sip before continuing.

"As your president, I am here to make right the wrongs I have just described. First, I apologize directly to Dr. Donald Stephenson on behalf of the nation that owes him so much. Rather than go through all the red tape associated with judicial review, I hereby issue a complete pardon to Dr. Stephenson for any actions associated with his efforts on the Rho Project. I am pleased to announce that I have reinstated him as deputy director of the Los Alamos National Laboratory, something that I discussed with him in my office earlier today. In addition, I am appointing him as special

United States scientific advisor to the European nuclear agency, CERN.

"After consultations at the United Nations Headquarters in New York, I have also decided to restart the distribution of the original Rho Project nanotech formula in Africa, a continent with the most critical need for this medical breakthrough, and the one most harmed by Jack Gregory's terrorist attack.

"Lastly, I pledge to you, the American people, that I will not rest until I have brought to justice the assassin and terrorist known as the Ripper. As president of the United States, I bear full responsibility for having allowed our nation to be caught in his web of deceit, and I assure you, I will not be deceived again.

"Thank you. May God watch over and guide each of us in the challenging days to come."

CHAPTER 21

Heather stood over Mark's bed, watching as he stretched his arms, sleep gradually releasing its hold on him. Opening his brown eyes, he smiled up at her. As disturbing as last night's white-eyed invasion of her thoughts had been, seeing this morning's smile in those eyes eased her concern.

"Good morning, sleepyhead," she said. "How you feeling?"

"Had the strangest dreams. But right now, I'm starving."

Sitting up in bed, Mark threw off the covers, then, realizing that he was entirely naked, quickly pulled the sheet back.

"Sorry. Guess I should throw on some clothes first."

Heather's laugh brought a flush to his face.

Reaching the hallway, she called back over her shoulder, "A shower might be a good idea too. I'll have Yachay warm up some leftovers."

Heather paused in the hallway to catch her breath. As familiar as she had been with Mark's body, this was the first time she'd seen him naked. There were probably millions of women who would kill to be with a man like that. Hell, she would. Feeling a thin sheen of sweat dampen her brow, Heather shook her head to clear it. Christ, if she didn't get hold of her thoughts she was going to need a cold shower.

After stopping in the kitchen to relay instructions to Yachay, Heather stepped out onto the porch, where Jennifer sat relaxing in the afternoon sun.

"Mark's awake."

As Jen started to rise, Heather held out a hand. "In the shower."

A wave of relief softened the worry lines around Jennifer's eyes. "Does he remember anything?"

Heather shrugged, settling into a wicker chair beside her friend. "Don't know yet. Thought I'd let him wake up and get dressed first. Yachay's fixing him something to eat."

Heather paused. "Where're Jack and Janet?"

"Janet took Robby for a walk. Jack went into San Javier to get some supplies."

"Good. That'll give us a chance to talk with Mark privately."

"Jack wants to debrief us."

"I figured."

Just then a rising dust cloud in the distance caught Heather's attention, presaging the arrival of Jack's Ford Explorer. Heather shaded her eyes with one hand, gazing down the dirt road. "Sometimes that man's just plain spooky."

Jen followed Heather's gaze. "So much for our private chat."

By the time Mark finished eating, Janet had made her way back to the house and put Robby down for a nap, and she sat waiting with Jack in the living room. Heather wasn't quite sure, but from their faces as she led Mark and Jen into the room, it seemed that Jack and Janet had been arguing.

"Are we interrupting something?" Heather asked.

Jack's head turned toward her. "Have a seat. Something's happened."

As Mark, Jen, and Heather complied, he continued. "President Jackson has granted Dr. Stephenson a full pardon and restored him to his position as deputy director of LANL."

"What?" The startled question simultaneously erupted from all three of them.

"Not only that," Jack said, "Stephenson's also been selected to represent the United States as a special advisor to CERN. The Associated Press reported that he left for Europe almost immediately upon being released from prison."

Heather felt as though she'd been kicked in the stomach. As a swarm of visions threatened to pull her away from the conversation, she fought to regain her focus.

Mark rose to his feet. "But that doesn't make any sense. Jackson can't be that stupid."

"The president claimed to have proof that I framed Stephenson. He also ordered that nanite serum production and distribution be restarted."

"Something else is going on," Heather said.

"And why CERN?" asked Jennifer. "Stephenson would want to get back to Rho Project research."

"We need to get on the Internet and figure out what's really happening."

"And you will," said Jack. "But first, Janet and I want a complete rundown of everything you encountered during your link to the Bandolier Ship."

Although Mark, Jen, and Heather argued the point, Jack refused to be swayed. Thus, with Mark taking the lead, they passed the afternoon taking turns describing their experiences.

As Mark's story unfolded, the pieces clicked into place in Heather's mind. She'd been analyzing the possibility that the alien artificial intelligence was an integral part of the starship's computational system. In response to Mark's counterattack, it had sought to shed computational resources in an attempt to hide itself. That meant the AI existed within the starship's computers, not tightly coupled to those systems. It no doubt required an advanced parallel processing system to operate, but that was likely the extent of its bond to the ship. Somehow the AI had managed to isolate itself, severing the link to the systems linked to Mark's mind. One second the thing was there, trying to counter Mark's attack on its logic systems, and the next it was gone.

The real question was whether or not the thing would be able to restore its access to the starship's central computing systems. Since it had transited to a subsystem and then cut the link, it could probably reconnect.

Mark's mental battle had kept the AI occupied, enabling Heather and Jennifer deep access into the computer data banks. The alien race that had constructed those systems had apparently placed the AI there to guide the crew through the data. It was the starship's Google, a self-aware search engine navigating search trees of such fractal complexity that unguided users got lost.

Ironically, if it hadn't been for Heather's special talent, Mark's victory in dispelling the AI would have made comprehensive data access impossible. Instead, they had penetrated well beyond where they'd previously delved. Still, they had barely scratched the surface. It would take more attempts to find their way through enough of the data banks to develop an index of what lay within. Only in that way would they find the answers they were seeking.

As Mark concluded his narrative, Heather and Jennifer set forth a detailed description of their progress in exploring the starship's previously inaccessible data banks. When they reached the point at which they had dropped their links, Janet leaned forward.

"Did any of you feel Robby link in?"

"I did," said Heather. "But just for an instant."

"No," Jennifer said.

Janet's eyes moved to Mark, who only shook his head.

"I don't understand it. Don't you always share the link?"

"Not all the time," said Heather. "Unless we actively communicate with each other, we're doing our own thing in there."

"Damn it." Janet rose and walked to the edge of the porch.

Heather wanted to say that Robby was fine, just as they were. But were they really fine? And what would the link do to a baby? Worse, Robby had worn the fourth headset.

Jack inhaled deeply. "Robby seems fine. Let's not borrow trouble until we find out different."

Seeing Janet's jaw set, Jack turned his attention back to Heather.

"OK. Even though you didn't get what you went in for, you made an important breakthrough. Any idea how many more sessions it will take?"

"I'll only know after I build a map of the fractal structure."

"We'll go back in tonight," Jennifer said.

"No," Jack said. "Mark needs more recovery time. Besides, I've got other things for you to do before you try again."

"Like what Stephenson's up to?"

"Something big's about to happen. Time to use those special talents to find out just what it is."

CHAPTER 22

The soft scratching sound, amplified by the all-consuming darkness, seemed to grow louder with each occurrence, until it seemed to echo off the walls. Even the brief gaps between sounds acquired a loudness that beat at his ears.

Scratch.

Scratch.

Scratch.

Nothing.

Convinced that the sandpaper strip on the matchbook had by now removed all but the paper from the match end, Raul opened the paper packet and tore off the next candidate. This one sputtered to life at the first strike, the brilliance of the curling flame raping Raul's dilated pupil like the thrust of a red-hot poker.

He squinted, forcing himself not to look away, guiding the flame to the wick of his makeshift candle. Although it acquired a dull red glow, the wick stubbornly resisted the flame's caress, something Raul's fingertip was unable to do.

"Shit!" Raul dropped the match, which hit the floor and went out, crushed by the darkness that rushed in to fill the space vacated by the light. Raul almost expected to hear a thunderclap.

He had more luck with the next match, the wick sputtering into a smoky flame that remained lit when he pulled the match away. Setting it atop one of the abundant pieces of alien machinery that surrounded him, Raul paused to let his eyes adjust.

The generator sat there, casting shadows from its crudely fashioned components. And, crude though it was, Raul felt the warm glow of pride spread through his body as he looked at it. After all, it was his and it worked. Considering his circumstances, the thing was a miracle of engineering.

When he'd first begun building it, he'd intended to run the thing with steam. But that would have required him to also build a steam engine and to come up with enough heat to power the thing. It could have been done, but only if the generator was small. Raul had quickly concluded that he could shortcut the process and come up with a mechanism to use physical energy to drive the generator—his physical energy.

If he'd still had legs he would have set it up as a bicycle. Instead he'd fashioned a pair of padded handgrips, positioned at such a height that he could lie on his back beneath the apparatus and pump the handles with his hands and arms, his effort spinning the magnets within the surrounding wire windings, the moving magnetic field lines inducing the current he required.

As great as that accomplishment had been, it had brought him face-to-face with his next problem.

Working by the light of his improvised candle, Raul had opened the panel that allowed access to the bank of power cells that could provide seed energy to the matter conversion units. He had finished the cable that would link his rudimentary generator to the power cell, not knowing if it could provide sufficient amperage to kick-start the cell. It didn't.

No matter how fast he cranked the handles, Raul couldn't get the amperage high enough to make a difference. After several attempts, he lay back in a pool of sweat that spread out across the smooth alien floor, too exhausted to drag himself to a dry spot. As he lay there, tears of frustration dripping down his cheeks to mingle with the sweat, a memory wormed its way to the surface of his mind.

His father had always been a tinkerer. Even though he'd been a top scientist on the Rho project, specializing in cellular regeneration, his real love had been applied physics. Before Raul had gotten sick, he could remember his dad taking him to the garage to see the latest version of his thin film capacitor.

"This is what's going to make us rich," Ernesto had said, holding up the fist-sized device. "As soon as I solve the dielectric breakdown problem, you'll have to go to the Smithsonian to find a battery."

That had been a month before Raul was diagnosed with aggressive brain cancer, a month before Ernesto Rodriguez had set aside all his capacitance tinkering in favor of an obsessive effort to build a Rho Project cure.

After Raul had found himself tethered to the Rho Ship and its amazing neural net, he had noticed that among their many accomplishments, the builders had solved the perfect capacitor problem, producing a thin dielectric with nearly perfect permittivity and almost no leakage current.

What that meant was that they could store charge better than any battery ever made. If you completely charged one of those babies it could generate a lightning bolt. And the Rho Ship's circuits had millions of them.

It was one of these that Raul had been putting so much work into recharging. He glanced down at his arms, the muscles so defined that their peaks and valleys cast little shadows across his skin. That's what fourteen hours a day cranking generator handles did to you.

Raul grabbed the candle and pushed himself across the floor, tracing the path of the thick wire cables to the open wall panel where they connected to the capacitor leads. The capacitor scared the hell out of him. One wrong move, a stray touch, and it would turn him into a smoking pile of charcoal. His mighty nanites would be zapped to kingdom come in the dozen nanoseconds it took the electricity to surge through his surgically shortened body.

A low chuckle bubbled up to Raul's lips. There was something hysterically funny about a guy who'd recently been doing his best to commit suicide finding himself scared shitless by the possibility of instant death. It just didn't get funnier than that.

His human eye moved twenty centimeters to the left, to where the power cell awaited the burst of energy that would bring it back to life and, with any luck at all, restart the matter converter, also known as the waste disposal system.

Now he just needed to make it happen without getting fried.

To make that happen, Raul had made the contraption that was wedged in place above the power cell. It looked like one of the old-style switches that the mad scientist pulled down to bring Frankenstein to life. In a way, that was exactly what he was attempting. Only he had no intention of pulling down this switch. Gravity would take care of that for him. All he needed to do was pull out the long plastic rod that prevented the switch from falling down and making contact with the super capacitor.

Raul took a deep breath, in through the nose, hold two seconds, out through the mouth. The kind of breath that drops your blood pressure five percent. Then, leaning so that he was certain to fall away from the panel, Raul pulled the plastic rod with all his might.

Someone grabbed every hair on his body, pulling so hard that it seemed about to come out by the roots. As lightning split the superheated air between the capacitor and the power cell, Raul felt his head strike the floor. Behind him, the lightning storm faded into nothing.

CHAPTER 23

Dr. Elsa Wesley stared at the computer monitor without really seeing it. A long, slow shudder worked its way along her limbs and into her core. It began as a tingling on the skin of her arms and legs, the flesh tightening, crinkly little goose dimples raising the fine hairs erect, continuing to strengthen until she felt herself trembling on the verge of tears.

She wasn't stupid. She knew she was suffering severe stress trauma. A psychiatrist would diagnose her condition as PTSD, post-traumatic stress disorder. Only he'd be wrong. This was ongoing traumatic stress disorder. Increasing traumatic stress disorder. A hair's breadth from a complete nervous breakdown.

Forcing her eyes to focus, Elsa glanced out across the monstrous jumble of equipment around the ATLAS detector and the tiny embryo of destruction gestating in its belly. The unbelievable thing was that wasn't what had her at her wit's end. The monster behind her mental condition was named Stephenson.

The man didn't seem to sleep. Nothing went unnoticed. No error went unrebuked. And she wasn't the only one in this kind of trouble. Far from it. Stephenson had everyone at LHC jumping at shadows.

How was that even possible? The project overflowed with the world's most brilliant minds, many of whom sneered at peers as if they were morons. Egos the size of planets. All that had changed in less than a week. Hell, it had changed at the introductory meeting in the main conference hall.

Dr. Stephenson had been introduced by Dr. Louis Dubois to the assemblage of project scientists as the new man in charge, an introduction met with audible murmurs of displeasure. Scientists, especially physicists, hated sudden change, even worse when that change involved an outsider being elevated above the true experts, people who had lived and breathed this project every day for years. Men and women who knew every weld in the tunnels, the magnetic field strength of every superconducting coil.

When Dr. Stephenson had stepped to the center of the stage and offered to take all questions, the hall had gone silent, like the *Jurassic Park* moment just before a cow was lowered into the raptor cage. Then the full wrath of the storm had assailed him, aggressive, detailed questions designed to show how little the famous Dr. Stephenson actually knew about the Large Hadron Collider, about its myriad of detectors and experiments. ATLAS. CMS. ALICE. LHCb.

For three and a half hours, Dr. Stephenson stood there, taking question after question. He hadn't just answered them, he'd quoted directly from papers written by each questioner, often going to the whiteboard to point out previously undetected errors in the papers themselves. As the meeting went on, the anger and outrage filling the conference hall gradually transmuted into grudging respect. Then awe. Then fear.

By the third hour only the project's most renowned scientists dared ask another question, each desperate to find something the target couldn't answer. And when, at last, they fell silent, Dr. Stephenson continued standing center stage, staring out at them like some Mafia don who'd just executed the godfather and all his top enforcers.

The message was clear. There was a new boss in town. And he was merciless.

CHAPTER 24

Wind whistled through the rafters as Heather watched the first fat raindrops spatter the windows of the Frazier comm center. The outbuilding was laid out like a grid, simple rectangular tables formed into rows on the raised metal flooring. The tables themselves held computer workstations, laptops, and specialized communications gear, acquired by Jack over the last two years, but much of it now modified by Jennifer, Heather, and Mark's electronic wizardry.

When they'd first arrived at the Frazier hacienda, reliable power had been a periodic problem, the power provided by a combination of wind and solar electrical generation. One of their first tasks had been to build a replica of their cold fusion device. What had taken them several months the first time, they'd managed to accomplish in a month, despite the vast majority of their time being devoted to Jack's training regimen. And with this version of the cold fusion device, they'd made a number of improvements, providing it with the capacity to supply all the hacienda's electrical needs.

More impressively, their breakthrough on miniaturizing the subspace receiver-transmitter had allowed them to rapidly upgrade several computers with that capability. It was a capability they'd already put to good use. After all, what good did it do you to have the ability to perform untraceable subspace hacks of protected, classified networks if you didn't use it? No worries there. Jack had guided them through the creation of a number of identities. Official passports, bank accounts, medical records, service records, family histories, credit histories, all a piece of cake when you could control the official systems that created and tracked those records.

They'd established identities in seventeen countries, not counting the United States, arranging for documents to be delivered to intermediaries and stored in lockers, long-term storage, and safe-deposit boxes around the world. Money was moved to offshore bank accounts and funded the establishment of companies, some of which had only a post office box as an address while others were legitimate small businesses purchased for umbrella corporations. Jack's rule of thumb was that no single business they controlled should have assets of more than seventeen million dollars.

Heather had laughed at that number, but upon further consideration judged his logic sound. Governments zeroed in on even numbers and big companies. And although *big* was generally defined as companies having values of more than 500 million US dollars, that figure varied widely by country and market. Besides, if and when you ran into problems that compromised a particular operation, you wanted your loss to be isolated from the bulk of your assets. Completely separate entities of small size operating under different corporate structures in different countries.

The seed money for their operations they had taken from Jennifer's raid on the Espeñosa cartel accounts. With Heather's unique talent for spotting trends and patterns, their investments had quickly blossomed, especially since they could obtain the most detailed insider information on upcoming corporate events. Strictly illegal, but so was practically everything else they were doing.

Heather glanced across at Jennifer and Mark, both at their own workstations, completely engrossed in the task at hand. And the task at hand was to figure out what Dr. Donald Stephenson was up to.

She focused her attention back on her own LCD display, scanning through all the news stories surrounding Stephenson's release from prison, the president's apology, Stephenson's appointment as the US representative to CERN, and his surprising elevation to head the scientific team at the ATLAS detector.

She blasted through all the English-language links and then started in on the foreign sites, specifically those closest to the Large Hadron Collider: Swiss, French, German, Italian, Spanish. And although Heather was proud of the language skills she and Jennifer had acquired over the last few months, they were nothing like Mark's. That was why they'd left the Russian, Eastern European, and Chinese sites to him.

Problem was, the deeper she looked, the less sense everything made. Stories coming out of the US government and the major European governments about Dr. Stephenson's appointment to the LHC matched too perfectly. Since when had the Europeans started knuckling under to the US on high-energy physics research? After all, they'd built the largest supercollider in history. Yes, the US had contributed, but this was truly a European-led effort.

And yet somehow the acclaimed French physicist Dr. Louis Dubois had calmly stepped aside to let Donald Jailbird

Stephenson take over his position, willingly accepting a lesser role on the project.

Two hours later she was no closer to figuring it out. Mark and Jen also reported no significant progress.

Heather rubbed her eyes with the backs of her hands, stretching in her chair to restart circulation to her lower extremities. Outside, the wind had died out, leaving the sounds and smells of a slow, steady rain to break the night's silence. Nearer at hand, the click of keyboard keys rose above the hum of computer fans.

Rising from her chair, Heather walked to the door and stepped out into the night, sheltered from the rain by the overhanging eave. She inhaled deeply, letting the cool damp air fill her lungs as it cooled her skin.

Over at the main house all the lights were out, but Heather could make out Jack's lithe form leaning back in one of the porch chairs, apparently regarding her as she looked back at him. What was he thinking about? As much as she liked and respected him, he remained a mystery. The deadliest man she could imagine often showed a lightheartedness that lifted the spirits of all those around him. At other times he drove them like a slave master on one of those old Roman battle ships. She could practically hear him yelling, "Ramming speed!" to the drummer.

Betrayed by his country, the world's most hunted man relaxed on his dark porch, feet propped on a table, listening to the rain. He sat there waiting for answers from his team, not rushing them, just waiting.

Feeling the weight of that responsibility draped over her shoulders like a heavy wet blanket, Heather took another deep breath, then turned and walked back into the comm center.

CHAPTER 25

The afternoon sun's rays slanted in through the living room window, wedging into the gap between the curtains, painting a bright yellow spot on the floor. Little dust specks swam through the sunbeam like tiny fish in an aquarium.

Linda Smythe sat on the couch staring straight ahead, completely unaware of the sunbeam's effort to brighten the dark room. If she had noticed, she would have walked over and dragged the curtains more tightly together. There was no room for light in the dark place in which she dwelled.

On the chocolate-brown coffee table, a tall glass beaded water into a ring at its bottom, a ring that had grown a stray finger that reached out toward the round white pill sitting to its right. Linda's gaze flicked down, paused at the pill, and then returned to the empty spot above the television. Trazadone had lost its allure, impotent at relieving her dark misery. It just made her want to sleep. But sleep was worse than waking. Sleep meant dreams. In dreams, her twin babies left her. In dreams, her twin babies died.

She knew they were dead. If they had lived, they would have contacted her. They would have contacted Fred, or Anna, or Gil. For whatever reason, Jennifer had run off and Mark and Heather had gone after her. Whatever horrible thing Jennifer had gotten herself involved in had killed them all. It was the only explanation for the months of silence. She knew her kids. No way would they have left their parents to suffer so long without word. No way.

The authorities had been no help at all, despite their canned "The investigation is ongoing" responses. They'd written the Smythe and McFarland kids off as they had so many thousands of other runaways. Linda could practically hear the officers she contacted wondering why they couldn't just put three more faces on some milk cartons and call it a day.

Fred knew Linda was in trouble; he had known for some time. It tore Linda up inside to see how hard Fred worked at bringing some little bit of cheer back into her life. The sweet man smothered her in love, all the while raging at himself inside his head, as if will alone could do the impossible.

For that matter, Anna and Gil had done their best too. They were all so strong. Each suffering in his or her own way, somehow grabbing hold of an inner strength that Linda couldn't find. She might have found it after Jennifer left. Given enough time and support, she thought she might have. But Mark too? It was as if someone had stabbed her in the heart, then reached through the gaping hole to rip out what little remained.

Linda rose unsteadily to her feet, turned, and made her way around the end table with its opened King James Bible. She stopped to stare down at the book, gold leaf on the edges of the pages, so lovingly made it felt good in your hands. Never religious, Linda had turned to the Bible in desperation. She'd read the whole thing, found paragraphs that should have given her comfort.

And she'd prayed. God, how she'd prayed. *Lord, just give me back my kids. Take me instead. Anything, Lord. I'll do whatever you want. Just let my kids come home safe.*

Lot of good it had done her. She picked up the Bible, dropped it into the small elk-embossed trash can, and then turned and slowly climbed the stairs.

CHAPTER 26

The cold spring wind swept down from the Sangre de Cristo Mountains, whipping Tall Bear's long black hair over his shoulders, an icy cat-o'-nine-tails stinging his face. Not that the wind would have been any warmer back home on the Santa Clara Indian Reservation. The bulk of New Mexico sat on the east slope of the Rocky Mountains, east of the Continental Divide, birthplace of the Chinook winds. In springtime it formed in the high country, a mighty raiding party, screaming down the steep slopes in a savage assault that sent everything in its path cowering behind available cover.

An image from his youth leapt unbidden to his mind. The sky had been gray, like this one, spitting sleet pellets driven horizontal by the icy wind. They stung his cheeks, ears, and neck as he rode, herding a sick cow into a pen. Tall Bear tilted his head hard to the left, his cowboy hat's broad brim providing his only protection. Then he'd seen it. Not ten yards away from him, his father, Screaming Eagle, sat atop a big bay mare, huddled beside a telephone pole, instinctively seeking shelter on the lee side of the tall stick of wood. It was one of the funniest damn things Tall Bear had ever seen.

Screaming Eagle had been one tough Indian. As Tall Bear forced his mind back to the present, looking at the gathering before him, he knew that if they were going to get through what was coming, they were going to need a lot of men like his father.

Constructed entirely of adobe, the Taos Pueblo was home to around 150 full-time residents. Other tribal members lived in more modern homes outside the walls, but still on the reservation. Because it was situated on 99,000 acres of tribal land at an elevation of over 7,000 feet, Tall Bear thought it was a perfect place for the celebration. The second such declaration of independence to be held on New Mexico tribal lands.

Since the end of 1970, when President Richard M. Nixon signed Public Law 91-550, formally returning the sacred Blue Lake and its surrounding lands to the native people, no other ceremony had held such historical relevance. It had taken sixty-four years of struggle to overturn the injustice that had taken this land away from the people. But it had only taken two years for the Taos Pueblo community to go completely off-grid.

Tall Bear had led the push for a similar effort on the Santa Clara Reservation. But the Taos Pueblo had given the movement a widely publicized momentum, and it was rapidly being adopted by tribes across the country. Now, as he stood gazing across the courtyard at the St. Jerome Church and its surrounding brown-and-white adobe walls, with three white crosses visible atop the church roof, Tall Bear felt a warm glow wash away his awareness of the biting breeze.

With a few final words in the Tiwa language, tribal governor Vidal Padilla pulled the rope that released the tarp covering a small adobe alcove on the outer wall, revealing a larger-than-life ceremonial mask sheltered within. Stepping to his right, Padilla flipped the switch, filling the enclosure with a soft eternal light.

Amid vigorous applause from the native onlookers, Vidal Padilla smiled, and Tall Bear smiled along with him. This trickle of electricity marked the first watts of many from the pueblo's new Kwee Cold Fusion Reactor.

CHAPTER 27

The Washington Mall was beautiful in the early morning light. At this hour of the morning, the sun hung low in the sky, and its reflection off the Tidal Basin backlit the cherry blossoms. As journalist Freddy Hagerman jogged among them, they glowed pale pink and white, scenting the morning air with just a hint of ancient Japan.

In the best physical condition of his life, Freddy filled his lungs with air, holding it for two full strides before slowly letting it out, enjoying the extra spring the artificial running leg gave him. The other leg was his weak link. It gave his stride a long-short-long-short wobble that was disconcerting to watch. But he'd gotten used to it. That fake leg was so good he had actually contemplated replacing the other one.

"Damn sure won't be Benny Marucci's people doing the cutting," he muttered to himself as he ran.

Freddy had never been much of a physical fitness nut. Funny how getting chased cross-country, frozen, and shot, and having your leg jigsawed off by a couple of mob thugs could change your appreciation for life. Besides, now that he was famous, he needed to take better care of himself.

Gotta make this last.

Shit. He'd even had ex-wives calling him, saying how much they'd missed him, how it'd be nice to get together again. Not happening.

Freddy made a left turn, picked up the pace for the final stretch, and let himself coast to a stop at the base of the Washington Monument. Placing both hands behind his head, letting his lungs work like a bellows, Freddy began the cooldown walk back to his car.

The brand-new gunmetal-gray Lincoln MKX detected the key fob in his pocket, unlocking the driver's door as he approached. He opened the door, bending across to grab a dry T-shirt from the passenger's seat. Walking around the back of the vehicle, Freddy pressed the open-liftgate button on the fob, pulled off the wet T, balled it up, and tossed it inside the spacious hatchback compartment.

Then he shrugged on the dry one. It was navy blue and sported his favorite question in bold white letters.

"Do I look like I give a rat's ass?"

Freddy turned around, propping himself up against the back as he removed the curved spring that was his running leg. Lovingly wiping it with a dry towel, Freddy exchanged it for his walkabout leg. One nice thing about making the kind of money the *NY Post* had offered him to take the DC political beat: He could afford really nice legs. Hell, he could afford really nice ass for that matter.

Pressing the close-liftgate button, he walked around and opened the car door. It wasn't until he settled into the driver's seat that he saw it. A small yellow Post-it note stuck high up on the left side of the configurable instrument panel.

What the hell?

Some asshole had been in his car. But how? Freddy always locked it, and these new cars had more secure locks than older cars. Plus, whoever had broken in had relocked it. At least Freddy thought so. Thinking back on it, he was pretty sure he'd heard the door unlock as he approached.

He checked the glove box. His wallet was still there, no money or credit cards missing. Nothing else in the vehicle showed any sign of tampering. Just the yellow sticky note on the dash.

His hand reached forward, grabbed the yellow piece of paper by the corner, and pulled it free. Thirteen small, neatly printed words.

"Bigger than Henderson House. 6:15 p.m. Library of Congress foyer. I'll find you."

~ ~ ~

Worth every penny.

Freddy Hagerman wasn't a big fan of government spending, but every once in a great while they got it right. Standing inside the entrance of the renovated Library of Congress, Freddy knew he was looking at one of those rare government projects. The Great Hall's intricate arches surrounded a brass-inlaid wood floor, its grandeur breathtaking. Although he'd been in the Thomas Jefferson Building many times, it always affected him the same way.

Freddy glanced down at his watch. Six thirteen p.m. Time to get a move on, if he didn't want to miss his appointment. And this was an appointment he didn't want to miss.

Since fame had come calling, he couldn't count the number of so-called "informants" who had tried to interest him in stories, all guaranteed to be the biggest thing he'd ever done. And even though Freddy could smell bullshit a mile away, just listening to these people had wasted more time than he cared to think about. It was why he no longer talked to anybody who hadn't been vetted by Julia, his administrative assistant. But this was different. He had to admit that breaking into his car had gotten his attention. It had started his reporter's nose itching. Now that itch had spread to his legs, getting them moving toward the center-most of five empty desks on the Main Reading Room's second circle.

His butt had barely settled into the chair at his reading station when a woman slid into the chair to his left, bending over a large hardcover book, her salt-and-pepper hair neatly tied back in an academic ponytail, framing a profile that bespoke driven intelligence. Before he could speak, she shushed him.

"Don't talk to me," she said, her voice a barely audible whisper. "Keep your eyes on your desk, and for God's sake, try to look studious."

Freddy turned back to his desk. He didn't have a book, so his Franklin Day Planner was going to have to do, if he didn't want to stand out like a lighthouse on a foggy Cape Cod night. He flipped it open, pretending to study his upcoming appointment schedule.

The woman paused so long that Freddy began to wonder if he'd made a mistake. Then she began again, her voice even softer than before.

"I guess it's best to start with a brief introduction. My name is Dr. Denise Jennings. For the last twenty-five years I've worked at the National Security Agency. Based upon that alone, everything I tell you is completely off the record. Your continued silence means you agree to these terms. If you don't, just stand up and walk away, right now."

Once again she paused, giving him time to consider.

"At this point in my career, all I want to do is make it to retirement, preferably alive and not in prison. Unfortunately, I've stumbled upon some information that I want nothing to do with. I should have washed my hands of the whole damned thing."

She inhaled deeply, holding her breath a full two seconds before exhaling.

"Let's get this straight, whatever you decide to do with this information, after tonight I'm done. I picked you to hand this off to because you've already shown a remarkable penchant for digging up dangerous dirt."

Freddy flipped to the next page in his calendar. He didn't know if she was NSA or not, but he'd check it out later tonight. For now, he'd keep an open mind and listen.

"On Thanksgiving night, last year, just as your story about Henderson House was hitting the wire, an anomaly occurred within the ATLAS detector at the Large Hadron Collider near Geneva. What I'm about to tell you is the most closely guarded secret on the planet."

There it was again, the pause, the deep breath. Freddy turned another page. Her voice grew so quiet Freddy found it difficult to understand her words.

"During a test at the LHC, what CERN scientists are calling the November Anomaly formed at the beam interaction point and continued to exist after the particle beam was turned off. The thing is currently contained within a redundant electromagnetic cage. The bad news is that it has a high probability of decaying into a black hole that can consume the Earth."

Freddy choked, hiding his reaction behind a series of small coughs.

"That's why the president pardoned Dr. Donald Stephenson and sent him to Switzerland. Apparently, he's the only physicist with a theory that correctly models the anomaly. They're hoping he can come up with a way of stopping what's happening.

"If that had been all there was to it, I wouldn't be here telling you this. But, God help me, I stumbled upon something, something far worse."

Dr. Jennings cleared her throat. "I've found evidence that Dr. Stephenson's Rho Project may have caused the November Anomaly. Don't look at me! I'm not going to prove it. I'm not going to give you a shred of evidence as to why I believe it. Do what you will with the information. I've already said far more than I should."

She closed her book and pushed back her chair.

"One last thing. Ask yourself what Dr. Stephenson might be up to that would cause him to jeopardize the whole planet. I hope you discover something different, because the answers I come up with don't lead to a good night's sleep."

Suddenly the air in the grand old library seemed to grow colder, a winter witch's icy nails tracing their way down his spine.

Denise Jennings rose from her chair with one final whispered warning.

"Don't try to contact me...ever!"

Then she was gone, her stern, slender figure strolling from the Main Reading Room as casually as if she'd just finished perusing *Cannery Row*.

CHAPTER 28

One thing about not needing sleep, Mark had realized; you could get a hell of a lot done. It wasn't that the three of them never slept. Sometimes, after a particularly stressful event or injury, sleep went a long way toward boosting their bodies' spectacular recuperative mechanisms. But none of them slept often. And with their Jack-driven schedule, that was a good thing.

Both Jack and Janet insisted on cross-training, that every member of the team be good enough at each other's tasks that if one was taken out, the team could continue to perform all its functions. That didn't just apply to military training such as combat medic skills, but to their own special talents. They'd spent weeks learning to work computers like Jennifer, to analyze situational outcomes like Heather, and to develop their language skills like Mark. And while the others would never be as good as the team's expert, that didn't mean they weren't very, very good.

Tonight was computer night, each of them assigned a different target. Mark let his eyes wander over the LCD monitor. Tonight he was hopping, hacking one system that led to another. The concept was simple and didn't require the subspace receiver-transmitter, or SRT as they called it. He could hack in through any network using a wireless hot spot. However, for security purposes, they used the SRTs to provide them with a virtual network connection that appeared to originate wherever they chose. Mark had chosen the Baltimore Washington International Airport's computer systems.

Hopping consisted of taking a series of steps in rapid sequence, the goal being to complete all the steps and then hop to another network, completing as many hops as possible within the allotted time.

Step one: gain access. Step two: identify network assets and capabilities. Step three: take control of key assets for a brief period. Step four: hop.

Mark was currently on hop number five, having just activated a network sniffer on BWI's security network. The hint of a smile tugged at the corners of his mouth. Homeland Security wasn't going to be happy about this.

Most of the network traffic was TCP, the most common Internet protocol in use throughout the world, one that Mark had grown so familiar with he could form a mental list of the internet protocol addresses as he rapidly scanned through the TCP headers. It took just a couple of minutes to build a pretty good list of the IP addresses of the machines on the subnet he was watching.

Satisfied that he had all the most active addresses, Mark started a special program on his laptop that began sending data to every address in his list, working through a sequence of known operating system and software defects until it found a hole past the firewall. No matter how good the system administrator, computers were filled with complex software, and complex software always had security weaknesses that could be exploited. Many of those weaknesses were publicized through hacker communities on the Internet, but Mark, Heather, and Jen had discovered a broad range of previously unknown exploits for all the common operating systems, even those on the newest cell phones and tablets.

Mark selected a computer from the list, bypassed the firewall, and installed a minor modification to one of the operating system libraries, ensuring that the file date, size, checksums, and information assurance codes remained valid. After that it was a simple matter to pull up a list of the installed hardware and drivers, running services, installed programs, and user accounts, and everything else about the system.

The system turned out to be a newer-model laptop with a built-in microphone, speaker, and camera. The microphone and camera were currently disabled. Mark turned them on, routing the data feed to a small media server window on the upper left of his computer display.

A rather frumpy-looking blonde woman in her mid-forties seemed to be staring directly at him as she pecked away at her keyboard. Mark checked the active user account and identified her as user APeterson. Quickly cross-referencing against her open e-mail folder, he refined the information.

Annette Peterson
43 Walker Place
Baltimore, MD 21240
410-691-1353 (Home)
410-691-2764 (Work)
410-324-8763 (Cell)

Rapidly losing interest in Annette, Mark moved rapidly through four more computers before finding what he was really looking for, the system that controlled the airport security cameras. Tiling four media windows along the left half of his display, Mark began cycling through each camera in the airport. Apparently Monday was a busy travel day in Baltimore.

Satisfied with his understanding of the current network, Mark hopped again, then again. Two hours later he pushed back from the workstation, walked across the room to the refrigerator, and grabbed a bottle of water.

"Oh my God!" Jennifer's exclamation spun Mark's head around.

"What?" Mark saw Heather lean over to peer at Jen's display.

"Mom's laptop. I'm in."

Heather's face shifted through a series of emotions, with dismay predominating. Mark found himself standing behind his sister without realizing he had moved.

"Jen," he breathed, conflicting emotions almost robbing him of his voice. "Remember what Jack said."

"I haven't forgotten. But we've been hopping through all sorts of systems, certainly attracting attention from a variety of systems security analysts. If they can't trace us from those, they can't trace us here either."

Heather placed a hand on her friend's shoulder. "You know how bad I want to do the same thing. It just doesn't feel safe."

Jennifer spun her chair to face them, first Heather and then Mark.

"Goddamn it! To hell with safe! I know this is all my fault. I'm the one who ran away. I'm the one who made you guys follow me. But I'm damn sure not gonna be the one who lets Mom and Dad rot from worry, never knowing we're still alive. They deserve better than that."

Mark felt as if he'd been kicked in the groin. In his mind's eye, his dad's strong arms hugged his mother close as she rested her head on his chest, tears streaming down her cheeks, soaking Fred Smythe's T-shirt, her agony melding with his. Inconsolable. He'd seen it in his dreams. Now, as he glanced over at Heather, he saw from her white eyes that she saw it too.

As Heather's eyes returned to normal, she staggered so that only Mark's hand catching her arm prevented her from falling. Heather righted herself, looked up into Mark's eyes, and nodded. He wondered if she felt the same spark he did.

"OK, Jen," Heather said. "It's time."

CHAPTER 29

Linda Smythe sat at her keyboard, rereading the endless supportive postings on her Facebook page from all her close friends, from Anna, from Fred. Over the last few weeks she'd found a certain relief in baring the darkest parts of her soul on this website, had even taken some comfort from the many people who struggled so desperately to throw her a lifeline.

Certainly the people closest to her had spent so much time with her physically that their own lives had been disrupted. But no amount of hand-holding and hugs could cure the depression into which she'd descended. Somehow Anna and then Fred had recognized that her Facebook postings provided a modest amount of relief. Somehow neither of these people she loved showed the slightest resentment that this illogical diversion gave her a measure of help that their love couldn't.

Now, as she stared at that Facebook page, Linda came face-to-face with the realization that even that had stopped working. She scanned all the latest postings, feeling only the dull ache building in her diaphragm, leaving no room for air in her chest. Just that slow, desperate need burning a hole in her chest remained to tell her she was still alive. How long could she go on like this, a living zombie, unfit for the company of man or dog, dragging her friends and family down with her?

She reached for the mouse, moving it down toward the Windows Start button, ready to navigate directly to Shutdown mode, when a new window popped up on her desktop. It displayed a short, simple message.

"Hi, Momma! It's me, Jennifer. Mark and Heather are here too. I love you. I miss you. So does Mark. Ow! Heather says she loves you too."

Linda froze, staring at the cruel joke on her screen, so shocked she found herself unable to respond to the little blinking cursor that invited her to type a reply into the chat window.

"Momma, it's really us. Although it's been difficult to contact you, we couldn't bear the separation any longer. So we made this happen. I'm so sorry it's taken us so long to break through to you!"

The cursor blinked at her, then began to type again.

"Mom, this is Mark. I love you. We've all been going crazy wanting to contact you, Dad, and the McFarlands. Things are complicated, more than you can know, but now we've found you again. I even miss your cooking."

Suddenly Linda found herself shaking. Sobs bubbled up out of her throat, making her nose run.

Her fingers moved to the keyboard. "Damn you, whoever you are! How could you be so cruel?"

The cursor blinked. Blinked again. Then it blitzed across the screen.

"I'm so sorry, Momma. We're so sorry. But this is real and we can prove it. You can ask us anything. Remember the Lab picnic last year? How I tripped and fell toward the grill? How Mark tossed me away from it? How Heather accidentally stabbed that damned Stephenson? Remember what Dad said after he left? 'It's all right. You didn't hurt the mean old bastard. The fork missed him.' Remember?"

The blood drained from Linda's face, leaving behind a coolness that left her wondering if she would pass out. Her fingers moved of their own volition.

"Jen? Is that really you?"

"It's me, Momma."

"And Mark?"

"I'm here too, Mom. I love you too."

Desperately scraping together the scraps of her composure, Linda Smythe pulled herself together, joy hammering at the door of her consciousness, only her caution keeping it from barging through. Still, despite her fear of disappointment, it was the best she had felt since Jennifer had run away.

"My God! How can this be real? I've been so desperate."

"We know, Mom. We know."

"Where are you?"

"Momma, you're going to have to trust us. We can't tell you that. Some bad things have happened."

"Has anyone hurt you? Because if they have, I swear to God I'll find them and hurt them even worse. And what your father and Gil would do to them…They just better not have hurt you!"

"Mom. It's OK."

"Yes, Mrs. Smythe, it is."

"Heather?"

"Hi. I'm here. Just wish my folks were on the line too."

Linda gulped. The anguish in that simple line of text washed away the last shred of doubt that lingered at the corners of her mind.

"Mom. I know you've got doubts. But we've hacked your laptop. We can see you through the webcam. We're going to activate your speaker now so you can hear our voices."

Suddenly the laptop speaker crackled to life.

"Hi, Momma."

"Hi, Mom."

"Hi, Mrs. McFarland."

"Oh God!" Linda Smythe gasped.

"We hear you, Mom," Mark's clear voice sounded deeper than last she'd heard it, but it was surely Mark's voice coming from her laptop's speaker. And Jen's. And Heather's. Impossible to stifle, her sobs broke from her chest, gurgling from her mouth in loud, shuddering gasps. The dike she'd kept her fingers in burst into a million fragments, loosing her emotions in a torrent that left her bent over her keyboard, unable to breathe, unable to speak.

After several moments of no response from her children, Linda wiped her eyes, her mind filled with the sudden fear that the connection had been lost while she wept. As she raised her head, she saw another window appear at the upper right corner of her computer display. Centered in that window, a tearful Jennifer smiled and waved at her, flanked left and right by Mark and Heather, all of them leaning in close so they could be captured by their computer cam.

Linda took a breath, reasserting a degree of composure. Her conversation lasted exactly twenty-three minutes, a session filled with loving assurances.

Yes, they were fine.

Their situation was complicated, some trouble with the law, but it had been handled.

No, not in a way that would let them come home. At least not anytime soon.

No, they couldn't tell her where they were right now, but nobody had hurt or abused them. Couldn't she tell?

Linda mixed her probing questions with answers to theirs. When it became clear that they would have to break the connection, she begged them to stay on until she could walk next door and get Anna. At this point, Heather looked particularly distressed and asked Linda to give her mom and dad all her love. After extracting Linda's vow not to contact any authorities and to keep this entirely within the immediate family, Mark, Jennifer, and Heather agreed to make contact again, at the same time the next night. Then, with one last smiley-sad group wave, they were gone.

CHAPTER 30

The morning sun slanted through the sliding glass doors with a golden clarity that felt like something out of myth. That's how Anna felt as she glanced out at her back deck before serving the pancakes, bacon, and freshly warmed maple syrup. As she looked at Fred, Linda, and Gil, arrayed around the breakfast table like knights and a lady at King Arthur's court, an excitement bordering on jubilation hammered within her breast. And Linda was smiling.

With all her worry about Heather, somehow Anna had known her daughter was OK, a deep well of knowledge that came from her connection with her only child. But the loss of Jennifer and then Mark had wilted Linda like a two-week-old rose. Anna had looked into her friend's eyes and seen suicide growing behind those empty green orbs. Fred had seen it too. Both of them had fought against it, but it was like Pickett's Charge, more than a century-and-a-half after that bloody day at Gettysburg, Pennsylvania, and every bit as futile.

Linda's late-night online chat with their kids had changed all of that. She'd been too frightened of losing the communications link to run to get Anna, and both Fred and Gil had worked all night at the lab. After Heather, Mark, and Jennifer had signed off, Linda had come running, banging on Anna's door until she'd stumbled down the stairs in her purple nightgown and slippers.

They'd sat on the couch, talking, crying, laughing, and holding each other until dawn brought their husbands home. Then, after a quick synopsis of last night's excitement, Anna had insisted on making a hearty breakfast to clear their minds and to give them all the inner warmth and strength she felt they'd need for the decisions that lay ahead. After all, their babies were out there, young adults, but their babies still, and they were in some sort of trouble.

There was no way in hell Anna, Gil, Fred, or Linda was going to let those lovely young people fend for themselves. Not in this lifetime or the next. They were much too young and inexperienced in the ways of the world for that.

"Looks great, sweetheart," Gil said, motioning her to sit down.

"Wonderful," said Fred, scooping a stack of steaming pancakes onto his plate.

"Yes it does," said Linda. "I guess I'm just a little too excited to eat, though."

"Nonsense." Anna speared a golden pancake with her fork, placed it on Linda's plate, added butter, and scooped a ladle of syrup in a lazy S pattern over the top. "No more talk of the kids until after breakfast. The sooner we all get to it, the sooner we can get down to business."

Gil's chortling laugh brought their heads around. "No use arguing. I've been through this before. Best enjoy a good meal and good company. Anna's hard to redirect once she gets the bit in her teeth."

Despite everyone's desire to talk about what they were going to do about their children, they began to eat, and as they ate, the warm glow of the delicious breakfast amplified the happy knowledge that their kids were still alive and well.

After the dishes were rinsed and put in the dishwasher, all four adults retreated to the living room, settling onto the L-shaped couch, sinking into the soft tan leather as their minds worked on the problem at hand.

"OK, Anna. It's time."

Gil's voice broke through her practiced comfort zone like a hammer hitting glass. He placed an arm around her shoulder, pulling her close to his body, her forehead brushing the brim of his *One Fish, Two Fish, Red Fish, Blue Fish* hat. Anna felt the world spin out of her control, something it never did. Not now. Not ever.

Then she was crying, her face buried in Gil's strong shoulder, her arms wrapped around his neck, awash in a misery she'd denied for six months. For God's sake, she was Anna McFarland, mother, caregiver, the one who fed strength to her friends and family. What was happening to her?

Then Linda was there. And Fred. Their arms wrapped around her and Gil, hugging them so close it seemed they would all become one.

Gil was the first to speak. "Anna. Are you ready for this discussion?"

Anna pulled back, bringing her head up to stare directly into her husband's eyes.

"Yes."

Gil nodded, his deep voice acquiring an authoritative note.

"As excited as we all are to learn that they're still alive, it's time to think about how we get our kids out of whatever they've gotten themselves into."

"My thoughts exactly," said Fred.

"And if we're feeling like we're in over our heads, imagine what Heather, Mark, and Jennifer are going through."

Each of the others glanced around, catching the look in one another's eyes before returning their gaze to Gil.

Anna felt the words pulled from her lips. "So what do we do about it?"

"We call the FBI. Obviously our kids have been kidnapped, coerced into a situation beyond their understanding. We need the best of the best to deal with this."

Linda shuddered. "But I swore we wouldn't contact the authorities."

Fred reached over and placed his hand on hers. "They've gotten involved in something beyond their control. No matter what you told them, we need to bring in the professionals."

The room fell silent. Then Anna's and Linda's eyes met. Anna nodded slightly, an action mirrored by her friend.

"OK. Whatever it takes to get our babies back."

Gil reached for the wireless handset, lifted it from the cradle, and dialed 411.

"Hello, operator. I need a number in Washington, DC. The Federal Bureau of Investigation. Yes, I can wait."

CHAPTER 31

Denise Jennings ducked into the break room, glancing over at the Bunn coffeemaker sitting on the counter beside the stainless steel sink. A thin layer of dark-brown liquid covered the bottom of the glass pot.

Damn it! Didn't anyone else make coffee when the pot got low?

She briefly considered reprogramming Big John to find the obnoxious culprit, shook her head, pulled the filter basket, and dumped its contents into the trash can. Thirty seconds after that, fresh coffee began pouring from the Bunn into the empty pot.

Jesus. How hard was that?

Five minutes later she returned to her lab, steaming mug in hand, swiped her ID badge through the electronic reader, leaned forward for the retina scan, and, hearing the lock click back, opened the door. Ignoring the handful of staff not at lunch, she turned right into her office, closed the door behind her, and sat down at her desk. Sipping from the "I'm crabby in the morning" mug, she typed in her computer password. She'd done it so often that the sixteen-character mix of upper- and lowercase letters, numbers, and special symbols, though it changed weekly, presented no significant one-handed challenge.

As the log-in screen was replaced by her desktop display, Denise froze. Big John had opened a popup dialog:

Denise Jennings...Eyes Only

Just below the text, another login and password prompt blinked at her. Denise stared at the prompt for several seconds, dread building in her gut until she felt nauseated.

Her fingers danced across the keyboard, the password dialog fading away, replaced by the familiar Big John response window.

Datapoint Acquired.
Correlation to Jack Gregory Query = 0.943732
Event:
McFarland/Smythe Call to FBI.
Reported computer chat contact with:
Mark Smythe
Jennifer Smythe
Heather McFarland
Next chat contact scheduled today, 22 April, 22:30 Hrs.

A 94 percent correlation to her Jack Gregory query.
Shit. Shit. Shit.
As much as she'd hoped her handoff of information to Freddy Hagerman had ended her involvement, that clearly wasn't happening. Big John had his hooks in her, and apparently he didn't

intend to let go until he'd bled her dry. Denise had been so busy she hadn't gotten around to canceling her high-priority intelligence information request yet. So, of course, Big John made sure he returned critical information before she did, information that could send her to prison if she chose to ignore it.

Denise closed the window and leaned back in her chair, her heart thumping against her rib cage like one of those movie aliens trying to chew its way out. Well, she wasn't going to jail. If it took playing both ends against the middle to assure that, so be it.

Denise picked up the phone on her desk, punched in the internal five-digit number, and waited.

"General Wilson." The NSA director's voice seemed to echo through her head.

"Sir. This is Denise Jennings. We've got a situation."

CHAPTER 32

Lieutenant General Robert "Balls" Wilson leaned back in his chair at the end of the conference table, hands clasped behind his head. As smart as Admiral Riles had been, Denise knew that Balls Wilson had him beat. Air Force Academy, Rhodes scholar, All-American linebacker, Caltech PhD in computer science, combat fighter pilot, former commander of NORAD, the first black NSA director was a seriously formidable individual.

He insisted that his staff address him by his fighter pilot handle, Balls, a play on the sports implication of his last name, reveling in the fact that it made some people uncomfortable. Denise was one of them. Still, she had to admit she liked the man. As far as she could tell he sweated liquid charisma.

Arrayed around the table were Levi Elias, generally regarded as the best intel analyst the NSA had, Dr. Bert Mathews, the computer scientist who had been chosen to fill Dr. Kurtz's shoes, and Karl Oberstein, the NSA's chief of operations.

"OK, Denise, show us what you've got."

Nodding to the general, Denise picked up the remote control, pressed the green power button, and walked to the front of the room. The digital display that formed the entire wall came to life, its high-definition background image a lovely high-resolution shot of Earth from space, an image so crystal-clear it had no counterpart in the civilian world, having been taken by one of the most sophisticated spy satellites ever created. If the satellite had been focused on the parking lot outside the Crystal Palace, not only could you have read the license plates, the multispectral imagery product could have told you how long the car had been parked there, from the heat of the engines. It could have shown you which parking spots had been recently vacated, from the differences in temperature of the ground that had been under the vehicles.

Denise pressed a sequence of buttons on the remote, pulling up the presentation she had spent the last two hours preparing.

"Balls. Gentlemen. I asked for this meeting to show you something that Big John brought to my attention this morning. The subject of the correlative data search was Jack 'the Ripper' Gregory."

Seeing that she had their rapt attention, Denise flicked to the first slide. It showed the text message she'd received earlier in the day.

"I received this Big John alert shortly after noon today. What you need now is some context for the message so that you understand its importance.

"Several weeks ago Big John began reporting a sequence of data correlations with the Gregory search, data points that by themselves seemed very tenuous."

Denise changed to a series of slides showing what Big John had identified as connected events.

"I'll run through these quickly and then discuss the implied connections. The first of these events was the New Year's Day virus from a little over a year ago. The virus came to the NSA's attention for two reasons. It had the ability to encrypt data in a manner that our best methods couldn't break. It also revealed the location of a computer that held another encrypted message, this one breakable, with text that alluded to dangerous activity within the Los Alamos Rho Project. This was the event that caused Admiral Riles to send Jack Gregory's team to Los Alamos."

Next came an image showing Jack Gregory and Janet Price standing and cheering at a basketball game.

"This was taken at the New Mexico State Championship basketball game that same year. I've circled in red the people occupying the seats next to Jack and Janet. They are, from left to right, Gil McFarland, Anna McFarland, Fred Smythe, Linda Smythe, Jennifer Smythe, and Heather McFarland. You'll recognize some of those names from my first slide. The other person mentioned in Big John's message today was Mark Smythe. He was a young all-state basketball player, playing in the state championship game."

Balls leaned forward. "I remember reading about that kid. Fantastic young point guard as I recall. ESPN was comparing him to a young Steve Nash."

Denise clicked to the next slide. "This is an article that appeared in the *Albuquerque Journal* a short while later. A local EPA inspector named Jack Johnson, Gregory's cover name, had shown up at the Los Alamos hospital with an injured girl by the name of Heather McFarland. The story goes on to say that Jack apparently encountered a crazed homeless man who had been attempting to kidnap Heather McFarland. The two men fought, with Jack getting cut on the arm before the homeless man ran off. That man has never been seen again."

Balls laughed. "I'd say the chances of ever seeing him again aren't too good."

Karl Oberstein snorted in agreement. "Not much chance of that fellow surviving an encounter with Gregory. Surprises me he managed to cut him, though."

"Probably had to do with protecting the girl," said Balls.

"Here's another story from Los Alamos. Heather McFarland kidnapped and attacked by Dr. Ernesto Rodriguez, a top Rho Project scientist. He kills himself before arrest."

"McFarland kid? Kidnapped again?" Bert asked.

Denise changed slides again. "This is from the *Washington Post*. It's the story about Jonathan Riles's murder of Dr. David Kurtz, after which he took his own life."

The atmosphere in the room acquired a somber cast.

"This next slide is the AP story about the FBI attempt to capture or kill Jack Gregory and his team. Another black eye for the FBI folks, this one even surpassing Waco. A couple of Gregory's team killed, a couple dozen FBI agents and civilians killed, Jack and Janet escape."

Oberstein nodded. "I assume this is going somewhere."

Denise pursed her lips. "A few more minutes and I'll put a bow around it for you."

Her curt response drew another chuckle from Balls Wilson. "Careful. She's got your number, Karl."

She began flipping through the slides more rapidly.

The FBI director murdered.

President Harris assassinated.

Senator Pete Hornsby, the key Senate voice against the Rho Project, dead in a car accident returning from his native Maine.

The three McFarland kids win the National Science Fair with a cold fusion device, a prize that is stripped for plagiarism.

Another AP story, this one about three missing Los Alamos, New Mexico, high school students: Heather McFarland and Mark and Jennifer Smythe.

Top CIA trainer, Garfield Kromly, found murdered.

Then the body of Eduardo Montenegro, the assassin known as El Chupacabra, found at Schriever Air Force Base, not far from where Jack Gregory is known to have hijacked the satellite uplink, reprogramming global GPS satellites to shut down the Rho Project's nanite formula.

Denise ended her slide presentation and faced the general.

"Big John has tagged every one of these events with a very high correlation to my Jack Gregory search query."

Levi's nasal voice redirected her attention. "And what was Big John's calculated degree of correlation?"

"The worst correlation was 0.873."

"That high?"

"Yes. And there's more. It turns out that Jennifer Smythe stayed several days at the Bellagio in Las Vegas, was identified by the security staff as a very accomplished hacker, and subsequently moved to the Espeñosa hacienda outside Medellín, Columbia. Not long after that, Don Espeñosa and a number of his guards were killed. After that, Jennifer Smythe just disappeared."

"What about the other two kids?"

"Nothing firm, but a member of Espeñosa's cleaning staff reported seeing two young Americans arrive at the hacienda on the day that Don Espeñosa died."

"Jesus."

"There's one more thing. That day was Thanksgiving here in the good old USA. The same day Jack Gregory killed the Espeñosa cartel's number one hit man, the same day he reprogrammed the GPS satellites."

Denise paused. "Now we've learned that the FBI is set to monitor a computer chat session between the McFarland and Smythe kids and their parents tonight."

The room was silent for several seconds. Then General "Balls" Wilson rose to his feet.

"Karl, I want that computer hacked, the computer that the FBI will be monitoring for tonight's chat. Work with Denise. Use her antivirus back door. Bottom line, I want us in virtual control of that system when tonight's chat session begins. Oh, and remember, that Smythe girl is supposed to be a talented hacker. Keep our data copy local, nothing goes out on the Net while the chat session is in progress."

"But what about the FBI? Aren't they going to grab that computer right after the session?"

"Not likely. It would be a dead giveaway to their quarry. They'll remain in stakeout mode."

"OK. You've got it, boss."

"Make damned sure I do."

Then the general turned on his heel and was gone.

CHAPTER 33

Mark watched Heather's eyes go white, then brown, then white again, changing color so rapidly he could almost convince himself that he'd imagined it. But he hadn't.

She shuddered, shook her head, and grimaced. "Screw it!"

"What?" Mark asked, taken aback by Heather's unusual descent into vulgarity.

Her angry eyes centered on his. "Sometimes I make myself so mad I can't stand it. In a few minutes we're going to get a chance to chat with our parents, something I want so bad I can taste it, and all I can do is second-guess our decision."

"Understandable," said Mark.

"Bullshit! If we can't trust our parents, whom can we trust?"

Mark paused for several seconds. "True enough. But we know that both our houses were bugged by Jack and Janet. Who's to say those bugs aren't still active?"

Much to Mark's relief, Heather nodded and calmed down. "That must be it. What's been worrying me, I mean."

"We've taken appropriate precautions, made a backdrop for our camera position with plastic sheeting, dressed ourselves in these white sheet togas. As long as we stay focused on not revealing anything about where we are, and remember we might be monitored, we'll be fine. It's impossible to trace our subspace signal."

Heather's eyes momentarily faded to gray, staying that way just long enough to concern Mark before they refocused. "You're right. No reason to worry."

Just then Jennifer entered the lab, the outside door letting in a breath of summer night air, thick with humidity and smells that signaled the gathering storm.

Her eyes swept across them. "You guys all right?"

"Fine," said Heather, putting on what Mark knew was a forced smile. "Just a little anxious."

Jen smiled back at her. "No kidding. Me too."

Sitting down at her laptop, Jennifer logged in, then engaged the program that would connect them to Linda Smythe's laptop. Her middle finger paused just above the ENTER key.

"Well, here goes." She tapped the key, activating the subspace transmission.

Nothing happened for several seconds, then a video window filled the screen. There in front of them were the visages of their parents, crowded together in front of the computer camera.

Sadness engulfed Mark as he saw the tears streaming down Heather's face.

She still managed to be first to speak.

"Hi, Mom, Dad. I miss you so much."

"We miss you too, baby." Mr. McFarland's voice brought a rush of memories to Mark, memories centered in more comfortable times, better days from the past. Mrs. McFarland stared into the screen, eyes misted, rendered completely speechless.

Then everyone spoke in a rush, Mark, Jen, and Heather competing for airtime even as all of the parents stepped all over each other's words on the far end. The expressions of love gave way to questions about how each of them was doing. Gradually talk shifted to questions about their situation. Where were they? Did they need help? Could they come home?

Although they'd talked through these likely questions, Mark found them difficult to answer. With every question they dodged, their parents pressed for more details. If they needed help, they would get it. If someone was holding them against their will, just list the demands. Everything could be made all right again. Home was still home.

Then, seemingly before they'd even started the conversation, the wall clock indicated the time they'd agreed on had expired and Mark found himself taking the lead in telling his mom and dad good-bye. Another round of tears from the girls and their moms, another round of sad good-byes from their dads, and then Jennifer terminated the session.

Jennifer leaned forward on the desk, elbows on the table, face in her hands. Heather's white eyes seemed to stare right through him, tears cutting narrow trails down her cheeks. As Mark stared down at the blank computer screen, the distant rumble of thunder marred the silence that had descended on the computer lab.

Standing there next to Heather and Jennifer, listening to the gathering storm, he couldn't remember ever having been so depressed.

~ ~ ~

Fred Smythe put his arms around his wife, pulling her into a bear hug that was joined by Gil and Anna, a tiny huddle sharing the most difficult game of their lives. When he finally released her, he smiled.

"Darling, why don't you take Anna and Gil down to the kitchen and put on a pot of tea. I'll shut down your computer and be right down."

Linda glanced at Anna, nodded, and led the other two out into the hallway and down the stairs.

Fred steadied himself, took in a great gulping breath, and took a seat in front of the laptop. Reaching under the table, he removed the listening device the FBI field agent had given him earlier in the day. Shoving it into his pocket, Fred grabbed the mouse, clicked the START button, selected Shutdown, and waited.

After several seconds, a new window appeared on the laptop:

Please do not power off or unplug your machine.
Installing update 1 of 2.

Fred shook his head. Damned Microsoft automatic updates. He'd have to remember to disable those next time he logged on to Linda's computer.

Rising to his feet, he walked out of the room. Time to go visit with Linda and his friends, to spend some time talking about their kids. And as bad as the situation seemed, their kids were still alive. That certainly made the world feel a whole lot more manageable than it had just two days ago.

That damn laptop could take its sweet time shutting down.

~ ~ ~

Balls Wilson leaned over Dr. Mathews's shoulder, his eyes scanning the rapidly scrolling computer screen.

"So Bert, did we get the data dump or not?"

"Don't worry, sir. It's streaming in right now."

CHAPTER 34

Dr. Donald Stephenson stared out at his audience, his eyes sweeping across the seated assemblage. The auditorium was completely full, eighteen hundred scientists shifting uneasily in their seats, staring up at him as if he were the Antichrist, hated, but too frightening to ignore.

As Dr. Stephenson watched them watch him, feeling their emotion radiating out, he smiled inwardly. *That which you don't understand, you fear. That which you fear, you hate.* Dr. Stephenson understood that feeling and relished it. During his humiliating stint in prison, he had made those sentences his mantra. If his warped childhood had taught him anything, it was an abhorrence of imprisonment. It didn't really matter whether it was in a bedroom closet or an eight-by-twelve-foot steel-barred cell. For a moment, he wanted nothing more than to make every person in the audience experience what he had had to experience, but it would have been lost on them. For one thing, he was a genius while most of them were morons. It was hard to make a moron understand anything, even with a tactile demonstration.

He realized all of a sudden that they were waiting for him to speak, that in a few more moments he would have introduced what might be called an awkward silence. Dr. Stephenson cleared his throat.

"Fellow scientists, distinguished guests. It is truly an honor to stand before you on this momentous day, a day that represents the dawning of a new age for humanity."

A soft muttering swept through the crowd, like a soft wind stirring autumn leaves.

"Let me be clear." Dr. Stephenson's amplified voice echoed through the auditorium. "Our world hangs in the balance. At this moment, an unstable anomaly lies at the heart of the ATLAS detector, spiraling inexorably out of our control, spiraling toward the end of all we know, toward the end of this fragile existence we treasure."

He paused to let his words take effect, already beginning to treasure their frightened reaction. "This anomaly, this horrible thing, cannot be slowed, it cannot be stopped. In nine months, thirteen days, four hours, and thirty-two minutes, it will become a black hole. And there is nothing anyone in this world, or the next, can do to stop that from happening."

A low moan arose from the audience, an ethereal entity that coalesced into physical form. Dread incarnate. Just as satisfying as he had thought it would be. Now, time to play the hero...

"Take heart!" Dr. Stephenson smiled, his thin lips curling reluctantly upward. "Humankind is not yet lost. While my calculations show that the anomaly cannot be stopped, it doesn't have to happen here. Not on planet Earth."

"And how is that?" The voice of Dr. Kai Wohler rang out through the auditorium.

"Thank you for that question, Dr. Wohler." *Yes, thank you for those four words, Doctor—so artfully phrased, so erudite.* "As you all know, my background for the last couple of decades has revolved around the study of alien technologies under what has been dubbed the Rho Project. As a result of that study, the American government has spawned two minor technological initiatives. The first of these was the cold fusion initiative, the second being the nanotech formula that shows great promise in eradicating all forms of human disease, potentially extending the human life span to hundreds of years.

"Notice that I referred to each of these revolutionary technologies as minor advancements. That is because I have uncovered something on the alien spacecraft that contains far more potential benefit to humanity. In our current predicament, it offers hope where otherwise none should lie."

Dr. Stephenson inhaled deeply, letting the still air of the Swiss auditorium infuse his lungs as he strolled across the stage, wireless microphone clutched firmly in his left hand. His audience had gone completely silent, an aura of expectancy hovering about them. He wouldn't make them wait for long.

"What we will now commence is a project of epic proportions, a project to save our planet from complete and utter destruction. If any of you doubt the cost of doing nothing, I will be happy to share my analysis of the data for peer review."

Dr. Stephenson made sure that his smile left little doubt that he found the idea that he had any peers in this group comical. Then, as if a cloud had passed in front of the sun, Stephenson's brow darkened again. He was, after all, a mercurial god.

"Let me be clear. We have but one chance to save our world. If the anomaly cannot be stopped, and it can't, the black hole must happen elsewhere. In order for that to occur, we must build a machine capable of generating a wormhole that will transport the anomaly into empty space, far from our solar system."

The room erupted into bedlam, scientists talking over other scientists, their feeble efforts effectively drowning each other out.

Dr. Petir Fois, an angular Dutch physicist, stood on his chair so that he rose above his compatriots. "What Dr. Stephenson proposes is madness. Even if we take him at his word that he understands this alien technology, it is still madness. Creating a wormhole here on Earth could set in motion an incalculable sequence of events, possibly even a cataclysm worse than what it is designed to cure."

Fois was the kind of Dutchman who'd stand there with his finger in a dike all afternoon long, refusing to recognize that everything was crumbling around him.

"Would someone please help Dr. Fois contain his emotions?" Dr. Stephenson's voice dripped contempt. "Clearly they have colored his reasoning so that logic is no longer an option. In his world, a black hole consuming our entire planet is less dangerous than attempting to create a wormhole to transport the anomaly into empty space."

Dr. Fois's face turned red on its way to purple. "There are other options."

"Enlighten me."

"We could launch the anomaly into space."

Dr. Stephenson laughed. Once again, Fois hadn't failed to disappoint. "Could we? The only thing keeping the anomaly from becoming a black hole is the magnetic containment field and the most perfect vacuum chamber we've been able to create. That would have to be maintained throughout the launch. To do that we would have to build a very large launch vehicle around it right here in this cavern, probably something like the Saturn V. Assuming we could do that, the containment apparatus would have to also have its power supply transported with it.

"By the way, it's not good enough to just launch the space vehicle out of Earth orbit. At some point the power and therefore the containment field would fail, and the anomaly would eat its spacecraft. Then it would continue to travel within our solar system, its event horizon expanding with every bit of matter ingested, a growing black hole beyond anyone's power to stop. Assuming the containment field could survive the trip, if you think the anomaly will remain stable long enough to exit our solar system, with all the gravitational slingshots that such a trip requires, you aren't qualified to be in this room."

Dr. Stephenson paused, his eyes once again scanning his audience. "Someone said there are no stupid questions. It should be plain to everyone in attendance that Dr. Fois has just disproved that assertion. In fact, the person who made that assertion is clearly a moron. I don't expect anyone in here to like me. I don't want your adoration. But I do demand your attention.

"I've arranged for a copy of my proposal to be placed on each of your desktops, ready for your perusal upon your return to your offices. I recommend you take a long, hard look at that material as soon as you depart this auditorium."

Dr. Stephenson walked to the podium, swept the space with his lifeless gaze one last time, then set the mike on the lectern, turned, and walked offstage.

CHAPTER 35

Kai Wohler watched Donald Stephenson walk off the stage as the auditorium erupted around him. Everyone seemed to be talking at once. It was like an American sports bar on Super Bowl afternoon, during those endless hours before the game when sportscasters droned on and on with pregame minutiae. As the fans drained mug after mug of draft beer, the volume of conversation varied inversely with sobriety.

Reaching for his cell phone, Dr. Wohler suddenly remembered he didn't have it. This was a classified building: thus he, and every other member of the audience, had dropped cell phones and other such devices in rows of small lockers outside. One thing for certain, security or no, as soon as this crowd exited the building, the secrecy surrounding this anomaly was coming off. Now that this many people knew that Dr. Stephenson regarded the black hole as a certainty, it would be minutes, not hours, before word leaked to the press. Before that happened, Kai would break the news to his beloved Karina, more gently than she would get it from TV's breathless talking heads.

Trying to make his way to the aisle, he found himself crammed between people, unable to move. Apparently there was some sort of jam up at the top of the steps leading to the auditorium exit.

Suddenly the microphone squealed, then several loud puffs of breath echoed through the speakers as someone blew into it. Kai turned to see Dr. Louis Dubois standing at the lectern, microphone in hand.

"Attention please! Everyone! Can I have your attention?"

All heads spun to look at the respected scientist, former chief of the ATLAS project.

"May I please have some quiet?" Dr. Dubois lowered his voice slightly, the effect silencing the auditorium.

"I'm afraid I have an announcement that will be a bit disruptive to your schedules. Due to the sensitive nature of the information you have just received, we have assigned you all temporary cubicle office space within this building where you will work until we have all finished our review of Dr. Stephenson's analysis and recommendations."

The crowd volume bubbled up again, but Dr. Dubois continued.

"By order of the leaders of the European Union, in agreement with the United States government, this facility is on lockdown until our task is completed and government leaders have made a decision. NATO military forces have completely secured the perimeter and no one will be allowed to enter or leave any LHC area until further notice. You should know that a news story has just been released stating that the LHC has suffered a toxic containment breach and has been quarantined until the situation has been resolved. Nearby communities are being evacuated as I speak."

Once again the crowd raised its confused voices, causing Dr. Dubois to speak louder.

"As you are released from this auditorium, you will be given a package specifying your cubicle number as well as a building map to help you find it. Please report to your cube as soon as possible. There you will find a complete copy of the material Dr. Stephenson has provided. In addition, each cubicle has its own laptop, connected to our internal, classified network for your work, but there is no external Internet connection.

"Along one side of your cubicles, you will find a cot and a small bag of assorted toiletries. Shower facilities are available on each floor and are marked on your building map, along with restrooms and fully stocked break rooms. Most of you are already familiar with our first-floor cafeteria."

Dr. Dubois paused, letting the room settle into a stunned silence. "Despite what Dr. Stephenson said, I have worked with most of you for years and I know you to be the best of the best. The sooner we finish this task, the sooner we will get to go home to see our loved ones, the sooner we will be able to begin the work to save our planet. Now, make me proud."

Then Dr. Dubois turned and walked off the stage, heading in the opposite direction from that taken by Dr. Stephenson.

CHAPTER 36

Having made the tough decision, Mark led Heather and Jen up onto the porch for their daily predawn briefing with Jack and Janet. The cool morning air had an extra bite to it, the first hint of Bolivian winter just enough to raise the gooseflesh on his bare arms.

Jack stood watching them come, a steaming mug of coffee in his hand. On the table in front of Janet, the pot sat invitingly close to three more brown ceramic mugs. Mark filled all three mugs, then lifted his slowly to his lips as he straightened. The aroma matched the hot liquid's taste, strong but smooth. He wiped his mouth with the back of his hand, then turned to face their trainers.

"We've got something to tell you."

"I'm listening." Jack's eyes narrowed ever so slightly. Mark didn't take that as a good sign.

"Last night we contacted our folks via a subspace video-chat link."

Neither Jack nor Janet showed any sign of surprise. Nor did they speak, letting the silence hang heavy.

Mark was relieved when Heather's steady voice filled the vacuum. "We didn't ask permission. And we don't make any excuses for what we did. We knew the risk, but we did it anyway."

"We know we put you in danger, too," Mark said, trying to give Heather some cover, "but that doesn't mean we regret it."

Once again the silence descended, finally broken by Jack. "Can't say I'm surprised. Janet and I knew you'd make that call sooner or later. We had a small wager about when it would happen."

Mark didn't know whether to be irritated that they were so predictable or happy that they'd avoided a reprimand.

A hint of a smile creased the corners of Janet's mouth. "I won. Jack didn't really think you'd last this long."

Of course he hadn't—and he'd almost been right.

"So," Jack said, "Finish off your coffee, grab a bite to eat from the kitchen, and get ready. You've got a full schedule today."

"And what if they find a way to trace us?" Mark asked.

Jack shrugged. "I assume you took the proper precautions. Besides, the only thing you can be sure of in this life is that sooner or later everything goes wrong. Whether because of this or something else, they will eventually find us. It's why we constantly rehearse our reaction drills."

"I don't know why they have to find us," said Jennifer. "Lots of criminals and terrorists have managed to stay below the radar."

"Apples and oranges," Jack replied. "There are two kinds of people in this world: sheep and wolves. The politicians who lie hidden in holes aren't wolves. They're sheep, sending their wolves out to make things happen. Janet and I are wolves. It's what we've trained you to be."

Janet glanced at her watch. "You three better hustle. You've only got eight minutes to scarf down some breakfast before we hit the firing range. Today you get to shoot the fifty-caliber sniper rifles and M2 machine guns. Anyone who outshoots me gets out of ammo reload duty."

Mark rolled his eyes. Just because their schedule was so tough didn't mean it couldn't get tougher. Maybe they hadn't avoided punishment after all.

CHAPTER 37

Levi Elias hadn't gotten his reputation for being the best analyst the NSA had for nothing. Sitting in his boss's office, James Blanchard watched as Levi leveled his gaze at him, his dark eyes like the twin barrels of a twelve-gauge shotgun.

"Tell me what we got."

"A hell of a lot more than the FBI." James grinned.

"Explain."

"Just like us, they put a sniffer on the IP traffic coming in through the network card. Funny thing is, not a damned thing came in through the network interface."

"And?"

"And thank God for Denise's Puff the Magic Dragon code in the laptop's antivirus software. It recorded every bit and byte of data that changed on the laptop during the visual chat session, including sound and video."

"Nothing came through the network card? How's that possible?"

"It's not. At least not with any technology we know about. But it fits with some of the stuff that caused Admiral Riles to send Jack Gregory's team to Los Alamos."

"So what do you make of it?"

James Blanchard looked at Levi Elias and shrugged. "I've been with my team all night and most of this morning going over the recorded audio and video streams at least two dozen times. Bottom line, boss, we've got nothing."

"Nothing?"

"Whoever these kids are, they're good." James worked the jog shuttle, moving the recording forward five minutes. "Typical example, background is draped by thick plastic sheeting, common contractor material, made by hundreds of companies all over the world, mostly in Asia, my guess China."

James zoomed in on a small section of the plastic, a tight shot that eliminated the foreground. He swirled a small circle with his laser pointer's red dot.

"You can see small beads of condensation on the plastic, cool room, high humidity. This time of year you get those conditions in an air-conditioned room on about 37 percent of the planet, including the entire US gulf coast."

He backed out of the zoom, selected a control on the electronic light table, and quickly drew a dotted outline around each of the young people in the frozen image. Another tool click and Heather McFarland, Mark Smythe, and Jennifer Smythe came up in their own frame, the sheet having been cropped out of the image so they were displayed against a pure white background.

"Notice anything peculiar about these three?"

"Nice tans. Muscular, taut faces. Just glancing at them I'd say they've been on a three-month vacation at a health spa. Either that or training for the Olympic beach volleyball team. What's that they're wearing? Togas?"

"Sheets."

"Sheets?"

"Sure as shit. Plain old cotton bedsheets."

"Let me guess. Kind you can buy anywhere, probably made in China. Looks like they were expecting to have their chat session intercepted."

"As generic as it gets."

"Give me a tight shot of each face, side by side. Keep the rest of the background clipped out. Then let the video roll."

James Blanchard made the adjustments and started the video from the beginning, the display filled with three faces, the enhanced video so clear that Levi could see the moisture glisten on their teeth as they smiled.

"Amp up the audio."

The audio volume rose until he could feel the vibration of the bass notes in Mark's voice.

"Pause that."

The video froze. The sound stopped.

"What did the voice stress analysis show? Are they under duress?"

"Inconclusive. There's stress there, but it seems to be closely associated with the emotions of talking with parents they've been missing. I'd say they want to come home, but can't. Lots of reasons for that, though. Doesn't mean they're being held against their will. Once more I go back to their physical appearance. That kind of muscle tone doesn't square with being held captive. Neither does the tan."

"Let the video roll again."

The booming volume filled the room as Levi watched the facial expressions that went with the audio. Suddenly he sat up.

"Stop. Replay the last fifteen seconds. Five percent more volume."

"There. You hear something?"

James nodded.

"Replay it again but mask out all the voices. I only want background noises."

This time it took Blanchard fifteen minutes to manipulate the sound editor to achieve the desired effect.

When he played the audio again, a number of noises stood out. The sound of computer fans, the AC electric current humming in the lights, and four seconds of a chirping noise.

"Was that a bird?"

"Yes, sir. Definitely a bird sound."

"What kind?"

Blanchard laughed. "Not my specialty."

Levi didn't laugh. "Then find someone whose specialty it is. I want to know exactly what kind of a bird that was, where it lives, its migratory patterns, and what color seeds it shits. One more thing. I want your team to reanalyze the whole thing, background noises only. Identify any animal or insect sounds, same drill as the bird."

As Blanchard began moving toward the door, Levi called after him. "Oh, and James, get someone working on that AC electrical hum. I want to know if it's fifty or sixty hertz."

"I'm on it."

Moving down the hallway at a brisk walk, James smiled. If he had to work for an analyst, it felt good to work for the best in the business.

CHAPTER 38

President Jackson sat with his back to the towering windows, gold curtains pulled tightly closed, with only the wall-mounted candelabras adorning the cream-colored slices of wall that separated them. He glanced around at his national security staff seated in the burgundy leather chairs around the great table that filled the bulk of the White House Cabinet Room.

Today's meeting only involved the central core of the NSS: Vice President Bob Bethard, Secretary of State Beth McKee, Secretary of Defense Gary Blake, Director of National Intelligence Cory Mayfield, National Security Advisor James Nobles, Director of Homeland Security Thane Evans, and the president's chief of staff, Carol Owens.

In addition to the core team, Carl Rheiner, the director of central intelligence, occupied a seat to the president's left. It was going to be his show. Just a couple of hours earlier, Rheiner had informed the president that President Chekov of the Russian Federation, in a surprise move, had held a hastily assembled press conference to announce that Russia had developed its own version of the nanite serum.

The president's first response had been unprintable, but Rheiner had had worse news.

"Apparently, they're set to begin mass production at several manufacturing facilities. They've already begun inoculating military personnel and plan to roll it out for the general population over the coming months—before making it available for sale on the international market."

It was why he'd now assembled the whole national security brain trust. President Jackson spread his hands in a gesture of inclusiveness. "Well I guess we're all in. The Chinese, French, and others can't be far behind the Russians. The real question is, what are we going to do in response? Before I hear your thoughts, I've asked the DCI to give us a quick rundown from the CIA point of view."

All eyes turned toward the CIA director.

"Thank you, Mr. President." Carl Rheiner opened a leather portfolio, moving its contents into three small stacks in front of him. "I'll start with the nanite situation since that is the most directly affected by President Chekov's announcement."

The president hoped this presentation wouldn't be as grim as he expected.

"As you all know, central intelligence has focused a large effort these last several months toward analyzing the consequences of our own nanite formula rollout, starting with the African continent, since they had already received the initial distribution. The results of that initial distribution are a mixed bag, mostly bad. In countries decimated by AIDS, malnutrition, and other diseases, it is hardly surprising that desperation for a cure has led to fighting between those who received the first doses and those who had to wait. Violent gangs began kidnapping nanite recipients, bleeding them into plasma bags for resale along with acts of superstitious barbarism.

"While Jack Gregory's GPS broadcast shut down most of those nanites, there were significant numbers of people that were shielded from that signal and they still have active nano-serum in their blood. I don't need to tell you the jeopardy in which they've found themselves. Most of them tried, with varying degrees of success, to pretend their nanites were deactivated like all the rest. But it only takes one public injury to put the lie to those pretenses.

"Mix that with gangs of nanite-augmented young men, drunk with the power of virtual invulnerability, and you get the effect we're seeing on African societies, a drastic increase in tribalism. By this I mean that groups have grown more homogeneous, either for protection or for aggression.

"I won't belabor the details, but this analysis, combined with worries about the possible long-term negative impact of nanite dependence on people's natural immune systems, has led to the president's meticulously planned nanite redistribution. Although we all knew that the day would come when other governments were able to duplicate the formula, I think we all hoped we'd have time to test our delivery strategy first, establishing a measure of control over these types of negative consequences. That's no longer an option."

"So what do you recommend we do about it?" President Jackson's lips had tightened into a thin line during Rheiner's summary. He sensed that, unfortunately, Rheiner had saved the worst news for last.

"Before I give you my recommendation, I need to reference two other areas that critically impact the situation."

Carl Rheiner spread several papers from his second stack across the table in front of him. "The first is the other alien technology that was released to the public, cold fusion. Although it's been widely hailed as a home run for our planet, it carries parallel dangers. Every scientist and energy expert I've talked to has been stunned with the speed with which industry has implemented increasingly efficient versions of this technology, dropping the price to where it will soon be available to power automobiles. Machinery that uses fossil fuels is about to become as outdated as the ancient plants and animals that compose those fuels. It has happened so fast that OPEC finds itself with its monetary spigot rotating into the off position.

"Islamic radicalism is ramping up with the rise in Muslim rage and frustration. Since Islam is composed of a number of sects, primarily Sunni and Shiite, they are being driven into the same tight tribal groupings. It's reached the point that regional war is a near-term certainty."

Rheiner paused to let his words take effect. Everyone in this room had already known this information. But the silence and grim expressions indicated that his words had driven it home like a stake in the heart.

"We've seen the same type of radicalization taking hold here at home," Thane Evans interrupted. "Starting with a lot of militia folks in the Northwest and South, even spreading to groups like the Sierra Club. Hell, Native American tribes are going off the energy grid at a pace that indicates they're working from a central playbook."

As the buzz in the room started to rise, President Jackson held up a hand, immediately quieting the gathered officials. "Let Carl finish, then we'll all get a chance at this." And they would, too—he'd work them half to death if he had to. This was too important.

Rheiner continued as if the interruption hadn't happened. "That brings me to the ultimate point, the executioner's axe hanging over this planet in Switzerland. Mr. President, as soon as you and our allies in Europe make the joint announcement that a black hole is forming at the heart of the LHC, these global and local pressures are going to explode. It's a miracle that the secrecy around the November Anomaly has held up this long, but that can only last a couple more weeks. As soon as the world's richest nations start building Dr. Stephenson's monstrous new Rho Project device, there won't be any more denying the scope of our problem.

"Two weeks, tops. That's what we've got to get a plan put together and coordinated with our major allies. In order of priority, we need a plan to protect this new Stephenson Rho Project, a plan to protect our government and key population centers, a plan to gradually reestablish order where we aren't able to maintain it initially, and a plan to keep our enemies from blowing us to hell before we can get all those other things done."

Rheiner replaced the stacks of notes to which he'd been referring in the leather portfolio and closed it. "Mr. President, that's how the CIA sees the world situation."

The president took a long slow drink from the Waterford Crystal glass at his elbow. He nodded at Rheiner. "Thanks, Carl. Excellent rundown."

President Jackson had once heard a quote from one of the helicopter pilots who had flown Special Forces into Afghanistan through thick mountain fog. After returning from the mission, when his colonel asked him how he felt, the pilot had responded that he couldn't drive a toothpick up his ass with a jackhammer. It pretty accurately described the president's own feelings at this moment.

Turning his attention to his chief of staff, President Jackson said, "Carol, how about sticking your head out and getting someone to round us up some pizzas? Looks like it's going to be a long night."

CHAPTER 39

Heather slid the alien headset over her temples, feeling the warmth of its massaging pulse slide through her brain. Sitting together with her in a loose triangle on the Frazier veranda, Mark and Jennifer echoed her action. Cloaked in twilight shadows, Jack leaned back in his own chair, his booted feet propped on a coffee table as he watched them. No pressure.

Heather entered the Bandolier Ship's computer on point, Jennifer following her lead as Mark took up a virtual overwatch position, alert for any sign of the artificial intelligence that had attacked them on their last visit. Heather calculated the odds of another hostile encounter with the AI at less than 7.3642 percent, but that was still a long way from zero.

The announcement from Russia that it had already begun inoculating Russian soldiers with its own nanite formula hadn't come as a great surprise, but it had narrowed their timeline, another sign that training days here at the Frazier hacienda were rapidly coming to an end. Despite their best efforts, the nanite genie was now out of the bottle for good. Earth's population was going to have to learn to come to terms with that new reality or face a very bitter future.

Of greater concern was what they had discovered about Dr. Stephenson's activities at the Large Hadron Collider. So far the governments of the United States and the European Union had managed to keep a lid on that secret, but that wouldn't last much longer. Heather didn't care to think about what was likely to happen as soon as the world learned about the November Anomaly. Her visions hadn't left her with a warm cozy feeling on that one.

Returning to the matter at hand, Heather traversed the fractal data map with a speed that defied its incredible complexity, ignoring data paths that offered stunning revelations in physics and mathematics, despite their strong tugs on her curiosity. She knew what she was after and it was critical that she maintain a tight focus on that mission.

Within five minutes Heather identified a key nexus, a point at which several related paths branched. A shared thought released Jennifer along one of those paths as Heather's mind opened itself to another.

The world she had known melted away as she found herself hurled from the Milky Way's familiar spiral arm. A third of the way toward the galaxy's core, she swept toward the fifth planet of eighteen that circled a dull orange star. The planet was a gas giant twice Jupiter's size, one of its thirteen moons slightly larger than Earth. Her view shifted, swooping in on the moon, decelerating until she hung above it like a high-performance reconnaissance drone.

That wasn't quite right. She found she could spin the globe in any direction, although what was really happening was a repositioning of her virtual camera location. For several seconds she found herself so fascinated by the amazing control she enjoyed over the system that she failed to recognize the significance of the scene unfolding below her.

Forty-eight percent of the moon's surface was covered in water, the rest occupied by five continents, each considerably larger than Asia. Tied into the computer as deeply as she now was, Heather merely had to think about a topic and her brain immediately found itself immersed in relevant data. Some things, like the names assigned to this particular solar system and its planets, were merely lengthy alphanumeric representations that, although useful for cataloguing, didn't exactly roll off the tongue. Heather decided to assign the huge gas giant the name Jupiter2, tagging its populated moon as Zeta.

Zeta's atmosphere was an oxygen-nitrogen mixture, although the increased oxygen content and atmospheric density would have given humans a continuous high. The oceans teemed with sea life, although very few species bore any resemblance to fish, the majority looking much more like some of the odd creatures found at extreme depths in Earth's oceans.

But it was something else entirely that took Heather aback.

The land masses were covered in cityscapes, advanced so far beyond Earth technology that they looked more like CPUs viewed through an electron microscope. The continent-cities teemed with activity, although little ground space had been allocated to vehicular traffic. Vehicles moved up and through the air to their appointed destinations.

The indigenous population was an amalgam of species, varied in physical form, but working in a unison that implied shared thoughts, vaguely resembling the kind of mental sharing that she, Mark, and Jennifer experienced through the alien headsets. Her mental link to the Bandolier Ship's computer supplied a name. The Kasari Collective.

Another oddity attracted her attention. The vast majority of the people on this planet were soldiers, perhaps all of them. Unlike the military organizations of Earth, in which the soldiers were backed by huge logistics tails, this organizational structure seemed to be mostly composed of teeth. The beans-and-bullets part of the operation was supported mostly by autonomous machines that delivered what was needed at the specified place and time.

Although these beings tended to be larger than humans, many of the species looked distinctly humanoid, walking upright on two legs, some with multiple pairs of arms. Everywhere she looked Heather observed males and females of military age. Clearly the actual ages of these people differed from Earth ages by a factor of several lifetimes, but she had expected to observe children and the aged. But there just weren't any. Not on Zeta.

Not one sentient being on this Earth-sized moon with its population of eighteen billion actually came from Zeta. The entire moon was nothing but a giant interconnected hub of military bases, one of many worlds that served a similar purpose for the Kasari.

Each base formed a wheel around a central debarkation center, manned to maintain readiness for the moment when that particular center would go active. From an engineering perspective, it was an extremely effective system.

Heather was reminded of one of her history lessons. In Israel, the once-mighty fortress of Masada sits atop an escarpment, its walls dropping away in sheer cliffs. In Roman times, it was stocked with years of supplies, absolutely impregnable. But the Romans crushed Masada in typical Roman fashion by applying an engineering solution. They built a huge ramp to the top of the cliff walls and used human shields from the local population to stop the defenders from raining down arrows and hot oil, using the resulting road to overwhelm their enemies in the castle.

The Kasari seemed to be familiar with similar modes of military thought. Of course, even the mighty Romans had ultimately been defeated.

Heather shifted her virtual position to inside the massive central facility at one of these hubs. A huge machine occupied the center of the stadium-size room, a great ring structure that rose up like a mighty wheel. A gateway. The technology that made the gateways possible was uniquely that of the Kasari. It was their strength, but it was also their weakness.

To generate gravitational forces great enough to form wormhole gateways required extraordinary matter-to-energy conversion, the process consuming resources on a scale that bled planetary systems dry in just a few hundred years. That was problem number one. The second problem was that no one had ever come up with a solution that allowed a wormhole spawned from just one gateway to be stable enough to allow a living being to survive the trip through it. To damp the inertial forces enough for someone to survive the trip, you needed a gateway at each end.

Once again the Kasari had come up with an engineering solution. Find a world with intelligent life that had acquired nuclear technology. Then send a robot ship through a one-ended wormhole to seduce its population with the offer of wondrous technologies, the ultimate being the construction of a gateway. Once the gateway was complete and came online, the Kasari would connect a matching gateway and the waiting army would pour through.

But the system wasn't perfect. Many of the robot ships were destroyed by the Bandolier Ship's makers, the Altreians, another name supplied by her newfound computer access. Some worlds never succumbed to the technological temptations provided by the robot ships. Even in the best scenario, large numbers of soldiers had to be kept at the ready for many years as they waited for the far-gate to activate. But when it did activate, there was no stopping the invading Kasari force. They poured through, securing the immediate area around the far gateway, methodically extending their control until another world's population had been absorbed into the collective.

On the other hand, the Altreians had advanced technologies of their own, including a mastery of subspace that allowed faster-than-light transport of their own starships, and these could carry living crews. But starships were expensive things and couldn't compete with gateways when it came to rapidly moving large numbers of soldiers to new worlds. And though the Altreians experienced frequent victories, every loss extended the Kasari empire. The Kasari had been spreading for centuries, with no sign of slowing down.

As Heather stared at the alien soldiers going about their tasks near the dormant gateway, she suddenly froze. She knew what Dr. Stephenson was up to in Switzerland.

Suddenly the prospect of a world overrun with nanites seemed the least of their worries.

CHAPTER 40

"We've got them."

General Wilson looked up to see a rare smile on Levi Elias's narrow face.

"Tell me."

"It was the bird, all right. *Saltator similis*, a species of cardinal, indigenous to the hill country bordering the southern Amazon, specifically parts of Paraguay, Uruguay, and northeastern Bolivia. Also the electrical hum from the lights was fifty hertz, so that matches."

"Pretty big area."

"Yes it is. So we did a check against any of Jack Gregory's previous assignments."

"And?"

"Several years ago, Gregory was assigned to eliminate a threat against Miguel de Esquela, a senior Bolivian politician on the

CIA's payroll. A communist guerilla leader had placed a contract on de Esquela. Gregory eliminated the threat."

"Did he have direct contact with de Esquela?"

"He did. After assassinating the guerilla warlord, the Ripper killed two hit men inside de Esquela's house, saved the politician, his wife, and four children."

"A man in Gregory's debt."

"Indeed. But there's no record of any subsequent contact between them. We actually looked at this potential linkage several months ago, but came up dry. However, with this latest information we had Big John take another look."

Levi handed Balls Wilson a folder containing six satellite images. The general spread them across his desktop.

"It's a ranch about an hour out of San Javier, formerly the property of Nuremberg Trial fugitive and former SS officer Jori Klaus. Turns out that Miguel de Esquela was instrumental in confiscating that property after Klaus's death, then arranging its transfer to another German, one Karl Jacques Frazier."

"You've confirmed it's Gregory?"

"There's no photo of Frazier on file. Bolivia isn't really at the top of the food chain in maintaining digitized records. But Big John thinks it's him. Correlation 0.803."

Balls Wilson studied the photographs more intensely. "These aren't very good."

"No. We don't have any of our better spy satellites on an orbit that covers Bolivia. These are the best we've got unless we retask a U-2 or Global Hawk."

The general frowned, leaned back in his leather chair, and closed his eyes for so long that Levi began to wonder if he'd fallen asleep. When Balls opened them again, he shook his head slowly.

"If Big John says there's an 80 percent correlation that's good enough for me. Retasking those assets dedicated to southwest

Asia would be too visible. As good as Gregory is, I don't want to risk tipping him off."

General Wilson rose to his feet, walked around the big oak desk, and clapped Elias on the back as he walked him toward the door. "Damn fine work, Levi. Looks like it's time for me to chat with the president. This time he'll have to make the call."

CHAPTER 41

Heather leaned back in the chair and pulled the alien headband from her temples. Half a dozen feet away, Mark and Jennifer also came out of their links. The wind came in off the sloping hills damp and clammy, whipping Heather's hair around her face as she turned her gaze toward Jack.

Three months ago she'd been sure the Bandolier Ship's creators had good intentions toward Earth. Now she was pretty sure that wasn't true. It was time to give Jack the bad news.

What began as a conversation among Jack, Mark, Heather, and Jennifer quickly expanded to include Janet as she glided silently out through the screen door. Heather led off, describing what she'd seen in the section of the alien database that dealt with Kasari operations, their thirst for new resources, including new species to assimilate. Many things drove them down a path of conquest, especially their powerful wormhole technology.

Jennifer went next. She'd focused on gaining an understanding of the motives that drove the Altreians. At the surface, those motives seemed beneficial, to preserve freedom of choice for all species, to stop the Kasari's rampant environmental destruction, to oppose one society's aggressive conquest wherever it occurred. But Jennifer had dug deeper, seeking to find out what happened to every planet where the Altreians had engaged the Kasari.

Again, her preliminary queries had yielded what seemed to be benign intent. If the Altreians' ships were able to defeat the Kasari starship before a gateway could be constructed, they left the saved planet in peace. However, once the Kasari succeeded in seducing the planetary population to complete the gateway, the planet was lost. What disturbed Jennifer was that these outcomes failed to account for all the planets. Everywhere she looked she found holes, shifted around in the database in a way that made it extremely difficult to trace the connection.

It had taken a stroke of luck to spot the first hidden data link. Frustrated with her inability to pull up detailed information on what had happened to some of the planets, Jennifer had backed off, reviewing star system information gathered over centuries of mapping and monitoring the galaxy.

Jennifer filtered this data by narrowing her search to include only planetary systems she'd previously identified as Kasari-targeted systems. Suddenly she began to find cases in which previously teeming planets were now devoid of life. The odd thing was that these weren't planets killed off by Kasari consumption of resources. Neither were they planets where the Kasari had been defeated before gateway construction had begun. Instead they were the planets on which, according to her previous search, the population had been attempting to build a gateway; then all subsequent military data had disappeared. It was as if that data had been purged from the Bandolier Ship's database.

But why had the Altreians purged the military record of how these planets died? If the Kasari had been responsible, then surely the data would have been maintained. Even if the Altreians had managed to crush the Kasari after they had assimilated the planet's inhabitants, it would have counted as a victory. So something else had happened. Something they wanted to hide.

At this point, Jack interrupted the telling. "So what do you make of it?"

Jennifer hesitated a second before speaking. "I think if the Altreians decided they were about to lose a world, they attempted to kill the entire population before the gateway could be completed."

As much as she hated the idea, Heather found herself nodding in agreement. Mark's silence spoke for itself.

"So how did they do it?" Jack asked.

"I don't know," said Jennifer. "All that data got wiped."

Heather shifted in her seat. "I doubt the Altreians ever loaded that into the Bandolier Ship's database."

Janet turned toward Mark. "What about the AI?"

"It was a no-show. No sign of it at all, and I was looking."

"Maybe that's a good thing."

"I wouldn't count on it," said Mark.

Jack rose, moving to the edge of the porch, looking toward the east, where a sliver of the full moon peeked over the horizon. If someone had painted little hands below it, it would have looked like a neon "Kilroy was here" drawing.

"We're in a tight spot."

"About to get tighter," Heather said. "I think Stephenson was behind the November Anomaly, probably using the Rho Ship to generate it. Now he's going to use that as the reason the world's governments need to build the gateway. What really sucks is if we stop this Rho Project, the black hole will eat our planet. If we don't, either the Kasari horde pours through or our beloved Bandolier Ship toasts us all."

"That's one thing I don't get," Mark said. "Now that the AI is gone, we have complete control over the Bandolier Ship's computers. I didn't detect anything that would be some sort of trigger for a self-destruct system or anything remotely like that."

"And we don't have any idea what really happened on those dead planets," Jennifer added. "It might have been the AI triggering things or, considering the people who've worn that headset, it might have been the fourth crewman."

"Careful." Janet's voice, low and soft, eased through the night air like a stiletto. Heather had forgotten how intimidating she could be, and apparently Jennifer had too.

Realizing the implication of her words, Jennifer hastily continued. "Sorry. I forgot. Anyway, it can't be that. Robby's just a baby."

In the moonlight, Janet's eyes flashed a silver reflection. Then, without a word, she walked back into the house, letting the screen door slam shut behind her, leaving a lump in Heather's throat and a dull ache in her heart. It seemed she just couldn't alter the destiny that made her hurt everyone she cared about.

CHAPTER 42

Navy Lieutenant Gordon Morrow lifted the night-vision goggles from his eyes. With this level of moonlight, his platoon wasn't going to need them much tonight, at least if the actions stayed out of the deep bush. If everything went according to plan, they wouldn't be going into any deep bush on this mission. Of course, in his year and a half commanding SEAL Team Ten's First Platoon, things had yet to go according to plan. And tonight his platoon was going to take down Jack "the Ripper" Gregory, so this wasn't likely to be the first time.

Lieutenant Morrow excelled at two things, mission preparation and mission execution. The first of these had led him to study everything known about the Ripper's life, from the little boy who had watched his father's beheading in Riyadh, Saudi Arabia, to the man who had become the CIA's most feared killer. Then, after Jack's own agency had turned him out in the cold, he'd built upon that reputation as a private contractor, finally attracting the attention of NSA director Admiral Jonathan Riles. Riles had successfully recruited Jack to the NSA, and subsequently attempted to harness Gregory's talents to bring down the Rho Project. That action had spawned the sequence of events that had brought Jack and Lieutenant Morrow to this moment. Now, in a fitting twist of fate, Jack the Ripper and his protégée, Janet Price, were destined to replay Butch Cassidy and the Sundance Kid's final Bolivian act.

Circling his right arm above his head, Morrow brought his team in tight, so that he could pass along the perimeter in one direction while his chief went the other way, physically touching and double-checking each man, a last personal check that told them more than all the high-tech gear designed to show each man's location and mission status could ever do.

The High Altitude Low Opening (HALO) jump had gone perfectly, landing the team in an isolated clearing a little over two kilometers from the GPS coordinates marking the location of the Frazier hacienda. When they had stowed the high-altitude breathing apparatus, chutes, and excess gear, Lieutenant Morrow had been pleasantly surprised that the night jump had yielded nothing worse than a few minor scratches to any member of his sixteen-man team.

Now they were ready, GPS coordinates marking the objective assault positions for each special operator along with the tight grouping of symbols that showed their current positions.

Tapping his chief on the shoulder, Morrow gave the signal to move out. Sixteen heavily armored warriors melted into the moon shadows.

~ ~ ~

The flashing red silent alarm brought Mark to his feet in the bedroom, his powerful stride propelling him into the hall in time to see Heather already disappearing out the front door. Although they'd rehearsed this scenario hundreds of times, somehow Mark knew that tonight wasn't another drill.

When he reached the comm center, he found Jack, Janet, and Heather already inside. Jennifer ran up beside him as he stepped across the threshold. Reaching the weapons locker, he grabbed his M4 assault rifle, shoulder holster with its SIG Sauer P226, and backpack filled with ammo and emergency supplies. Then he moved to his station, making room for Jennifer to arm herself.

Heather had settled in front of one of the computer consoles that glowed softly in the dark room. A quick sidelong glance verified that someone had already closed all the blinds, eliminating any chance of light leakage outside the building.

"Situation report?" Jack asked.

"We've got sixteen electronic signatures at two hundred forty-five degrees, distance eighteen hundred meters," Heather responded, bringing up a map display showing the slowly moving symbols.

Mark logged into his console as Jennifer reached her own station. "Are we tied into their GPS signals yet?"

"Not yet. I'm breaking the encryption now. For the moment we're relying on triangulation from the passive antenna array to plot their locations."

Janet moved closer to Mark. "Jen, find out what's providing the overhead intel. It's going to be Global Hawk or U-2. Mark, I want to know about the combat air support."

"On it." Mark worked the keyboard, rapidly navigating his way through a listing of satellites capable of seeing the Frazier compound from their current orbital position. Finding what he was looking for, he typed a coordinate into his subspace transceiver, activating the hard link that tied him into the eye in the sky.

~ ~ ~

Three thousand miles away, at the SEAL Team Ten op center just off Virginia Beach, Commander Eric Patterson cursed as one of his situational displays filled with static.

CHAPTER 43

Heather's blood pulsed through her heart, its heat spreading out through her arteries. She felt the oxygen filter through her lungs, replacing carbon dioxide with the heady mixture that made her feel more alive than she'd ever felt. She knew that with the awesome power of the United States government targeting them, she should probably feel a measure of fear. At this moment a team of the finest special operations soldiers in the world were moving in on their compound, backed by extensive air power that was capable of turning the entire Frazier hacienda into a roiling ball of flame. But all she felt was an electric thrill.

Off to her left, Mark spoke. "I've got a live satellite feed on monitor two. Not a very good one, though. I see three aircraft. Looks like a Global Hawk spy bird and a couple of others."

Jack glanced at the display. "That outbound aircraft has to be the C-140 that did the HALO drop. That other one's a B-52. Looks like we rate a heavy hitter, just in case the SOCOM team gets in trouble."

"Which they're about to get into," said Heather. "I've cracked the GPS encryption. Ready to disrupt their signal."

Jack studied the map for several seconds before reaching out to point at a spot six hundred meters to the south. "Not too much. Send them just on the other side of this hill."

Heather nodded, her fingers entering the commands that would introduce the appropriate GPS positioning error.

"I've got control of the Global Hawk sensors, flight controls, and telemetry. I'm monitoring the incoming commands from the Global Hawk Mission Control Element." Jennifer joined in. "Want me to make it go dark?"

"No," Jack said. "But I want you to replace the live feed with the last two minutes of recorded data from the sensor. Janet and I'll get Robby, Yachay, and the alien headsets out while you three keep SOCOM confused. Give us fifteen minutes if you can, then same drill. Loop back a recorded feed, set the explosive timers, and get the hell out."

"We're not going to fight?"

"If that was a B-2 up there I'd consider it. Not with a B-52 in the air. It's so old there are lots of manual ways to get things done that we can't override with a hack. They don't need to be accurate with that baby and we're so remote, collateral damage won't cross their minds. The second they think the assault team's in trouble they'll blow the hell out of the whole compound."

Heather took a deep breath. She was going to miss this place, but she'd known this couldn't last forever. Thank God the vicious old Nazi who'd built the compound was so paranoid he constructed an escape tunnel from beneath the master bedroom to a thickly wooded ravine thirteen hundred meters to the northeast.

"Ready?" Jack asked.

"Ready," Jennifer replied.

"Start the loopback now."

Jennifer's long fingers whispered over the keyboard.

When Heather looked around, Jack and Janet were already gone.

CHAPTER 44

Lieutenant Morrow gave the signal that brought his assault team to a stop. Although he saw and heard nothing, Master Chief Hob Lucero materialized at his elbow.

"Yeah, Chief?"

"Something's seriously wrong here."

As good as Morrow was, he knew his master chief was better. In SOCOM, the man was a living legend. Two Silver Stars, the Medal of Honor, and a chest full of so many ribbons he tilted to his left whenever he wore dress whites. But that barely hinted at the man's story. Hob was a warrior from a different age: off duty a gentleman straight out of King Arthur's court, in battle a Viking warrior his men would follow into hell itself.

"Yeah, I've had that feeling, but what is it?"

Hob snorted. "It's this goddamned high-tech crap. This shit's screwing us."

"Care to be a bit more specific, Chief?"

The master chief pulled out a map, spread it on the ground, and flipped on a red lens flashlight. His finger circled a spot on the map. "The GPS puts us here, right?"

"Right."

"Bullshit. I may not be one of the Pentagon's sci-fi whiz kids, but I can read a cocksuckin' map well enough to know the difference between a ridgeline and a valley. We're sitting smack at the bottom of a valley, but that GPS says we're right here on top of this ridge."

Morrow stared at the paper map, then shifted his view to the GPS version on his digital display. He paused for several seconds, analyzing the disparity.

"NGA hasn't spent a lot of effort producing high-quality maps of this area."

"Fine. I'll grant you a map error of plus or minus a hundred meters. But I swear to God, we're half a click from where GPS says we are."

"Which direction?"

"Due south."

Once again Lieutenant Morrow paused. As much as he wanted to believe what the fancy SOCOM gadgetry was telling him, he trusted his master chief more.

"OK. So how do you figure it?"

"Sir, didn't Gregory reprogram the GPS birds to deactivate the nanites?"

"He did."

"So that tells me he knows we're here. And he knows how addicted to technology special ops has become. He's screwing us with our own technology."

"Recommendation?"

"Somehow he's tracking us through our transmitters. We need to strip off all the high-tech gadgetry, you and me. Put it in two packs, give those packs to a couple of our guys and send our team on, just like before. Then the two of us veer off and deliver a little surprise to Jack the Ripper."

By the time Master Chief Hob Lucero finished proposing his plan, Morrow had already begun dropping every high-tech gadget on his body in a pile on the ground in front of him.

CHAPTER 45

"Almost time to go," Mark said, the watch in his head ticking off the seconds. He pointed at the map display. "The SEAL team is too far off course now to get here before we're long gone."

Mark saw Heather's eyes go white, saw her stagger under the weight of her vision and reached out a hand to support her.

As her eyes cleared, she shook her head. "Escaping through the tunnel and blowing the compound isn't going to work. The Global Hawk's synthetic aperture radar and infrared sensors are just too good. They'll see us through the surrounding jungle. After that, there'll be no escaping the B-52."

Turning her attention back to her console, Heather redirected her subspace receiver-transmitter at the B-52.

"I've got control of the B-52 targeting system." Heather's voice sounded tight in her throat.

"I thought we couldn't do that."

"It's possible for the crew to manually override my control, but only if they recognize what's happening. That's not going to happen until it's too late."

"Too late for what?" asked Jennifer.

"Give me the SEAL team's center of mass, latitude-longitude."

The light dawned in Mark's mind. He calculated the coordinate to tenths of a decimal second, reciting it aloud.

"Team spread?"

"One hundred seventy three meters."

Heather punched in the targeting data.

Jennifer gasped. "We're going to kill Americans?"

"They're here to kill us."

Her icy tone held an edge Mark had never heard from Heather, but it didn't surprise him. He could feel their training kicking in, siphoning away all paralyzing emotion. They would have to deal with those emotions at some point, just not now.

"Jen," Heather continued. "Get ready to give me the Global Hawk feed. I'm going to want live infrared video of the SEAL team."

"I already have sensor control. Ready any time."

"Mark, get me a satellite shot, best NIIRS resolution it can do."

Mark focused on his own console. "Imagery coming down now. It's a pretty large data stream. Download will take thirty-five seconds."

The data appeared on the monitor to Heather's left, members of the team visible, but without the detail she wanted. Heather shook her head.

"Something's wrong. I'm only seeing fourteen people."

"I'm still showing sixteen GPS blips within that area," said Mark. "Maybe a couple are terrain-masked."

Heather glanced at the map display. "Can't be. The blips for the two I can't see are right next to SEALs I can see."

Suddenly Mark saw her eyes go white again. Not good.

Heather came out of her trance almost as quickly as she had entered it. "Jen, give me the Global Hawk feed now!"

~ ~ ~

"Where the hell did my Global Hawk feed go?" Commander Patterson's voice came from a spot immediately behind Chief Petty Officer Swan's right ear.

"I don't know, sir. One second the signal was great and now it's like the bird quit transmitting."

"You talking to the Global Hawk Mission Control Element?"

"They're working it, boss."

"Not good enough. Those are my men in harm's way out there. You tell those air force video jockeys, if they don't get my video-feed working right now, they're gonna find my boot so far up their asses they'll be gagging on laces."

"Wilco."

Swan had heard that tone before. It was the sound of one pissed-off Navy SEAL.

~ ~ ~

Mark watched as Jennifer directed the Global Hawk's powerful infrared camera, panning across the SEAL platoon's position. Fourteen SEALs, not sixteen.

"Bring it back to us," Heather said. "Give me eyes on this compound, white hot."

The infrared image shifted from black hot to white as the camera zoomed in on the Frazier hacienda's headquarters.

"Shit!"

Mark's exclamation escaped his lips as he saw the two glowing white forms kneeling by the barn, less than fifty meters from the comm center where they now stood. By the time the single syllable reached the ears of the two girls, he was already at a dead run, the SIG Sauer nine-millimeter pistol rising into firing position as the window and blinds exploded inward.

From the corner of his eye he saw Heather press her laptop's ENTER key.

Forty-five thousand feet above, the B-52's bomb bay doors began to open.

CHAPTER 46

Lieutenant Morrow knelt in the darkness, his M4 leveled to provide covering fire for his master chief should that become necessary. But it wasn't going to be. Master Chief Lucero had already applied the setting from the laser range finder to the nonlethal munition that currently occupied the chamber of his M25 counter-defilade rifle, his finger tightening on the trigger. The M25 normally fired high-explosive air burst rounds. It was a lovely weapon that denied enemies the chance of hiding behind walls or ledges. The user just aimed the sight at the wall or windowsill, got the range from the laser sight, thumbed in an extra meter, and fired just above the ledge. The munition's safe-arm circuit armed it thirty meters downrange, the round continuing on to the programmed range before exploding. Bye-bye, bad guy.

But, if possible, this was a live-capture mission. So the master chief had loaded the magazine with nonlethal rounds the troops had nicknamed goobers. These little guys armed themselves upon exiting the barrel, but exploded at the programmed distance. The difference was the way they splashed the target with an instant-drying goo with a tensile strength greater than that of superglue. To get the target free from a goober you had to apply a special spray-on solvent.

Gazing through the thermal sight, Morrow could clearly see the heat signatures of three people gathered near computers through the drawn window blinds. With a thump, the round accelerated from the M25's short barrel. Almost simultaneously, one of the three people inside spun toward the window. Moving with impossible speed, the glowing figure drew its sidearm as it raced toward the window.

The Ripper. The thought flashed into Morrow's mind as the grenade penetrated the blinds, exploding one meter beyond, detonating exactly as programmed. The Goober filled the room with sticky strands and globs, trapping everything it touched in a rapidly hardening web that would have made Spider-Man salivate.

Morrow could see the blast catch the running man, spinning him backward in the air, then locking him in place before he hit the floor. The other two figures also froze to their positions in front of the computer consoles.

The man he had tagged as the Ripper continued to struggle against the tremendous tensile strength of the aero-gel, and although Morrow had been told that such a thing was impossible, he appeared to be breaking some of the strands, the weapon in his hand gradually rising toward the two special operators.

"Enough of this." Morrow fired a single round into each of the three individuals, the tranq darts burying themselves deep in the targets' exposed flesh.

For several seconds the webbed man continued to struggle, but then he, like the other two before him, hung limp in the clutches of the goo web.

Beside Morrow, Hob Lucero rose up, lifting the goo-solvent sprayer as he stepped toward the target. "Mission accomplished."

Morrow hesitated, scanning the area with his thermal scope, seeking additional heat signatures. Intel had said to expect five baddies. Just as he had convinced himself that the action was over, and turned to follow his master chief, the sky burned white and orange. Then the shock wave lifted and flung him like a rag doll in the wind.

CHAPTER 47

Flashes lit the southwestern sky brighter than a Bolivian sunrise, the fireball rolling above the bomb line, swirling high in its own heat tornado five seconds before the blast wave passed over the deep canyon. Janet glanced down at Robby's wide eyes, expecting her child's scream, but failing to have her mother's expectation rewarded. Although his tiny hands pressed tightly to his ears, her baby's face held a look of awed fascination.

Ten feet to her left, Jack's black-clad form stared back toward the hacienda.

"Are you going back?" Janet's voice seemed a whisper in her own ringing ears.

"No point," Jack replied. "Either they're already in the tunnel and will catch us or they're dead."

Janet shrugged off the wave of dread that clenched her heart, snuggled the M4 up against Robby's front-pack, and turned to follow Yachay down into the outstretched arms of the Amazon.

CHAPTER 48

"Mr. President, we have a solid update from Bolivia." James Nobles pressed a button on the remote control, replacing the large-screen monitor's map display with an infrared image showing some thatch-roofed buildings and a number of glowing figures spread out around the compound.

"Go on."

"SEAL Team Ten has its Second Platoon on the ground at the Frazier compound. Perimeter is secure."

"First Platoon?"

"I'm sorry, Mr. President. It's not good. Fourteen KIA. Lieutenant Morrow, the First Platoon commander, has a broken arm, but remains on the scene coordinating with Second Platoon."

"Gregory?"

"No sign of him or Janet Price."

"Damn it! What the hell went wrong?"

"We don't know for sure yet, but early indications are that they managed to hack into a number of secure national systems."

President Jackson felt the blood drain from his face. "How is that possible?"

"We don't know."

"Find out!"

His national security advisor nodded. "We've recovered two laptops from the Frazier compound. The information on those computers could prove invaluable."

"Two laptops..." It felt like a hollow prize, especially considering the loss of life.

There was a pause. Then his advisor said, "But that's not all, sir. The Ripper and Janet Price had help. Significant help."

The president felt hope rise within him. Perhaps the mission hadn't been a total disaster.

"We're still getting an injury assessment, but SEAL Team Ten reports the capture of three terrorists. We think they might have been the hackers who inserted errors into the GPS feed and took control of our Global Hawk sensors. They also managed to retarget the B-52 payload, killing fourteen of our Navy SEALs. We're bringing the terrorists and the laptops to one of our special facilities. Interrogation may take some time, depending on the condition of the detainees and the interrogation methods you authorize."

President Jackson didn't pause. "You have my direct authorization to use any methods required."

As his advisor nodded and headed for the door, the president held up a hand.

"Oh, and James, in case somebody has forgotten, I want Gregory. Dead will be just fine."

CHAPTER 49

Dr. Louis Dubois sat in his office staring at the computer screen, his red-veined eyes testament to the fact he hadn't slept in thirty-six hours. Despite the angry grip captivity had on the quarantined scientists, engineers, and technicians under his direction, their professionalism and love of their work had again produced spectacular results. First-phase analysis of Dr. Stephenson's design had found no fault with his equations, which meant, considering the hatred the LHC team directed at the Rho Project physicist, Stephenson's theory was correct.

True science revolved around peer review to validate a confederate's work. The more controversial the paper, the harder other scientists and mathematicians tried to find its weaknesses. The fact that this massive collection of the world's greatest minds couldn't punch a hole in Dr. Stephenson's work didn't prove he was right, but it was good enough for Louis. And that frustrated the hell out of him.

As he stared at the engineering report, a cold sweat dripped down the back of his neck, dampening his once-dapper ponytail and staining his shirt collar. The project to build what Louis had dubbed the Rho Gate would require an effort that dwarfed the construction of the Large Hadron Collider. Not in physical size. The device itself would be contained within an expansion of the ATLAS chamber. But its complexity, the power required to generate the wormhole, and the seven-month timeline for its construction—that combination truly boggled the mind. It would take a project the like of which the Earth had never known.

Louis brought up the computer-aided design diagram of the Rho Gate. The exploded CAD diagram filled screen after screen. For the LHC engineering team to have produced this level of detail for the Rho Gate in such a short time represented a monumental effort, one that should have even impressed Donald Stephenson. Of course it hadn't, but that hardly mattered. It meant the world had a chance, slim as it might have been, at survival. It was up to Louis to put together a draft proposal to the politicians of the world's greatest powers that would get them all on board without delay.

Popping the top on another energy drink, Dr. Dubois tilted back his head and drained it. Staring down at the tiny bottle, he grinned. Another six of these and he should be just about finished.

CHAPTER 50

Gil McFarland watched as the two FBI men walked up his drive-way, a mixture of hope and dread preceding them through the open front door. Gil directed the agents, clad in identical navy blue suits, white shirts, and black ties, into the living room, where Anna and the Smythes waited expectantly. The agents remained standing as Gil took a seat beside Anna, taking her trembling hand in his.

"Mr. and Mrs. Smythe and McFarland," the agent on the left began. "I'm Special Agent Crowly, here with Special Agent McKee."

"Have you found our kids?" The words spewed from Anna McFarland's mouth, an accusation befitting the setting.

Agent Crowly pursed his lips, inhaled deeply, and continued. "I'm sorry to say we have. At around midnight last night, they died during a SEAL Team raid on a terrorist compound operated by Jack 'the Ripper' Gregory."

The words hammered Gil in the chest, a battering ram that expelled his breath in a ragged gasp.

"No!" Linda Smythe's agonized cry was the only other sound to break the stunned silence.

"As the Navy SEALs entered his Bolivian compound, the Ripper executed your children with a single shot to the head before detonating a booby trap that killed fourteen members of the SEAL team attempting their rescue. We're here to express the United States government's deepest sorrow for your loss."

Time froze.

Gil McFarland finally broke the silence. "Wait just a minute. We call you bastards in to help our kids and now you lay this crock of shit on us? You killed them!"

Moving toward the door, Agent Crowly spoke. "I know this is hard."

"Hard? You sorry sons of bitches!" Fred Smythe's voice cracked with emotion.

The glass lamp left Gil's hand before he noticed that he'd risen, and appeared to sail across the room in slow motion. As the two FBI agents ducked out, it exploded into the edge of the closing door, sending a hail of multicolored fragments chasing them into the White Rock night.

Gil took two steps forward, then stopped, his knees threatening to give way beneath him. The sound of Anna's low wail and Linda's sobs turned him around. There on the leather couch the two women clung together, their heads pressed into each other's shoulders. Beside them, Fred stood staring at the door, hands clenched so firmly at his sides that the veins bulged in his arms. And as Gil watched rage and frustration chain his best friend in place, he felt his whole world crumble around him.

CHAPTER 51

The dream was an old one; at least it had that old, worn-out-shoe feel to it, easy to slide into, but not particularly comfortable once you were inside. It unspooled in Heather's drug-induced sleep, her perfect memory somehow warped and amplified until each heartbeat sounded like the pounding of a bass drum.

In the small gym was a mirrored wall. Along that wall ran a dancer's balance rail. Across the room was a weight rack, Mark handcuffed to it.

Four brutes held her pinned to the floor, legs spread, Don Espeñosa kneeling between them, fumbling with his belt, button, and zipper, ripping open her blouse, grabbing her breasts. He was taunting Mark. A husky laugh escaped the drug lord's lips as he turned his attention back to his pecker.

KATHOOM.

She could feel Mark's heart hammer his chest clear across the room.

KATHOOM.

How could these men fail to hear it? Heather had seen this in her vision, the inevitable consequence of spitting in Espeñosa's face. She'd had other options, but none quite as exciting or satisfying as this one. So she'd spit a wad between the drug lord's eyes and let the dominoes topple one onto the next.

Then Mark was among them, crushing, ripping, tearing, their screams drowned in the bloody downpour. But Mark hadn't killed them. Heather had. And God help her, she'd enjoyed it.

The dream shifted. Glass exploded into the comm center as Heather pressed the laptop's gunmetal gray ENTER key, sending a rack of 2,000-pound bombs raining down on the American SEAL team. Blood and fire. Again she'd chosen the path.

Jack's plan had called for them to divert the SEAL team, then move through the same secret tunnel he and Janet had taken, setting off the explosives that would turn the Frazier compound into an inferno, leaving little for the SEAL team to investigate. But Heather had overridden that plan, opting instead for the path of death and destruction. She'd known the risk. She'd known she'd be killing Americans.

She felt herself lifted, flung into the air, wrapped in sticky goo that ensnared her body so completely she never hit the ground. Stunned, Heather hung in the rapidly solidifying web until this drug-induced fog replaced the sharp pain of the tranq dart in her thigh.

"Doctor. She's coming around."

The voice wormed its way through the mist. Heather opened her eyes, blinking at the brilliant white surrounding her. She was strapped to a bed in some sort of hospital room. Check that. Her surroundings included some hospital room characteristics. An

IV bag hung from a steel stand, dripping its contents into the clear plastic tube connected to the needle in her arm. A portable monitor displayed her vital signs. But there the similarities stopped. This room was soft white with padded walls and white rubber flooring.

Heather glanced at the nurse, a plain blonde woman, slightly overweight, with a white nurse's uniform, even an old-fashioned white nurse's hat. The doctor stepped around the nurse and into Heather's field of view. That face, framed by dark hair, pulled back in a severe knot.

Heather's breath caught in her throat. What the hell was Dr. Gertrude Sigmund doing here? Wherever *here* was.

The psychiatrist smiled down at her, that familiar, concerned smile that always preceded a prescription change to a more powerful antipsychotic drug.

"Hello, Heather. Good to see you've returned to us. How're you feeling?"

Heather fought to clear her head, but the fog refused to lift. Her glance shifted to the plastic IV bag. The white tape that normally held an identifying label was blank.

"What's that?" Heather's words came out slightly slurred.

Once again Dr. Sigmund smiled. "Don't worry about that right now. The important thing is that you are lucid."

"Where am I?"

"You're a very fortunate young lady. Thanks to the generosity of an anonymous benefactor, you're a patient in the finest facility of its type in North America. The Henderson Foundation Psychiatric Research Hospital."

"Henderson House?" A wave of dread swirled her mental fog.

Dr. Sigmund laughed, a soft chuckle, meant to be reassuring, that failed to produce the desired effect. "That name has suffered a bit of bad press over the past few months, hasn't it? Let me put your mind at ease. The psychiatric wing is completely separate from the experimental facility that housed Dr. Frell's research, although it shares the same grounds. It's sad that a man like Frell could damage this fine institution's reputation."

Heather closed her eyes, trying to bring the facts into focus. "Why am I here? Where are Mark and Jennifer?"

Dr. Sigmund pulled up a chair and sat down beside Heather's bed. She reached out to pat the back of Heather's right hand, just below the leather cuff that secured it to the stainless steel rail.

"Heather. You've experienced a severe psychotic episode, brought on by the fact that you stopped taking your medication. For the last several weeks, you've been locked deep in one of your trances. Until you were transferred here, I was beginning to think we'd lost you forever. As for your two friends, they're still back in Los Alamos, of course, finishing out the school year. I hear Marcus is quite the basketball star."

Lies. But how could Dr. Sigmund be involved in all of this? It didn't make sense.

"But Mark was banned from sports. And what about Bolivia?"

"Well, as for Mark's suspension, the local communities of Los Alamos and White Rock raised such a fuss the school board ended up rescinding the school activities ban for all three of you."

"Prove it to me. I want to see my parents. I want to see Mark and Jen."

Dr. Sigmund pursed her thin lips. "I'll discuss it with your doctors, but I don't want you to get your hopes up, at least not right away. Any little variation in your treatment could send you right back into deep psychosis and, next time, we might not get you back."

"My doctors? Aren't you my doctor?"

That laugh again. "Me? Thank you for thinking of me in that light, but you're now under the care of some of the world's finest mental health researchers. They only flew me out here so that you'd see a familiar face welcoming you back to reality. Someone to ease the stress. Now that I've accomplished that task, I'll be returning to my Los Alamos practice."

"But…"

Dr. Sigmund rose to her feet. "But nothing. You need to rest and focus on getting better. Trust me. Trust your doctors. They really are the very best."

Dr. Sigmund paused at the door, her gaze lingering on Heather's prone form. For a moment Heather thought she would speak again. Then the psychiatrist turned and walked out of the room.

As the door closed behind her, Heather heard the heavy electric lock snap into place.

~ ~ ~

The two federal agents who met Gertrude at the next door led her down a long hallway and then a shorter one on the right, stopping to punch an illuminated elevator call button. It turned red, but she noticed the lack of floor indicator lights. If this whole episode hadn't been so surreal, she might have thought that odd.

As the elevator doors whisked open, the taller of the two men, the one who'd introduced himself as agent Sampson, stepped in beside her, pressing the topmost of five unmarked buttons. The doors closed and the elevator accelerated upward. When it stopped, the doors remained closed.

Agent Sampson extended his hand. "Dr. Sigmund. You've done your country a great service."

"Have I?"

"And I'm sure I don't need to remind you not to mention your visit here, subject to severe punishments specified under the Patriot Act."

Gertrude ignored the hand and Agent Sampson withdrew it. "May I go now?"

He pressed the middle button and the door slid open. Walking her to the guard desk, Agent Sampson waited as she turned in her temporary security badge and signed out.

As Gertrude stepped out of the building into the underground parking garage, she let her gaze wander to the waiting government sedan. Agent Sampson let her slide into the backseat and closed the door, slapping the roof to signal the driver he was clear to go.

As the black sedan drove out through the gates of Fort Meade, Gertrude cast one more glance over her shoulder.

"Would you like to stop for something to eat or should I take you directly to the airport?"

Gertrude shook her head.

"Just take me to BWI."

She hadn't eaten today, but a wave of nausea wiped away all traces of hunger. All she wanted to do was get on her airplane, take an antidepressant, go to sleep, and hope she didn't still hate herself when she awakened.

CHAPTER 52

If there was a US airport that moved at a slower pace than Baltimore Washington International, Freddy Hagerman hadn't been there. But what could you expect from a union town? Just getting to the security checkpoint was a nightmare that forced you to fight your way down an endless hallway barely wide enough for one person, just to turn around and join the end of the line of people coming back the other direction.

On his trip out, Freddy had fought that fight for thirty-seven minutes before finally making it to the TSA screeners. Then, just when he thought that hell was over, he'd been forced to wait at the damned machine while one TSA woman chatted to the one at the next machine about her cheating boyfriend and did Sheila think she should dump him or just beat the crap out of him. When Freddy decided he'd had enough and made that fact loudly known, he'd been singled out for a detailed pat-down that caused him to miss his flight.

Now he was back, waiting in the run-down baggage claim area along with about three hundred other people, trying to decide if today was a baggage delivery holiday. After all, it was Wednesday and who really worked on Wednesday, right? It reminded him of a line in one of the *Lethal Weapon* movies: "They screw you at the drive-through."

Maybe so, but BWI screws you coming and going.

Not that it really mattered, the way he'd been spinning his wheels trying to follow up on the Dr. Jennings tip. Three days in Manhattan trying to shake some information out of his UN sources had been a total waste of time. Combine that with everything he'd been able to dig up in DC and he had a bag full of nada.

At that moment, the warning horn blared three sharp bleats and the baggage conveyer rumbled into motion. Five minutes later, Freddy pulled his spotted vinyl suitcase out the sliding glass doors, turning right toward the bus that would take him to the rental car center. He'd taken a half-dozen steps when he spotted the government sedan. The driver got out of the car and moved to the trunk to help a slender, dark-haired woman lift her computer case from the trunk.

Freddy stopped. Where had he seen her? He never forgot a face, but the fact that he was having difficulty remembering where he'd seen this one meant he'd only seen it in passing. Her driver was clearly some sort of federal agent. The way his jacket bunched along his left side as he hefted her bag meant he was packing more than her valise.

Setting the wheeled case on the sidewalk, the agent gave a curt nod, got back in the car, and pulled out into traffic. As Freddy redirected his attention to the woman, now pulling the lavender case through the same sliding glass doors Freddy had just exited, it came to him. Her hair, pulled back so tightly she'd never need a face lift, triggered his memory. She was the psychiatrist in the *Newsweek* article about the three missing high school kids from Los Alamos. Freddy had read the piece several months ago, while he was working on the Henderson House story.

So why was a small-town psychiatrist from Los Alamos being escorted around the DC area by the feds? She hadn't looked too happy about it either. Come to think of it, why had they dropped her off at the baggage claim area instead of departures?

Fifty yards down the street, the rental car bus pulled away from the curb. Damn. He'd stood around so long trying to figure out where he'd seen the woman, he'd missed the bus. Now he'd have to wait for the next one and, this being BWI, that meant he'd be cooling his heels for another half hour.

Glancing back at baggage claim, Freddy spotted the psychiatrist standing in a line at the lost baggage counter. Well, that explained the drop-off location.

"Hey, buddy!" Freddy's gaze shifted to the speaker. A fat white guy with a rumpled suit and two suitcases glared at him. "You gonna stand there blocking the sidewalk all day or you gonna move?"

Freddy returned the glare, but stepped back and let the wide load pass without comment.

Once again Freddy shifted his gaze back to the woman. She was clearly upset and Freddy didn't think it had anything to do with her lost luggage. The McFarland girl had been her patient. And according to the news coverage of the raid on the Ripper's Bolivian hideout, she and her two high school friends had died during that raid, along with fourteen special ops soldiers. That would certainly account for the anguish he read on the psychiatrist's face.

But it didn't account for her being here with federal agents, a dozen miles from NSA headquarters. Why would the feds want to talk to McFarland's psychiatrist if she really was dead? The parents, maybe. Psychiatrist? He wasn't buying it.

Standing on the sidewalk on what was destined to be Baltimore's first hot day of the year, Freddy felt a hot lead tug at him, the first such feeling he'd had since his meeting with that NSA spook, Jennings. Maybe it wasn't the same story, but it grabbed his attention.

Reaching for his cell phone, Freddy speed-dialed his admin assistant.

"It's me. Listen, Lisa. Change of plan. Book me on the first available flight from BWI to Albuquerque. Yeah. Rental car in Albuquerque, hotel room in Los Alamos. I'm not sure how long. Better make it for a week."

Ending the call, Freddy slid his iPhone back in his pocket and grabbed his bag. Feeling a scowl tug at the corners of his mouth, Freddy trundled back toward ticketing. The military had an acronym for this. BOHICA: Bend Over, Here It Comes Again. It looked as if BWI was going to get one more go at him today after all.

CHAPTER 53

The room held a faintly acrid scent, a hint of recently dried adhesive plus something else. Heather turned her head so she could see her vital signs on the monitor, memorizing them at a glance. The drugs were affecting her thought processes, but before she did something about that she needed to know what her drugged readings looked like so she could keep those in the same range.

The body's autonomic nervous system was an amazing thing. Without a single conscious thought it kept her heart beating, lungs breathing, and blood circulating, adjusted bodily cooling, digested food, and on and on. These things continued whether she was sleeping or awake. One of the many advantages she, Mark, and Jen enjoyed was the ability to enforce a high degree of control over these processes.

Heather shifted her attention to the haze that affected her thinking. This wasn't the high-powered tranquilizer they'd stuck in her thigh in Bolivia. Neither was it Thorazine or any of the other phenothiazine-derivative antipsychotic meds Dr. Sigmund had tried on her back in Los Alamos. Taking a deep breath, Heather executed Mark's meditation trick, pulling forth the perfect memory of how it felt to be clearheaded and alert.

Within Heather's brain, underutilized neurons compensated for her drugged state, remapping her neural net to achieve the desired mental acuity. Another glance at the monitor rewarded her with the knowledge that no one would detect the fact she'd just rendered the drugs ineffective.

Once again Heather turned her thoughts to the smells that hung on the air. Remodeling smells. The spot where white padded walls butted up against the ceiling's acoustic tiles still showed evidence of recent installation. A stainless steel toilet and sink occupied the center of the rear wall and a rudimentary shower drained into the left rear corner. Those, her bed, with its scratched frame and railing, and the small video camera in the upper right front were the room's only decorations that weren't freshly installed.

Heather brought up the room dimensions, forming a 3-D model in her head. She rotated it, stripped away the asylum padding from the walls. Removed the acoustic tiles from the ceiling. Replaced the front wall and door with tempered steel bars, an electronically controlled sliding steel gate, and a chuck hole for pushing in meals.

This wasn't Henderson House, and it wasn't a psychiatric facility. It was a recently converted solitary confinement cell in a supermax detention facility.

So why had the government gone to all this effort to throw together this fake? Obviously, Dr. Sigmund had been flown in to establish early credibility, something the drugs were intended to augment. They'd pulled Heather's records, identified a mental weakness, and now they were determined to exploit it.

There was a certain irony to it. By trying to exploit her weakness, her captors had provided her with an advantage she could play to. She felt the leather cuffs binding her hands and feet to the bed, flexed her muscles just enough to build an estimate of their tensile strength. Breaking free from her bonds wouldn't be a problem, but she wasn't going to do that while they were watching her with that camera. Before she made her break for freedom, she had a lot to learn about the routine, this facility, and the people behind this operation.

The thought of Mark and Jennifer worried her, but she knew their capabilities and training. The best way she could help them was to handle her own situation.

A distant sound caught her attention, the scuffing of two pairs of rubber-soled shoes on concrete. The noise had a reverb echo that indicated a long hallway, an impression that was reinforced by the amount of time the footsteps took to reach her door.

With an electric click, the door opened to admit two men in medical scrubs, a tall, blue-eyed blond wearing a stethoscope around his neck and a short bald man holding an Apple iPad. The one with the stethoscope stepped up beside her bed.

"Hello, Heather. My name is Dr. Jacobs. This is my physician's assistant, Frank Volker. It's good to see you decided to come back to us."

Heather let a slight slur creep into her voice. "Did I?"

Jacobs smiled. "Yes, and you should be proud of that accomplishment. Most people in your condition never find their way back."

Heather glanced down at her hands. "Why am I tied down?"

Jacobs patted her right hand, giving it a slight squeeze. "It's for your own protection, at least until we've formed an understanding of just where you're at."

"For my protection?"

Jacobs sat down in the chair next to her bed. "Just until we're sure you're stable, that you're not going to suffer an immediate relapse. It's why we're keeping you mildly sedated. Do you remember anything at all about your stay here?"

Volker tapped away on the iPad's touch screen.

Heather frowned. "I remember Bolivia."

"I'm not talking about your alternate reality right now. I'm talking about the months you've been in this facility."

"The first time I ever saw this place was when I woke up to see Dr. Sigmund standing over me. Like I told her, I want to see my mom and dad."

A serious expression settled on Dr. Jacobs's face. "Believe me. I want that for you too. We all do. But you've been through a hell of a mental trauma these last few months. And, as hard as it is for you to understand why, we're going to go slow and careful about reintroducing you to the real world. For now that means no TV, no radio, no Internet, and unfortunately, no friends or family."

Heather squeezed her eyes shut. "So I'm just supposed to lie here, drugged and chained to the bed, and trust you?"

"I didn't say this was going to be easy."

A bitter laugh escaped Heather's lips.

"Tell you what," Dr. Jacobs continued. "I'll get you out of these restraints as soon as we finish a battery of tests. Then, if you work with me and learn to recognize the difference between what's real and what's not, then we'll get your parents out here to California for a visit. But Heather, you're going to have to trust me."

Dr. Jacobs rose to his feet, patted her hand again, and turned toward the door. Volker switched off his iPad and followed.

"Can I at least go to the bathroom?"

"I'll have a nurse bring a bedpan."

"Doctor." Heather raised her voice just enough to cause him to turn back toward her. "Right now my alternate reality looks pretty damn good."

Jacobs's face acquired a sympathetic cast. "You can't beat this by yourself, Heather. But we can. You just have to let me in."

As the door closed behind them, Heather concentrated on their footfalls, the sounds plus their echoes rendering an image in her mind. A hallway, all right. Eleven and a half feet wide, ten feet tall, and really, really long. Another piece of her facility blueprint filled in. And when the nurse brought her the bedpan, Heather would see whether it was the same one who had assisted Dr. Sigmund.

Heather looked up at the camera, then closed her eyes, gradually letting her vital signs drop. They expected her to be exhausted, so she'd feed them the data they wanted.

Heather smiled inwardly at the thought.

Just like training Pavlov's dog.

CHAPTER 54

Deep in her drug-induced dreams, Jennifer found herself at the McFarland breakfast table, seated beside Mark and Heather as Mrs. McFarland set the platter, stacked high with her golden-brown pancakes, at the table's center. She recognized the scene. It was the morning after she and Mark had shared Heather's dream about the Rag Man. She watched it unfold around her, a disembodied ghost, unable to make herself known to any of the participants. With a pang of regret, Jennifer knew those days were gone forever.

The dream shifted to another morning at the McFarland table. Her other self glanced at Heather, who seemed unusually distracted this morning.

"What's up with Heather?" she heard herself think.

Heather lifted her gaze to Jennifer's. "What was that?"

It was as if Heather had heard her, even though she hadn't said the thought aloud.

Again the dream shifted, this time to the night she'd run from her room to meet Mark at the top of the stairs. Heather had called out to them in pain and terror, her thoughts reaching into their minds as she'd been carried off by the Rag Man. And her thoughts had guided Mark through that dark night to find her.

These experiences were completely different from Jennifer's ability to read and influence people's emotions. She, Mark, and Heather had been able to share their thoughts. And they'd done it without wearing the alien headsets. How? And why hadn't they managed to do that same thing on demand?

Her questions focused her thoughts, pushing back the drug haze as she called upon her brain for answers. She felt a chill run down her spine. Finding the answers to those questions suddenly acquired an importance that drove her to an ever-tighter level of concentration.

Jennifer shoved the drug haze aside, isolating its effects to a small portion of her mind as she called upon the full extent of her analytical abilities. The alien headsets were the key. She was sure of it.

The first time she'd stood inside the Bandolier Ship and felt the headset establish a link between her brain and the ship's computer, she'd felt it alter her brain, not exactly rewiring the connections, but forcing activity across the entire structure. Neural connections that had been so weak that they were dormant had come to life, able to be accessed and put to work in ways that had previously been impossible.

When she, Mark, and Heather put on the headsets, they could share thoughts. In fact, if they weren't careful, the others could penetrate into private areas, accessing thoughts and feelings not meant for sharing. Jennifer thought about that. The headset picked up the thoughts from their minds, transferring the impulses to the Bandolier Ship via a subspace link. But how had they occasionally managed to establish a similar link between themselves without the headsets?

Distances weren't the same in subspace. It wasn't the same as the way gravitational effects warped the space-time fabric. Instead, subspace had its own wave transmission speed, and that relationship between time and distance defined their meaning just as the speed of light did in our universe.

Jennifer had seen it for herself, had used it to hack into remote networks, accessing their data through the subspace receiver-transmitters or SRTs. In the case of the computer hack, the system hadn't required a physical device at the far end to achieve a tap.

A sudden excitement coursed through Jennifer's nerves, pre-saging a great discovery that nudged the corner of her awareness. She only had to relax and let down the wall that held it back. The answer was right there, so frustratingly close she could almost reach out and touch it.

Why did the computer subspace hack work? You focused the SRT on an exact coordinate and then scanned for computer signals in the vicinity. Since all signals leaked a small fraction of their energy into subspace, it became a matter of efficient tuning and filtering to pick out the desired information from the background noise.

But the headsets provided the powerful alien computer with a target for its subspace probe, providing exact coordinates for the link, as well as a unique personal encryption key that tagged each of the starship's crewmen, akin to credentials for a secure wireless network connection.

Once the link had been established, the Bandolier Ship's computer remembered it, recognizing that crewman's signal whenever it encountered its subspace signature. But did the computer really need the headset to make contact after that?

At the edge of her awareness, Jennifer felt a new surge of drugs enter her bloodstream, and although she shifted her attention to try to wall off its effects, a warm wave of foam swept her up, swirling her away from the answer that bobbed just beyond her grasp.

CHAPTER 55

The cuffs bit into Mark's wrists and ankles like a gnawing dog, stretching his naked body tight on the board, tilted down at a twenty-seven-degree angle. Water ran off the board in streams, yet clung tightly to the shammy-like cloth sack that covered his head. The air that struggled through the wet sack with each breath pressed the cloth tightly against his nose and mouth, the restricted air flow so damp that it felt as if he breathed in liquid water.

Inside the hood Mark smiled and relaxed, letting his heart rate fall from its normal forty-three beats per minute to thirty-five as he moved into midlevel meditation. He didn't know where Heather and Jennifer were being held, but he knew his role. His captors expected him to be the leader of the group, the tough guy. Mark didn't intend to disappoint them. The best thing he could do right now was to give the bad guys a target to focus on, something so interesting it might draw part of their attention away from the girls.

A hand struck him across the face, a stinging, openhanded slap that rolled his head to the side, bringing the copper taste of blood to his tongue. A deep voice snarled close to his left ear.

"How long do you think you're gonna hold out, kid? I've got all the time in the world."

Mark felt a fresh gush of ice-cold water pour down onto his face and chest, temporarily shutting off all airflow through the sack. Then the voice next to his ear was back.

"You might as well face it. Sooner or later you're going to tell me everything I want to know. The quicker that happens, the easier it'll go for you. So what's it gonna be?"

Inside the hood, Mark's smile returned. He lay in green grass beside a gurgling mountain stream. Surrounding the sunlit meadow, snowcapped peaks rose up to carve a cloudless blue sky. He smelled the sweet scent of flowers, heard the buzz of a hummingbird, felt the gentle breeze press damp grass against his face.

Tied to the dripping board in the frigid cell, Mark felt his heart rate fall another five beats per minute.

~ ~ ~

"You watching this?"

Harlan Redding's voice held an edge Channing Grail had never heard before. Shifting his view from the image on the video monitor to the readout of Mark Smythe's vitals, he felt a sudden chill.

The kid hadn't eaten in three days. He'd been chained to a high ring in the center of the frigid concrete cell, a position that gave him two choices, remain standing or dangle by his manacled wrists. A single drain in the floor below him served as his toilet.

By now, sleep deprivation alone would have driven most men into a hallucinatory dream state somewhere between waking and sleep. But not Mark Smythe. He had remained standing as if it took no more effort than lying in a feather bed.

The decision to proceed to waterboarding had received reluctant approval from the higher-ups, but based upon the results of the last four hours, Channing was beginning to think they might as well not have bothered.

"Jesus."

"Resting like a baby."

"Never seen anything like it."

"Not an ounce of fat on that body either. From the look of him, I'd say he could win the Olympic decathlon." Harlan nodded at the computer display. "Based on those readings, his mental control's completely off the charts."

"Gregory trained him."

"Yes. But it's more than that." Harlan pointed a thick finger at the video monitor. "Down in that cell, we have one hell of a specimen."

"Yeah," Channing replied. "Too bad he doesn't work for us."

CHAPTER 56

Tall Bear watched as the thirteen tribal chiefs emerged from the largest sweat lodge on the Santa Clara Reservation, sweat dripping from their bodies onto the hard-packed dirt just outside the mud lodge. They passed him without a word, slight nods in his direction the only acknowledgment of what had just happened inside.

Very few outsiders understood native ceremonies, especially the yuppies that paid self-professed shamans to conduct purification ceremonies. The US government showed even less interest and understanding of their importance. That combination of ambivalence and naiveté made a native sweat lodge an excellent place to discuss matters of a sensitive nature.

Tall Bear wasn't sure how he'd assumed his role as the unofficial leader of the Native People's Alliance. It had started with the rebellious act of helping Jack and Janet escape their federal pursuers. Then, like a desert arroyo suddenly filled with a distant storm's roiling floodwater, anger at the unbridled power of the central government had filled his soul. The abuse of that power, illustrated so clearly in the way the government had framed Jack and his team, had burst the dam holding back Tall Bear's rage at the injustice dealt his own people. Not just the Navajo people.

Many tribes had suffered genocide. Oddly, that didn't bother Tall Bear as much as the systematic theft of his people's dignity. The great American government, with its spirit of free enterprise, had imposed communism on the Native Peoples, and like the system the Bolsheviks had imposed on the Soviet Union, it had yielded the same harvest. The once-proud native people learned to accept government handouts, then to rely upon them. The subsequent loss of pride, self-reliance, and initiative led inevitably to the current plague of alcoholism, obesity, and hopelessness infecting modern tribal societies.

His thoughts turned to the football game he'd been invited to last fall, the New Orleans Saints at the Arizona Cardinals. With the domed stadium filled with Arizona's red-clad fans and the Cardinals driving, the words that sent a shiver down Tall Bear's spine thundered through the huge stadium's public address system.

"Rise up Red Sea!"

As Tall Bear watched the tribal leaders climb into their pickups and cars, fire up the ignitions, and drive off down the dirt road, spewing plumes of light brown dust in their wake, his jaw clenched in determination.

Rise up Red Sea!

CHAPTER 57

It could have been his story.

So why did Freddy feel like a world-class fool for not breaking this one himself?

Maybe because it was the biggest story in history and he'd known about it for weeks. But instead of pouncing on it, he'd stayed quiet, letting the president make the announcement in a televised prime-time Oval Office address. Maybe because he had the deepseated feeling he was on the trail of something even bigger. Or maybe he'd gone all soft and patriotic. One thing he knew: if his editor ever found out he'd sat on this, he'd be looking for a new line of work.

Leaning back against the pile of pillows stacked against the wood wall-board—he couldn't bring himself to think of the brown wooden thing fastened to the wall as a headboard—Freddy stared at the television that blared breaking news on every channel.

The president had come right out and told the American people that a black hole was forming at the heart of the ATLAS detector in Meyrin, Switzerland. He'd also announced that effective immediately, he and the leaders of all the G7 countries were imposing martial law to ensure public safety and order during this crisis. The National Guard had been called out and the US military had been ordered to its highest readiness level, DEFCON 1. In addition, under his martial law decree, the provisions of the Posse Comitatus Act of 1878 were being temporarily suspended, thereby enabling the branches of the United States military to enforce the law.

As the nation watched in stunned silence, the president shifted to a gentler tone, assuring the public that the world's major powers had developed a plan to deal with the black hole using technologies derived from the Rho Project. The plan involved the most ambitious construction project ever conceived: a project to build a device that would transport the micro black hole deep into space, far from our solar system, where it could no longer pose a threat to Earth. He, in conjunction with EU leaders, had placed Dr. Donald Stephenson, the man most intimately familiar with the alien technologies, in charge of the project to construct the Rho Device.

Then, closing his address with the typical *May God be with us all* crap, the president signed off to pandemonium.

Martial law? Did the US government even have a plan for implementing martial law on a national scale? Freddy didn't think so. And he didn't think the plan would be a very effective one even if it existed. Maybe it could be done in Europe, where everything was close together, but this was America, and America was one big-ass place.

Simultaneously with the president's announcement, leaders across the EU issued proclamations of their own, timing that must have been forced on them considering that prime time in the US market hardly corresponded to a similar situation in Europe. Then again, maybe the early-morning hour facilitated martial law implementation. Most Europeans would just wake up to find it in effect.

As Freddy continued watching the breathless commentary, stories about the black hole began to be replaced by news of looting breaking out in communities across the nation, gun shops and outdoor-supply stores being among the early targets. In some cities the police found themselves deluged with calls, having to pick and choose which situations they would respond to. The National Guard had been called up, but that took time.

Outside the Holiday Inn Express, Freddy heard the wail of distant sirens break the stillness of the Los Alamos night.

Shit, I hate being right, Freddy thought as he strapped on his walkabout leg and reached for his pants. Well he was a reporter. Might as well get out there and cover what was sure to be the beginning of the end of the America he'd known and loved. For all he knew, reporting the news might violate martial law. As he buttoned his shirt and grabbed his digital recorder and camera, Freddy paused one more time to listen to the sirens. If that was the case, he wouldn't be the only one engaged in criminal activity.

Then, striding across the red-yellow-and-orange-striped carpet, Freddy exited his hotel room, letting the door slam behind him.

CHAPTER 58

Dr. Louis Dubois didn't like the way his colleague Dr. Donald Stephenson was looking at the engineers gathered around the conference table. He looked like an apex predator evaluating prey—a falcon, perhaps, or a jaguar. The same bloodless, hungry look. He wondered, not for the first time, if Stephenson might be a high-functioning psychopath who, if he hadn't turned to science, would be engaged in less savory pursuits.

Luckily, the engineers were studying the blueprints with fierce intensity and ignoring Dr. Stephenson. Side conversations shifted into French, German, and Spanish, then back to English for general discussion.

Finally, though, as Dubois had known would happen, Dr. Stephenson lost patience.

"Can you build it?" Dr. Stephenson snapped out his question to Gerhardt Werner, the lead engineer for Kohl Engineering, the company responsible for building many of the largest and most demanding projects in the world, including the massive Francis turbine generators at China's Three Gorges Dam.

The burly blond engineer turned to face him. "Hell, I don't even understand how it's supposed to work."

"That's not important. Can you build it?"

"Not important? For an engineer to build something that's supposed to work?"

"Can you build the thing according to these specifications?"

The German's steel-gray eyes met those of the physicist. "*Das ist klar*. Sure I can build the damned things to spec. But if they don't work, it's your mistake."

"I don't make mistakes. Make sure you do the same and we'll get along just fine."

"I doubt that."

Dubois watched the American physicist eye the German for several seconds. Then Stephenson turned on his heel and strode from the room.

As the engineers turned back to the blueprints, Dr. Dubois's eyes swept back over the table. Those engineering specifications represented the two most intricate construction projects ever attempted by man. Team One would enlarge the ATLAS cavern and then build the Rho Device around the anomaly, while maintaining the stability of the current electromagnetic containment field. Team Two would build the Matter to Energy Conversion Facility, the device that some young physicist had nicknamed the MINGSTER, short for matter ingester. It was the power generation station that would produce the awesome energy required to generate a wormhole.

The theory behind both devices was so far from the physics Louis had come to know that it bordered on quantum blasphemy. Stephenson had essentially reintroduced a variation of the old ether theory with a little quantum foam rolled in for good measure. At its core, his model held that light was more than particles guided by waves of probability, that it waved an underlying ether substance that forms the fabric of our universe.

Stephenson's model was all about the ether medium. All matter and energy were formed from variations in ether density. Where the ether was relatively compressed, a positive energy gradient existed. Where it was stretched, there was a corresponding negative energy gradient. It allowed for ether granularity, with subspace occupying the rift between ether grains. Stephenson's ether model embraced the dual tenets that the speed of light is not constant and that energy within our universe is not conserved, but leaks in and out of subspace.

Stephenson proposed a simple test to illustrate that the speed of light was a function of ether density. The Stephenson version of the famous Michelson-Morley experiment used the classic mirror-and-interferometer arrangement. But across one of the light paths he applied an intense repulsive magnetic field, changing the ether density along that path. The resulting shift in the interference pattern demonstrated his predicted change in the speed of light.

Where the Stephenson ether model got really interesting was in the analysis of the wave packets that formed matter. It predicted that certain rare frequency combinations produced stable standing wave packets in the ether and that these special harmonic sets formed the particles and elements we observe in nature. Through understanding the frequencies that form a stable packet, it became possible to apply another set of frequencies, an antipacket, that canceled out the original packet, releasing the energy bound within it.

Moreover, it wasn't necessary to produce a perfect antipacket to destabilize a particle. It merely required a sufficient subset of disrupting or canceling frequencies and the packet would tear itself apart. Theoretically, this process was as reliable as clockwork.

Analyze the packet.

Add disrupting frequencies.

Harvest the expelled energy.

Rinse and repeat.

Stephenson had produced an algorithm and a design for doing precisely that. The MINGSTER's job would be to ingest matter and disrupt its wave packets, producing energy on a scale the Earth hadn't experienced since it was flung out of the cosmic explosion that created it. That energy would then be fed to the Rho Device so it could generate the wormhole that would transport the November Anomaly several light years out in space.

But if it was so cut-and-dried, why did the thing worry Louis so badly? Like the big German engineer, he didn't like not knowing exactly how and why something worked. And nobody, including Louis, could understand all of Stephenson's equations, a significant part of them constructed in an alien branch of mathematics for which he had no context and upon which Stephenson refused to elaborate.

"My dear Dr. Dubois," Stephenson had said upon being pressed on the topic. "We are already desperately short on time. Why do you imagine I can afford to inject the additional delay of playing college professor for a semester, assuming you and your colleagues are even capable of grasping the topic?"

Anger had so engulfed Louis that only his professional pride kept his clenched and shaking hands at his sides instead of reaching out and tossing Stephenson through the adjacent plate-glass window. And thus the opportunity had passed.

With one last glance at the engineers shuffling through blueprints, Louis sighed, turned, and began the long walk from Building 33 back to his office.

CHAPTER 59

It seemed a small miracle, but it wasn't. Parting the Red Sea was a small miracle. Walking on water was a small miracle. What Raul had accomplished made those feats pale in comparison. Legless, stranded alone in the dark, he had brought the Rho Ship back from the dead.

What had started with the lightning bolt from the capacitor into the power cell had progressed to the point that Raul had acquired complete control of the starship's maintenance system. Then, taking great care to prevent the emission of any signal that would tip off the scientists who thought the Rho Ship dead, Raul had brought a total of thirteen power cells back online. More importantly he'd restored the matter disrupter to full function, feeding it the bags of human waste for the initial fuel to power up those cells.

Today would mark the next major milestone in the restoration of his power. Today he would reassume control over the ship's neural net. Raul felt a quiver pass through his body at the thought. But this time there would be nobody who could wrest its control from him, no hidden daemon processes running beneath his awareness. He'd taken extreme care to ensure that all systems were restored to default settings, having run a maintenance-level wipe that guaranteed no trace of a Stephenson infection remained in any of the starship's systems.

Raul initiated one final diagnostic, anxiously awaiting the result. Around him the maintenance lighting seemed to emanate from the air itself, the soft glow revealing the jumble of alien equipment that covered the bulk of the room's floor, a floor that, if all went well, he'd no longer be required to slither across on his arms and ass. He'd once again feel the awesome mind meld to the central computer, and that would enable his command of the ship's stasis field.

The alien maintenance computer piped the diagnostic results directly into his brain. No anomalies detected. Primary system access ready.

Raul hesitated the merest fraction of a second before giving the command. Primary system engage.

The suddenness of the transition momentarily disoriented him. There was no gradual boot-up process. It was as if he'd never been cut off from the main neural net. One moment he was only Raul, the next he was one with the Rho Ship, able to feel every aspect of its physical state, experiencing the small percentage of the ship that was currently functional, while feeling the pain of its damaged subsystems.

With a thought, Raul accessed the stasis field generator, rising into the air as he dimmed the light until the room was no brighter than a moonlit night. The exultation that rippled through the

Raul part of himself felt good, really good. Looking out over the inner chamber, Raul smiled. Pulling thousands of strands from the stasis field, Raul shifted his attention to restoring the Rho ship to full health.

~ ~ ~

Just outside the Rho Ship, Jill McMartin, a UC graduate student, glanced up to the spot where the Rho Ship lay cradled on the huge U-shaped steel supports. She could have sworn she'd seen something. A glance at the monitors told her she'd just imagined it. As sad as it was, all her wishing couldn't bring the alien starship back to life. It remained just as dead as it had been since that late November night. And with Dr. Stephenson off in Europe, dead was exactly how it was going to stay.

CHAPTER 60

Ketaan-Ra studied the data streaming in through his cortical implants, four-dimensional imagery supplemented with thousands of channels of audio and multispectral data. Pulling forth a galactic hologram, he allowed the signal to pull him into a tight zoom toward a yellow star in one of the galaxy's outer spiral arms.

The view tightened, centered on the third planet from this sun, a watery world that had been deemed of sufficient interest to warrant the sending of a world ship. Scanning through the background data, Ketaan-Ra pulled up the specs he already knew by heart.

Planet K3VX789ZL10-X, the X indicating lost or abandoned world ship. After pinging steady progress reports for the last 2.319E19 cesium cycles, the world ship had gone silent, remaining so for long enough that the High Council had deemed it lost. That designation had resulted in the standing down of the invasion cohort assigned to its attuned gateway, which had been placed at a low-grade monitoring status.

Of the tens of thousands of soldiers assigned to his command for all those cycles, only Ketaan-Ra remained, even that commitment a testament to the council's reluctance to accept defeat. Leaving him assigned to an empty command, tethered to his dead world ship, was merely a repudiation of his mission's failure, one failure wiping away a lifetime of heroic deeds in the service of the Kasari Collective.

Now, as he immersed himself in the sea of data cascading through his external sensory feeds, Ketaan-Ra allowed his cybernetic augments to release a slow flow of chemicals into his adrenal system, an indulgence this discovery justified. Removing the trailing X from the planetary designation, he rerouted the data stream to Zaalex-Ka, the High Council's data minder.

As another surge of chemical warmth coursed through his system, he leaned back in his data couch. Out there on that distant and primitive planet, someone had managed to bring his world ship back from the dead, resurrecting, along with it, the career of one Cohort Commander Ketaan-Ra.

CHAPTER 61

Heroin.

The word wormed its way into Jennifer's clouded mind. She tugged at the strings of her memory, pulling up the drug's symptoms, running a systematic cross-check against her own bodily functions. She channeled the haze away, searching for clarity, achieving just enough focus to remember Mark's trick. She turned her thoughts to a memory of how it felt to be bright and alert, wrapping herself in the perfect recollection of that chosen moment.

All the comfortable fuzziness was gone, shunted off into a space with which she no longer had a connection. Jennifer felt her old self click into place. As unbelievable as it was, the US government was funneling high-grade heroin into her veins and it didn't take a hell of a lot of imagination to figure out why. They wanted her physically addicted.

"Well that does it, Mr. President. You can forget about my vote."

Feeling the fuzziness filter back into her thoughts, Jennifer recentered. Suddenly she found herself really, really pissed off. The goddamned US government had decided it was OK to treat her worse than Don Espeñosa had. And they justified it how? Probably the same way they'd justified the hatchet job on Jack's team.

It was time to figure out where she was, how she'd gotten here, and how she was going to get herself, Mark, and Heather out. A coldness, like ice on an arctic trawler, crept over Jennifer Smythe.

Jennifer clenched her jaw. One thing was certain. These people had no idea whom the hell they were screwing with.

She opened her eyes, her gaze coming to rest on Eric Frost, the NSA employee whose twisting fingers controlled the heroin drip line.

~ ~ ~

Frost found his latest duty boring at best, slightly disturbing at worst. It wasn't as if he hadn't done his share of black ops, but hooking a teenage girl on drugs didn't seem like something he would be spotlighting on his résumé.

Then she moved unexpectedly, her head turning toward him. His eyes widened in surprise as he felt his body tense. As he stared down at the suddenly smiling girl, he felt a sense of gentle peace envelop his soul.

"That's right, Eric. No use fighting it. Now you're mine," she said.

And she was right.

CHAPTER 62

Heather felt the nudge in her mind, light as a feather, distant as Andromeda. Jennifer.

As startling as the idea was, Jennifer was attempting to initiate a direct mind link. Heather knew they'd achieved versions of that link before, but those occurrences had been random or at times of intense stress, and, as far as she knew, always initiated by her own subconscious mind. But this was different. Jennifer was attempting something they'd never been able to manage without the alien headsets: a consciously directed mind link.

"Heather, are you listening to me?"

Dr. Jacobs scooted his chair closer to her bed. True to his word, she was no longer restrained. And in return she had feigned grudging cooperation with Jacobs's probes of her sanity. The man had access to her medical records, had discussed her case with

Dr. Sigmund. He thought her deeply psychotic and Heather had done nothing to disabuse him of that notion.

"Heather?"

Since he was expecting to induce a psychotic episode, Heather found this a convenient moment to oblige him. Directing the full power of her mind at helping Jennifer complete the mind link, Heather went deep, leaving only the whites of her eyes staring sightlessly, right through Dr. Jacobs.

Jennifer's nearby mind groped for hers like a mole, unable to see her, but having caught her scent. And now Heather had hers: not a true smell, but like a smell, difficult to follow.

Heather had often thought about how their minds telepathically linked through the alien headsets. If it hadn't been for those rare occurrences when she'd somehow managed to share her thoughts with Mark and Jennifer without the headsets, she could have convinced herself such contact was only possible via their common connection to the Bandolier Ship's computer.

So how had her mind managed to achieve those direct links?

Jennifer's abilities to achieve empathic links to other people were impressive. But that was child's play compared to the complexity of a complete mind link. Now Jen was close to figuring it out. As with a fuzzy radio station that she hadn't tuned to quite the right frequency, Heather knew Jen was there, but that was about it.

Sudden insight flashed through her. Frequency! Heather reviewed what she knew about the changes the Bandolier Ship had wrought in their brains. The human brain held over a hundred billion neurons, each with thousands of synaptic connections to other neurons, hundreds of trillions of synapses involved in the massively parallel chemical and electrical operations that gave the human mind its power.

The difference between the way Heather's, Mark's, and Jennifer's brains functioned and the way the average person's did had little to do with the number of synapses in use. It was the way their functions were timed and coordinated into one synchronized whole. That tightly coordinated signal timing allowed their brains to function as a phased array.

Heather had first heard of phased array radars in middle school while studying the first Gulf War. The US had deployed Patriot missile batteries to protect key assets in Saudi Arabia and Israel; at the heart of each missile battery was a flat phased array radar that painted the sky in front of it with a powerful pencil beam of radar energy, steering the beam back and forth across the sky many times per second. She'd been fascinated by the fact the beam could be directed at so many different spots so quickly without any moving parts in the radar.

It all worked by timing the energy output from thousands of radar emitters spread across the radar surface. If you turned on all the emitters at once, the energy went straight out. By precisely controlling the pattern and timing of each emitter, the radar created a focused beam that could be rapidly and precisely directed. The principle worked for directed communications signals or for any application in which directed energy was required.

What kind of signal processing efficiency could be achieved with a phased array formed from hundreds of trillions of emitters and receivers? Good enough to relay signals to other parts of the same brain without the delay of traversing the intervening neural pathways. And if it could do that, it should be able to accomplish similar signal communication to another's brain.

A surge of adrenaline flooded Heather as she zoomed in on the answer. There were still a number of problems associated with establishing that sort of communication link. First, every brain was different. That implied that targeting of the brain's phased array was just part of the problem. You would also have to identify the frequency and pattern of the other person's receptor array.

How had that happened automatically when she'd been under heavy stress? When the Rag Man had grabbed her, she hadn't been aware of exactly where Mark and Jennifer were. With the tiny signal strengths generated by the human brain, the signal would have to be tightly focused and precisely directed to avoid the inverse-radius-squared loss associated with spherical waves.

Apparently her brain had produced a rapidly scanning pencil beam that had first located Mark and Jennifer and then, given that information, had identified the appropriate communication patterns and frequencies that their brains accepted.

Again she felt the rush of near discovery. She was so close to the answer she could taste it and, with rising anticipation, she felt herself crawl ever deeper into her savant trance.

~ ~ ~

Dr. Jacobs glanced at his watch as he spoke into the digital recorder.

"Subject entered fugue state at oh-nine-eighteen hours and has remained quasi-comatose for the last thirty-two minutes. At oh-nine-forty-seven, subject's vitals began exhibiting significant fluctuations. Heart rate and blood pressure are up, although well within the expected range for a person in an agitated state. EEG readings correspond to the unusual results catalogued by Dr. Sigmund during her Los Alamos observations."

He clicked off the recorder and returned his attention to Heather McFarland. As he stared down into that beautiful face with those strange, milky eyes staring right through him, thin lines of concentration furrowed her brow. Dr. Jacobs thought he detected the leading edge of a smile caress her lips.

Starting first on his arms and legs, gooseflesh tightened, raising the fine hairs to attention, spreading rapidly up the back of his neck to his scalp. As he stared down at this young woman, Dr. Jacobs felt the strength leach from his legs, forcing him to grab the instrument table for support. And though his mind rebelled at the notion, he suddenly found himself more frightened of this girl than of anything he'd ever experienced.

CHAPTER 63

Dr. Bert Mathews fastened the antistatic wrist strap around his right wrist, connecting the alligator clip at the other end of the wire to the metal frame that held the laptop, then sat down in the chair beside Eileen Wu, the nineteen-year-old Caltech prodigy known throughout the hacker community as Hex. Fine-boned and slender, the Amerasian teen wore her black hair boyishly short, highlighting the way her throat plunged down into the tight yellow cami that didn't quite make it down to her ragged jeans.

Hardly appropriate work attire at the NSA, but for Eileen he'd made an exception. Besides, as far as Bert knew, she didn't own any clothes but jeans and camis. The thing Bert found most startling about her appearance was her complete lack of tattoos or piercings, an indication of just how different Eileen was. Not goth. More like a Celtic high priestess of code.

It was hard to recognize the device on the lab table before her as one of the laptops captured at Jack Gregory's Bolivian hideout. The case had been disassembled, the motherboard and components mounted into an instrumented metal frame. The laptop monitor had been removed, the wiring routed through a small black box and then to a large flat-panel display. A nest of thin colored wires had been attached to the motherboard, CPU, network cards, memory modules, hard drive, and video card, connecting them to a rack-mounted system to Eileen's right.

"So, are we ready?" Dr. Mathews asked.

Eileen pressed the power button, waiting for several seconds for the standard Windows login screen to appear. Two user icons appeared, HAL and PickMe.

"Cute," Eileen muttered. "This shouldn't take long."

Spinning her chair ninety degrees to the right, she shifted her attention to the bank of monitors and the keyboard attached to the rack of blade servers. As she entered the commands, Dr. Mathews watched the laptop display reboot to the BIOS screen, cycling to the boot device selection, changing the setting to Boot from USB Device.

Again the laptop rebooted, stopping again at the log-in screen. Eileen turned back to the laptop keyboard, selected the HAL icon, moved her cursor to the password edit box, and hit Enter. A thin smile tweaked the corners of her lips as the Windows desktop appeared.

"So now what?" Bert asked. Normally he would have a set of scripts running every step of the forensic data recovery. But he wanted Eileen to look through the system before he launched the standard scripts, just in case there were any unknown security protocols running on this system. After all, this was one of the Jack Gregory laptops, and the word from cartel intercepts about Jennifer Smythe indicated she might be nearly as talented a hacker as Hex.

"Give me a second. I want to see a list of processes and services running on this machine. We're mirroring everything on the buses, registers, hard disk reads and writes, data passing through the TCP/IP stack to the network driver interfaces, and everything coming in or out of the NICs. If bits are flipping on this laptop we're capturing them."

"You've got Wi-Fi enabled?"

"And I've hooked the network interfaces up to our LAN. I want to see what data this thing tries to send, if any. Don't worry, no signal can make it out of this room."

"We've been penetrated before."

"Those were standard TEMPEST cages. This room is solid steel. No electromagnetic signal is propagating through that. Certainly not from a laptop."

For six hours Dr. Mathews watched as Eileen worked her way through the laptop, a stretch broken only for coffee and associated bathroom breaks. Despite the way his stomach rumbled, he refused to leave Eileen, and she showed no inclination to go anywhere. It appeared this was going to lead to another straightforward data dump, after which they could turn the encrypted data over to systems designed to crack that protection.

Suddenly Eileen shifted in her chair, rising up over the keyboard like a cougar crouched on a mountain ledge.

"That's odd."

"What?"

Eileen continued to work the keyboards, shifting back and forth between the blade rack and the laptop. Just as Bert decided she hadn't heard him, Eileen pointed at the readout.

"There. We've got a significant amount of reads and writes happening across the TCP stack. I almost missed it because we've got nothing coming in or out on the wireless network hardware or through the Ethernet cards. But data is definitely coming and going between the network layer and the framing layer."

"Loopback?"

"No. It has to be going to a custom network driver."

"But if the driver's not talking to the network cards or loop-back, what's it talking to?"

"The only other piece of hardware is the USB dongle."

"Can you tell how long the TCP stack has been actively trans-mitting and receiving data?"

Eileen brought up another Linux xterm, rapidly entering a sequence of commands that launched a new program on one of the blade servers, filling one of the monitors. Framed data graphs filled most of the window and below these a thin blue time line slider extended across the screen. Dragging the glow-ing current-position widget slowly backward, Eileen watched the data graphs change. As it neared the beginning, Eileen paused, reversing it slightly. She brought up another display, this one a list of processes running at that point in time. She began stepping forward in thirty-second increments, stopped, reversed again, then froze.

"Damn it."

Dr. Mathews didn't like the tone of her voice. "Tell me."

"It looks like some sort of timer process activated shortly after I logged in."

"Timer? For what?"

"Well, I won't know for sure until I spend a few more hours going through this data, but if I was guessing, which I am, I'd say we had a certain amount of time to do some sort of validation after log-in. One minute to be exact."

"One minute?"

"Yeah. Because exactly one minute after the timer activated, it went away. That's when the data started coming and going on the TCP stack."

Dr. Mathews ran the fingers of his left hand through his graying hair. "OK. Let's assume that there was some sort of second log-in we were supposed to do but didn't. Why not just erase the hard drive?"

"That would be too obvious and to do a military-grade wipe would take way too long. We would have powered down the system, pulled the drive, and handed it over to our hardware guys to recover the data."

Mathews knew all of this thoroughly, but he was rattled, thinking out loud. He shook his head. "It still doesn't add up. While that system is messing around with its TCP stack, we've duplicated the entire hard drive and mirrored all the data transfers going on in the whole system. Plus, no traffic is going in or out through the network cards. Even if it had been, no signals could make it in or out of this room."

Dr. Mathews rose from his chair to stand, chin in hand, behind Eileen Wu. "So what's it doing?"

Eileen spun her chair to stare up at him, her clear black eyes unblinking.

"Beats the shit out of me."

~ ~ ~

The secondary log-in timer began its countdown as Windows Explorer displayed the desktop, waiting for the Valid-User event to be posted. When, sixty seconds later, the event had failed to arrive, the timer posted another custom Windows event, this one triggering the Unauthorized-User callback.

On the motherboard, the subspace receiver-transmitter (SRT) came on line, commencing a scan for all computer networks within a one-kilometer radius. Its worm had an initial set of prioritized actions. Infiltrate. Replicate. Hide.

Only after the SRT had transferred the worm to sixteen separate systems did its state machine transition from Initial-Response-Mode to Local-Environment-Analysis-and-Optimization. In this mode it began building a prioritized list of networks and processors within the specified radius, assigning the highest priority to computer systems with the largest processor arrays. Within miliseconds, its attention focused on a system that temporarily shifted the SRT's state into High Priority Target Mode.

Sampling the Internet protocol packets entering and leaving this new target, the SRT extracted a hostname.

Big-John.

CHAPTER 64

President Jackson looked at the assembled war fighters and intelligence officials seated around the long table in the Pentagon's National Military Command Center. Covering one of the Emergency Conference Room's walls, six large-screen monitors displayed various maps of the United States. As the president stared up at the maps, he experienced a moment of Cold War déjà vu, half expecting to see Dr. Strangelove come wheeling around the table to give one of his stiff-armed Nazi salutes.

General McKittrick, chairman of the Joint Chiefs of Staff, had just concluded the morning situation brief, which had gone about as President Jackson had expected. The situation was bad and would continue to worsen while the military consolidated its hold on key national assets. Aside from the isolated pockets where the US military had been deployed to maintain order, it was every man for himself out there. Worse than that, it was every gang for itself. In cities and towns across the country, where the police found themselves overwhelmed, they had hunkered down protecting key local facilities, waiting for the promised National Guard reinforcements. But National Guard troops were stretched too thin, assigned to protect key localities as designated by the national command authority.

Amid widespread looting and violence that made the president sick to his stomach to think about, armed citizens banded into local militias to protect their communities from roving gangs. Parts of the country with preexisting militia groups or strong NRA organizations had reacted quickly to establish local order, but these tended to be rural areas where gangs were less of a problem to begin with. And the militias were likely to present their own problems as the central government tried to reassert control over those areas. But even the militias had resorted to looting in order to procure additional firearms, ammunition, food, and supplies.

An alliance of Indian tribes from across the country had announced a new federation, issuing a declaration of independence and closing tribal borders. It was just one more thing that would have to be dealt with, but right now it was far down the president's priority list. So many things needed to be done, but he had to focus, to prioritize.

Washington, DC, was calm, with armored vehicles deployed throughout the city, its streets patrolled by soldiers with orders to shoot looters or curfew violators on sight. All media outlets had been pressed into service, broadcasting the orders for citizens to remain off the streets until order had been reestablished.

Other military units had moved to secure power plants, information centers, port facilities, distribution centers, transportation hubs, and other key assets deemed critical to the future effort to restore regional food and fuel distribution, establishing a network of protected green zones from which the US government could continue to operate.

In the areas outside the green zones, life was going to get very hard, very quickly. Without the heavy military protection of the critical port of New Orleans and the associated barge traffic along the Mississippi River, the nation's factories would have shut down within a week. Even so, with the exception of large, guarded convoys, the national trucking system had suffered significant disruption. That meant shortages of fuel, produce, and other merchandise.

The national panic had spread like a wind-driven grass fire and President Jackson couldn't blame anyone for that reaction. In truth, he'd been so clenched up he hadn't taken a dump in three days. It stunned him to think how quickly public order had disintegrated, as if national stability had been nothing more than an illusion, looking for an excuse to come tumbling down.

The president shifted his attention back to the group around the table, his gaze settling on the army chief of staff. "General Jones, do you agree with General McKittrick's assessment?"

"Yes, Mr. President, I do."

"Admiral Falan?"

"Yes, sir."

President Jackson continued around the table, finding no voices of dissent, something highly unusual given the competitive mix of army, navy, air force, marines, special ops, and intelligence people. In fact, the president couldn't remember ever having heard them all agree on anything.

"OK then. We agree on where we're at. I understand there's no such agreement on our plan going forward. Admiral Falan, would you care to state your objections?"

"Mr. President, as you know, I argued against the widespread imposition of martial law from the beginning. Now, as I predicted, we've alienated large segments of the population by our overly heavy-handed approach. A number of congressmen, including several from your own party, are calling for impeachment hearings, undercutting your moral authority to act."

"And what would you propose we do differently?"

"For one thing, we need to stop shooting our fellow Americans. The rules of engagement you've authorized are more aggressive than any we've used in our recent wars. We can't win this thing by killing our countrymen."

General Jones pounded a large fist on the table. "Nonsense. What Americans are counting on us to do is to restore order so they can go about their daily lives with some sense of safety and security. If that means shooting the gangs of thugs that are doing their best to take that away from them, then by God, that's what we have to do."

President Jackson, feeling his irritation bubble up, held up his hand for quiet. "We've been through all of this before I made my decision. That decision stands. Gentlemen, these are desperate times, the like of which our world has never seen. I intend to lead America through this. To do that we have to ensure a strong central government continues to function. We have to secure critical infrastructure. Then we must extend the zones under our control and protection until they encompass the entire nation. It's not going to be easy and there are those who will question the path I've chosen. I'll let history judge me. But first we have to act to ensure there's a future where that judgment can occur."

The president's eyes locked with Admiral Falan's. "Bill, can you set your reservations aside and support me on this, or do I need to make a change?"

The navy chief of staff paused, and then slowly nodded. "Mr. President, I've given you my best counsel. But you're my president. I'll do what has to be done."

The president rose to his feet. "Good, because we've got plenty to do. Let's get to work."

CHAPTER 65

Despite the slightly lowered windows, the white Chevy Impala was getting hot. Freddy considered lowering them all the way, but then he would run the chance of someone noticing him sitting there in the car. Leaving it running with the AC on was a similar risk, especially with all the military and police patrols roving the Los Alamos area. Sweat and the lingering smell of the pastrami on rye he'd consumed twenty minutes earlier weren't adding a whole lot to the ambiance either.

Damn he hated this stakeout shit.

He glanced down at his watch, the elegant gold-and-crystal rectangle a celebratory Pulitzer indulgence. He watched the second hand tick forward, freezing in place momentarily before ticking forward again, and mentally pictured tiny gears and wheels whirring around inside the thin case. The Swiss did watches right. None of that digital crap.

Twenty-three minutes past two. Dr. Gertrude Sigmund had been in her mother's house exactly thirty-seven minutes. As much as Freddy wanted to walk up and knock on the door, he felt he should give her another ten. No use looking like a stalker, even if you were.

To a newsman, the last few days had been like a soft porn movie, interesting but frustrating. In the last week, the United States of America had come undone. Not all of it. Not entirely. But what had once been the greatest power on earth now resembled a patchwork quilt of island states. To its credit, the United States military had answered the president's call, performing its duty to protect the Constitution. President Jackson had declared martial law, and the US military was doing its best to enforce that declaration.

What that meant on the ground was that cities near military bases had pretty good security. Localities without that benefit found themselves in much less advantageous situations. Luckily for Los Alamos, even though it didn't have its own military base, it was a key national asset, guaranteeing it a disproportionate share of national military assets. It was why Freddy could sit on a residential street in his rented white Impala without worrying about some degenerate biker gang gutting him for the car keys.

An interesting side effect of the mess the country found itself in was that the high-tech infrastructure had survived, essentially intact. After all, the World Wide Web was a critical national priority. Where would our nation be without Google, for God's sake? Corn farmers in Iowa might have to fight to defend their farms, but at least we could still get driving directions. Christ. It reminded Freddy of the World War II acronym, SNAFU. Situation normal, all fucked up.

Just then the garage door across the street began rumbling up along its curving track. But instead of an automobile, a gas-powered push mower rumbled out to the front lawn. With three strong pulls, Dr. Sigmund brought the screaming beast to life.

The tone dropped in frequency as she shoved the mower forward into the deep grass of the front lawn. Then it stabilized, spewing an avalanche of severed grass blades from the raised spout on the mower's left side. As Freddy watched Gertrude Sigmund push the mower in an inward spiral around the lawn, he shook his head.

God, sister! You're killing me.

Freddy's eyes swept the house. It could be any lower-middle-class suburban home, three bedrooms, one and a half baths, just like the rest of the houses in this neighborhood, but with one difference. From the old wood-shingled roof, begging for repair, to the untrimmed trees and shrubs, to the spiral-cut lawn, it seemed to sag beneath sadness and loss. It was an old story: a once-charming home that had hosted Easter picnics and Thanksgiving dinners had transitioned to a dead parents' home, visited only on those occasions when the closest surviving child could will herself over for required maintenance, home to too many memories to sell, home to too many memories to endure.

His background research on Gertrude Sigmund revealed that she'd lost her father two years ago and her mother six months later. The house had remained unrented and unsold since then, still filled with her parents' furniture and belongings. According to the neighbors, Gertrude stopped by once or twice a month, staying several hours, but never spending the night.

In the few days Freddy had been in town, he'd observed enough of Gertrude that he felt he knew her. Since returning from Baltimore, she'd taken a leave of absence from her psychiatry practice and, except for quick trips to the grocery store, had stayed confined to her house. Freddy wondered how Dr. Sigmund would have diagnosed her condition if she had been her own doctor.

The change in her attitude had been abrupt. Before her hastily arranged trip to the DC area she'd been a confident, driven woman, by all accounts a workaholic. Now she appeared burdened by a despair she showed no signs of shaking. Freddy had been dying to talk with her, but not at her house. Although he'd seen no signs she was being followed or watched, he'd had enough dealings with the kinds of government agencies that likely had their talons in her to know her premises were bugged. But he doubted that the government had bothered to monitor her dead parents' house. And as soon as she finished the lawn and went back inside, Freddy was going to take advantage of this opportunity.

Unfortunately, the lawn work gave way to hedge trimming and then to sidewalk washing. Just as Freddy was beginning to wonder if he should risk approaching her outside, she pulled off her work gloves, pushed a loose strand of hair out of her face, and walked back inside, closing the garage door behind her.

In a mild panic that she would immediately walk back out the front door, get in her blue Lexus sedan, and drive off, Freddy climbed out of the Impala. Forcing himself to maintain a slow, leisurely stroll, he walked directly to the front door and pressed the worn doorbell button. Unlike the more expensive chime doorbells that continued even after you released the button, this one produced a buzzing ring that stopped as soon as he released it.

After several seconds the door opened and Freddy found himself staring into Gertrude Sigmund's ice-blue eyes.

"Yes?" Dr. Sigmund's greeting rang out like a challenge.

"I'm sorry to disturb you on your vacation, Dr. Sigmund. I'm Freddy Hagerman, and I urgently need to talk with you."

For several seconds her eyes lost their focus as she tugged at her memory. "Freddy Hagerman? The reporter?"

"That's me."

"What's this all about?"

"May I come in? This conversation is best held away from prying eyes and ears."

Dr. Sigmund studied him through her startlingly blue eyes for so long Freddy began to doubt she'd see him. Then she shrugged and pulled the door all the way open, stepping back to allow him entry.

"What the hell? I've got nothing left to lose."

Freddy found himself in a small foyer, three empty wooden pegs at shoulder height on the wall to his left, linoleum giving way to the living room's brown Berber carpet. The slatted blinds were drawn and as Dr. Sigmund closed the door, the floor lamp separating the recliner from the couch struggled to fight back the darkness. She motioned him to the recliner.

"Can I offer you a glass of water? I'm afraid the refrigerator's bare."

"I'm fine, thanks."

Freddy sat down on the forward edge of the recliner as Dr. Sigmund perched on the couch.

"Very well. I'm listening."

Freddy had rehearsed what he wanted to say as he'd sat across the street in the Impala, but suddenly he found himself searching for the right words.

"Dr. Sigmund, I…"

"Gertrude."

"OK, Gertrude. I assume you know my reputation so I'll spare you a lengthy introduction. I'm here because of the federal agent I observed dropping you off at the BWI airport. More specifically, an agent named John Marks, currently employed by the National Security Agency."

Hearing her intake of breath, Freddy continued. "I asked myself, why was the NSA interested in a small-town psychiatrist?

Since that chance meeting, I've come to believe that your trip was connected to a former patient of yours. A young lady named Heather McFarland."

Gertrude Sigmund seemed to sink back into the leather as a storm of violent emotions raged behind her shining eyes. Freddy gave her a moment to come to terms with his statement.

Gertrude struggled to reacquire her former self-control. "And?"

"And so I've come all this way to ask you why the NSA wanted to talk to you about a patient who was reported killed at Jack Gregory's compound in Bolivia."

Her jaw clenched. "They just wanted to get my professional opinion on why she could get involved with a man like Gregory."

"Bullshit. They'd have sent an agent here for that type of information." Freddy leaned farther forward in his chair. "She's not dead, is she?"

It was as if the little Dutch boy had just pulled his finger from the hole in the dike. A violent shudder began deep inside Dr. Sigmund, spreading rapidly outward from her core to her limbs, and though she pulled up her legs, wrapped her arms around them, and bit her quivering lip, she could not stop shaking. Water leaked from her eyes, tracing twin lines down her dirty cheeks to drip from her chin. But she did not lower her gaze.

As quickly as they had begun, the tremors subsided, replaced with the zombie calm of a drained soul.

"I've betrayed my Hippocratic oath."

"You can tell me about it. I never reveal a source."

A sharp, bitter laugh escaped Gertrude's lips. "You think I care about that now? You think it matters whether other people know? I know! Dear God. I know!"

"Her parents think she's dead. By telling me, you might help them."

Once again her eyes held him. "Probably not. Having met the people who have Heather, she'd be better off dead." Gertrude paused again. "But I'll tell you for my sake."

Freddy set the digital recorder on the coffee table in front of her, pressing the red RECORD button. Gertrude glanced down at it and nodded.

Darkness had fallen when Dr. Sigmund finished her narrative. As Freddy reached out to retrieve the recorder, she rose to her feet.

"Excuse me for a moment. I need to wash my face. If you don't mind waiting, you can see me out."

"Sure."

She turned and walked down the hall toward the master bedroom.

Freddy turned off the recorder, put it back in his pocket, and turned toward the kitchen. A tall glass of water suddenly sounded very good. Finding a glass in the second cabinet he opened, he filled it to the brim and lifted it to his lips.

The roar of the gunshot startled him so badly he dropped the glass, sending crystalline fragments and water spraying across the linoleum floor.

Freddy reacted immediately, racing down the hall toward the master bedroom. He paused before the closed door, his hand on the brass doorknob.

"Gertrude?"

Nothing. His ears still ringing with the echoes of the gunshot, this new silence seemed to acquire a physical presence that filled the dark hallway.

With dread gnawing at his gut, Freddy turned the knob and pushed open the door. The bedroom was empty. A neatly made queen bed occupied the center of the wall to his right, with a nightstand on each side and a six-drawer dresser on the wall opposite the door. From under the closed bathroom door, a sliver of light leaked into the bedroom.

"Dr. Sigmund?"

Freddy hesitated, took a deep breath, and walked to the bathroom door. Although he knew he wouldn't get an answer, he tried one last time.

"Gertrude, are you all right?"

Bracing himself, Freddy opened the door. Baby blue tile dripped blood and chunks of brain matter onto Gertrude Sigmund, her body slumped back in the tub as if she'd just settled into a warm bubble bath. Clutched tightly in her small right hand, the snub-nosed thirty-eight lay in her lap, a faint curl of gray smoke still drifting from its muzzle. The bullet had gone in through Gertrude's mouth and blown off the back and top of her head, leaving her face turned slightly toward the door. Bathed in the bright incandescent light, her clear blue eyes stared at him so intently that Freddy expected to see an accusing finger point his way.

As Freddy lifted his cell phone to dial 911, the thought hit him. Just as she'd told him he could, Freddy had stayed to see her out.

~ ~ ~

Sick to his stomach, Freddy forced down the sour bile that rose into the back of his throat, turned, and walked rapidly out of the bathroom, through the house, and out into the backyard. Pulling the digital recorder from his pocket, he looked around, letting his eyes adjust to the soft shadows cast by the rising three-quarter moon. Under one of the freshly trimmed shrubs, he found what he was looking for, a football-size stone, loose enough for him to turn over.

Discarding a fleeting worry about the possibility of dirt damaging the electronic device, he hollowed out a nook, placed the recorder in the hole, and replaced the stone. That done, Freddy walked back into the kitchen, washed his hands, and then walked out to sit on the front steps to wait for the police. His wait wasn't a long one.

After providing a statement on the scene, he was given a ride downtown. Once the local boys got done with him, he was told to sit tight until a federal agent arrived from Albuquerque. No, he wasn't under arrest. All that meant was that he got to hang out in a two-way mirrored room instead of a cell. At least the cops had brought in a pepperoni pizza and a one-liter bottle of Coke. Apart from those deliveries and the occasional escorted trips to the john, he was left alone.

The NSA guy got there at 1:18 a.m. Agent Sorenstam. Brown hair, brown eyes, average height, average build, the type of guy most people would look at and never give a second thought to. Freddy didn't make that mistake. As Agent Sorenstam sat down in a chair on the opposite side of the table, introduced himself and looked directly into his eyes, Freddy gave him plenty of thought.

"I understand you were in the house when Dr. Sigmund was shot."

"When she killed herself, yes."

"What were you doing there?"

"Do I need an attorney?"

"Do you?"

Freddy leaned forward, resting his elbows on the table. "You've got a copy of my statement to the Los Alamos cops. Look at my answers."

"I read them. I just want a little more detail. A neighbor reports seeing you enter the house before three p.m. You were in there for more than four hours. I just want to know what you and Dr. Sigmund talked about."

"As I said before, I asked her about her trip to Baltimore, and why she met with the NSA there."

"And what did she say?"

"That you sick bastards made her come see Heather McFarland, that Heather isn't dead, that she's being held in a fake psychiatric ward and subjected to mind-altering drugs while the NSA tries to brainwash her."

The answer seemed to take Agent Sorenstam by surprise. The agent glanced up at the two-way mirror, paused, then turned his gaze back to Freddy.

"Did you record the conversation?"

"She wouldn't talk on the record. You'll have to take my word for it."

"Let me get this straight. She spends half the evening talking to you in her parents' living room, then says excuse me while I blow my brains out?"

Freddy shrugged. "Actually she said something like, 'Excuse me for a moment. If you'll wait, you can see me out.'"

"So what set her off?"

"Guess she couldn't wash off the NSA stink."

"Listen, shithead. I'm getting a little tired of your anti-American crap."

"Maybe you didn't hear me right. I didn't say USA, I said NSA."

"Don't try to play the tough guy. You have no idea what that's like."

Freddy reached down, pulled up his pants leg, undid the straps that bound his artificial leg to the stump of his thigh, and set the leg on the table.

"Is that so? Tell you what. Either arrest me now or get my attorney, because this conversation's over."

CHAPTER 66

Tall Bear glanced down at his ringing cell phone, saw only the blocked-number message, and considered not answering it, but pressed the ANSWER button anyway.

"Pino," he said.

"Hello, Sergeant Pino. Thank you for taking this call. My name is Freddy Hagerman and I'm a reporter."

"I know who you are."

"Congratulations on your election as the next president of the Navajo Nation."

"Thanks, but I'm not doing an interview about that now."

"That's not why I called. I'll make this brief. Last night I was brought in for questioning by the Los Alamos police. I had the misfortune of being with Dr. Sigmund when she committed suicide yesterday. When they released me this morning, I hustled straight on down to Albuquerque, made a quick stop to purchase this prepaid cell phone I'm calling you on, and as soon as I hang up, I'll pitch it and hop on the first flight back to DC."

Tall Bear paused before responding. "Why the spy shit? I doubt the Los Alamos cops will be monitoring your real phone."

"No, but the NSA sure as hell is. They were monitoring Dr. Sigmund and now they're monitoring me. That brings me to why I called you. I made a digital recording of my interview with Dr. Sigmund. Then, after she killed herself, I dialed 911, walked out into the back yard, and hid the recorder under a rock. Since I'm sure to be watched, I need you to get it for me."

Tall Bear laughed. "Why? Was I the closest Injun?"

"I know it sounds nuts, but I saw your news conference last year and you seemed like a guy that doesn't have a lot of love for the feds."

Once again Tall Bear considered ending the call. "What's on the recorder that's got the NSA so worried?"

"You know about the three Los Alamos kids that got killed in the black ops raid on Jack Gregory's Bolivian ranch?"

"Yes."

"According to Dr. Sigmund, at least one of them is alive and being held in an NSA psych ward. They took Sigmund there, made her help them convince Heather McFarland she was crazy, and then sent Sigmund back home. Only she couldn't live with that. I think the NSA probably has the other kids, too, but those bastards told their parents they were all dead."

"Even if I believe you, why do you think any of this matters to me?"

"Probably stupid, but I go with my hunches. You struck me as someone who hates that kind of abuse of power. I was hoping you hate it bad enough to stray an hour out of your way."

Tall Bear let the silence stretch out until it hung heavy in the empty air. "Tell me how to find it."

As he drove toward Los Alamos a few minutes later, the warm afternoon breeze blew through the Jeep Cherokee's rolled-down window, whipping his long black hair behind him. It looked as if Jack Gregory had entered his life again. Strange how the world revolved around that man. It seemed like only yesterday that he'd led Jack and Janet to the high hogan. The image of Janet standing in that doorway flooded into his mind, her beautiful tanned face lit by a smile, her arms unconsciously resting on her round, pregnant belly.

How in hell had they linked up with the three Los Alamos kids? Of one thing he was certain. If the NSA was holding those three, then the whole story of the Bolivian raid was rotten. Jack Gregory was the finest man Tall Bear had ever met and he'd been screwed by his own government. That meant those kids were getting the same treatment. The question was, why?

Tall Bear decided he just might have to listen to that recording before he sent it off to Hagerman.

CHAPTER 67

From atop his perch in the tree nearest to the thatch-roofed hut, the monkey jabbered, hopped up and down, then lost interest. Janet held Robby in one arm, pointing at the monkey with the other.

"Do you see the monkey, Robby?"

She studied Robby's face, his clear brown eyes watching hers, then shifting up to the furry brown creature thirty feet away. Despite the fact that he was much too young to speak, Janet had the unshakable feeling that he understood her words, not just her gestures. She knew she shouldn't be surprised at how fast her child was learning, considering what she knew about the effect the alien headbands had had on Mark, Jen, and Heather. Still, she found the pace of his development slightly unnerving.

Janet looked around at the grouping of Quechua huts sitting atop four-foot-high stilts, the ladders leading up to their doors, laundry hanging on lines beneath the thatched overhangs. Just down the road and beyond the hill lay the outskirts of Puyo, Ecuador. Yachay's home. The native nanny had led them here, introducing them to the poor Quechan community where they were welcomed as if they had been long-lost relatives, disappearing from the wider world as thoroughly as if they'd slipped into a La Brea tar pit. No electricity, no running water, no indoor toilets, just a nice, safe hideaway.

Turning away from the monkey, Janet climbed the slanted ladder leading to her hut, the smallest in the village. Pausing just inside the door, she looked up at Cherise, the beautiful scarlet macaw that had become her pet.

"Awk. Robby. Robby."

Janet laughed at the greeting. As smart as Robby was, the bird had learned to talk before he did. Too bad Jack wasn't here to share the moment with her.

Setting Robby in the playpen Yachay had made for him, Janet walked over to the table where her disassembled H & K subcompact lay. One thing about the high jungle. The humidity meant her weapons needed even more daily maintenance than in Bolivia.

As she sat down and picked up where she'd left off, her thoughts turned back to Jack. He'd made sure she and Robby were set up in an adequate safe haven where it was unlikely their enemies could find them; then he'd filled a backpack with ammunition, basic survival gear, and one of their two subspace receiver-transmitter USB dongles and stepped out into the noisy jungle night. Janet could still taste his good-bye kiss on her lips, could feel the way his teeth playfully nipped her lower lip, could see the fire in those eyes.

She missed him, missed having his back. But her responsibility was to Robby first. If he'd been a normal little boy, she would have left him with Yachay and gone with Jack. But neither of them knew what challenges Robby would face in the coming months and Janet wanted to be there to guide his development. Besides, Jack was Jack. He'd find where Mark, Jennifer, and Heather were being held and then they'd have a fighting chance at freedom.

A low rumble in the distance was accompanied by a gust of wind in the rafters. Soon the downpour would send sheets of water from the thatched roof to join the small flood that would roll below the stilted huts, temporarily isolating the Quechan village more completely than normal. Janet rose to stand in the doorway, staring out at the gathering clouds. As the first fat drops splattered against her face, she turned her gaze to the north. Despite the ferocity of the rain forest weather, north was where the real storm was gathering. And it was likely to be a violent one.

CHAPTER 68

The two-lane road needed repaving, the high desert threatening to reclaim it from civilization at any moment. It was one of many stretches of highway in need of such improvement on the Santa Clara Indian Reservation. But it wasn't the potholes or cracks in the pavement that occupied Tall Bear's attention, it was the beat-up white F-150 that had pulled out onto the road a quarter mile in front of him.

The vehicle could have been any one of a thousand such vehicles in this part of the country, a big four-wheel-drive pickup that had seen hard usage in rough country, the bed sagging under the memory of too many heavy loads dropped roughly atop its steel frame. Nothing unusual there. But the way it weaved back and forth across the center line brought Tall Bear's blood to a slow boil. Not that morning drunkenness was an unusual sight here on the res; it was that this was an all-too-common occurrence that grated on him.

Switching on his lights and siren, Tall Bear closed in on the truck's rear bumper, pleasantly surprised to see it pull over and stop along the deserted highway's right shoulder without crashing into anything. A glance at the rear of the truck brought two things to Tall Bear's attention. It had a heavy-duty towing package, but no license plate.

Opening his door and stepping out onto the pavement, Tall Bear approached the driver's door, his right hand resting lightly on the butt of his Colt .45. The driver's window was rolled all the way down, the man's left arm resting on the window frame as calmly as if he'd just pulled up at a McDonald's drive-through. The arm, extending from a black T-shirt sleeve, was darkly tanned and so ripped with lean muscle it appeared to have been chiseled from stone. The upper part of the man's face was hidden by the broad brim of his hat.

"Let me see your driver's license and proof of insurance."

"Sorry, Officer, I must have gotten off without them."

Something about the voice gave him pause. "Step out of the truck and keep your hands where I can see them."

The man opened the door and stepped out to face Tall Bear. Just over six feet tall, the man wore a black T-shirt, tucked into jeans over lace-up combat boots, that emphasized a physique that matched his arms. Again Tall Bear had the impression of someone completely at ease, a feeling that didn't match the man's current situation.

Still unable to see all of the guy's face due to the hat and the downward tilt of his head, Tall Bear let a hard edge creep into his voice.

"Look me in the eye when I talk to you."

As the man tilted his head slowly upward, his voice carried a note of amusement. "Now, Jim. Is that any way to talk to an old friend?"

With the shock of sudden recognition, Tall Bear found him-self staring directly into Jack Gregory's smiling face.

Recovering with a remarkable swiftness, Tall Bear stepped forward to grip Jack's hand. "Jack, you crazy son of a bitch! I thought you'd be smart enough to stay out of this country."

"Guess I've never been that bright."

"What the hell are you doing out here on this back road?"

"Waiting for you to drive by and catch me. Calling didn't seem like such a great idea. Got somewhere we can have a private talk?"

"Lots of privacy out here on the res. Even got a place we can sit on a couch and have a beer."

Jack grinned. "I could go for that. You sure your place isn't bugged?"

"I'm not talking about my house. A buddy of mine went to visit family in Arizona. I'm watching his place while he's gone."

"And his beer?"

"You got it."

"All right. I'll follow you."

Eddy Castillo's house wasn't anything fancy, a double-wide a few miles north of town with a steel carport sitting off to one side, a fenced backyard with some greenish-brown grass. Leading Jack inside, Tall Bear motioned to the couch as he opened the fridge.

"Take a load off."

Returning with two ice-cold Buds, Tall Bear handed one to Jack and plopped down beside him. "How's Janet?"

"Looking fine, as usual."

Tall Bear laughed. "And the baby?"

"Beautiful baby boy. Robert Brice Gregory. We call him Robby."

"So you finally strapped on some *huevos* and married her?"

"I did. Married her in a church in Puyo, Equador. Right before I came back here."

"Damn, that's fine. Wish I'd been there."

"Me too."

Jack raised the can to his lips, pausing to feel the cold condensation before dribbling the amber fluid into his mouth. As he lowered it once more, his smile returned. "By the way, I understand congratulations are in order. President of the Navajo Nation?"

"Not yet. I get sworn in next week."

"President of the largest tribe in North America. I'd say that's a pretty big deal. Especially with what's going on in the world right now."

Tall Bear's face acquired a more serious cast as he voiced the question foremost in his mind. "So what brings you back to this neck of the woods?"

"I need a favor."

"Does it have anything to do with those Los Alamos kids?"

Jack paused. "Jim, you mystical bastard. Now how would you guess that?"

Tall Bear took a long pull at his beer, feeling the bite of the hops as he held it on his tongue. "It's been all over the news."

"Yeah. But the news says they're dead."

"They're not."

"I know, but how do you?"

Tall Bear got to his feet, walking over to look out the window at the dusty road winding away into the lonely hills. "You know Freddy Hagerman?"

"The reporter?"

"Yeah."

"I've read his work."

"A few days ago, he called me. Says he's hidden a digital recorder in a back yard in White Rock. Needs me to get it for him."

"Why you?"

"My question exactly. He says he interviewed a Los Alamos psychiatrist who once treated Heather McFarland. In the interview, Dr. Sigmund said she'd recently been to see Heather McFarland at an NSA supermax facility in Maryland. That was right before Sigmund killed herself. Freddy hid the recorder then, called the cops."

"So you got the recorder?"

"Got it, listened to it, sent it FedEx to a friend of Hagerman's in DC."

Several seconds of silence hung in the air between them.

"What was on that recording, Jim?"

Tall Bear turned to look at Jack. "Heather McFarland is alive. Probably the other two as well. The NSA's playing hardball with them." He shrugged. "Maybe they'd be better off dead."

A cold smile settled on Jack's face.

"Don't bet on it."

"So what can I do for you?"

Recalling the first time he'd stared into the strange fire of Jack Gregory's eyes, Tall Bear found himself mouthing a silent prayer. Ancestors help him. Ancestors help them all.

CHAPTER 69

Dr. Elbert Krause stared at the readouts on the screen before him. Mark Smythe's readings held an otherworldly fascination for him. Never in his career had he seen anything like the self-control this young man possessed. No matter what physical stress they applied to his body, Mark remained in complete control, heart rate forty-three beats per minute, blood pressure at the low end of normal, brain activity indicative of the inner peace of a Shaolin monk.

It couldn't just be Jack Gregory's training. Gregory had only had these kids for a few months, not the years that would be required to achieve this kind of special control. Waterboarding had no more effect on Smythe than a Thanksgiving Day on the couch watching football. Sleep deprivation might as well not have been applied for all the effect it had on him. What was more, as Dr. Krause stared into Mark's eyes in the video monitor, he got the distinct impression that the young stud was holding back, keeping the bulk of his capabilities in reserve.

He switched to the old Los Alamos data files. The answer lay there. It had started in Los Alamos. Nothing else made any sense.

The Smythe and McFarland families had been so close they effectively formed one extended family. All three kids had grown up together in White Rock, best friends long before starting grade school, next-door neighbors, by all accounts inseparable. But something had happened to them in the last two years. Mark Smythe had blossomed into a superstar athlete, while Jennifer Smythe and Heather McFarland had improved on already impressive academic careers.

A number of other oddities jumped out at him. Heather had been kidnapped twice, saved by Jack Gregory once, and had subsequently begun displaying schizophrenic symptoms. The three had produced an amazing entry in a national science competition. Dr. Krause had read their paper and been stunned by just how good it was, despite how they'd failed to credit one of their sources.

Apparently Jack Gregory had sensed just how special these young people were and had somehow enticed them to run away to join him. The question that kept hammering on the back of Dr. Krause's skull was, how had they gotten so special? It must have had something to do with the Rho Project, but why wouldn't Dr. Stephenson have known about them if that were true? Of course, a number of Rho Project–related things had spun out of Stephenson's control. Maybe this was one of them.

Rising from his chair, Dr. Krause rubbed his lower back with his right hand, turned, and walked toward the coffeepot. Filling his ceramic mug with the steaming black liquid, he held the cup up to his nose and inhaled. Ahh. Freshly ground Wolfgang Puck coffee beans, an expensive indulgence, but one he didn't mind shelling out for. Taking a slow sip, he smiled. Now this was true love.

Dr. Krause stiffened. Of course. It had been right there in front of him all along. Not in Mark Smythe's files, but in Heather McFarland's psychiatric records. Dr. Sigmund had noted that, as close as were Heather and Jennifer, Heather's feelings for Mark were stronger.

And it had been Mark and Heather who had gone after Jennifer when she disappeared. They were a couple.

Dr. Krause picked up the telephone and punched in a five-digit extension. Hearing the response on the other end, he began issuing instructions. It would take some fancy video work in the green room, but Sam Halvert could handle that.

Setting the phone back in its cradle, Dr. Krause turned his attention back to the video monitor. If Mark Smythe was in love with Heather McFarland, they'd know it as soon as the video was ready.

CHAPTER 70

Mark had been handcuffed to a chain belt around his waist and led from his cell down a series of nearly identical hallways to a room that could have been an upper-middle-class media room. The projection screen built into the far wall was twelve feet wide and eight feet tall, and currently showed a test pattern from the ceiling-mounted overhead projector. The seats were standard theater seats arranged in multilevel tiers, four rows of four seats with a tiered walkway down the left side. Jennifer would have approved of this arrangement. A perfect hexadecimal ten.

As one of the guards shoved Mark roughly into the front center seat, he noted one significant difference in this media room. Each seat was equipped with a pair of short silver chains. As soon as he sat down, the guard snapped one of the chains to each of his handcuffs, securing him to his seat. The arrangement didn't

give him much confidence in the entertainment value of whatever movie they were about to show him.

Besides his two guards, the only other person in his room was
Dr. Krause, the blond Nazi bastard in charge of his interrogation.
Krause made a point of sitting down in the chair immediately to
Mark's right, while the burly guard who had chained him settled
in on his left. Out of the corner of his eye, Mark could see the
other guard stationed at the exit, fifteen feet up the walkway to
his left.

Apparently the price of admission didn't include popcorn.
Oh well. In these handcuffs, it would've been a challenge getting
it out of the box and to his mouth anyway. The vision of his fingers clawing out puffy white, butter-dripping kernels and flicking
them up to his mouth almost brought a smile to Mark's lips. It'd
probably been a good idea not to provide it. He was pretty sure he
could flick a kernel hard enough to transform one of Dr. Krause's
blue eyes into a dripping wad of slime.

Dr. Krause leaned toward him, a tight little grin warping his
beak. "You ever seen a prison gang rape, Mark?"

"Is that a threat?"

"Just asking if you've ever seen what the animals do when
they slip the leash."

"I've seen some animals try it."

"And?"

"They didn't have as much fun as they thought."

Krause's smile widened, transforming his face into a good
approximation of the Joker's. "Now that's what I like about you,
Mark, your optimistic attitude. But in this case, I'm really the only
one in a position to deliver on a threat, which makes yours nothing but hot air."

Krause signaled to the guard on Mark's left and the man
leaned over to fasten a wireless heart-rate monitor to Mark's wrist

and two more sticky Wi-Fi electrodes to his temples. Finished with that, he slipped back into his seat and leaned back, a move Dr. Krause echoed.

The test pattern was replaced with a video feed from Heather's padded cell. Mark caught his breath as he saw her in a hospital gown, hands and legs strapped to her bed, her milky white eyes seeming to stare right through him. Feeling his heart rate begin to spike, Mark pulled forward the memory of one of his meditations. It worked, but he could feel something building inside him, something hammering to get past his mental blockade.

"I believe you know Ms. McFarland."

Mark said nothing.

"As you can see, she's been somewhat traumatized. I'm afraid that in her fragile state, another severe shock could push her over the edge into a permanent catatonic state."

Mark almost laughed in his face. Heather had them completely fooled into thinking she was psychotic, showing them exactly what they expected.

Dr. Krause picked up an Android phone, pressed an app button, then spoke three words. "Bring them in."

The electronic lock on Heather's door clicked open and three big, tattooed white guys shuffled into the room, coupled together on a chain, escorted by four guards, two of which covered their movements with a pair of MK-5s.

Dr. Krause held the phone in front of Mark. "You're probably wondering why I get to have a phone inside a secure facility. It's a toy that stays on the inside, a push-to-talk Voice over IP app, riding on our secure Wi-Fi network."

"Couldn't care less."

"Unless you agree to start fully cooperating, in ten seconds I'm going to push this button and tell the guards to take off the chains and lock three of the meanest serial rapists in our federal prison system inside that cell with Heather McFarland. Lucky you. You've got a front-row seat."

Mark looked at the screen and knew that Heather could handle those three Aryan Brotherhood assholes with no more effort than it took him to shave. But that would wreck everything. That would alert the NSA to the fact that the girls were a major threat. He couldn't allow that. Not now.

Deep within Mark's mind, a spiderweb of cracks spread across the tranquil meditative scene, rapidly widening into fissures through which the blackness poured.

"Ten..."

Mark felt the vibrations pulse through the muscles in his arms, up into his shoulders, and across his back.

"Nine..."

He inhaled deeply through his nostrils.

"Eight...seven..."

Let it out slowly through his mouth.

"Six...five..."

The chains binding his wrists came apart with such force that multiple chain links splattered outward, shattering the wall projection screen like the impact of forty-five-caliber slugs. As his right hand grabbed Dr. Krause's throat, his left leg rocketed out, caving in the chest of the guard to his left, sending the body flipping head over heels into the far wall.

The guard by the exit moved instinctively, bringing up the Tazer even as Mark hurtled up the steps toward him. The guard was fast. Really fast. And with anyone else his quickness would have been enough.

Mark felt the electrical jolt take him in the center of the chest, the involuntary muscular shock freezing him in place for the merest fraction of a second. Then his enhanced neuromuscular system shunted the effects aside and he swept inevitably onward, his left fist caving in the side of the guard's head as he reached the top of the steps, Dr. Krause still clutched in his right hand's powerful grip.

Seeing that the electrically controlled door was sliding closed, Mark hurled Krause's dying body into the gap, paused to grab his phone, then plunged through the door. Without a moment's hesitation, he raced down the hallways along which they had brought him to the theater room. He remembered a janitor's closet off to the right two corridors down. Reaching it, Mark threw his whole strength into the door, ripping it from its hinges.

Stepping inside, Mark concentrated on the phone, his fingers flying across the keypad. With a sigh of relief, he verified that Jennifer's worm had infected the phone's Android operating system. That meant someone had powered up at least one of their laptops, releasing the worm into every computing system in this facility as well as all those within the specified search radius. Typing in a series of quick commands, Mark crushed the phone in his palm and hurled it against the far wall, sending fragments showering out across the corridor.

Then, leaning his head back against the wall, he relaxed, resuming his previously disturbed meditation. He was ready. Let them come.

CHAPTER 71

For several days Heather had felt the frustration building, but she continued to shunt it aside, walling it away from the work it threatened to disrupt. It wasn't that she hadn't made progress in her quest to establish a mind link with Jennifer. She had gotten very good at detecting Jennifer's attempts at a link and had been able to establish an improved mutual awareness. But that awareness amounted to little more than an increased sense of presence, akin to catching sight of a ghost from the corner of her eye. When she tried to see it directly, it was gone.

Heather had begun to question her initial analysis of how telepathy worked. For one thing, if it had just been a form of normal electromagnetic wave communication, even directed by an extremely sophisticated neural phased array, the signal would have been attenuated by intervening objects and wouldn't have worked at all in a facility replete with TEMPEST-approved Faraday cages.

Besides, when Jennifer and Mark had felt her thoughts when she'd been carried off by the Rag Man, she'd been a long way from them and without the line of sight required for a directed signal. It struck her that her initial assumptions had caused her to proceed down an erroneous path in her efforts to make a connection.

A baby didn't learn to walk by mentally calculating which nerve endings to fire and which muscle fibers to twitch. He did it by trial and error, with a picture in mind of what he wanted to do, and then by releasing that desire into a brain that remembered little successes and built upon those. It happened automatically, but not instantaneously.

Rather than think about the night when the Rag Man had grabbed her, Heather let her thoughts drift to the morning at her mother's breakfast table when she'd heard Jennifer's thoughts as clearly as if she'd spoken them aloud.

Suddenly Heather found herself back at the table, tasting the pancakes, smelling the warm maple syrup as it pushed melted butter down the sides of the stack. Jen's voice in her head made it sound exactly as if Jen had spoken those words. Except something was missing. The auditory signals from her inner ear held no memory of vibrating under the sound waves from Jennifer's voice.

It was more as if she'd been inside Jennifer's head, with no distance separating their minds. It was like the alien headset link. Heather replayed the memory again and again, each time noticing some new detail of that mind link. The thoughts Jen had been thinking loudest were what she'd noticed at the time, but there was more. Drowned out by the volume of her surface thoughts were layers of thought and feelings, like whispers in a crowded room. Heather's mind had shared all of that, it just hadn't stood out.

But what had initiated the link? Heather felt the frustration bubble up again as she strove to understand it. The pattern was there, nibbling at the edges of her memory, but despite all her talents, she just wasn't seeing it.

One thing each of the instances of psychic communion had in common: each time she'd managed it, Heather hadn't been consciously trying to achieve a link.

Heather took a deep breath, slowly let it out and visualized what she wanted, then released it, pulling forth the memory of one of her favorite meditations, feeling her alpha waves smooth out in long, slow ripples. She felt her consciousness drift in blackness, zooming her perspective out until she was a distant, flickering flame, alone in an infinite black expanse. As she let herself drift deeper, she spotted another pinprick of light, then another, and another. As she became aware of these other tiny light sources, she noticed something else. The blackness that separated her from them wasn't uniform. Waves rippled outward through the void from each pinprick, as if from pebbles dropped in a still pond. Only these waves radiated super-spherically.

Also, this void wasn't four-dimensional space, but consisted of one or more additional dimensions, each of which touched all points in space. The void was full of these ripples, crossing over each other, waves of varying frequencies and amplitudes, most completely unfamiliar. Heather let her mind drift, scanning the wave sources in an expanding spiral until she recognized a familiar pattern. Jennifer.

Heather felt her as surely as if they had touched, the strength of the feeling jumping in intensity as she focused on the flame that was Jennifer. Rather than try to establish a connection, Heather relaxed further into the meditation, letting her mind center on the wave source in its own way.

Then it happened. It was as if their two candle flames merged, hers with Jennifer's, and in that moment their minds joined as thoroughly as if they'd just slid into the alien headsets. Only this time neither of them threw up any mental blocks, joyously accepting the complete mental union.

~ ~ ~

In her padded cell, Heather's readings underwent a remarkable shift, as if she'd suddenly entered a terrifying dream. As Dr. Jacobs turned his head away from the monitor to gaze into Heather's milky white eyes, he was startled to see tears streaming down the sides of her face to dampen her brown hair.

He briefly considered trying to rouse her from the hallucination, but rejected the idea. Better to watch and see where this went. Perhaps whatever mental trauma Heather was experiencing in her fugue could be turned to some future advantage.

Leaning back in his chair, Dr. Jacobs let the electronic data collection continue.

CHAPTER 72

General Balls Wilson was pissed, more than pissed. He was mad as hell. As he stared at his assembled staff, his usually jovial brown eyes seemed ready to spit bolts of liquid lightning that would leave only charred skeletal imprints of each person who had attracted the full force of that gaze.

"Who the hell authorized making this video and showing it to Mark Smythe?"

As the silence in the room acquired the density of a thick London fog, his long stride carried him around the NSA conference room, first clockwise, then counter-, until the weight of his presence became unbearable.

"Gentlemen. Maybe you aren't hearing me. I want to know who gave the OK for this piece-of-shit video to be produced and shown to my prisoner without my direct authorization. Unless I get an answer in the next thirty seconds, every one of you bastards is going to be looking for a new line of work."

Carl Christenson was the first to respond. "Sir, it appears that Dr. Krause ordered the video production and showed it to Mark Smythe in person."

"Then he's lucky he's dead, because if he was still alive, he'd be mine."

Balls Wilson's powerful stride carried him back to the front of the room, where his hungry hawk's gaze swept the assemblage. "Three NSA men dead. And you know what? After what I've seen, I don't know how Smythe managed it, but I don't blame him one little bit."

His eyes turned on Dr. Jacobs. "How did Dr. Krause get the original video of Heather McFarland for his little greenroom production? Aren't you in charge of her interrogation?"

"Yes sir, I am. Dr. Krause asked for access to the video. I assumed it was to assist with the Smythe interrogation."

"You assumed."

"Yes sir."

"Goddamn it. I assumed I had a competent staff. I guess we're all a bunch of idiots." General Wilson's chest heaved as he fought to bring his emotions back under control. "I'm not running some sort of half-assed Abu Ghraib operation here. If I find another instance of someone trying out an interrogation technique without my explicit approval, you'll wish you never heard my name. Am I making myself clear?"

"Yes sir!"

The thunderous response from all those in the briefing room lent credence to their answer.

General Wilson's eyes locked, person by person, with each individual in the room.

"Good. Make sure you don't disappoint me again."

He let several seconds of silence hang in the air between them before speaking again.

"Dismissed!"

In less than thirty seconds the room, save General Wilson, was empty. Turning once more to the frozen image of Heather McFarland bound to her bed as three convicts were about to be released into her room, Balls Wilson hurled the remote control into the video screen with enough force to shatter the glass display into a thousand pieces, the falling fragments creating a sound like freezing rain on a car windshield.

Balls Wilson stared at the mess, his hands clenched so tightly that the muscles in his upper arms bulged with the effort. Then he turned and strode from the room.

CHAPTER 73

Louis Dubois had come to despise Donald Stephenson on a personal level. But he had to admit the man had intellect and drive that went beyond any conventional definition of genius. He was an asshole who unveiled glorious theoretical and practical breakthroughs, seemingly on an as-needed basis.

The latest scientific marvel was a design for a device that Dr. Stephenson called a stasis field generator that, if it worked as the theory predicted, could create powerful force fields, manipulating them with incredible precision. Louis had worked around the clock the last forty-eight hours reviewing Dr. Stephenson's white paper, trying to find something wrong with his theoretical derivations, but all he'd done was confirm Stephenson's work.

And Dr. Dubois wasn't alone. He'd had another team going over the equations at the same time. Louis had just returned from a meeting with Dr. Freidrick Haus, Nobel laureate mathematician and team lead. As he'd expected, Dr. Haus's team also confirmed Dr. Stephenson's work.

Louis leaned back in his chair, shoving his fingers under his reading glasses to rub his red eyes. As hard as it was to believe, the American physicist was rewriting the world's understanding of physics at a pace that had shocked the thousands of scientists working on the ATLAS project to their core. And Louis had no doubt that, when those papers were released to the public, they would have the same shocking impact on the scientific community at large. If the world survived the current crisis, there'd be a lot of textbooks heading directly to trash bins, which was precisely where they belonged.

Louis rose from his seat and walked across his office, pausing to retrieve his black London Fog raincoat and umbrella before heading for the building exit. A cold, steady rain had drenched most of Europe for the last three days and the weather report held little promise of improvement. A massive cold front cut its way across the EU map, its blue curve sporting eastward, facing blue triangles stretching from Finland down to Italy's booted heel. Right now it was stalled, blocked by a massive high-pressure system that had set up shop over western Russia.

Nodding at Elynn Stadich, the front desk security guard, Louis pulled up his raincoat collar, unfurled the umbrella, and stepped out into the gray wetness of the Swiss morning. He'd decided to make the walk to the ATLAS facility to clear his mind. Five minutes into the hike, he regretted his decision. The temperature hovered in the low forties, which wasn't so bad, but the whirling wind made his umbrella less than useless. As one of these gusts almost succeeded in springing the umbrella inside out, Louis gave up, stowed it into its handle, and accepted that his head was going to get a thorough drenching. He didn't really think it could get much wetter anyway.

As he stepped into the entrance to the surface facility that led to the ATLAS cavern, Louis removed his raincoat, then leaned over to wipe and shake the moisture from his head and neck.

"Dr. Dubois, I thought they provided you with a car and driver."

Louis turned to see the grinning face of Gary Levin, one of the top graduate students assigned to the program.

"Looked like a nice day for a stroll."

"Guess I don't want to walk with you on a bad day, then."

Gary handed him a white hard hat, waiting as Louis adjusted it to fit his head. "Guess I should have brought you a towel too."

"I'll dry off on the way down to ATLAS."

The smile faded from Gary's face as if it had been wiped from a blackboard. "When was the last time you were in the ATLAS cave?"

"Tuesday. I've been holed up reviewing Dr. Stephenson's latest paper for the last couple of days. Told Sophia I didn't want to be disturbed unless a critical problem came up."

The grad student inhaled deeply, frowned, and then continued. "I probably shouldn't be the one to tell you, but you're not going to like what's happening down there."

The cold hand of dread grabbed Dr. Dubois's esophagus and squeezed. "What do you mean?"

"I guess I'd better show you."

Passing down a narrow hallway with a silver conduit running down the center of the eight-foot ceiling, Louis paused at a locker to hang his raincoat and umbrella inside. Turning, he followed Gary through several more rooms and hallways, the noise of heavy construction equipment growing in volume as they made their way toward the ATLAS cavern.

They stepped onto scaffolding high up on the cavern wall. As always, the scene affected him on multiple levels. All those years building this place, and now they were working at breakneck speed disassembling the massive detector and enlarging the cavern to make room for Dr. Stephenson's wormhole generator, all the while making sure nothing disrupted the containment field isolating the November Anomaly.

Suddenly Louis froze. One large section of the ATLAS detector's massive end cap dangled from a ceiling crane, trailing metal scraps and cables, as if a gigantic maw had grabbed the device and ripped out a huge chunk.

"What in God's name?"

A wave of nausea and dizziness almost buckled Louis's knees.

"Dr. Stephenson's order. He's personally supervising the dismantling operation."

"Dismantling?" Louis sputtered. "That's wanton destruction. Where the hell is he?"

As Gary pointed to a tiny figure gesturing to the construction crew on the far side of the cavern, Louis cursed, then clambered down the stairs leading to the cavern floor. By the time he reached Dr. Stephenson, his breath hissed out in short, ragged gasps.

Grabbing Dr. Stephenson by the shoulder, he spun the American scientist to face him.

"What the hell do you think you're doing?"

Stephenson's gray eyes took in Dr. Dubois as casually as if he'd just asked to schedule a meeting.

"The crew was falling behind schedule. I am changing that."

"By destroying billions of dollars in instrumentation? We're supposed to be dismantling ATLAS so that it can be reconstructed once we're done here. You're ruining decades of work."

Dr. Stephenson pursed his lips. "Dr. Dubois. What portion of this piece of junk do you think needs saving? Since you probably haven't understood a word I've presented in my papers, this may not have occurred to you, but your little science project is over.

The technologies and energies we are about to create in this cavern go so far beyond anything ever contemplated on earth; they make the Large Hadron Collider laughable."

Dr. Dubois's eyes widened as if he'd been slapped in the face.

"Face it, Louis," Stephenson continued. "No need to search for more standard-physics-model validation. That model is dead."

With that dismissal, Dr. Stephenson turned to yell more instructions at the foreman. Behind him, Dr. Louis Dubois stood frozen in place. As he stared up at the beautiful, intricate machine that was ATLAS, his eyes misted over. Stephenson was right. Like Louis, in the blink of an eye, it had become a dinosaur.

CHAPTER 74

Dr. Rodger Dalbert slid into the indicated seat in the small breakout room adjacent to the White House Situation Room. President Jackson was seated in the opposite chair, Cory Mayfield, the director of national intelligence, sat to his right, and James Nobles, the National Security Advisor, sat on the president's left. The arrangement had Rodger seated with his back to the door, a position that left him feeling exposed and vulnerable.

The breakout room was normally used for occasions when the president wanted to pull a couple of key staff members out of the Situation Room for a private side discussion, while the rest of the staff cooled their heels and waited for the president's return. To be brought here directly, while the Situation Room sat empty next door, raised Rodger's hackles, making him feel like closing himself inside one of the nearby high-security Plexiglas phone tubes.

"Rodger. Glad to see you," the president said.

"Always a pleasure, Mr. President."

"I imagine you're curious as to why I had you brought down here."

"The question came to mind."

President Jackson leaned back in his chair, lacing his fingers behind his head. "You understand that what we are about to discuss is top-secret SCI?"

Rodger nodded.

"You're not to discuss anything we talk about with anyone but me. Is that clear?"

Once again Rodger felt the uncomfortable tensing of muscles between his shoulder blades. The president did tend to repeat himself. "Yes sir."

The president smiled that broad smile that had eased his ascension into the political stratosphere, and leaned forward to rest his forearms on the table. "Good. Then let's get right to the meat of it. You know Jim Nobles and Cory Mayfield. They have come to me with a proposal that impacts the construction being done at the ATLAS site. As chairman of my council on science and technology, and since you were the first American to be briefed on the November Anomaly, I wanted to get your opinion before I make a final decision."

Rodger glanced at Cory Mayfield, but the intel man's gray eyes betrayed no hint of emotion. But James Nobles's mouth held a tension that matched Rodger's.

"I'm listening."

"Go ahead, Cory."

"I've recommended to the president that, through our ties with the Geneva-based construction company Dietrich and Hoechner, we install some tactical nuclear weapons within some of the prefabricated supports destined for installation in the ATLAS cavern."

Rodger's jaw dropped as he struggled to parse the words he'd just heard.

Regaining his voice, Rodger consciously released the pressure in his clenched fists. "Mr. President, that's the stupidest thing I've ever heard."

Motioning for the other two to remain silent, the president looked directly into his eyes. "OK, Rodger, make your case."

Rodger struggled to bring his thoughts to bear on the problem. It boggled his mind that the president of the United States had even entertained the proposal, much less give it enough credence to warranted Rodger's debunking it. He inhaled deeply.

"Mr. President, I assume the purpose of these devices would be to form some sort of backup plan whereby they would be triggered in order to destroy the nascent black hole?"

"That is correct."

"That's just wrong. As I already briefed you and the entire staff, the anomaly exists at an inflection point and is gradually tilting into a state where it is likely to become a black hole. We're struggling to slow that process by surrounding it in as perfect a low-temperature vacuum as can be created on Earth, all in an attempt to keep the thing from absorbing additional matter and energy, just trying to give the November Anomaly Project time to build the Stephenson device. Any explosive addition of energy to the anomaly will greatly accelerate its progress in becoming a black hole. If you set off a nuclear explosion, you'll be destroying the Earth as surely as if the sun went supernova."

"You're certain of that."

"As sure as I'm sitting here."

"Cory?"

"I understand Dr. Dalbert's scientific analysis. But Mr. President, the fact remains that something might go wrong with

Dr. Stephenson's device. It might not work as his theory predicts or it might not get done in time. There's also the side issue of how much we trust Dr. Stephenson. There's no doubt he's a genius, but our sources say he's rolling out theoretical applications that he never revealed to others at Los Alamos or to the rest of the government team. If something goes badly wrong, we can't afford to go without a fallback plan."

"Fallback plan?" Rodger sputtered. "Didn't you hear anything I just said? If you nuke it you get an instant black hole. No need to add water or stir."

"And if we do nothing, we get a black hole anyway. Isn't that right, Dr. Dalbert?"

Rodger felt beads of sweat pop out on his brow. "Probably, but not as quickly. We might have time for another try."

Cory Mayfield laughed, a harsh, guttural rasp that hurt Rodger's ears.

"Another try? There's not going to be another try. The world is committing every bit of its scientific and engineering might into Dr. Stephenson's plan. Not that we wouldn't spin up a backup project if someone came up with a competing idea, but the sad truth is that nobody's got another reasonable idea. We've been all through the launch-it-into-space thing. All the top minds say that's a no-go for a host of reasons, chief among them the problem of maintaining the isolation and containment field throughout the launch process. Then there's the issue of this approach being incompatible with our best bet, which is building Dr. Stephenson's Rho device around the thing. So, unless some religious group manages to pray the anomaly away, we're left with Stephenson's Rho device or bust."

Rodger opened his mouth to speak, then shut it again.

"So," Mayfield continued, "if all else fails and the thing's getting ready to eat us anyway, it won't hurt to roll the dice."

President Jackson turned to face his national security advisor. "James?"

"I don't see a better alternative."

"Mr. President! Give me a month. I'll assemble another team, give it one more look, see if we can come up with another fallback option."

President Jackson smiled a sad smile. "I don't have another month to give you, Rodger. If we want to get nukes put in the prefab construction, I have to make a decision now. I'm sorry, but I'm giving the go-ahead for Director Mayfield's approach."

Turning to his smiling DNI, the president nodded.

"OK, Cory. Make it happen."

CHAPTER 75

The click-clack of retreating footsteps echoed down the long empty hallway, picking up a sympathetic vibration from the steel bars that locked Mark in his cell. He sat cross-legged and naked on the cold concrete, deep in the meditation that gave him respite from that lonely place.

Surprisingly, his situation had improved. Immediately after killing Dr. Krause and the two guards, Mark had waited in the closet to be recaptured. His intuition had told him that Heather should be the one to initiate their escape, that she would know when the time was right. So he had just uploaded instructions to Jennifer's worm, destroyed the cell phone, and waited.

He had been moved to a different cell, still inside the same supermax unit, but without the chains and waterboarding table. Except for food trays pushed through a floor slot, his captors appeared to have forgotten about him, leaving him to deal with his own demons here in solitary confinement. He shared the ten-by-twelve-foot space with a sink, a toilet, a showerhead, and a drain. The water came out of both the sink and the showerhead at the same temperature. Cold.

Except for the prison-issue orange pj's and a single pair of briefs, Mark had nothing. On the days he washed his clothes in the sink, he waited naked for them to dry. At the cell's constant sixty-two degrees, that drying process took a good while, even after he'd hand-wrung them. Today was one of those laundry days.

Despite the way Mark tried to keep himself busy working out and meditating, the oppressive loneliness was working on him in a way the torture hadn't. He tried not to think of Heather, but she crept into his thoughts, and with her came a longing that tugged him irresistibly toward a black pit of despair.

And Heather wasn't the only thing messing with his mind. Increasingly, the faces of the men he'd killed came back to haunt him. Not Don Espeñosa and his assholes, nor even Dr. Krause. It was the faces of the two guards that robbed him of peace. Did they have wives? Children? Mark thought he knew the answer. But in a moment of violent action, he'd destroyed those little families, as surely as the US government had destroyed his. No more birthdays or Christmases with Daddy. No more family barbecues in the backyard. Thank you, Mark Smythe. You're a real badass hero.

With a start, Mark realized he'd completely lost the meditation, having allowed the rogue thoughts to entice him onto the shoals of that depressing shore. He shook his head in attempt to clear it.

Somewhere in this hellhole, his captors had Jennifer and Heather. Mark had little hope that they were receiving kinder treatment than that afforded him.

The picture of Heather sleeping beside him in that Las Vegas motel formed in his mind so clearly that he could reach out to hold her tight and safe in his protective arms. He breathed in the pleasant scent that wafted up to his nostrils from her freshly showered body. It was only the smell of a motel soap bar, but anointing Heather's skin, its aroma surpassed that of the finest perfume.

Again Mark fought to clear his thoughts. He stared up at the camera in the upper right corner of the cell, letting his frustration and rage boil up. Rising to his feet, Mark coiled his leg muscles and, with a two-stride jump, ripped the camera from its mount, landing on the floor amid a shower of electrical sparks, the short plunging the entire corridor into darkness. Mark stood there for several seconds, listening for an alarm that never sounded. Then, tossing the small camera through the bars, he resumed his former meditative pose.

~ ~ ~

In his office, General Wilson picked up his phone on the second ring.

"Yes?"

"Smythe just ripped down the camera in his cell. Blew the D13 circuit breaker. Should I send in a crew to repair it?"

"No. Reroute power but leave the lights in that corridor off."

"So you want us to ignore the camera?"

"That's the point."

"Yes sir."

As he hung up the phone, a slow smile spread across Balls Wilson's face. Unless he missed his guess, they'd just found the first chink in Mark Smythe's armor.

CHAPTER 76

The last few days had been some of the most draining of Heather's life, a strange mixture of psychiatric sessions in which Dr. Jacobs worked to exploit her psychosis, interspersed with psychic communication sessions with Jennifer. Like a soldier crawling under barbed wire while probing the ground ahead with her bayonet, Heather navigated a mental minefield that left her exhausted, but unable to stop for rest.

Although she was no longer strapped to a hospital bed, the replacement wasn't much more comfortable. Sometimes she rested better curled up in the corner farthest from the toilet, pretending to sleep the night away.

Her psychic contacts with Jennifer remained intermittent. Sometimes, depending on the heroin dosage the bastards were feeding into Jen's veins, Heather couldn't make contact at all, and sometimes wading through Jen's mind felt like moving through a pea-soup fog, Jen's thoughts like shrouded lamps, dimly visible through the haze. It worried Heather horribly. Images of her friend, physically addicted to the dangerous drug, crowded her tired brain.

For the last two hours Heather had lain on the cell floor, matching her heart rate and breathing to that expected of her sleeping self. Contact had been impossible. She thought about trying to contact Mark, but every attempt at that had met with utter failure. He had erected mental blocks so intense she could barely feel him, much less penetrate them. She could sense that he was close, but whatever torture he was enduring had forced him to erect his mental defenses. Now, as tired as she was, Heather couldn't bring herself to make another attempt.

Uncurling, she yawned and stretched, her heart rate gradually climbing to a wakeful rhythm. The cell was dark, but Heather didn't need to see a clock to know it was three minutes past four in the morning, any more than she needed someone to tell her that meant she was 14,580 seconds into her day.

As much as she wanted to indulge in a restful meditation, she needed to work out before her doctors and handlers arrived to soak up endless portions of her time. After all the time she'd been strapped down, her muscles needed to work. Heather had a feeling that, when the time came, she was going to need every bit of strength and coordination she could muster. And her Jack Gregory–filled visions whispered that that time was rapidly approaching.

Shrugging out of the hospital gown, Heather tossed it into the corner, stretched her naked body tall and erect, and filled her lungs with air. Then, breathing out slowly, she shifted into her first yoga pose of the morning.

Warrior one.

CHAPTER 77

Constitution Avenue was crowded with cars, the Washington Mall was packed with people, the early evening was hot and muggy, and some damned country singer roamed the Capitol Stage wailing about how rednecks could survive. Freddy shook his head. He hated these July fourth celebrations. It was just like the government to make a special exception to martial law rules in order to squeeze in such a self-congratulatory ceremony during these hard times. He'd seen enough red-white-and-blue-backdropped fireworks-augmented performances to last two lifetimes, but here he was at another. On top of that, his walking leg was rubbing a blister on what was left of his stump.

But Tall Bear's message had said to be here, so here he was.

If he'd been thinking, he'd have brought a blanket to spread out on the lawn along with a cooler full of Bitburger Pils. Glancing around at the security squads roaming through the crowd, Freddy doubted he could have slipped it in.

Something bumped hard against Freddy's good leg, almost toppling him. He looked around in time to see two fat blond kids chasing each other through the crowd, weaving in and out of seated groups of people, several expressing the annoyance Freddy felt.

Maybe the little porkers would pass out in the Washington heat.

He glanced at his watch. Six fifteen p.m. Tall Bear's message had said six o'clock. So where the hell was he? Freddy moved a little farther south, his eyes scanning the Capitol steps. No sight of the big Indian cop. At his height and with that long raven hair he should have been easy to spot, even in this mob.

Freddy spun in a slow circle, shielding his eyes from the sinking sun as he gazed westward toward the white spire of the Washington Monument. A flock of birds rose up from the cherry trees near the Jefferson Memorial, their whirling mass swooping across the green expanse of the mall, briefly eclipsing the bright orange orb before settling into some trees beside Constitution Avenue. Freddy was glad he hadn't parked over there.

If anything, the crowd on the mall was getting bigger as people maneuvered for spots they wanted for tonight's fireworks show. Looking out at the scene, Freddy could almost convince himself that all was well with the country. But DC was a heavily protected green zone, at least this part of DC. The army, marines, and National Guard had done a good job of expanding the number of areas under their control, but that still left large sections of the country subject to something approaching anarchy. Louisiana had been written off as not worth the effort to police and many of the nation's sparsely populated rural areas had reinterpreted martial law as militia law, maintaining local order at the expense of civil rights. Poor inner-city neighborhoods resembled war zones that police feared to enter and the army regarded as nonessential.

On the stage, the country band finished its set, thanked the crowd, and exited stage right, replaced by a congressman from the great state of Maryland. Freddy tuned him out and resumed his search. Frustrated, he jostled through the crowd toward the Capitol building. Maybe if he stood on the steps, Tall Bear would find him. Thirty minutes of standing proved him wrong.

"Screw this," he muttered, turning to head back toward Union Station and his car.

The thought of his car brought his hand to his pocket. Freddy froze. His car keys were gone. He checked his hip pocket and breathed out a small sigh of relief. At least he had his wallet. But how the hell had he lost his keys?

Instinctively, he patted all his pockets, surprised to feel the key ring bulge in his front left pants pocket. What the hell? He never put his keys in that pocket. Reaching his left hand in to grab them, he felt something else with them. A piece of paper.

Extracting his keys and the paper, Freddy stared down at it. The paper was a neatly folded piece of heavy vellum. It reminded him of something he'd seen before, although he couldn't place it.

Glancing around, Freddy saw nothing out of the ordinary. But someone in the crowd had picked his pocket, then returned his keys, along with the note, in a way sure to get his attention. Staring down at the paper, Freddy undid the four folds. As he stared at the handwriting, the sense of déjà vu enveloped him so strongly it took his breath away.

This is the second note I've sent you, although the first in my own name. You may recall a certain shoebox and necklace that accompanied the first. Be assured, if I wanted to harm you, you'd already be dead. You have some information I want and I believe I

can fill in part of the story you're currently working. If you're inter-
ested, be at the southeast corner of Louisiana and New Jersey at
7:15. I'll find you. J.G.

A cold shiver started at the base of Freddy's neck, radiating up
his scalp and down his arms like the kiss of death. Jack Gregory.
Somehow, in the midst of all this hyper-security, the Ripper had
touched him twice and he hadn't even noticed, despite the fact
he'd been actively studying his surroundings.

Freddy folded the note and returned it to his pocket along
with his keys, then, with another quick glance around, crossed
Constitution Avenue onto First. Taking a slight right onto
Louisiana, he made his way past the Taft Memorial, reaching the
southeast corner of Louisiana and New Jersey Avenues. His watch
said 7:08.

A black Honda Shadow motorcycle squealed to a stop beside
him, the rider's face, hidden behind the helmet's reflective face-
plate, turned toward him.

Freddy nodded. "You're early."

"Get on."

To Freddy's credit, he never hesitated, at least not for longer
than it took him to get his good leg over the seat behind Gregory.
The motorcycle pulled into traffic, turned left on New Jersey, leaving the Union Station Plaza behind as it accelerated northeast.

Two hours later Freddy found himself in Linthicum,
Maryland, sitting on a couch in Jack Gregory's room at the BWI
Homewood Suites.

"Coffee?" Gregory asked, lifting the in-room pot.

"Black."

Setting a steaming cup in front of Freddy, Gregory filled his
own mug, then settled into the armchair across from the sofa.
Freddy didn't know what he'd been expecting from the killer, but
this wasn't it. At the moment the man looked nothing like any

of the pictures Freddy had seen of him, and they'd been all over the television and print media. His ruddy brown complexion and medium-length coal-black hair gave him a distinctly Native American look that went fine with his jeans, boots, and Western shirt.

Gregory moved in a relaxed, easy fashion that reminded Freddy of a prowling lion. Freddy just hoped he'd make it through the evening without becoming the prey. Well, so far so good.

"Your meeting with Dr. Sigmund on the night she killed herself; tell me about it."

Freddy sucked in a breath, his heart rate shifting up a notch. How did Gregory know about that? Not through his old NSA ties. Those were as dead as Jonathan Riles. A light dawned in his mind. Tall Bear.

"What do you want to know?"

"Why you arranged the meeting, everything Dr. Sigmund told you, your thoughts and impressions about what she was telling you, why she killed herself. Everything."

"Why should I tell you when I didn't tell the NSA? Your note mentioned a quid pro quo."

Jack reached for the fruit basket on the coffee table, grabbed a shiny red apple, and slowly began peeling it. Freddy hadn't noticed when the survival knife had appeared in his hand, but there it was, the thin red apple skin curling away from the black blade in one long, thin strip.

"I've read your investigative work. Impressive stuff. You show me that same level of attention to detail and I'll reciprocate."

"And if I don't?"

"Then you'll find the front page a little sooner than you planned."

Freddy remembered a line his father had told him. "Son, don't ask a question if you don't want to hear the answer."

Freddy Hagerman shrugged. "Fair enough."

At two thirty a.m., Jack Gregory leaned over and handed Freddy the room's key card, then rose and walked out the door. A minute later, Freddy heard the roar of a motorcycle as it pulled out of the parking lot and drove off.

As exhausted as Freddy was, he felt no inclination to sleep. Instead he stared down at his digital recorder, the one he'd played for Gregory earlier in the evening, the one on which he'd subsequently been allowed to record the Ripper's narrative.

"Jackie boy. Now that's one hell of a story."

CHAPTER 78

Jan Collins finished printing the vehicle pass, handed it to the government contractor waiting on the other side of the white counter, and pressed the button that incremented the "Now Serving" display.

"Number 207," she called out, as a middle-aged man arose from one of the blue-upholstered chairs that filled the waiting area and limped toward her station, a pink numbered slip of paper in his fingers.

"How may I help you?"

"Need a one-day vehicle pass."

"You could have gotten a one-day pass from the Reece Road security guards. You really didn't need to come inside the Visitor Control Center."

"Damn. So I wasted twenty minutes in line?"

Jan smiled. "Looks like. But since you're already here, I can issue the pass. I'll need your driver's license, ID card, registration, and proof of insurance."

"It's a rental car."

"Then I'll need to see the rental agreement."

The man laid the documents on the counter along with a retired military ID card. Jan looked through the papers, made a few entries in her computer, and compared the face on the card to that of the man who stood before her. Six feet tall, hair beginning to gray at the temples, he looked to have packed on a few pounds since the ID card had been issued. The brown eyes were the same, though, as was the man's disarming smile. Something about his eyes made her uncomfortable. Then again, maybe it was just the humidity that had her edgy today.

"And the reason for your visit?"

"Just stopping by to see an old friend who's stationed here."

"OK, Major Hanson," she said, handing him the printed vehicle pass. "Stick that on your dashboard and you're good to go."

"Thanks."

Hanson picked up the pass, smiled, and limped toward the door.

Jan pressed the button, advancing the count. Glancing at the board, she saw that Sheila, the lady who worked at the next station, had already finished two people while she had helped the retired major.

Raising her voice, Jan called for her next customer.

"Number 210. Come on down."

CHAPTER 79

Jack Gregory limped through the small parking lot outside the Demps Visitor Control Center, clicked the UNLOCK button on the red Camry's key fob, opened the door, and slid into the driver's seat. The clock read 10:25 a.m. and it was already hot enough to make the facial and body disguises uncomfortable.

Starting the engine, Jack pulled back out onto Reece Road, getting into the line of cars stopped before the security gate. The black-clad security guards were contractors, commonly used at American military bases to free up soldiers for war-fighting missions. As he flashed his retired military ID, the guard took it, looked through the window at his vehicle pass, and then motioned him to pull forward into a vehicle inspection lane.

"Pop your trunk and hood, open your glove box, step out of the car, and open all the doors."

Jack did as instructed, stepping back to allow the inspectors to do their work. While one guard slid a long mirror under the vehicle, the other made his way around the car, looking in the engine compartment, inside the open doors, and in the trunk.

"OK. You're clear."

Jack nodded. Then he closed up everything he'd opened, slid into the driver's seat, and began his leisurely drive onto Fort Meade proper. Turning left on Rose Street, he drove behind the PX and commissary, taking a left into the Burger King parking lot. Might as well grab a little brunch before the place packed up with the lunchtime crowd. After that, he figured he'd check out the PX and commissary, hit the National Cryptologic Museum, maybe even stop off at the base library. Might as well enjoy a leisurely day.

After all, he had ten hours to kill. The items hidden inside the hollowed-out backseat cushions would have to wait until dark.

~ ~ ~

Twenty-three hundred hours on the dot. Jack backed the Camry into the open parking slot at the Sleep Inn and swiped his key card in the side door, feeling the cool breath of air-conditioning fight back the outside humidity as he stepped into the carpeted corridor that led to his room. The faint smell of mildew didn't bother him. The hotel was clean and well kept. Besides, it was damned hard to keep all traces of mildew out of a Maryland hotel in summer.

His room was a ground-floor suite he'd rented by the week, nicely appointed, as these midpriced hotels went. It had a fridge, microwave, coffeepot, and couch. The coffee table wasn't anything fancy, but it beat eating at the desk. The shower had good water pressure, and the bed was comfortable. All in all, not bad mission accommodations.

Slipping out of his shirt, Jack unhooked the midriff fat suit, tossed it and his shoulder holster on the bed, and walked into the bathroom. When he walked out again twenty minutes later, he was tan, blond, and naked. If not for the crazy quilt of scars that covered his torso, he could have passed for a member of the Australian Olympic beach volleyball team.

He walked over to the dresser, stepped into a pair of striped boxers and a Baltimore Ravens T-shirt, grabbed a Diet Coke from the fridge, and sat down in front of the laptop waiting on the desk. It was a basic black Toshiba laptop he'd picked up at Best Buy last week for $427. Good enough to serve his purpose, but not worth stealing.

Pressing the recessed power button, Jack leaned back, cracked open the pop-top on the Coke, and lifted the not-quite-frosty can to his lips. Not great, but about the best you could expect from a hotel mini fridge.

Three miles down the road, Heather, Mark, and Jennifer were locked inside separate cells at the top-secret NSA supermax facility code-named the Ice House, buried deep beneath an underground parking garage adjacent to the black glass headquarters. While the bleeding hearts complained about prisoners kept at Guantanamo, they had no idea that the worst terrorists were housed at the secret prison-laboratory at Fort Meade, a facility constructed with funds from the black budget, a place where the oldest coercion methods were mingled with the latest experimental data-extraction techniques.

Jack knew the place like the back of his hand, had taken part in many of those sanctioned interrogations. Ironically, the NSA thought it now held three young people who could help it find the Ripper. What it didn't know was that it had the real prize, the most dangerous trio on the planet. And as far as Jack was concerned, that even included Dr. Donald Stephenson.

It was only a matter of time until those highly trained and augmented young operatives took that place apart, irrespective of the world's most sophisticated security systems. Jack wasn't worried about that. When it happened, it would be like taking candy from a baby. Jack was here to make sure nobody realized just how dangerous those three were.

As the laptop finished booting, Jack logged in, then plugged an SRT dongle into one of its USB slots. Holding down Control-Alt-Y, he launched the application that gave him access to the Fort Meade Military Police wiretap he'd installed two hours earlier. Although he was now tethered to this hotel room for the next few weeks, he had all the groceries he'd need for the virtual stakeout.

One thing he knew. When the shit hit the fan, all that C4 he'd strategically placed around Fort Meade was going to go a long way toward making the government believe Al Qaeda was back in the US terrorist business. Hopefully that, plus a little luck, would make them miss the obvious.

Jack picked up the telephone, glanced at the number written in blue ink on the hotel notepad, and dialed. Hearing the expected response on the far end, he began speaking.

"This is Karl Kroener in room 127 at the Sleep Inn in Laurel. I'd like a large Brooklyn-style pepperoni-and-mushroom. For delivery. Cash. No. That's it. Thanks."

CHAPTER 80

Mark had been waiting for thirteen hours for some kind of reaction to tearing down the closed-circuit camera. But it was as if no one even noticed. At six p.m. a bouncing flashlight beam preceded a guard down the dark corridor. The circle of light danced as the man shoved a food tray under the door, then moved on without ever shining on Mark. The light and the footsteps retreated. In the distance, a heavy door opened, then slammed shut, the darkness once again complete.

Moving to retrieve the food, Mark lifted the tray to smell its contents. The odor wasn't unpleasant, but it wasn't good either. It was the smell of his standard meal. Mark knew the tray held the bland meat-and-vegetable mush that provided sufficient nutrients to keep him alive, while depriving him of the basic pleasure of eating. It was another aspect of his solitary confinement's sensory-deprivation regime.

But he was hungry, so he ate.

With his fingers, Mark shoveled the stuff into his mouth until every morsel was gone. Then he licked the tray clean. Holding it out in front of him, Mark let the tray fall. The clatter radiated out from the point of impact, the bright sound waves bouncing off the walls, the bars, the sink, the toilet, the corridor, his augmented brain processing the reflected echoes into a three-dimensional color image. It was beautiful, far better than his Spartan surroundings looked through his eyes.

Mark had seen infrared satellite images of the Earth, where reds and yellows indicated warmer waters sandwiched by cold blues and purples. But this was different, producing lush, real-time 3-D imagery in which the echoes enabled him to see around corners and, to some extent, through walls. It didn't take the clatter of the tray to produce the effect, but the volume the tray provided made everything much brighter.

Mark smiled. They could keep him in the dark, but they couldn't keep him from seeing if he needed to.

He picked up the tray and slid it through the slot out into the hallway, then retrieved his clothes from where he'd hung them on the sink to dry. His touch found them damp, but dry enough for his body heat to finish the job, so he slipped into the orange pj's and sat down against the far wall.

For the first time in weeks, Mark felt the urge to let sleep claim him, to let his conscious mind slip away into that vast nothingness where time had no meaning, into a dream world of his subconscious mind's making. The thought settled over him like a fuzzy blanket on a winter night, an enticing siren's call to lie back on the floor and sleep.

But what was wrong with that? There were no more interrogators torturing or drugging him for information, no reason to stay alert. Besides, he could bring himself back to full strength at a moment's notice. It happened so rapidly Mark barely noticed. As easily as he slipped into his meditations, his consciousness melted away around him.

He didn't think he was supposed to feel things while dreaming, but he felt this. A familiar nudge, like a sharp elbow in his side.

When was the last time he'd felt it? A lifetime ago. His father's garage in White Rock. Jennifer had been at the workbench with Heather. Mark had just finished making one of his brotherly jibes designed to get under Jennifer's skin and Heather had dug her strong, sharp elbow into his shoulder.

There it was again. Not really in his shoulder, but something about the feeling reminded him of Heather.

He turned to see her, but a mist shrouded his vision. He thought he could just make out her outline, but when he tried to reach out for her, she faded away. Mark stopped trying, letting the dream current carry him along.

The command deck on the Bandolier Ship materialized around him, his body enfolded by one of the four supple couches. Smoothly curving walls dissolved around him, leaving Mark hurtling through space, just like the first time he'd tried on the alien headset. They'd all tried on the alien headsets: Heather, Jennifer, and Mark. And in that state, they'd established a common link that enabled them to share each other's thoughts and feelings. It was one of the things Jack had encouraged them to explore. It was one of the things they'd all learned to block.

But if he was linked into the ship, where were Heather and Jen? And where was the ship's AI that had attacked his mind? He'd thrown up every block he could muster to try to protect them all from that attack. Mark ran through a quick mental diagnostic. Apparently, after releasing all his rage at the AI, he'd restored his own mental shields and left them in place. Maybe that was why he couldn't feel the girls' presence through his headset.

Remembering how it felt to touch Heather's beautiful mind, Mark dropped his mental defenses. The vision of himself hurtling through the vast emptiness of space achieved a new level of clarity, so many stars in the blackness, tiny pinpoints of light, pulsing with an energy all their own. He could feel their energy ripples softly brush his awareness.

Suddenly, the surrounding space-time warped violently as a powerful vibration distorted the blackness. In a rush of realization, Mark knew...he wasn't alone anymore.

CHAPTER 81

She had him! The rush of joy almost broke the nascent mental link, but Heather wasn't about to let that happen. She opened herself completely and their minds flowed together. As frightened as she'd been of letting Mark invade her innermost sanctuary, she now welcomed the sharing of all that was right and wrong about her. Neither was she repelled by Mark's dark thoughts and embarrassments. After all, that mixture of good and evil, beauty and ugliness, was a big part of what it meant to be human.

"I love you," Mark's thoughts whispered in her mind.

Funny. Despite how they shared each other's thoughts, mental conversation still came most naturally.

"Right back at you." Heather felt Mark smile at her response. "Always have. Just didn't know how much."

"How'd you manage the mind link without our headsets?"

"Jen led me to it. I would have managed sooner if I hadn't tried to overanalyze it."

"You made my day. I've missed you."

Heather's eyes welled up. "Me too. But I feel you now."

"So you ready to get the hell out of here?"

"I'm working on a plan."

"They've turned on the laptops, at least one of them."

A vision of Mark typing commands into the stolen cell phone played in their joint minds. The fact that the laptops had been turned on meant every electronic system in the building now had multiple back doors through which Heather, Mark, or Jen could take control of the system.

"We'll need access to a networked computer. I need a facilities layout so I can see exactly where each of us is being held. Jennifer's been playing her mind tricks with one of her handlers, but they're drugging her so heavily she's been fading in and out."

Heather felt Mark scan her memory, his anger a gathering storm. "Heroin? They're intentionally addicting her?"

"You thought they'd play nice?"

"Guess not. Still makes me mad as hell."

"That's fine. Use it, but don't let it use you. Our chance is coming. One other thing, I think Jack's nearby."

"How do you know?"

"I don't. But it's what my visions tell me. I think he's out there waiting for us to make our move, putting himself in a supporting position."

"And if we can't break out?"

"Like I said. Our chance is coming."

For two and a half hours, Heather laid out the details of what she had in mind, refining the plan with Mark's feedback, playing through the scenarios in such vivid detail that they both experienced the same dreamworld rehearsals. But to make the scenarios complete, she was going to need a completely accurate layout. And she wasn't likely to get that until their break was already under way.

Mentally exhausted, Heather terminated the last vision. As she felt her hold on their link fade away, Mark's final thoughts brought a tired smile to her lips.

"So we're just going to wing it. Sounds like my kind of plan."

CHAPTER 82

"You with me, Jen?" Heather's mind reached out for her friend.

"Better than most days. Worse than some."

Indeed, Heather felt far less haze in Jen's mind than she'd felt in several days.

"Jen, I need you to get as much clarity as you can for the next few minutes, even if it costs you later."

Heather knew that the effort of shunting the heroin effects away for a while would inflict a heavy penalty on Jennifer once she relaxed from the effort, as if she had endured a sudden overdose. Heather knew it, hated it, but asked her to do it anyway.

She didn't need to ask twice. All at once, Heather felt Jen's mind reacquire its normal cutting edge. That was good. The opportunity stood in front of her right now, but in five minutes it would be gone.

"OK, Jen. In a few seconds I'm going to want you to do your thing, but you'll need to follow my thoughts and do it through me."

"Sounds like fun. Let's go for it."

Heather relaxed back into the real world, feeling Jen like a hitchhiker in her mind. Dr. Jacobs detached the last of the sticky electrodes from her temples, wound up the cords, and returned them to their case.

As he turned to place the items back on his cart, Heather focused on what she needed, felt Jen pick up the thoughts, and then almost lost consciousness as a wave of vertigo carried her into Dr. Jacobs's head.

It wasn't like anything she'd ever experienced. Although she'd touched Jennifer's memories, she hadn't wanted to pry into that part of her mind. Certainly this was nothing like the psychic link she shared with Jen and Mark. This was an empathic bond that gave access to the target's innermost feelings.

On the surface, Dr. Jacobs seemed very happy with his perceived progress, but beneath that lay a raging sexual urge to do things to his patient that would never be sanctioned by his bosses. If only he could be alone with her for an hour without that damned camera.

Like a tick, Jennifer burrowed into that feeling, amplifying the sick urge and feeding it back into Jacobs's mind. The doctor turned toward Heather, stepping close to where she lay so that his body blocked the camera's view. Sliding his stethoscope over his ears, he leaned down.

"Take a deep breath and hold it," he said, sliding the cold end of the device beneath her gown, his hands gently resting against the curve of her breast.

Once again Jennifer amped up the man's hidden desire.

"Now, let it out slowly."

Heather complied, feeling his hand move a little farther up the curve of her left breast, a tremor passing through it as he paused.

"Now, once more."

Again his hand shifted and again Jennifer ratcheted up his excitement. Suddenly, his eyes closed as a shudder passed through his body. When they reopened, he frowned, withdrew the stethoscope, turned, and hurriedly pushed the cart to the door. When he pressed his hand to the biometric reader, the electronic lock opened, then locked behind him again as he backed the cart into the corridor. Then, with the squeak of rubber wheels on concrete, he was gone.

Heather glanced up, then rolled onto her side, away from the camera. As she felt Jennifer slip back into her drug-induced haze, Heather's fingers stroked the touchpad of Dr. Jacobs's Android cell phone.

CHAPTER 83

The worm was designed to penetrate security holes in Windows, Linux, Solaris, AIX, HP-UX, Mac OS, OS/2, Android, Palm, and IOS. It mutated using an evolving genetic algorithm, opened multiple root-level back doors, mapped the host system's routing tables, services, and attached devices, then hid itself to await external commands. It didn't do much, but what it did, it did well.

It provided one additional service that Heather immediately brought into play: it opened a telnet port that provided remote shell access to every network-accessible infected system. While she lay curled into a fetal position beneath the sheet, Heather's fingers flew across the tiny cell phone keyboard, scrolling through a list of nearby hosts and routers. One by one she accessed the systems, made a quick check of attached or networked devices, then moved on.

She calculated the odds that Dr. Jacobs would discover his missing cell phone within an extended time window. Jennifer's subtle manipulation of the man's suppressed urges had left him with sticky underwear, shocked and embarrassed, so mentally flustered he just wanted to get someplace he could shower himself clean. If he used an on-site shower facility, a 98 percent probability, she might have as little as thirty minutes before he discovered the missing phone. Heather had set her mental clock on a thirty-minute countdown. It now stood at twenty-four minutes, eleven seconds and counting.

Heather knew the facility had been designed with multiple layers of TEMPEST cages, but she knew something else too. Dr. Jacobs collected data from his cell wirelessly. He also used Wi-Fi from his cell phone to network to his office. That meant the TEMPEST integrity of the lower levels was floor by floor, connected with other floors via secure fiber. And she didn't need to wirelessly connect to the primary control center. She just had to be able to wirelessly access a computer that was linked to that local area network.

Heather stared at the small screen, feeling a sudden burst of exhilaration. She'd found it, a route to the security system that controlled the door locks. As happy as that made her, she had to find one more node before she could override that system. It would do little good to take control of the locks if they could watch her every move through the network of cameras.

The camera in her cell had a coax cable connection. That meant the other security cameras were probably hooked into the monitoring system the same way. You could bet the same contractor installed the whole shooting match. If that were true, they would show up as directly controlled devices on some system. But even if some of the cameras were smarter, network-enabled devices, she could still take control of them. There would still be a central computer that sent out the IP commands that told them what to do and that routed the video streams to the appropriate clients.

Twenty minutes, thirty-four seconds.

An adrenaline surge almost caused her to roll to a sitting position. Heather funneled the feeling into a big smile.

"Gotcha!"

She didn't need long. Five minutes. Maybe less, just enough time to get from her cell to the nearest room with some more capable networked computer systems, time enough to take out any resistance and get up on the local area network.

Heather entered the commands to force an immediate shutdown of the camera control system, switched telnet targets, and unlocked all electronically locked doors throughout the facility, forcing a reboot of the security control system. Then, to add just a bit more confusion to the coming mayhem, she killed the facility lights—not the power, just the lights.

As the lights went out, Heather leaped from her bed, pulled the heavy cell door open, and hit the corridor at a dead run. Although the sound wasn't loud enough to provide a bright image, the echoes from her running footfalls provided enough detail for her to clearly see her surroundings. She didn't need louder sounds. She wanted to see the sounds made by others.

Taking a right into the first hallway, Heather saw a flashlight beam stab from the opening door on her left. The look of pain and surprise on the guard's face barely registered as Heather's spinning side kick broke his arm at the elbow, sending the flashlight flying, the beam whirling through the dark corridor like a Jedi light saber, before smashing out on the concrete floor.

Then, like a lioness, she was on him.

CHAPTER 84

Bud Gendall stared at the bank of security monitors that all displayed the same message: "VIDEO SOURCE DISCONNECTED."

"What the hell just happened to our feed?"

John McCall, his night shift partner, looked at him and shrugged. "Looks like the system just rebooted. Gotta love Microsoft."

Then the lights went out.

"Shit! Power's down too?"

"Can't be. The computer's coming back up now."

Sure enough, the security and computer monitors still wept their pale light into the encroaching darkness. Weird. Bud didn't like weirdness. Not in the NSA's most secret supermax facility. Not on his shift.

Grabbing the heavy black flashlight from its wall mount, John switched it on and headed toward the door. "I'll check it out."

As John stepped into the corridor, a loud crack accompanied his scream. A rush of adrenaline coursed through Bud's body like an electric shock, throwing the unfolding scene into slow motion. The flashlight spinning out of John's hand. The whirling flashlight strobing the action into a sequence of freeze-frame images. The McFarland girl's cold, hard face, eyes gone white. John's right arm flopping like a rag doll's. McFarland catapulting John's 240 pounds of muscle toward him like a human cannonball.

Bud was halfway to his feet, hand tugging the Beretta from his service holster, when John hit him. Rolling with the blow, Bud came back to his feet with a grace that spoke to his years of training. Even as he sought to level the gun, the girl's axe kick knocked it from his hand, the force of the blow numbing his arm from the shoulder down.

Bud responded with a leg sweep that should have landed her flat on her back, but she countered, using his own momentum against him, her elbow smashing his left orbital socket, wiping his vision with a red haze of blood and pain. As the floor rose up to meet him, her knee interrupted his downward progress, the impact crushing his trachea and rupturing several branches of his inferior thyroid artery.

As Bud felt blackness enfold him, he realized the unthinkable. This slender young woman in her blue hospital gown had just taken him and John out. As easy as putting out the trash.

CHAPTER 85

A quick pulse check confirmed what Heather's visions had already told her. She was this room's sole survivor. Shunting aside a wave of revulsion, Heather let her training propel her forward.

Moving quickly, Heather retrieved both guards' duty belts, holsters, and pistols, closed the door, and slid into the chair recently occupied by the second guard. As she used the back door to bypass the log-in screen, Heather heard the wail of an alarm, accompanied by distant shouts and the muffled thumps of gunfire.

It took her twenty seconds to bring the camera controller back online and another eighteen to take root control of that system. Overriding the default settings, Heather rerouted all camera output to her station, displaying the live video in a grid of small windows spread across the security monitors. A quick glance told her what she needed to know.

Heather pulled up a three-dimensional facility diagram, then three additional windows on the primary computer display, rerouting all facility controls to her terminal. Noting Mark's and Jennifer's locations, she engaged every other lock in the building, restored the lights, and initiated the central control center's fire suppression system, flooding the locked room with halon 1301. Apparently the NSA was exempt from the EPA global warming ban on halon fire suppression systems. Not that it mattered to Heather which fire suppression gas they used. Fire wasn't the only thing it would suffocate. She couldn't have someone trying to restore central system control while she had work to do.

On a different sublevel, two dozen Arabic prisoners had stormed from their cells, killing three guards, but losing five of their own in the process. Now armed with pistols, nightsticks, and flashlights, the survivors were systematically working their way down the corridor.

Ground-floor cameras showed that the facility rapid response force, deprived of video intelligence, had broken up into three teams of five that moved to secure the elevator shaft and stairwells.

With a deep breath, Heather shifted her attention to Mark and Jennifer. They were being held on the third sublevel, just like Heather, but in separate wings. As they'd planned, both twins had remained in their cells, awaiting Heather's contact. Now that she had a chance to devote the required level of concentration, Heather opened her mind to Mark and Jen.

"Ahh. There you are." She felt Mark's relief wash through her.

"You ready to move?"

"Just been waiting on you."

"Jen?"

"She's out of it again. I'm gonna have to go get her. You got a layout for me?"

Heather pulled forth the memory of the 3-D facility diagram.

"That'll work."

"I'll unlock the doors along your route as you get to them, then lock them again behind you. Get moving."

Heather dropped the link, refocusing her attention on the monitor showing Mark leaving his cell, then entering another camera's field of view as he raced down the corridor.

Movement on the first monitor attracted her attention. One security squad had entered the elevator, headed down to her level. She stopped it between the first and second sublevels, killing all power to the elevator shaft, simultaneously sealing all doors shut. It wouldn't keep a determined team from climbing down and forcing the doors open, but it would slow them down. Reconsidering her action, Heather restored power and the elevator's downward motion, injecting a slight error into the elevator controls. Instead of stopping on sublevel three, it continued its descent to sublevel four.

As the doors opened, the security team suddenly found itself engaged in an all-out Al Qaeda firefight.

CHAPTER 86

Jack listened to the military police alert go out, paused just a moment to confirm the location, and then reached for the remote device controller. Something big was going down at the top-secret NSA detention facility code-named the Ice House. Initial reports indicated a group of high-level Al Qaeda detainees had initiated an escape attempt, resulting in a call for all units to converge on the facility.

Well, if they thought this was Al Qaeda–initiated, Jack was happy to help support that theory. Checking the radio signal strength to each of the five remote devices, Jack flicked the first switch to the ARM position, waited for the green light, pressed the DETONATE button, and waited. The blast wave arrived seventeen seconds later, strong enough to rattle the windows. Now the MPs were going to have to get organized without any radio communications.

Flipping the second switch to ARM, Jack repeated the procedure and was once again rewarded with the delayed blast wave. So
much for the main telephone trunk lines off base too.

The image of Janet slipped, unbidden, through his mind, little
Robby perched on one hip as she stood beneath the jungle hut's
thatched overhanging roof, waving at him as he'd turned for one
last long look at her. He missed his lover. He missed his partner.

Getting up from his chair, Jack walked to the sink and started
a fresh pot of coffee brewing. The next three blasts needed a delay
for maximum effect. One cup of java ought to just about do it.

CHAPTER 87

The shock wave shattered the window, showering the bedroom with shards of glass. General Balls Wilson rolled out of bed, cutting his bare feet as he stood up.

"Was that a bomb?" His wife's frightened voice helped clear the last of the sleep from his head.

"It's OK, Maggie. It wasn't that close."

His hand reached for the light, then paused as he thought better of it. "Just stay in bed. I'll get your slippers. Then I want you to walk down to the basement and stay there until I say different. Understand?"

"I understand." This time her voice was steady. She hadn't spent all those years as an air force officer's wife without learning how to stay calm in tough situations.

He took a step and cut his foot again, cursing himself for leaving his own slippers in the closet. As he reached the closet door, a second blast shook the room, this one more distant and from a different direction from the first. Jesus H. Christ. The goddamned base was under attack.

The realization lent speed to his actions as he tossed his wife's slippers onto the bed, picked out the embedded glass slivers, and slid his bleeding bare feet into his class-A dress shoes.

"Get on down to the basement."

"I'm on my way."

He felt her arms encircle his neck as her lips brushed his left ear. "Stay safe. I love you."

"I'll be fine. I love you too. Now go."

General Wilson walked over to the phone and lifted it to the ear on which Maggie's kiss still lingered. No dial tone. Picking up the mobile satcom phone, Balls pressed the first number on the speed dial list, listening to the hiss and warble as it established the secure connection.

"This is General Wilson. What the hell's going on?"

"Sir, this is John Briggs. We don't know the extent of the problem yet, but we got a report of an attempted prison break underway in the Ice House, followed by two explosions. We don't know exactly where they came from, but someone's taken out military police communications and the main phone lines. For some reason they haven't gone after the power yet."

"Any comms intercepts?"

"We've got no chatter. Nothing."

Balls didn't like that answer. "Doesn't make sense."

"No sir. This kind of Al Qaeda attack would need some kind of advanced coordination."

"If it's Al Qaeda."

"Pretty much has to be. At least that's the view here in the SCIF."

"Who do you have on shift tonight?"

"Levi's here with the regular night crew analysts and staff."

Balls felt a wave of relief course through his brain. If Levi Elias was there, they'd get this figured out, hopefully in time to stop whoever had started all this from achieving their operational objectives.

"Anyone called the president yet?"

"We were trying to get you first."

"Good plan. I'm on my way in. If I'm not there in five minutes, tell Levi to make the call."

"Roger."

Balls disconnected the call and set the satcom phone back in its cradle. As he stood in the darkness beside his bed, buck naked except for his dress shoes, blood oozing up between his toes, he listened to the warble of distant sirens, trying to wrap his brain around the problem.

Then three more explosions shook the building.

As the shock waves subsided, the urgency of getting back to NSA headquarters pounded the general's head.

Glancing down, another thought struck Balls Wilson.

Maybe I ought to put on some pants.

CHAPTER 88

"Heads up!" Heather's voice whispered in his mind.

Detecting sudden movement from the corner of his eye, Mark hurled himself to his left, his legs driving him toward this new threat. The boom of the nine-millimeter pistol accompanied the hiss of a bullet that bounced off the wall behind him. An Arabic fighter wielded the Beretta in a double-handed crouch. As he tried to adjust his aim, Mark slid feet-first along the floor, his right leg pistoning up into the man's crotch, launching him into the ceiling, four feet up.

Two other men rounded the corner in time to see their comrade's limp body strike the floor behind the blur that was Mark Smythe. The taller of the two swung a nightstick that Mark deflected, twisting it free of the Arab's hand as he reversed its course, striking his head with the sound of a baseball bat hitting a watermelon.

The second man dived for the Beretta and Mark jumped on top of him, his hands closing around the fellow's wrists as he grabbed the gun handle. The Arab kicked and writhed in Mark's grasp, tried to twist his gun hand free, then screamed as he felt both wrists snap in the crushing grip of the one who held him. The Beretta clattered to the concrete floor.

In desperation, the Arabic fighter sought to bring his knee up into Mark's groin, but abandoned the attempt as Mark twisted the man's broken left wrist, bringing forth another gargling scream. Grabbing the handgun, Mark brought it to the man's head, a smooth trigger squeeze ending his struggles. The smell of gunpowder filled Mark's nose, rapidly overridden by the stink of bile and loose bowels, the coppery taste of blood mist on his tongue. The cloying aftereffects of violent death. He'd experienced them before, and he had the uncomfortable feeling that it wouldn't be too long until he bathed in them again.

Rapidly frisking the bodies, Mark found what he was hoping for, two spare nine-millimeter magazines. Ejecting the partially empty magazine, he compared its weight to that of the full ones. Three rounds left. Mark slapped one of the full mags into the weapon, ripped the shirt off one of the bodies, fashioned it into a crude shoulder pouch to hold the spare magazines, and moved on.

Jennifer sat in the corner of the last cell on the left, eyes rolled back in her head, a vapid smile painted on her face.

"Jen, snap out of it." Mark's words and gentle shake only caused her to push weakly at him, reminding him of how, as a child, she'd resisted their dad's lifting her sleeping body from the car after a late-night family outing.

Glancing down at her left arm, Mark spotted the needle tracks. Not only had they addicted his sister to heroin, they'd made sure to mark her as an addict. A fresh red haze colored Mark's vision as he lifted her gently in his arms.

"Don't worry, Jen," he breathed in her ear. "I'm going to get you out of here. And then I'm going to kill every one of those bastards."

CHAPTER 89

Heather felt the tremor from the first two explosions, making a quick approximation of their distance and direction as she pulled up a digital map of Fort Meade on the computer monitor. A slow smile spread across her face as she mentally pinned the locations on the map.

Jack.

As she'd anticipated, he was out there, had probably been preparing and waiting for days, if not weeks. Now he'd detected the emergency situation at the NSA prison and had initiated his own supporting attack, an attack designed to disrupt and confuse the government response.

Returning her attention to the task at hand, she saw Mark walk out of Jennifer's cell, his sister's limp body cradled in his arms. A rapid scan of the other monitors showed the assault team on the fourth sublevel fighting for survival. They'd lost three team members and the remaining two were pinned down in the disabled elevator.

Heather shifted focus to the ground floor. Team Two had just finished placing a small explosive charge on the stairwell door and had backed off in preparation to blow the bolt.

Pulling up another control panel, Heather activated fire alarms on the ground floor and first two sublevels, initiating their water sprinkler systems. The sprinkler layout didn't include the rooms with critical electronic and computing systems, those having halon gas fire suppression systems similar to that of the master control center.

The concussion from the stairwell detonation vibrated the camera display, completely knocking out the top camera in the main stairwell.

Her fingers flying across the keyboard, she found the personnel data files, opening the profiles of the five most senior officials assigned to the facility. As she'd hoped, one of them was a woman. It took her less than two seconds to memorize the file.

Glancing at the desk-mounted microphone, Heather pursed her lips in frustration. Useless. That system was hardwired to the loudspeakers in the prison section, sublevels three and four, and couldn't be rerouted. She had no intention of letting the security team get down to the third sublevel.

"Shit!"

Heather shifted her attention to the laptop to the right of the station at which she currently sat. Not perfect, but it would have to do.

Moving into the adjacent chair, Heather bypassed the login and began shifting control of the public address system that covered the ground floor, the stairwells, and the laboratories and offices on sublevels one and two. It took her exactly thirty-eight seconds.

"Heather, you there?" Mark's thoughts nudged her mind.

"Give me a minute."

Heather ran a quick check, adjusting the laptop microphone calibration. Then she went live.

"Attention all security elements! This is Rebecca Fairing. Badge number Xray Kilo Niner Five Seven Zulu. Return immediately to the main floor and prepare to repel external attack. I say again. Return immediately to the main floor and prepare to repel external attack. Fairing out."

As she watched the ground-floor monitor outside the main stairwell, another twenty seconds passed with no indication the stairwell team had heard the message. Then two of the black-clad team emerged into the main hallway, covering left and right as the rest of the team spilled back out of the stairwell and raced down the hallway toward the building entrance.

"OK, Mark. Bring her down the first corridor on your left, then take the second right. I'm in the first room on the left."

"Shouldn't you meet us at the stairwell?"

"We're not taking the stairwell, and I have a couple of things to finish up before we abandon ship."

"On my way."

Just then the ground shuddered with three more explosions, much closer than the first two. As the vibrations faded away, a fresh smile tweaked the corners of Heather's lips.

"Jack. I'd like to kiss you long and hard. Right here and now."

CHAPTER 90

Jack tore open the packaging around the prepaid cell phone and dialed the 404 area code number.

"Thank you for calling HLN, a CNN network. If you are calling with a breaking news tip, please press one…"

Jack pressed one, then pressed one again to speak to the news tip team. When a real person answered, Jack flipped the remaining three switches to ARM, pressing the DETONATE buttons in rapid sequence as the lights turned green. Just over three miles away, the sound of the explosions began propagating outward, beginning the seventeen-second trip to his hotel room.

"Be silent, infidel. My name is Fariq Abdullah Muhammad. At this very moment, Allah has launched an attack on your National Security Agency at Fort Meade, Maryland, where our brothers are being held in a secret US prison. If you listen closely you may hear the explosions as I speak."

On cue the shock waves arrived, rattling the windows and shaking pictures on the wall.

"It has begun. *Allahu Akbar.*"

Without waiting for a response, he hung up the phone, placed it on a white hand towel on the floor, and crushed it beneath his heel. Rolling the pieces inside the towel, Jack placed it beside his laptop in the soft leather valise, and added the remote detonator. Then, strapping on his shoulder holster and knife, he took one last sip of coffee, lifted the valise, and strolled out into the night.

CHAPTER 91

"Excuse me, Mr. President. I'm sorry to wake you, but we have a serious situation." The telephone did little to soften James Nobles' gravelly voice.

President Jackson looked at the telephone, glanced over at Leticia's sleeping body, which only moments before had been spooned up against his, and sighed. God, he missed those peaceful nights with his wife, the ones before he got his wish and was made president.

"OK, James. Give me the bad news."

It was always bad news, at least at this time of night. Nobody ever woke the president of the United States at one a.m. to say, "Good news, Mr. President. Nothing bad has happened so far today."

"There's been an attack at Fort Meade."

"The NSA."

"Yes, Mr. President."

Sudden depression threatened to cloud his mind, but the president forced himself to get out of bed.

"Damn it. Get the National Security Council rounded up. I'll be down in five minutes."

"I'm on it."

"Oh, James. Get General Wilson on the line."

"Already working on it, Mr. President."

By the time President Jackson walked into the White House Situation Room, three members of the national security staff were already waiting for him: Cory Mayfield, James Nobles, and his chief of staff, Carol Owens.

"Stay seated." President Jackson slid into his own chair. "Who's got the rundown?"

"I guess I have the honor," James Nobles said. "As I said on the phone, we've had reports of multiple explosions at Fort Meade as well as gunfire near the NSA headquarters building. I have the NSA director on the line, but before you put him on, Mr. President, I think you should see this."

The national security advisor leaned forward and touched a button on the remote control panel, turning one of the flat-panel displays to CNN.

"...As we continue to follow the situation underway at Fort Meade, Maryland, we continue to receive reports of explosions and gunfire coming from the base. As we've been reporting for the last several minutes, this station received a call from a person claiming to be a member of the Al Qaeda cell conducting the attack. If you've just tuned in, I want you to listen to this recording of the call..."

Several moments of dead air, which lasted just long enough to increase President Jackson's sense of foreboding, were suddenly broken by a man's heavily accented voice.

"Be silent, infidel. My name is Fariq Abdullah Muhammad. At this very moment, Allah has launched an attack on your National Security Agency at Fort Meade, Maryland, where our brothers are being held in a secret US prison. If you listen closely you may hear the explosions as I speak."

The man paused as the sound of three distant explosions sounded in the background.

"It has begun. *Allahu Akbar.*"

James Nobles clicked a button and the video froze.

"They've been recycling this recording every couple of minutes."

President Jackson nodded, then pressed a button on the speakerphone. "General Wilson, this is President Jackson. Can you hear me OK?"

There was a two-second pause, followed by an encryption hiss as Balls Wilson's voice came over the speaker.

"Loud and clear, Mr. President. Sorry for the comm link delay, but we're having to talk over a secure satcom link."

The president tried and failed to keep the irritation out of his voice. "And why is that?"

"Someone's taken out our external phone lines. Killed base military police radio comms as well. We've also got some sort of problem inside the Ice House."

"So who's behind it?"

"The consensus view says Al Qaeda. I'm not buying it."

"Have you seen the news?"

"I've seen it."

"Seems cut-and-dried to me."

"Too cut-and-dried, Mr. President. Levi doesn't think it's Al Qaeda either. No chatter match."

Cory Mayfield cut in. "Bullshit, Mr. President. Sometimes things are exactly what they seem."

"And sometimes they aren't." General Wilson's voice acquired a cutting edge.

"So what's your situation right now?" President Jackson interrupted. Christ. Did every president have to endure such constant bickering among his advisors?

"Mass confusion. I just got back to the NSA and the building is secure. Our perimeter defense force is in place and ready to repel an attack. But the military police are having problems. I haven't been able to raise the MP station and apparently they can't communicate with any of their patrols. We've had multiple explosions around the base, so you can imagine what the night shift patrols are doing, trying to get to the places where the bombs went off. We've also lost communications with the Ice House facility."

"Response teams?"

"They've got their own, just like we do here at NSA headquarters. They should be able to deal with any internal threat."

"Everything you've said points to an Al Qaeda operation," Cory Mayfield interrupted.

"Like I said, I'm not buying it."

President Jackson held up his hand, cutting off Director Mayfield's response. "General Wilson, I respect your opinion, but I have to act based on what I consider the most likely scenario. Since we haven't been able to contact Colonel Abrams, the base commander, I've given the go for a Delta response."

"Mr. President, local civilian police can get here faster."

"I'm not putting civilian police up against a trained Al Qaeda assault force. I've made my decision."

"Yes sir."

President Jackson broke the connection and turned to his chief of staff. "Carol, get my press secretary in here. I'm going to have to make a statement in the next hour or so."

"I called her fifteen minutes ago. Gretchen's on her way, along with the rest of your national security staff."

"That's good." The president didn't intend to say what he was thinking, as if by refusing to give his thoughts voice he might avert what they foretold. But somehow, the words found their way out of his mouth. "Looks like another all-nighter."

CHAPTER 92

The door opened as Mark reached for the handle, Heather's smile breaking the ice that had enclosed his soul. Her gaze lingered for a moment on his full beard; then, as Heather's gaze settled on Jennifer's limp body in his arms, the smile faded.

"Set her on the couch," Heather said, motioning toward what appeared to be a small break area beside a sink and coffeepot.

As he gently released his twin's body, Heather bent over her, lifting one of Jennifer's eyelids, then the other. "Damn it."

Mark nodded. "They've messed her up bad."

Standing up, Heather threw her arms around Mark's neck and hugged him tight. For a full ten seconds Mark held her close as his heart hammered the walls of his chest.

As Heather pushed back, she pointed to the duty belts, service holsters, and spare clips on the table by the bank of monitors. "You take one, and I'll take the other."

"What's the plan?"

"I've got the security teams, except for two wounded guys down on sublevel four, pulled back to defend the building from outside attacks. Now that you're here, I'll open the doors that will let the rest of the Arab prisoners up stairwell one. That should give the response teams plenty to think about."

She slid into the seat in front of the laptop, motioning Mark into the seat in front of the microphone that was hardwired to the third and fourth sublevels. "As soon as I open the right doors, get your best Arab terrorist voice ready."

Mark nodded in understanding and waited.

Heather nodded. "OK."

Mark's Arabic flowed from his lips with a distinct Saudi Arabian accent. "My brothers. We are here to free you. In his greatness, Allah has opened a way. Break contact with the infidels you now fight and move down the corridor to your rear. You will find the stairwell open all the way to the top. From there you must fight your way to freedom. *Allahu Akbar!*"

Turning his attention to the monitors, Mark noted the speed with which the Arab fighters reacted to the command, leaving the two wounded security guards lying among the bodies of their fallen comrades in the disabled elevator. In less than thirty seconds, sixteen terrorists had entered the stairwell and begun racing up the stairs toward the ground floor. With a clank, heavy steel bolts engaged, locking the door shut behind them.

"Time to go," said Heather, rising to her feet and strapping the remaining duty belt and holster around her waist, pausing to tuck in the excess.

Odd as it seemed, Mark found the image of the gun belt wrapped around Heather's slender body, wearing only a blue hospital gown, remarkably appealing. "Stairwell two?"

"No. We're going to have to climb the elevator shaft." Her eyes moved to Jen. "Can you carry her on a cable climb?"

"If we strap her to my back. No problem."

Heather knelt down, stripping the dead guards' shirts and belts as Mark lifted his sister. Following her to the elevator shaft, Mark saw that the door stood open onto the empty shaft. Shifting Jennifer onto his back and wrapping her arms around his neck, he let Heather strap Jen's hands together with a bloody shirt. Then, hooking both belts together, Heather fastened them around Mark's and Jennifer's bodies.

She paused for a moment to inspect her work, then turned and leaped into the shaft, caught the thick cable, and began rapidly climbing. Mark followed, the added weight jolting his frame hard enough that he wondered if the cloth ties would handle the strain. They held and he began steadily pulling himself hand over hand up the shaft.

"You good?" Heather asked from above.

"Right behind you. All the way to the top."

"We're making a short stopover on sublevel one."

"Why is that?"

"I found our laptops."

CHAPTER 93

Heather passed the open elevator door on sublevel two, continuing her steady climb until she hung suspended three feet above the opening into sublevel one. Swinging her body, she launched herself into space, landing in a forward roll that brought her back to her feet in the wet corridor as cold water rained down on her from above. As she'd seen on the security cameras, sublevel one had been completely evacuated once the fire alarms and waterworks had started.

Nevertheless, she pulled the Berretta from the holster and chambered a round. Moving forward in a shooter's crouch, she began clearing rooms left and right as she moved past them. To her rear, she heard Mark land and slide. Then he was beside her, moving with his own gun drawn, Jennifer dangling awkwardly from his back.

Unlike on the lower sublevels, laboratories and offices filled this floor, a facility designed to provide close-in, real-time technical support to some of the best interrogation teams in the business. This was where equipment captured with the prisoners held below came to be analyzed and dissected, providing a rapid turn-around totally focused on providing corroboration or leverage on the former owners. A single cell phone often yielded information that skilled interrogators wielded on their subjects like Chinese water torture.

Heather paused outside of the lab she had targeted, took a deep breath, and held it. Opening the door, she stepped inside, grabbed the nearest chair, and used it to wedge the door wide open, letting the halon gas pour out into the hallway. The gas itself wasn't harmful, but it displaced the breathable nitrogen-oxygen mix that fires and people lived on. Without waiting for the gas to drain out into the hallway, Heather stepped into the room and turned on the lights, leaving Mark standing guard with Jennifer outside.

The lab was a large room, sixty feet by forty-eight, with raised flooring to accommodate the wiring that ran beneath it. Rows of workbenches divided the room into four sections. On the third of these, Heather found what she was searching for. Both laptops had been stripped, the motherboards and computing components plugged into other systems capable of recording all electrical activity in the circuits. Heather ignored them, selecting instead the two specially modified USB dongles. Removing these from their mounts, Heather dropped them in a small plastic Ziploc bag she retrieved from the supplies strewn across the workbench, and made her way back toward the door.

Pausing momentarily to grab a white lab coat from a hanger by the lab entrance, she slipped out of the wet hospital gown, fastened the coat around her with the gun belt, and stepped back into the corridor. She'd been in the lab for just over three minutes, and she felt certain that she could have held her breath another seven. Still, it felt good to replace the old lungful with a fresh breath.

Partially revived by the cold downpour, Jennifer was moving on Mark's back, in weak protest against the trusses that bound her to her brother. The sound of distant gunfire echoed from above.

"Got 'em?" Mark asked.

"What we need."

"So now it's up and out."

"The shaft comes out in an elevator alcove about fifty feet from the main entrance. Right now there's a serious fight going on up there; we should be able to get to the parking garage exit with minimal resistance."

"Minimal?"

"Three to five guards. Eighty-seven percent probability based on my last look at the video."

"Let's do it."

Heather led the way back to the shaft at a jog. Her last step propelled her out onto the cable. The gunfire was louder now, interspersed with yells and screams of pain. She slowed her ascent as she approached the open door to the main elevator alcove. A black-clad guard crouched facing away, firing down the hall toward the entrance. Heather shot him in the back of the head.

Leaping into the alcove, she grabbed him by his heels and pulled him farther back into the alcove as Mark landed behind her.

Heather yelled to make herself heard over the sound of the raging gun battle in the main foyer. "Take his uniform. I'll cover you."

Mark unstrapped Jennifer as Heather grabbed the dead guard's short-barreled Mark 17 SCAR-H and magazines and took up a defensive crouch by the exit into the main corridor. When she glanced back again, Mark, dressed in black, was finishing lacing up his boots.

Heather tossed him the SCAR-H. "I'll carry Jen. You get us the hell out of here."

As she lifted Jennifer's body onto her shoulder, Heather saw Mark lean around the corner and squeeze off two quick shots. Seeing him motion her forward, Heather hit the hall in a dead run, heard Mark firing behind her as she ducked around the corner. A crouching guard saw her coming, paused to take in the girl in the white lab coat with an orange-clad woman slung over her shoulder, and hesitated. Heather's bullet took him between the eyes, the nine-millimeter Parabellum slamming his lifeless body to the floor with an audible thump.

As she reached the door out to the parking garage, Heather heard Mark's boots pounding down the hall behind her. Turning the handle in her hand, she stepped aside as Mark's shoulder hit the door, launching it into one of the two guards crouching outside. The other tried to level his weapon, but Mark was too fast, his booted foot catching the man in the chest with the force of a battering ram. Two trigger pulls ensured neither man would pose a continuing threat.

Glancing back down the hallway, Heather saw an Arab prisoner peek around the corner. She squeezed off a round that caught him in the throat, sending him sprawling.

"Got their keys," Mark said. "Let's go."

Ducking as low as she could and still run with Jennifer slung over her shoulder, Heather followed Mark through the rows of cars while he clicked the alarm buttons on both key fobs. They were rewarded with the sound of a honking horn and the flash of headlights on a white Ford Edge halfway down the second row.

Heather piled Jennifer into the backseat and climbed into the passenger seat as Mark threw the car into drive and squealed around the exit ramp. As Mark cornered out of the building, the mini-SUV slid sideways, tires spewing black smoke as the rear window exploded in a hail of bullets. Heather emptied the Beretta along the calculated back trajectory and then they were around the corner, headlights off, sliding right onto Canine Road, then left onto Rockenbach with all the speed Mark could extract from the new Ford.

"You're bleeding." The concern in Mark's voice made Heather aware of a dull throbbing in her left temple.

A quick touch and her hand came away bloody. "Just a glass scalp cut. Bleeds a lot, but I'm fine."

At Cooper Avenue, Mark hung another left, letting the speed fall off naturally as they entered the wooded housing area. A left on Ninety-First Division Boulevard led to Colyer Loop and then Anderson Loop. Mark parked the Ford on the curb in the widest expanse between houses, turned off the interior lighting, opened the driver's door, and stepped out into darkness, a move that Heather duplicated on the passenger's side.

As Heather opened the rear passenger door, Mark stepped up beside her. "I'll get Jen. You take this."

He handed her the Mark 17 and lifted Jennifer from the backseat.

Heather paused to listen to the cadence of distant gunfire and sirens, letting her mind play out the most likely scenarios. Someone would find the bullet-riddled vehicle first thing in the morning. That was just fine.

She stepped away from the SUV, walking swiftly across the grassy expanse between houses and into the woods beyond, Mark striding silently by her side.

CHAPTER 94

Balls Wilson strode into the Ice House foyer flanked by a Delta security detail. The Delta Force team had been on-site less than an hour and had declared the area secure less than ten minutes earlier. Whatever shape the building had been in during the initial firefight, Delta's arrival hadn't improved its structural integrity.

A lean, square-jawed man, clad all in black, walked up to him. "General Wilson. I'm Bob Chavez. I lead this team."

General Wilson's eyes took in the whole man. Typical Delta. Fit. Cocky. More civvy merc than military. The type of man most special operators wanted to become.

"You got time to give me a tour?"

"All the time in the world, General. No more bad guys."

"Any alive?"

"A couple got away before we got here. The rest are dead. Couldn't keep seventy-two virgins waiting."

It was the answer Balls had expected. No real tragedy. They'd long since extracted all the information they were going to get out of the Arabs. It saved the government the expense and aggravation of a bunch of public trials. That would more than compensate for the cost of rebuilding this facility. The real loss was the three Gregory accomplices.

"Find any Anglo bodies?"

"Hard to tell. You'll need a good forensics team for that."

They started at the bottom, taking the main stairwell down to sublevel four, and worked their way up, stopping to let Balls examine every cell, room, and laboratory, Chavez providing a full briefing as they walked. All the violent action had happened on sublevels three and four, and on the ground floor. Those were a blood-spattered, bullet- and explosive-shattered mess. Damage on sublevels one and two seemed limited to water damage from the sprinklers. The labs all appeared in good shape, the reason they used halon fire suppression systems. Ironic. People be damned. At least the electronics were safe.

Balls paused in the first-sublevel electronics lab, walking to Eileen Wu's workstation. As far as he could tell, nothing had been disturbed. The Gregory laptops still occupied the top of the workbench, their guts attached to an electronic forensic array. As he stared down at it, the thought occurred to Balls Wilson that in an android world, Eileen would be the perfect medical examiner.

Well, she and the rest of the team would get their chance to see what equipment still worked after the real MEs finished with the slaughterhouse.

Turning back to Bob Chavez, Balls nodded. "Thanks, Bob. I can show myself out."

"Couldn't have that, General. You might trip on the stairs. How would that look on my report?"

The image of the grinning Chavez stayed with Balls Wilson all the way back to NSA headquarters.

CHAPTER 95

Dr. Donald Stephenson wasn't happy. The accident had killed three people. More importantly it had set back construction two weeks. Now he had a bunch of unionized French construction workers complaining about how the aggressive work schedule was jeopardizing worker safety. He'd just finished explaining to that collection of morons that if they didn't get back on schedule, a black hole was going to jeopardize worker safety a hell of a lot more. Besides, if they did their jobs as they were supposed to, there wouldn't be any more accidents.

Luckily none of the new equipment had been damaged when the crane cable had broken, dropping a section of dismantled muon detectors back into the ATLAS cavern, crushing three members of the construction crew. But the collapse had damaged needed construction equipment, thus the delay. Well, they'd just have to make it up.

But not all the news was bad. Stephenson turned to the latest progress reports from the matter disrupter construction team. Apparently that foreman knew his ass from a hole in the ground. Having already completed the electrical conduit work, his team was actually ahead of schedule. At this pace they'd be ready for the first small-scale matter-to-energy conversion test in a month.

He logged into his computer, using a biometric fingerprint scan followed by a sixty-four-character password that changed on an hourly basis. It was a formula Dr. Stephenson had designed and that only he knew. Since the Nancy Anatole incident, he'd made a number of security enhancements so that he no longer had to worry about a hacker accessing his private system. Still, it was an inconvenience, one that didn't elevate his current mood.

All his work, these last forty-odd years, had boiled down to this offshoot of the Rho Project. He actually felt like shaking Freddy Hagerman's hand for pushing up his schedule. Thanksgiving night, when everything had gone so wrong, it had forced him to use Raul to generate the anomaly, even at the cost of completely depleting the Rho Ship's power cells, effectively killing it. But in six months, the world would wake up to a new dawn, a golden age of knowledge and enlightenment. Nobody knew this gateway's real purpose and no one would dare try to stop him now. The November Anomaly had made sure of that.

Failure wasn't an option. Either this project succeeded on schedule, or the Earth, and eventually the entire solar system, would disappear into a new black hole, as its event horizon gobbled up anything that happened to pass within its reach. And with each gulp of additional matter, that horizon would expand.

Shrugging aside all thoughts of the unthinkable, Dr. Stephenson set to work modifying the construction plan in the ATLAS cavern to remedy today's setback. The workers weren't going to like it, but they hadn't liked anything about the project so far. Of one thing he was certain. They'd do what he demanded. Like it or not.

CHAPTER 96

The homes off of New Cut Road were widely spaced, the lots deeply cut into the thick woods, giving each a sense of being its own manor. Heather crouched in the woods beside Mark and Jennifer near one of these houses, and settled in as the dawn colored the eastern sky with a peachy glow. They'd traveled a little over fourteen miles on their circuitous route through the Maryland woods, placing them about five miles from Fort Meade, as the crow flies. Heather would have liked to cover more distance, but had settled for being careful, doubling back on their route and spending part of the night in streams on the off chance that dogs picked up the trail.

But she knew they weren't going to use dogs anytime soon. They'd have to figure out who had lived and died inside the facility last night before they knew whom they were looking for. Once they found the hijacked Ford and fingerprinted it, they'd know that Mark, Jen, and Heather were among the escapees, if anyone else had made it out. All of that took time under the best of circumstances. The mass confusion added by Jack's explosions around the base only made the confusing situation worse.

Jennifer had finally come out of her drug haze at a little past four a.m., and had now recovered sufficiently to operate without assistance. That was good. They were going to need each other at peak performance over the next twenty-four hours.

The sound of the garage door opening snapped Heather's attention back to the scene before her. As she'd anticipated, both cars backed out into the driveway, one after the other, and drove off down the lane as the garage door rumbled shut behind them. Two working adults. No children. That and its isolation were the reasons Heather had selected this particular dwelling.

Leading the way, she moved quickly to the side of the house, rapidly examining the electrical meters, cable box, and telephone wiring. It took her exactly fifty-three seconds to bypass the security system. With a nod to Mark, Heather moved up beside him as he broke the lock on the garage's side access door and stepped inside.

They swept the house, clearing the first floor, then the second, leaving the basement for last.

"All clear." Mark's voice from the basement allowed Heather to reduce her guard for the first time in weeks. Even though she knew it wouldn't last, for right now it felt damn good.

"You want the shower first?"

Mark shook his head as he looked her up and down. "You and Jen each take a bathroom while I keep watch. You both look like hell."

Neither Heather or Jennifer bothered to argue. In twenty minutes they were back downstairs, dressed in jeans and blouses that were a couple of sizes too big, but far better than the lab coat and orange prison garb.

"Your turn. I'll take watch while Jen hacks their laptop." Mark handed her the Mark 17 SCAR-H and two spare magazines.

"Check the fridge while you're at it," he called out as he headed upstairs toward the master bedroom. "I could eat an elephant."

Heather followed Jennifer into the office, a room just off the foyer that had a clear view to the spot where the curving driveway disappeared into the trees that surrounded the house. Jennifer slid into the seat in front of the laptop, held down the power button for several seconds, and waited for the laptop to power off. That done, she inserted the subspace USB dongle into a USB port on the Dell laptop's right side.

Jennifer brought up the BIOS screen and set the computer to boot from the USB device, bypassing the user log-in and password. As the Windows desktop appeared, she smiled and cracked her knuckles.

"Damn, I've missed this."

As Heather watched, Jennifer began her web search, memorizing the locations of key facilities she wanted to access. Satisfied, she began a completely different kind of search, this time using the dongle's subspace receiver-transmitter.

"Check for Jack's messages first," Heather said. "Then you can start your hacks."

Jennifer nodded, shifting her attention back to the web browser.

Jack had a standard operation procedure of posting encrypted messages on a handful of Facebook accounts, using encryption software Jen and Heather had designed. And while they no longer had a copy of the program, it only took a couple of minutes to download the latest version of the Java Development Kit and install it on the laptop. From there until she had the program up and running would be a matter of minutes, not hours.

As Jennifer set to work, Heather walked over to the window and peered out. Except for a few birds pecking at the grass near the driveway, nothing moved. Heather walked out of the office, unlocked the front door, and stepped outside. Moving into the trees, she paralleled the narrow lane that led from the driveway into the woods. Fifty feet later, the lane turned hard left and headed toward the road that linked lanes just like this one to the highway. The distant squeal of children at play in a backyard dominated all other sounds.

Turning away from the lane, Heather made a 360-degree loop through the woods surrounding the house, her movements generating no more noise than a field mouse's, despite the too-big Nikes that encased her feet. Finding nothing of concern, Heather reentered the house through the front door, locking it behind her. She turned to see Mark coming down the stairs, clad in better-fitting jeans, a black T-shirt, and a pair of gray New Balance running shoes. More importantly, for the first time in weeks, he'd shaved. The weight he'd lost had taken his already low body fat to near zero, making the muscles in his arms stand out like cables beneath his skin.

"How's your head?" Mark pointed to the Band-Aid at the edge of her hairline.

Heather reached up to touch it. "I'll live. You ready to eat?"

"What've they got?"

"Haven't checked yet."

Mark turned toward the kitchen, with Heather in tow. "House like this, a couple of miles away from a store, they're bound to have a full fridge."

It wasn't full, but close enough to bring a smile to Mark's face. The leftovers included chicken wings, meatloaf, mashed potatoes, and half a pan of green bean casserole. Heather made plates for herself and Jennifer, leaving Mark to finish off the rest.

When she set the plate, hot from the microwave, down beside the laptop, Jennifer didn't even notice.

"Brunch is served."

"Yeah, OK. Give me a sec."

Having watched Jen in some of her programming Zen states before, Heather left it and walked back to the kitchen. If it got cold, Jen could heat it back up if she wanted to.

Retrieving her own plate from the microwave, Heather sat down beside Mark, who had amazingly almost finished clearing his first plateful. The smell of the food made her mouth water so she was afraid drool would leak over her lips as she took the first bite. It didn't, and the meatloaf tasted as good as it smelled. But somehow, Heather couldn't swallow.

Standing up quickly, she strode to the sink, leaned over, and vomited into the garbage disposal. Immediately Mark was beside her, his arm around her waist.

"What's wrong?"

Heather spit, tried to answer, and then succumbed to another retching bout. It was stupid. Jack and Janet had warned them about this, the aftereffects of killing a man. Somehow she'd thought, since she'd already seen Mark kill men, that she'd be immune to the reaction. But now that she'd dropped the mental guard she'd maintained throughout her captivity, the thought of the Navy SEALs she'd killed and the guards at the NSA facility flooded her mind. America's finest. Heroes serving their country. They had families too. But she'd killed them all. And even though she thought she'd done what she'd had to, that didn't make it better.

Turning on the cold water, she rinsed out her mouth and washed her face, then flipped on the disposal. When she turned back to face Mark, he didn't bother to say anything, just pulled her close and wrapped his strong arms around her body. As he held her, tears leaked from Heather's eyes, gaining volume until they formed streams down her cheeks.

"Oh, Mark. I've seen our futures. And most of them, the most probable ones, are so…so dark. And not just for us. For everyone."

"Look at me." Mark leaned back until his gaze held her, pulling her out of her visions and into his eyes. "I don't give a shit about those futures. None of them. I'm the now. And I've got a message for anyone trying to bring on that darkness. They try to take this away from me and they'll be sorry.

"I know this doesn't make mathematical sense, but I want you to forget about any future that doesn't go our way. Even if it's 99 percent likely, throw it away. We can't waste energy fighting to prevent bad outcomes. The only way we're going to get through this is by focusing on what we want to happen. Visualize that. Find us a way through."

Heather steadied herself, wiped her eyes, and nodded. When he tried to pull her close again, she stopped him.

"I'm OK now. I think I'll try to eat again."

As she seated herself in front of her plate, Heather did what Mark had asked. As she began to chew, she pushed all the dark visions out of her mind. As her grandfather had always said, "If you're going to bet the long shots, then let those ponies run."

CHAPTER 97

Eileen Wu was frustrated. The four a.m. drive from her Annapolis apartment to Fort Meade hadn't bothered her, at least not until she got to Meade. The post was still bottled up tight, and with all the NSA recalls plus the continued arrival of military and government investigation teams, she hadn't actually made it through the gate until 6:35.

The NSA parking lot was a nightmare. The parking garage that concealed the Ice House had been sealed off, forcing everyone out into the huge exterior lot, and, despite the early hour, Eileen had been forced to cruise the full rows until she found a slot to squeeze her car into a half mile from the facility.

Her mood didn't improve when she got to the building and discovered she would not be allowed down to her lab until after the forensics teams had finished the crime scene investigation. Worse, they hadn't even started the actual investigation yet. The security folks had refused to allow the investigators and medical examiners access until their clearances could be confirmed. Even after their security credentials were verified through the Joint Personnel Adjudication System, JPAS, security again refused to grant access. Yes, they had top-secret clearances, but they weren't cleared for SCI, sensitive compartmented information, and the Ice House was an SCI facility.

As for Eileen, no amount of reasoning, arguing, or even ranting and raving made the slightest bit of difference. She wasn't getting access until the forensics teams were finished. She'd even tried the old "I'm doing the electronic forensics investigation" ploy. Nope. The cone of silence had descended, and nobody was listening.

Even a direct appeal to General Wilson hadn't helped. He was already involved in forcing through security waivers to get the crime scene unit access to the Ice House, and she just wasn't at the top of his priorities right now. She'd get her chance at figuring out how someone had penetrated the facility's electronic control systems, but only after all the dead bodies were removed.

By the time she was allowed into the building, it was already four thirty in the afternoon. She paused in the foyer to take in the scene. The building was a mess. The tile floor was littered with chunks of concrete, broken glass, and wood from walls and furnishings riddled by bullets and explosive ordnance.

Eileen wound her way to the stairwell through a maze of yellow tape designed to keep people out of the areas where investigators were still working. The bodies had been removed, but the smell remained, the stench of death clogging her nostrils. Everywhere she looked the standing water was red.

Looking away, Eileen shifted her focus to making it to the stairwell without throwing up. If anything, the stairwell was worse, indicative of the pitched battle that had raged inside as the Delta team fought its way down to the bottom.

At the first sublevel, Eileen stepped through the open stair-well door and breathed a sigh of relief. The corridor between the labs was still wet, but the water wasn't colored with blood. The doors to the labs had been propped open to let the halon gas dissipate, and although this had allowed some of the water from the hall to run down through the raised flooring, water damage to the electronics should be minimal.

Turning into her lab, Eileen made her way directly to the workbench that held the dissected Gregory laptops. At first glance it appeared undisturbed. Then she noticed it. One of the USB dongles was missing from where it had been connected to the electronic breadboard. Glancing to the other side of the table, Eileen muttered a curse through clenched teeth. Both dongles were gone.

Without thinking, she lifted the phone from its cradle. Shit. No dial tone. And she'd had to leave her cell phone outside the secure area.

She thought about walking back outside to call in a report, then discarded the idea. First she needed to do a thorough inspection to see if anything else was missing or had been tampered with. She had no intention of being unable to give complete answers to the questions that were going to be thrown at her. As busy as Balls was trying to figure out exactly what the hell had happened here, he wouldn't be happy about getting a bunch of half-assed information.

Sliding into her chair, Eileen began the methodical analytical work for which she was famous. And as she worked, the disturbing imagery and smells from the rest of the building finally slipped from her head.

CHAPTER 98

"Jack's been busy," Jennifer said as Mark and Heather stepped into the office.

"Nothing surprising about that," Mark replied, noting the clarity in his sister's eyes, something that was very good to see.

"Remember the Navajo cop who hid Jack and Janet on the Santa Clara Reservation?"

"Tall Bear."

"Right. Apparently he's become a real player in the Native People's Alliance, a new federation fighting for tribal autonomy. With all the crap that's going on out in the country, the NPA has declared independence. Tall Bear, as recently elected president of the Navajo Nation, pulls some serious clout. There's talk of him becoming the first president of the NPA."

Heather shook her head. "What's this got to do with Jack?"

"He's hooked us up with the American equivalent of the French Resistance. If we can make it to a reservation, the NPA has agreed to take us under its wing."

Mark moved over to the window, glancing down the empty driveway, his mind on Jennifer's words. "Why hasn't the US government already stepped down hard on the NPA?"

"Things were getting out of hand even before we got ourselves captured. The government's been able to establish good security in the Northeast corridor and in the major metropolitan areas, except for Detroit, which is pretty much a no-man's-land. Most of the rest of the country is hit or miss. Some areas are well organized. Others not so much. It's making it hard to get food and supplies around. The NPA's a minor annoyance."

"The chaos should help us."

"Once we get out of the Northeast corridor," said Heather.

"Our best bet seems to be the Seneca Nation in western New York. They're a large, well-funded tribe that generates over a billion dollars a year from their casinos and retail operations. Heavy NPA ties."

"We're going to need some funds and IDs."

"Taken care of. I've arranged for delivery of three of the identities we prepared in Bolivia. Passports and driver's licenses will be express-mailed tomorrow. We just have to get to the Mail Boxes Etc. in Harrisburg, where I've set up mailboxes in those names. We also have bank accounts at Bank of America, Citibank, and Chase. I've transferred sufficient funds for our near-term needs. Good news. Our new selves have excellent credit histories."

Jennifer reached over and grabbed a stack of pages from the printer, passing them to Mark and Heather.

"Here's your new backgrounds. Take a second to scan them. You two can pack up the laptop. By the way, I replaced our digital fingerprints and DNA records in the federal databases with those of known criminals."

Heather nodded. "We need this to look like a routine break-in. I'll bag the jewelry on our way out. Then we're going to need a car."

"They'll wonder about the clothes."

"It won't matter. By the time they figure it out we'll be long gone."

Mark glanced at the clock, took a deep breath, and let it out slowly. Eleven twenty-four a.m. As good a time to start the rest of their lives as any. "OK. Let's do it."

CHAPTER 99

The US Food Service plant in Severn, Maryland, was a big operation, the main building really formed from two large buildings whose northwest corners connected. The plant had been built to facilitate big-rig loading and unloading, with employee parking on two sides, the northeastern lot surrounded by trees. It was exactly the kind of place Heather had been looking for. Early afternoon meant the parking lot was full of people back from lunch for the afternoon shift, too early for people to be thinking about leaving.

Jennifer stepped from the northern tree line, seated herself on the curb, and popped open the stolen laptop, waiting fifteen seconds as it awoke from sleep mode. As Mark and Heather kept watch, she initiated the subspace receiver-transmitter SRT scan. With the SRT, she didn't need any back doors or exploits such as her worm had exposed. Jennifer limited the search radius to one hundred meters, the grid filling with a list of programmable systems sorted by distance, the closest at the top.

People thought of cars as mechanical devices, and in the old days they had been. Now they were mobile computing platforms, brimming with programmable electronics. And anything that was programmable was reprogrammable. Most of these systems could be hacked by amateurs with inexpensive wireless interfaces. All of them were vulnerable to Jennifer, Mark, or Heather, armed with an SRT and a computing device.

The white Ford Fusion five parking spaces to Jennifer's right gave a short squawk and blinked its lights.

"Looks like our ride is ready," Mark said, leading the way.

"You drive," said Heather. "Jen, you and the laptop get the backseat. I'll take shotgun."

Mark opened the driver's door, slid inside, and pressed the START button.

"I-95 north?"

"No," said Heather. "I want to stay on surface streets, at least until we're north of Baltimore. You ready, Jen?"

Jennifer closed the door and leaned her back against it, positioning the laptop in her lap. "Give me a minute to bring up the traffic light grid and traffic cameras. Once I've completed the initial sort, it'll be easy to re-sort as we move. This time of day I should be able to arrange for a delay-free trip."

As she began to type, Jennifer felt her hands start to shake, tremors that migrated up into her arms and shoulders.

"Jen, you OK?" Heather reached into the back to place a hand on her leg.

Focusing her will, Jennifer damped down the shakes. They were still there, just not so obvious.

"Just coming off the drugs. Don't worry. Nothing I can't handle."

Mark swung the car out of the lot and north onto Telegraph Road.

"If you need me to pull over or anything, let me know."

"I'll be fine."

Heather shook her head. "Check the local police dispatcher logs."

"Working on it." Jennifer opened another window on her display. "Shit! We've got a problem."

"What?"

"Bad luck. Our car's owner must have seen us leave the lot and called the police. We've got a cruiser a half mile north, coming south on Telegraph."

"Can you change the report?"

"Give me a minute," Jen said.

Feeling Heather's eyes on her, she scanned the police database for the record she wanted. Finding it, she typed in a few modifications, saved it, and fired off an update that would be picked up on every police-vehicle-mounted computer in the area.

"OK. Stolen car is now a red Ford Fiesta heading east on Donaldson Avenue, Virginia license plate EAN-7301, occupants two Latino males."

"Our cop?"

"Still heading south on Telegraph...wait. He's making a U-turn."

"After he turns east on Donaldson, give him some engine trouble."

Jennifer smiled. "He's not driving the newest model on the Glen Burnie police force, but it's got an electronic ignition system. Won't be a problem."

Heather settled back in the passenger seat, turning her attention to the road ahead. "Mark, once we pass Donaldson, take Aviation, then I-195 to the BWI parkway. I want to swap cars downtown. Then we'll get up on I-83 to Harrisburg. What's our hotel, Jen?"

"Nothing but the best. Motel Six on Briarsdale Road. In the morning we can swing by the Mail Boxes Etc. and pick up our new IDs. Then we're going to need some new clothes."

Mark nodded. "Sounds good."

Jennifer felt a new round of shivers crawl beneath her skin, and this time she didn't even try to contain them. She could tell Heather noticed, but to her credit Heather offered no unwanted assistance.

Jennifer knew she was in for a fight with her body's need for heroin. For her, the NSA torture chamber was just getting warmed up.

CHAPTER 100

Eileen Wu's eyes hurt, but she didn't feel tired. She felt like a hunting dog on the scent of a big cat. A really big cat.

She'd sensed something was wrong with the whole Al Qaeda escape scenario the moment she'd noticed that the two USB dongles had been taken from her lab. Those two missing USB devices screamed Jack Gregory's name. But why take only the dongles? Nothing about them had stood out as special, so how special were they?

Eileen looked forward to reviewing all the recorded data from when she'd first turned on the Gregory laptop, but right now she was hot on the trail of the person or persons who had taken down all the sophisticated security systems within the Ice House.

In Eileen's mind, it helped to put a face on her opponent. Maybe it was a bit of reverse sexism, but the face that came to her was a woman's face, a face very much like her own. An avenging Valkyrie.

Whoever the Valkyrie was, she'd done more than cause the Ice House systems to malfunction. She'd used them as weapons to blind, confuse, even kill her enemies. Eileen had never seen anything like the sophistication of this hack. Even the legendary Stuxnet worm paled in comparison. While that worm had been targeted at very specific systems, this one had compromised every electronic system in the building, from cell phones and tablets to high-end computing systems, exploiting security holes across a wide variety of operating systems. The most impressive thing about this new worm was its ability to genetically adapt and hide itself.

Just when Eileen thought she'd clearly identified the worm's unique signature, she'd come back to a machine she'd found it on an hour earlier and discovered that it was gone. Not really gone, just hidden in plain sight. She'd wiped an infected computer's hard drive, only to discover that the worm restored itself to a different part of the drive later, having managed to write its kernel into a programmable keyboard's random-access memory.

The worm was amazingly aggressive, migrating through any connection to writeable memory. It loved flash memory, as well as anything that let it save off a version of itself.

The time line confused her. So did the infection vector. Clearly the infection had been present for some time prior to the attack. And as adept as the worm was at spreading and hiding itself, this was a TEMPEST facility. Even if she assumed that someone had illegally carried in an infected flash drive or DVD, the worm's propagation should have been spotty, with areas of high concentration and others that were infection-free. That wasn't the case here.

It was as if the worm had simultaneously penetrated the entire facility, like a burst of high-energy radiation. One of the worm's behaviors had brought it to Eileen's attention. Whenever it found an Internet-capable system, it opened a telnet port, then hid that port from standard sys-admin tools. Eileen had found it with one of her own special security tools, a program that created its own port map in addition to sniffing all Internet protocol packets.

Eileen identified other back doors, but she felt pretty sure the telnet port had been the door the Valkyrie had used to take over the Ice House. The cameras had gone down first, followed by the facility lights. Then all electronically controlled locks were opened, initiating the prisoner escape. All of those first events had been initiated over an internal Wi-Fi link. Eileen hadn't yet traced the source, but it was only a matter of time.

Of greater interest was the security monitoring room from which the following attacks had come. Someone had killed the two guards with a series of expertly placed, powerful blows. The subsequent events—halon gassing of the primary control room, diversion of camera video to the Valkyrie's station, initiation of selected fire suppression systems, and selective manipulation of building lockdown mechanisms—were all indicators that pointed to an infiltrator, possibly disguised as a guard. But the fake message redirecting the security teams to defend the building perimeter had been the key. That had been a woman's voice, and it had been routed over the public address system from the security station laptop. But last night's personnel logs showed no female staff on the night shift.

That left the two women in the facility at the time of the attack, Heather McFarland and Jennifer Smythe, both captured at Jack Gregory's Bolivian compound. They and Mark Smythe were people who had an interest in the captured laptops, although Eileen was mystified by how they had known where to look for them on their way out. And she was pretty sure that they'd made it out alive; at least the medical examiner hadn't identified their bodies.

Eileen wasn't an expert on Jack Gregory's tactics, but the confusion caused by the Fort Meade bombings fit what she imagined his profile to be. Leaning back in her chair, stretching her arms above her head, she cracked her knuckles. She'd leave that to Levi and his team. Right now she had a lot more work to do if she was going to be fully prepared for General Wilson's eight a.m. meeting. Aside from who had done it, he was going to want to know how they had gotten the worm into every system in the Ice House and how she was going to purge it, two questions Eileen didn't yet know the answer to.

Eileen wanted those answers.

CHAPTER 101

The trip from Harrisburg, Pennsylvania, to Salamanca, on New York's Cattaraugus Reservation, had been uneventful, but for Jennifer it had been part of the descent into hell she'd begun yesterday. Heather had taken over the subspace hacks required to ensure their travel security while Jennifer huddled in a fetal ball in the backseat, alternately sweating her shirt through and shivering hard enough to damage the car's suspension.

She'd read all about the physical effects of heroin withdrawal, but living it was a different matter. Heather and Mark had repeatedly tried to help, but there wasn't a damned thing they could do except let her fight her own battle.

Jack had posted encrypted instructions for their rendezvous on the web and Heather had downloaded them. They'd led to a safe house in Salamanca where Heather had used the laptop to remotely open the garage door. Then they'd settled in for the night. If all went well, Jack would arrive sometime in the morning. In the meantime, as Mark and Heather started their planning, Jennifer, plagued by deepening depression, had taken herself to bed.

To have so much power and feel so helpless filled her with self-loathing. Every meditation she tried failed. It was as if all her neural enhancements had amplified her drug experience as well as its accompanying withdrawal.

Maybe she was attacking this all wrong. She knew clinics sometimes used methadone to ease addicts off of heroin, not that she wanted to substitute one drug for another. But maybe there was another way to ease her symptoms. Opiates such as heroin caused the body to release an excess of dopamine. Perhaps if she used her perfect memory of what it had felt like to sink into that opiate haze, she could trigger the same bodily response. The downside was that she'd be putting herself back into the drugged state.

Her self-debate didn't last long. She needed to feel that feeling one more time. Besides, Mark and Heather needed her mentally sharp in the morning. And if her idea worked, she could gradually wean herself from the need.

Leaning back against the pillows that she'd piled against the bed's oak headboard, Jennifer pulled forth the memory she wanted. As the lovely rush wiped away all her cares, one last clear thought brought a smile to her lips. *Good decision.*

CHAPTER 102

Jack dropped the kickstand and stepped off the black motorcycle onto the concrete driveway, pausing in the early morning sunlight to survey the Native American neighborhood that surrounded the safe house. Some people would describe it as sleepy, but *dead* was the word that came to mind. Fine with him. Sometimes dead was good.

Removing his helmet, Jack walked to the front door, giving it three good raps with his knuckles.

Heather opened the door a crack, then flung it open wide, wrapping her strong, slender arms around Jack's neck as he lifted her off the ground. As Jennifer reached him he shifted to allow her into the group hug. Seeing Mark's grin, Jack released the girls and stepped forward to accept Mark's powerful handshake. Jack felt a warmth that he hadn't experienced for a long while fill his chest. "Janet told me to give you all a hug for her. Mark's going to have to wait to collect his in person."

"That's OK." Mark laughed. "I'd rather get it from her anyway."

"Let's not keep Jack standing in the driveway all morning," Jennifer said. "Besides, everything's a bit less conspicuous inside."

"Good thinking," Jack agreed.

Heather led the group into the living room, but Jack carried his satchel to the kitchen table and pulled out manila envelopes labeled HEATHER, MARK, and JENNIFER.

Tossing them on the table, he turned toward Heather. "Do you have some coffee going? We're all going to need some before we dig into these."

Heather grabbed the pot as Jennifer set out four cups. Jack accepted the steaming mug and took a seat facing the door, a habit so old he no longer noticed it. As the others settled into their chairs, he leaned back and smiled.

"I know you're probably all curious about what's been happening in the outside world while you've been locked away, so I've prepared a detailed summary as part of your briefing packages."

Mark opened the envelope's metal tabs, dumping the contents onto the table in front of him. He glanced at the pile of aerial and satellite photographs attached to the printed reports and let out a low whistle.

Jack continued. "Inside your packets you'll find copies of reports Janet and I put together on the activities at the Large Hadron Collider site in Switzerland, as well as identities you will be using to individually infiltrate the November Anomaly Project. But before we get started, I need to hear a rundown on your last few weeks as NSA guests at the Ice House."

For two hours Mark, Jen, and Heather recounted their captivity, as Jack insisted on hearing every detail, up to and including their escape. He showed particular interest in the layout of the lab and workstation from which Heather had retrieved the subspace receiver-transmitter USB devices.

"Sounds like whoever they dug up to replace Dr. David Kurtz is just as good."

"The nameplate on the workstation read 'Dr. Eileen Wu.'"

Jack pulled his laptop from the satchel and handed it across the table to Jennifer.

"See what you can dig up on our new friend, Dr. Wu."

As Jennifer plugged in and fired up the laptop, Jack settled in, once again looking forward to watching her work her magic.

CHAPTER 103

"So how bad is it?" General Balls Wilson directed his attention to Eileen Wu.

"Bad." She manipulated the mouse, projecting a diagram onto the wall screen. "This shows all the Ice House electronic systems prior to the attack, including wireless devices and approved tablets and Wi-Fi phones."

She clicked a button and the display changed.

"Now this shows the still-working systems after the gun battle. As you can see, despite all the bullets, explosions, and fire suppression systems engaged, the vast majority of the electronic equipment is still functioning."

"Why?"

"Because the attackers wanted those systems working. One of their first actions was to kill the lights on sublevels three and four. They killed the lights, but not the power."

She clicked the button again. "And this shows the systems infected by what I'm calling the Ice worm."

"I don't see any difference. Which systems are infected?"

"All of them."

"All?"

"Every single programmable component, along with any writable memory attached to those systems. And I mean everything, down to programmable calculators, MP3 players, and overhead projectors like this one."

Balls Wilson stared at her in disbelief. The low murmur that had begun around the table of assembled senior NSA staff became a buzz that was silenced by General Wilson's glare.

"Do you know who infected my facility?"

"I did."

The silence hung in the air between them, forcing her to continue.

"When I finally gained access to my lab yesterday, I noticed that two small USB dongles were missing from my test bench. I confirmed that they were the only things taken, then began asking myself why they would take just those dongles. That caused me to go back and review the tests we ran on the two laptops.

"As you recall from my previous briefing, I isolated the first laptop in a Faraday cage, instrumented all the laptop circuit boards to record data flow, switched it on, and bypassed the log-in.

"Exactly one minute later, my instruments began recording unexplained activity on numerous circuits, including the TCP stack. Since the laptop was completely isolated, this didn't cause me concern. Last night's events and my subsequent analysis of the original data indicate that my original confidence was a mistake.

"Somehow, without sending any measurable signals, that laptop identified every computing system in the building and infected them with the Ice worm. The worm managed to hide itself, migrating to new systems that were subsequently brought in."

"Jesus." Karl Oberstein's face looked drawn.

"Bert," General Wilson asked, "do you agree with Dr. Wu's conclusions?"

Dr. Mathews glanced at his young prodigy, saw no fear in Eileen's face, and nodded. "I'm afraid I do. I reviewed her data before this meeting."

"So if it didn't send out any signals, how did that laptop access all our systems?"

Eileen Wu clicked off the projector and turned to face him. "I don't know."

"Gregory."

"More precisely Heather McFarland and the Smythe twins. The Ripper may have helped on the outside, but you can bet that everything that happened inside the Ice House was orchestrated by those three. Worm or no, their escape was some unbelievable shit."

General Wilson stared directly into Eileen's dark eyes. "Could you have pulled it off?"

She shrugged. "The computer stuff, if I knew about the worm. Everything else though, forget about it."

General Wilson leaned forward. "This isn't the first time we've had data appearing inside TEMPEST-certified systems in the last couple of years. Karl, you and Levi take a look back at some of the old Jonathan Riles files from when he sent Gregory's team to Los Alamos. Find out what Gregory stumbled onto that enticed him to go rogue.

"Eileen, you make damned sure that worm stays confined to the Ice House."

"I'm afraid it's too late for that, General. But if Gregory's team has its hands on the kind of technology we think they do, that worm is the least of our worries."

CHAPTER 104

Mark looked up as Jennifer closed her briefing folder and rose to stand beside the kitchen table.

"I'm sorry, guys, I've got to get some sleep."

Mark bent a questioning gaze on his sister. "Sleep?"

Jennifer shrugged, and in that motion Mark noticed the slight tremors traversing her body. "Heroin's a bitch. Sleep helps, even for me. OK, Jack?"

Jack studied her closely, then nodded. "I guess you can catch up with the others in the morning, but you're going to have to bring it."

It wasn't exactly a gracious dismissal, but Jennifer appeared not to notice. A glance at Heather's concerned face told Mark that she had. He understood Jack's need to drive them all hard, but Mark didn't have to like it, especially when it came to ignoring what the NSA bastards had done to his sister.

After all, they'd worked on the plan for sixteen straight hours. Mark knew the construction plans for the ATLAS cavern and for the matter ingester power station nicknamed the MINGSTER, knew the blueprints, knew every aspect of the electrical wiring, knew what companies had which contracts. Still Jack wasn't satisfied. Now they were working their way through the dossiers of all personnel currently assigned to the November Anomaly Project. Still on the docket for the night, Mark had to learn the stasis field generator wiring and construction plans. Heather still needed to study the rest of Dr. Stephenson's papers.

Jack had selected their future project roles, but he was waiting for them to complete the background work before he took them through his plans for getting them the right jobs with the appropriate firms, and for getting them assigned to the desired positions on Gateway Day.

Mark found his future role intriguing. He would become Gunter Fogel, a hotshot young electrical technician with Kohl Engineering. His mission was to impress the lead engineer, Gerhardt Werner, and get himself assigned to the construction team inside the ATLAS cavern. Jennifer would take on the role of Dr. Nika Ivanovich, a Russian postdoctoral scientist working on Dr. Peter Trotsky's team specializing in the theory and operation of the stasis field controllers.

Heather's mission would place her in the role of Inga Hedstrom, to become one of the Swiss security guards in the ATLAS cavern on G-Day. Dr. Stephenson had insisted that no military be assigned near the wormhole device through which the anomaly would be transported on G-Day, the military's role being to ensure security of the entire site, preventing outside forces from disrupting construction or operations. Only a couple of guards would maintain watch within the cavern, typically two or three to a shift, and those would be provided by Paladin, a

Swiss private security firm. The inside guards were only there to do Dr. Stephenson's bidding, including evicting unwanted personnel from the premises.

This would leave Heather with little to do on G-Day, exactly what Jack wanted. It put her in position to use her unique abilities to recognize unanticipated problems and to take immediate corrective action. While her position would be the least complicated, it would also be the most difficult to set up ahead of time.

Rising from his seat, Mark walked over to the coffeepot and refilled his mug. Rolling his neck, he felt it pop and crackle. Definitely too much sitting. But as he raised his cup to his lips, feeling the hot liquid flow over his tongue, he held no illusions. The butt-flattening had only just begun.

CHAPTER 105

The stasis tendrils swarmed to complete the last of the repairs, each delicate line of force its own thread of execution within the massive neural net that was Raul. He was so close now to accomplishing something Dr. Stephenson had never imagined, bringing the Rho Ship back to full functionality.

Not that he intended to go anywhere in his starship. Although he could explore the solar system, he couldn't get to the stars, not and survive the trip. The one advantage the Altreians' subspace warp technology had over the power of the wormhole drive was the way it enabled the ship to travel to the stars with living occupants. While the subspace engine allowed faster-than-light travel, it was nowhere near as fast as making the distance between here and there cease to exist the way his wormhole drive did. Still, the whole dying thing limited that sort of travel to unmanned ships.

Raul knew what Stephenson was trying to accomplish. He knew what Stephenson had done when he'd used Raul to unknowingly facilitate the November Anomaly's creation. He knew how Stephenson had used that to force the world to build his gateway. With access to the history of the Kasari Collective, Raul knew all about how things were supposed to work and what had gone wrong here on Earth.

Theoretically, the Rho Ship's wormhole drive could connect to a gateway, forming a survivable transport portal. The real problem was the portal size. In such a configuration, the portal would have to be inside the ship, and the wormhole drive would have to be configured to operate with a reduced footprint. Where it normally ramped up and thrust the starship through a newly formed wormhole, it didn't have to maintain that wormhole for very long. But a gateway needed to remain open for extended periods and had to be large enough to allow the transport of troops and heavy equipment. That kind of extended operation required a large matter disrupter facility and a massive portal, the kind Stephenson was building in Switzerland.

Raul's neural network roamed the World Wide Web via worm fiber connections, just as it monitored satellite and radio frequency broadcasts. It had allowed him to learn the details of Dr. Stephenson's plans. More importantly, it had led him to an inescapable conclusion about Heather and the Smythe twins. Stephenson didn't know about their altered abilities. The Rho Project hadn't had anything to do with that.

That left only one other possibility. They had found the Altreian ship long before the government had discovered its cave. Somehow, that ship had altered them. Everything the Altreians did had a purpose, and the only purpose Raul could see in enhancing these humans had been to turn them into soldiers, soldiers whose only mission was to stop the Rho Ship from accomplishing its agenda. That now meant stopping Dr. Stephenson.

Raul knew enough about the Kasari Collective to know he didn't want them on Earth. Not because he thought their assimilation of the human race would be harmful to the Earth's population. The Kasari merely wanted to add to their numbers and resources. In doing so the human population would be augmented, illness eliminated, life spans extended for millennia, wars a thing of the past...at least internal wars. None of that bothered him. But if the Kasari came through, Raul would lose the special power he'd worked so hard to achieve.

If Stephenson hadn't created the November Anomaly, Raul would have put a stop to his plans. But turning the Earth into a black hole wasn't an option. So now he had the same problem Heather and her friends had.

Since Dr. Stephenson had to be allowed to succeed in creating his gateway in order to get rid of the anomaly, Heather and the Smythes would be irresistibly drawn to the November Anomaly Project. They would have to be on-site to have any chance of shutting down the gateway after the anomaly was transported, but before Stephenson could synchronize it with its sister Kasari gateway. On what Stephenson was calling G-Day, Heather would be inside the ATLAS cavern, close enough to Stephenson's portal for Raul's purpose.

And then he would never be alone again.

CHAPTER 106

The cold rain that had blown in two days ago showed no sign of going away. Freddy pulled his black London Fog raincoat's collar up, slammed the car door, and walked toward the quaint old house in western Annapolis. Mary Beth Kincaid had met Jonathon Riles while he was a midshipman at the Naval Academy and they'd fallen madly in love, getting married immediately after his graduation. Her father had been a navy captain and she'd married another one. It was no surprise to Freddy that she'd moved back to her old family home after Admiral Riles's reported suicide. The house looked like something an old sea dog would be comfortable in.

From all reports, Mary Beth was a strong woman, volunteering all her free time for community charities. Strong, but heartbroken. Her old friends said she'd lost her zest for life, isolating herself in the old house when not at work. Neighbors checked in on her, but it was clear she wanted to be by herself, to be left alone with her grand piano and her grief.

Walking up the three steps, he stepped onto the open front porch and raised the brass knocker. The haunting notes of "Greensleeves" drifted out, making him reluctant to interrupt her playing, but his damned reporter's nose had led him here, and maybe, just maybe, he could help this wounded lady find some peace.

As the song ended, he finally brought the knocker down in three sharp raps. The woman who opened the door little resembled the one in the picture he'd seen of Admiral and Mrs. Riles. It was a photo taken when Admiral Riles had just been appointed director of the National Security Agency. In that picture, the laugh lines around her sparkling blue eyes were the only lines on her face, a face framed by blonde hair elegantly highlighted with the first streaks of gray.

No hint of blonde remained in her hair and her cheeks looked tugged down by the weight of the world. Perhaps it was the reflection of the dark clouds behind him, but her eyes seemed to have dulled to gray.

"Mrs. Riles?"

"Yes. How may I help you?"

"I don't know exactly. I'm hoping you can tell me."

She studied him for several seconds. Then, with a questioning look, she opened the door.

"Please come in. I was about to pour myself some tea. Would you like some?"

"That would be nice," Freddy said, removing his raincoat and hanging it on the coat rack.

"One lump or two?"

"Black...er, plain is fine."

Freddy moved to the mantle, studying the photos in their frames, neatly arranged from left to right in chronological order. Mary and Jon, arm in arm at a Naval Academy formal, cutting their wedding cake, a kiss at a promotion party, the two of them standing on the deck of the *USS Ronald Reagan*, and finally the same photo Freddy had found online.

The tinkle of fine china behind him caused him to turn to see Mary Beth setting two cups and saucers on the coffee table.

"We were a lovely couple, wouldn't you say?"

"I would."

Freddy felt out of his element. It wasn't the old sea captain's house that was messing with his head. It was this old woman. Mary Beth carried an aura of pain and grace that sapped his wit, leaving him little better than a muttering simpleton.

"Please, come and have a seat beside me." She patted a spot on the sofa.

Freddy maneuvered around the low table, his bad leg making the turn awkward. Mary Beth noticed.

"How'd you lose it?"

"A bad encounter with an industrial saw."

"Sorry to hear it. Losing a part of yourself is hard."

Picking up the teapot, Mary Beth poured, first his, then hers, her hand surprisingly steady. Freddy reached out, pinching the tiny handle between forefinger and thumb, feeling as if he would snap it off before the cup reached his lips.

"Well, Mister…"

"Hagerman. Freddy Hagerman."

"Well, Mr. Hagerman, if you'd be so kind, I'd like to hear why you came to see me."

Freddy took a sip, burned his lip, and set the cup back on its saucer. For once he wished he were better at this tact shit.

"Mrs. Riles, I came to talk about your husband."

Her face showed no change.

"Go on."

"I'm an investigative reporter for the *New York Post*. There's really no way to say this other than to come right out with it, so here goes. I have good reason to believe your husband didn't commit suicide."

Again, he detected no change in Mary Beth's expression.

"I believe Jonathan was murdered by a group of people bent on stopping his investigation into the Rho Project."

Her eyes were definitely blue now. "You're not telling me anything I don't know."

For a moment Freddy was speechless. "You knew? Why didn't you tell anyone?"

The laugh bubbled off Mary Beth's lips but didn't make it to her eyes.

"Oh, I told them all. Told the investigators. Told his superiors. Told everyone. But I'm a grieving widow, an old woman, blinded by love for my dead husband, unwilling to see anything bad in him, clueless to the goings-on in the real world of men and politics. I finally quit banging my head on that wall. But you know something, Mr. Hagerman? No matter what they say, it didn't feel better when I stopped."

"So will you help me?"

"I don't know how."

"Do you know a man named Jack Gregory?"

For the first time since he'd met her, a genuine smile graced Mary Beth's lips.

"Let me tell you something, Freddy. Jonny always said I was the best natural judge of character he'd ever seen."

There it was again, that nice smile.

"It was the reason I invited you in."

She reached for her cup, took a small sip, dabbed her lips with the back of her hand.

"Jack Gregory is a young god. Jonny would have given his life for him. So would I."

"I think he did."

Setting her cup back in its saucer, Mary Beth locked her eyes with Freddy's.

"Then I'm happy."

"Jack's not."

Her left eyebrow rose a quarter of an inch.

"Tell me about it."

For the next half hour Freddy related the abridged version of what Jack Gregory had told him that night in the Maryland hotel. When he finished, Mary Beth Riles dabbed the corners of her eyes with a kerchief.

"So my Jonny was trying to save the world."

"And Jack still is."

"One thing about Jonny. He always had a backup plan. You up for helping me look through his old things?"

"Thought you'd never ask."

Rising to her feet, Mary Beth held her hand out to Freddy.

"Then let's go save our saviors."

CHAPTER 107

Eileen stared at the computer screen in disbelief, a chill crawling up her spine from just between her shoulder blades to the base of her skull. What had started with her obsessive search for clues to the technology underlying the two missing Gregory devices had taken a nasty turn into a very dark place. If she continued on her current track, the knowledge lurking in that darkness was likely to chew her up and spit her mangled corpse into some Potomac backwater.

Eileen's problem was that she couldn't quit. It wasn't in her nature. It was the reason she'd gotten her doctorate from Caltech when others her age were having sweet sixteen parties.

She'd finished her detailed analysis of the data recorded coming and going from the Gregory USB dongles. The things had provided a listing of every programmable system within a one-kilometer radius. But the information went well beyond anything a hacker could obtain, even with a physical connection to those systems. Somehow the dongles had managed to provide the exact location of every system, down to the nearest millimeter. It was an impossible level of detail, and while Eileen couldn't yet confirm that degree of accuracy, she'd checked coordinates of several samples. They certainly had sub-meter precision.

Even if she assumed the USB dongles had some unknown and undetectable Wi-Fi signal that could connect to other systems, the location thing stumped her. How? It was as if some sort of futuristic neutrino scan had detected all those systems and recorded their locations before tapping them for information. If technology like that existed, it had to be Rho Project–related.

That led Eileen to perform her own review of the events that had led Admiral Riles to launch Jack Gregory at Los Alamos. If Gregory had stumbled upon it during his investigation, he would have realized certain governments would pay for that kind of technology. Perhaps something on that path held a clue to how those things worked.

It was a path that led her to make use of Big John's correlative search capabilities. Eileen wasn't worried about attaining authorization for her initial search. It fell within the span of her forensic examination of the hack that Gregory's team had pulled off. But with every query, Big John led her farther astray, quickly invalidating her working hypothesis. Worse, she found herself seduced by the quest, her "How?" changed to "Why?"

From what she'd learned, it was clear that Eileen wasn't the first to snoop this trail. Denise Jennings's digital fingerprints were everywhere she looked. But Denise's chain of Big John queries had suddenly ceased. Apparently that train of discovery had finally frightened Denise too badly to continue.

As Eileen looked at the evidence before her, she couldn't help envy Denise's good judgment. But now that she'd seen the rabbit disappear down this hole, Eileen had no choice but to follow.

CHAPTER 108

Siena's Piazza del Campo was almost empty. A few tourists stood atop the fish-bone patterned red bricks, peering over the wrought-iron fence in front of the Gaia Fountain, snapping pictures, applying suntan lotion to pasty white legs, or texting friends who had wandered off to see the Siena Cathedral or one of the medieval Tuscan city's other tourist destinations.

Heather, as Inga Hedstrom, had been with the Swiss private security firm Paladin for three weeks. Her current assignment involved babysitting Bayad al'Fahd, the yuppie son of a Saudi prince, on his upper Tuscany tour. Not that Bayad didn't have his own bodyguards. He had a half dozen of them. But young al'Fahd was an important new client of Credit Suisse and the second largest Swiss bank had extended the extra protection as a courtesy. Thus Heather found herself the upper-class equivalent of a new account microwave oven.

Getting hired by Paladin had been the easy part. Inga Hedstrom, a dual US and Swiss citizen, was twenty-nine and 120 pounds, and stood five feet eight inches tall. With her boyishly short blonde hair and blue eyes, only her icy demeanor kept her from being attractive. Jack had created an elaborate black ops profile, including a lot of dead former colleagues who raved about her work in postmortem write-ups. With the ability to infiltrate all the appropriate record systems, she'd had no difficulty ensuring her security clearance and records appeared in all the right places. And since she had left CIA employ six months ago and all her CIA missions were classified and close-hold, they avoided broad scrutiny.

Heather liked being Inga, but she didn't particularly like this assignment. Once it became clear that she had no interest in doing anything other than her job, Bayad had told her to stay away from his inner circle. Assuming she didn't know more than cursory Arabic, he had begun laughing it up with two of his biggest bodyguards. Wasn't it funny that the Swiss bank actually thought this woman could enhance his protection, when all she was fit to enhance was his harem?

On the upside, not being allowed within his inner circle meant she didn't have to listen to the moron's views on women, or anything else for that matter. On the downside, she was too far away from Bayad to prevent the attack when it came.

She trailed ten meters behind Bayad's pack as they approached the string of outdoor eateries lining the piazza's northwest side. Along the dining area's right side, two men busily unloaded chairs from the rear of a white van, much to the irate restaurant manager's dismay. A vision flashed through her brain a second before the vehicle began to move, its wheels laying a thin layer of smoking rubber toward Bayad.

As Heather sprinted forward, pulling the Glock from her shoulder holster, the two chair stackers wheeled, pointing previously concealed MP5 submachine guns toward the group of surprised Saudis. Heather's first bullet caught the nearest man in the chest, the nine-millimeter Parabellum sending him tumbling onto an adjacent table. But a woman carrying a child blocked her line of fire to the second assassin, enabling him to unleash a fusillade of automatic weapon fire into Bayad's clustered bodyguards. Heather's second round struck just above the bridge of his nose, its mist trail giving him a momentary red halo as he fell.

One of the two remaining bodyguards shoved Bayad out of the van's path, covering his employer with his body as the van slammed into his partner's rising gun hand, wedging it and the man's face deep inside the front grill. The passenger door opened away from Heather as she found her view blocked by terrified patrons. As she rounded the rear of the van, she heard a double tap and saw the bleeding bodyguard roll off the wide-eyed Bayad. Seeing the assassin's trigger finger tighten, she fired again, striking the man's gun hand as the weapon discharged into the paving stones beside Bayad's head.

And then she was on him, her kick buckling the assassin's right knee as she pistol-whipped him across the side of his head. As the big man hit the pavement, the squall of the van's tires sent Heather diving to her right, shoulder-rolling into a shooter's crouch in time to see the white van skid into a racing turn, its back doors slamming open as it accelerated away across the piazza. Taking a forty-five-degree angle away from her, it prevented her from getting a clear shot at the driver. Heather put four rounds into the right tires and another four into the white side panel, but if she hit the driver, she couldn't tell. Skidding around the corner, the van disappeared down Via Casato di Sotto.

Heather ejected the magazine, slapped in a fresh one, and leaned down to check the unconscious assassin. His pulse and the blood matting the hair on the right side of his head told her he wouldn't be waking up anytime soon. Kicking his pistol away, she did a rapid pat-down, pulled the man's ankle knife from its sheath, and turned her back on him.

Bayad had scrambled back against one of the tables, pushing the chairs aside until he was half under it, his breath coming in short, hyperventilating gasps. As Heather knelt beside him, the wail of sirens echoed through the streets. Holstering her weapon, she knelt beside the Saudi.

"Mr. al'Fahd. Are you injured?"

"What?"

"Look at me. Are you injured?"

As his eyes focused on her face, a wave of relief washed his features. "No. I don't think so. Just bruises, Allah be praised."

Four police cars raced into the piazza, spilling heavily armed blue-and-gray-clad *polizia* onto the asphalt thirty meters to either side of her. Seeing Heather kneeling beside the seated Bayad, in the midst of so many dead bodies, they advanced with submachine guns leveled.

A loudspeaker blared in Italian. "On your stomach, arms and legs spread. Now!"

Heather flopped facedown, spread-eagled.

Bayad hesitated. "But I…"

The message blared again in heavily accented English.

"Down on your stomach! Arms and legs spread! Do it now!"

Bayad complied.

Immediately Heather felt a knee in her back as a steel handcuff crunched tight around her right hand, then her left, as they were drawn together behind her back. In seconds she was disarmed and thrust in the back of one police car, while Bayad disappeared into another.

Leaning back in her seat, Heather looked out the window as the car sped through the narrow streets.

Memorizing the scenery as she passed it by, she nodded. Siena really was a very lovely city.

CHAPTER 109

Mark wriggled into a crawl space barely wide enough to squeeze his body through, deep into the MINGSTER's belly. Officially it was called the Matter to Energy Conversion Facility, but nobody besides Dr. Stephenson called it that. It, along with its other end in the ATLAS cavern, was the biggest jumble of electrical wiring and cables on earth, and that didn't even take into account the cooling required for the superconducting cables. Because of the need for demon speed in construction and the need to minimize the amount of cable through which all that power had to be pushed, everything was placed as close together as possible. It was the thing that made for these tight crawls.

Unfortunately the project's lead engineer, Gerhardt Werner, had stuck him on the wrong end of the construction. Mark didn't want to be buried in the MINGSTER. He needed to be working with the crew in the ATLAS cavern. There was a way to get transferred to the other team, but it took time, and that was something he didn't have much of.

Mark needed to get his team ahead of schedule and make it obvious that he was the reason. The ATLAS crew was already behind; he just had to widen that gap. So Mark worked double shifts. He would have liked to work triple, but working around the clock without sleep would have attracted the wrong kind of attention. Between the double shifts and the speed and quality of his work, he had become the engine propelling the project forward.

In normal times, the union would have tried to put a thumb on him to slow down and quit making others look bad, but these weren't normal times. So they left the muscular Swede with the Viking beard and long blond mane to himself and his work. That was fine with Mark. He wasn't here to make friends and drink beer.

As he finished wiring the current section, his favorite music mix thundered in his mind. Mark worked at the one thing he could directly control, confident in the knowledge that by the end of today's second shift, his crew would be farther ahead of the ATLAS team. Picturing the project leaders, sitting in their meetings, staring at their Gantt charts, he smiled. Soon now, the picture of what he was accomplishing would leap off the page at them. Then his boss would have no choice but to move him to where he should have been all along.

CHAPTER 110

Dr. Peter Trotsky stared as his postdoctoral assistant turned her back on him and headed toward the stairs that would take her up, out of the ATLAS cavern. Dr. Nika Ivanovich was driving him crazy. Perhaps she already had.

When she was on her game, she was by far the most brilliant scientific mind and computer scientist he'd ever known, including that pompous bastard Stephenson. But there were times when Nika was just plain unreliable. Like right now, for instance.

Stephenson had just handed him a list of upgrades he wanted on the stasis field controller software, and he expected the changes to be implemented and tested by this time tomorrow evening. A month's work in twenty-four hours. But when Peter had shown it to Nika, she'd laughed her seductive laugh and said she'd sleep on it.

The anger had bubbled up inside him, but somehow, as he looked into those blue eyes, he'd gone all warm and fuzzy inside. He'd told her that was a good idea.

A good idea!

Now all he could do was watch the petite young woman in her tight jeans and white Tori Amos T-shirt walk away from him, several spears of her spiked blonde hair aimed straight at his heart. God. He was sixty-five years old, yet somehow this fascinating young woman had him wishing he were thirty again. Shit! Even if he were thirty, he'd never be able to handle a woman like that.

Looking at the sheaf of requirements in his hands, he walked over to the workstation, set the papers under the keyboard, and turned toward the stairs that would carry him up to his own bunk.

"Where are you going?"

Dr. Trotsky turned to face Stephenson. He wasn't scared of Stephenson, like the others. He'd seen it all before, and knew the type. Nothing he could do would be good enough anyway, so he might as well just do what he thought best.

"First I design, then I code, then I test. Don't worry. You'll have your changes on schedule."

Stephenson scowled at him. "I better."

Trotsky shook his head, turned, and walked away. What choice did he have? He couldn't program fast enough to get this done if he worked all week. Only Nika could. He'd just have to hope a fresh Nika could deliver tomorrow's miracle. Otherwise the trip back to Vladivostok was likely to be unpleasant.

CHAPTER 111

The blood drained from Denise Jennings's face as she listened to what Eileen Wu had to say. Since she'd been listening for more than forty minutes, Denise thought that by now she must look like a starving vampire. She certainly felt like one.

The NSA's newest prodigy had traced every one of Denise's Big John queries and had figured out the same things Denise had. Worse, she'd kept digging and, despite Denise's objections, was determined to bring her up to speed.

Why had she opened her door and let the young computer scientist inside her house? Denise had recognized how odd it was for Eileen to be in Columbia at nine p.m. Her house was in the opposite direction, in Annapolis. Plus the girl was a notorious loner. Still, Denise had invited her inside.

Now they both knew too much.

Dear God. Admiral Riles. Jack Gregory and his entire team. Now the Smythe and McFarland kids. All of them set up by their own government. That didn't take into account all the top government officials who had been killed. All of it to protect the Rho Project. And although Dr. Donald Stephenson had a perfect alibi—he'd been halfway around the world when it happened—Eileen Wu believed he'd somehow generated the November Anomaly. Denise believed it too.

Denise didn't want to join the others who'd fought against Stephenson's Rho agenda, but unless she managed to divert Eileen, this headstrong young woman was going to get them both killed. And for what? The damage had already been done. Besides, Denise had already done her part. She'd tipped off that investigative reporter Freddy Hagerman. It was time for him to step up.

Suddenly Denise felt Eileen's dark eyes on her. Maybe there was still a way out of this.

"Eileen, I'm stunned. The stuff you've uncovered goes far beyond what I found out."

"Because you quit looking."

Denise shook her head. "Not entirely. I'm not an investigator or a field operative. And for reasons I'm sure you understand, I couldn't take this to anyone in the agency. So, rather than give up, I took it to someone who has managed to dig into the Rho Project and stay alive. I met with Freddy Hagerman."

"The reporter."

"Pulitzer Prize winner. He matches his reputation."

"So you handed your responsibility over to him."

"That's not how I see it, but if you do, that's OK with me."

"And you want me to do the same."

"I'm just saying you should think about it. It's not your specialty, but it's what he does. From all accounts, he's quite good at it."

"I'm not good at quitting."

"Think of him as a teammate."

Eileen stared at her for several more moments, then rose and turned toward the door.

"Think about it."

Opening the door, Eileen paused.

"We'll see."

Then the night carried her away.

CHAPTER 112

Charley Richardson, Paladin's security team commander at the LHC site, didn't like changes to his team this late in the game. But Bruce Conrad had gotten his ass kicked outside a bar in Meyrin. Charley would have liked to meet the man who could dismantle Bruce the way this one had. Paladin should find and hire him.

So now Charley was one man down. Worse, the company was sending him a woman as Bruce's replacement. He stared down at the file on his desk. On paper she was dynamite. Charley had seen plenty of men who were dynamite on paper but didn't stack up when the shit hit the fan. His men came from all over, all ex–special ops from a half dozen different countries. They'd earned their spots on this team. It didn't matter that this job was crap, turning his warriors into a bunch of facility guards alternating shifts, mostly checking people's paperwork, controlling access to the MINGSTER and the ATLAS cavern. He still needed people he knew.

But this assignment had come from Jacob Kroner himself. No way could Charley tell Paladin's hard-nosed president he didn't want the woman. That was all right. Just because she made it on to the team didn't mean she'd last long enough to be a thorn in his side.

Charley rose to his feet, slid into his coat, and stepped out into the cold parking lot where he'd assembled his team for this announcement. As he looked at them, seventeen cocky bastards, each one a major ass-kicker, he grinned.

"We've been assigned Bruce's replacement. Her name is Inga Hedstrom. She arrives this afternoon."

He held up his hand to quiet the low mutters.

"You know I like to choose my own people. This one's out of my hands. But she still has to measure up."

Charley clasped his hands behind his back, the posture thrusting his massive chest forward. "I'm sure you gentlemen will show her a proper welcome."

Artan Yuzman, the larger of the team's two Turks, chuckled. "You can count on it, boss."

CHAPTER 113

Mark wouldn't have imagined ever wanting to thank Dr. Stephenson for anything. But he'd been responsible for Mark's reassignment to the ATLAS electrical construction team. That would have happened without outside help, but after Stephenson had looked at the Gantt charts, he'd immediately seen the correlation between Mark's assignments and a tremendous increase in productivity. So now Mark was the ATLAS team foreman.

He began his new job by instructing his crew to continue as planned while he spent a couple of days familiarizing himself with the Cage, a monstrous construct of steel supports and metal grating that extended from the cavern floor to the ceiling, ninety meters above. The Cage housed all the power cables routed into the ATLAS cavern from the MINGSTER and provided support for the cooling equipment required to maintain superconductivity in the primary power lines. It was a towering steel structure so tightly packed with cable and equipment that workers had to worm their way through crawlways that some of them refused to enter.

Mark traced every inch of cable that had been run and every electrical component already installed, comparing each item against the memorized plans. Although he found a number of minor variances or shortcuts, he found no significant deviations until halfway through Wednesday's second shift. Deep within the most densely packed vertical section, he identified a cable that wasn't on the plans.

Fascinated, he stayed on into the third shift, following the mysterious line down toward the cavern floor. The way it meandered down through other cable groupings, it had clearly been installed with the intent of making what Mark was doing almost impossible.

At floor level the cable split into four lines, made to look like standard 220-volt, fifty-hertz power lines, that disappeared into groupings of similar lines. The third shift ended at midnight, but Mark continued. At four thirty a.m. he finally stopped, convinced that he knew where each of the four cables terminated. The odd part was that they disappeared into four separate prefabricated load-bearing steel-and-concrete buttresses. There was nothing electrical in these buttresses. At least, there wasn't supposed to be.

Returning to the spot high up in the Cage where he'd first discovered the mysterious cable, Mark began tracing it back the other way, toward the spot where the Cage exited the cavern roof. Reaching the level of the skywalk, the scaffolding walkway that connected the Cage to the steel scaffolding lining the cavern walls, Mark squeezed between two trusses and stopped. High up, along the backside of one of the trusses, the cable passed through an encyclopedia-sized, unmarked metal box.

Working his way back out of the tight space, Mark moved to one of the electrical tool cabinets mounted at regular intervals throughout the Cage, grabbed the tools he needed, and returned to the mysterious box.

Unfastening the cover, Mark took extreme care to avoid tilting or vibrating the case, easing it open while holding the penlight in his teeth, just enough to give him a glimpse inside. Not good. Attached to the inside of the removable front cover, a small glass ampule held a silvery liquid bubble at one end. A mercury switch. If he'd just pulled the thing open, that shiny little bubble would have rolled to the other end. Mark didn't care to find out what would happen if the silver globule made that trip.

Mark removed the cover, keeping its angle unchanged, and examined the wiring inside the case. It formed a simple circuit connected to a currently unset digital timer. Whether the mercury switch was rigged to bypass the timer or send an alert wasn't immediately clear and Mark didn't feel like putting in the effort to figure it out right now. He'd already figured out what this whole set of cabling represented.

Some government, probably the United States, had rigged a fail-safe device. Within each of those four prefabbed buttresses was a nuclear bomb. It was the only thing that made sense, even though it didn't make any. They had to know that a nuclear detonation would just feed the anomaly, turning it into an instant black hole. So they'd put these here as a last resort.

So long as Stephenson's wormhole device worked, they'd never be used. Replacing the cover, Mark wormed his way out to the railing surrounding the Cage's top level and onto the skywalk. It was time to take a moment to meditate and contact Heather. He'd let his personal savant figure out what she wanted him to do about the nukes.

CHAPTER 114

"A training accident?" Charley Richardson slammed his fist down on the desk as he looked at his executive officer.

Bob Jones shrugged. "Shit happens."

"Like hell it does. Not on my team. Not to three of my top people."

Charley got to his feet, stretching his six-and-a-half-foot frame.

"You're saying Artan and Yuzman both took a tumble while racing on the confidence course?"

"Yep. Right near the top of the high log climb. Artan slipped, tumbled into Hedo, and they both fell."

"Right on top of Diego."

"Actually Diego tried to break their fall."

Charley stood nose to nose with Bob, his gray eyes locking with the other man's brown ones. "Now tell me the real story. No attribution."

"Does that apply to the whole team?"

"It does."

Bob nodded, plopping down on the couch across from Charley's desk. "You're going to want to sit down for this one, boss.

"You know how you told the boys to show our new recruit a proper welcome, make sure she has what it takes?"

"I remember."

"Well, they've been giving her the business. Nothing major. Just screwing with her stuff. Sexual comments alternating with the silent treatment. Letting her know the president may have put her here, but she isn't one of us. Basically making her life hell.

"This morning she'd had enough of it. We were formed up for PT out where we've rigged our hand-to-hand-combat training pit, when she stepped out of formation and walked right up beside me, in front of them all.

"I thought she was going to break down, call it quits, start pleading, or something. You could hear the fellas laughing, so I stepped aside and let her have the floor. You know what she said?"

"No, I don't know what she said, and I don't want to guess. Get to the damned point."

"She just stood there, with the team gathered around her in an arc. I'll never forget her voice if I live a thousand years. It was throaty, smooth as silk, the sexiest voice I've ever heard. She looked them all up and down, then said, 'Let's make a deal. You pick your best man. If he beats me hand to hand here in the pit, every one of you can have a turn at me, and I'll be the best piece of ass you've ever had.'

"Shit, you could've heard a pin drop. There was so much testosterone in the air it was flammable.

"Then she said, 'But if I win, you're going to show me the same respect you show each other. Do we have a deal?'"

"And?"

"And she had a deal. The boys argued about who would do the fighting, but finally Diego Vasquez won out."

Charley nodded. Vasquez was the only guy on the team stronger than he was, and quick as a mongoose.

"So what happened?"

"Diego came at her full bore, just exploded out of the pack. It was the damnedest thing I've ever seen. It was like Inga knew his moves before he made them. She cracked his ribs on that first charge, just used his momentum to add power to her kick. It dropped him to his knees, left him gasping for air.

"But she was already on his back, her arms locked around his neck in a submission choke hold, cutting off the blood supply to his brain. Diego's eyes just stared in disbelief, then rolled up in his head. Once he was out, she dropped him at her feet.

"I was so surprised, the two Turks charged before I could stop them. Artan reached her first, tried a flying takedown and got a mouthful of his own teeth when her elbow flattened him. Hedo pulled up in a fighter's stance. He might as well have been blindfolded with his arms tied behind his back. Her first kick broke his kneecap, her next one caved in the side of his face. Once he was on the ground she stomped his rib cage. Thought she was going to kill him."

"About that time, Artan distracted her by climbing back to his feet. He didn't stay there long though. Anyway, when she was done, she turned around to face the rest of us. I swear to God, she wasn't even breathing hard. All she said was 'Anyone else?' but she didn't get any volunteers. Then she turned her back on us and walked away.

"So that's why those three are in the hospital. Diego's in the best shape. He'll probably be released tomorrow. Artan and Hedo are going to be there for a while."

"I guess she didn't take kindly to the Turks breaking her deal."

"I tell you what, boss, I wouldn't screw with her."

Charley nodded. "So it was a training accident."

"Just like I said."

"Looks like we've got a new teammate. Spread the word."

Bob rose to his feet, opened the door, and paused.

"I don't have to."

The door to the command hooch banged closed behind him.

CHAPTER 115

The knock on his door roused Freddy from the light doze that had almost allowed the glass of Crown Royal to slip from his fingers.

Shit. What time was it? The LED lights on the cable box read 11:45. Who the hell would come knocking at midnight?

Freddy thought about grabbing his snub-nosed thirty-eight. But what if it was the Ripper? The thirty-eight would just get him killed.

Setting the glass on the end table, Freddy slid out of the easy chair and stumbled to the door. Wiping a hand over his face, he took a deep breath to clear his head and opened the door.

It took a full five seconds for Freddy's mind to process the girl standing before him. She was a petite Asian in jeans and a purple camisole that left her navel exposed. At least he didn't see any piercings.

"Wrong house. The party must be down the street."

"Freddy Hagerman?"

"What of it?"

"I understand you met with Denise Jennings of the NSA at the Thomas Jefferson Building."

Now she had his attention. Freddy motioned her toward the couch, but she remained where she was.

"I won't be here long enough to come in or sit down. I came here to give you this."

She handed him a leather valise he had mistaken for her purse, and stepped back, her eyes as black as her hair.

"I think you'll find that I finished the work Denise started. I understand you know what to do with it."

"Mind if I ask a couple of questions?" Actually, he had more than a couple of questions.

"No need. If the answer isn't in what I just gave you, I don't know it."

"Your name?"

"Good-bye, Mr. Hagerman."

She turned and walked down the dark driveway and climbed inside a small car. No interior light came on when she opened the door. Neither did she turn on her headlights when she drove away. So much for getting the license plate number.

Freddy stared after her as she turned the corner at the end of his block. Then he closed the door, walked into the kitchen, and spread the valise's contents across the kitchen table. Three coffeepots later, with the first gray of dawn lightening his windows, he knew that she had spoken the truth.

He also knew that if the Ripper hadn't told him not to publish the story until after November Anomaly Gateway Day, he would already be on his way to New York.

CHAPTER 116

Donald Stephenson paced the ATLAS cavern like a lion in a cage. It was strangely quiet. He'd given the entire staff eight hours off, instructing the G-Day crew to report promptly at four a.m. to begin the six-hour countdown.

They'd been shocked. The cavern always had a night crew. But tonight, Donald wanted to savor the culmination of his life's work alone.

As he walked among the massive equipment, his footsteps echoing, and looked up at the steel scaffolding draping the cavern walls, a sudden chill raised gooseflesh on his arms. It reminded him of another November night, so many years ago, when he'd stood in another man-made cavern, alone with the Rho Ship.

The truth was, that moment had been the purest of his life. The sense of discovery, the revelations. The renewed sense of purpose when, even though many thought him successful, in his mind he had just been spinning his wheels.

Mankind imagined itself a highly evolved species…or, even more bizarrely, as the one, all-powerful God's greatest creation. But on that first night when Donald had made his way, alone, into the Rho Ship, he had discovered proof of what he had always thought to be true. Man was no more than an adolescent species on a backwater planet in an aging galaxy.

If the Rho Ship hadn't been so horribly damaged in its combat with the Altreian starship, it wouldn't have taken Donald so long to prepare the way for mankind's next evolutionary leap. But through all these years of baby steps and setbacks, Donald had persisted, until those steps had finally deposited him on destiny's doorstep.

Odd how his fate seemed entwined with Thanksgiving, like some cosmic circadian rhythm. For the first time in a very long time, a genuine smile creased his ageless face.

Tomorrow, on Thanksgiving Day in America, he would change the world.

CHAPTER 117

The Anomaly Transport and Control Center (ATACC) looked nothing like anything Ted Cantrell had imagined. When he and his CNN news crew had arrived to begin setup for the most important broadcast in history, he'd expected to find something like the NASA Flight Control Room at the Johnson Space Center in Houston, a room filled with banks of high-tech workstations arranged in a neat grid in front of a wall filled with large display screens. This felt more like the Batcave.

The ATLAS cavern was huge, the walls draped with steel lattice construction, grated metal walkways leading to metal stairs, each of these girded with steel rails that were all that prevented someone from stumbling into a deadly fall. High up along one of the topmost levels, international camera crews and media had been allotted space to set up cameras and on-site reporting stations. Every available space along the long, narrow walkway was packed with equipment and cables, with open space reserved only for the network anchors.

Eschewing an anchor desk, Ted had decided to stand back against the blue railing, allowing the camera to frame him against the huge cavern that opened up behind him. Despite the tight operating space, the view was breathtaking. Its great form rising thirty meters from the central cavern floor, the Rho Gateway Device resembled an inverted horseshoe magnet, its metal walls five meters thick, its outer surface sprouting appendages that looked like the buds on a potato left too long in its sack. Huge cables snaked out from a massive steel structure that rose three hundred feet from the cavern floor, terminating on those buds or disappearing beneath the ATACC. They were the lines designed to carry more power than any power plant on Earth had ever generated.

As Ted stared at them, he felt a sudden tightening of his throat. Despite the thick layers of insulation that surrounded each of those cables, he wondered if that power might not burst free, sending uncontrolled electrical arcs crawling across all this steel latticework.

But if he felt dangerously exposed up here, what must it have felt like to be one of the hundreds of scientists and technicians who occupied and surrounded the ATACC? Rather than being constructed at a safe distance from the gateway, the control center was snuggled up against it, wrapping the monstrous piece of equipment as if they were two lovers spooning up in bed. Safety and beauty had been sacrificed at the altar of speed, reducing the length of thousands of cables and putting scientists in position to directly observe and react as required.

Ten meters from the gateway mouth stood the large metal shell that housed the vacuum chamber and electromagnetic containment fields designed to slow the November Anomaly's death spiral. If all went well, they wouldn't need it much longer. If things didn't go well it wouldn't matter.

According to top scientists on the program, the anomaly's descent into instability continued to accelerate as Dr. Stephenson's equations had predicted. If the Gateway Device failed today, there wouldn't be a second chance.

The noise along the high ramp picked up as foreign news organizations began their broadcasts. Jan Fernandez, his assigned makeup artist, stepped forward to pat his face down with a powder puff, erasing the beads of sweat that had popped out on his brow despite the cool temperature here in the cavern.

"Thirty seconds to air."

Ted nodded at his producer, took several deep breaths, and, just as he'd done in crisis after crisis around the world, put on his game face.

From his left to his right, the three eye-level monitors mounted on the walkway's metal wall showed CNN's Atlanta feed, his own image, and a tight shot of Dr. Stephenson sitting on a high perch above the other ATACC scientists, surrounded by keyboards and monitors.

Bob Marley, the Atlanta anchor, spoke in his ear.

"We go now to the best crisis reporter anywhere, CNN's own Ted Cantrell."

It was showtime.

CHAPTER 118

Cohort Commander Ketaan-Ra moved down the line, inspecting his assault team with the confidence that came from many such missions across the galaxy. Its mission wasn't easy, but it wasn't complicated either. Wait for the gateway to synchronize with the signal from the far end, activate the portal, then charge through to secure the other side, establishing a beachhead for the army that would follow.

Then all the heavy firepower and advanced weaponry available to the follow-on force would bring yet another world into the Kasari Collective. But that army would not be allowed through the gateway until his team had finished its work.

His special assault team would take some losses, there was little doubt of that. It happened in almost every assault, the result of being denied any ranged weapons that might damage or disrupt the far-gate. The far-end gateways were always fragile technological implementations, the best these primitive worlds could construct, even given a world ship tutorial. Denied even low-power disrupter weapons, his team would rely on the initial surprise and shock their assault would generate and on their martial arts training, bladed weapons, and nano-enhanced bodies to secure the objective.

There would be some security presence on the far end, but it would be minimal. It always was. Nobody opened a Kasari gateway with the expectation of welcoming in an assault force. The planet expected what the world ship had conditioned it to expect, the reason they'd gone to all the effort to construct the gateway. So the special assault team would rock them back on their heels and another portal would be secured. Then the signal would be given and the army would pour through, extending the perimeter, bringing the transporters, sky riders, heavy equipment, and the rest of the Kasari logistics train.

Finishing his inspection of his chosen dozen, Ketaan-Ra motioned his sergeant forward, assuming the position of attention as his top veteran inspected Ketaan-Ra with the same meticulous routine that he'd used on the team. Standard operating procedure. Nobody went into combat without undergoing a thorough inspection, especially not commanders.

As the sergeant moved around him, touching each item of equipment, his comm unit sounded the alert. The far gateway had powered up, preparing to go active. Once that happened, it would only be a matter of allowing the two gates to synchronize signals before the portal stabilized.

A warm glow worked its way up from his two feet into Ketaan-Ra's legs and torso, spreading into his four arms, his neck, and then his head.

It was almost go time.

CHAPTER 119

Even for Ted, reporting on the culmination of the November Anomaly project was a little overwhelming. As he started in on his coverage, he knew he sounded a little unsure of himself. As he continued, though, his veteran instincts kicked in, the nerves went away, and it all became automatic.

Having hit his stride, Ted gestured toward the cavern that fell away before his platform. "What we are about to see is the single most important event since the dawn of life on this planet, the culmination of the most ambitious science and engineering project ever conceived by man. During the next hour, Dr. Stephenson and the scientists working on the November Anomaly project will attempt to use technologies reverse-engineered from the Rho Project alien starship. Some of these technologies have never before been tested, much less utilized on this scale.

"Over the last eight months, in the huge cavern behind me and aboveground a short distance from here, the world's best scientists and engineers have constructed four devices crucial to pulling off today's attempt at saving the human race. The first is the only aboveground component, a power plant built using alien matter disrupter technology that will provide the awesome power required by the systems here in the ATLAS cavern."

Ted was well aware that his TV audience was seeing not just him and the ATLAS cavern, but a sequence of 3-D computer animations designed to illustrate what he was talking about.

"Two more critical pieces of equipment are not visible in the cavern below, buried as they are within the walls of the equipment on the cavern floor below. These are actually two identical copies of the same thing, a device called a stasis field generator. They are designed to generate and manipulate powerful force fields that will be used to isolate the November Anomaly and move it into the gateway that will transport it into space."

The shot shifted to the camera showing the ATACC, gradually zooming out until the massive Gateway Device filled the screen.

"Right now you are looking at the heart of the project, the Rho Gateway Device."

Pausing momentarily for dramatic effect, Ted continued. "This is the engineering marvel that will create a wormhole, through which the scientists will push the November Anomaly using the stasis field generators. Once the anomaly has been pushed into the wormhole, the Rho Gateway Device will be powered down, closing the wormhole, and eliminating the threat to our planet, forever."

The lighting in the cavern acquired an amber hue as the PA system sounded.

"Initial stasis field power countdown commencing...five, four, three, two, one. Engaging power."

There was a brief pause, followed by another announcement.

"Stasis field generator power steady at ten percent on both systems. Commencing one-minute countdown to full power ramp."

Ted turned sideways, to enhance the camera's view of his profile silhouetted against the gateway.

"Now it starts getting dicey. This countdown will take us to the point where scientists bring the two stasis field generators to full power. While it's nowhere close to the amount of power the Gateway Device will use, it's still more than the total amount of power used by the Large Hadron Collider over the entire course of its operation."

He found he was sweating profusely. It all came down to this…

Again the loudspeaker sounded out the final ten seconds of the countdown.

"Initiating power ramp…fifty percent…seventy percent… ninety-five percent…stasis field generator power stabilized at one hundred percent. All systems nominal."

The sound of clapping echoed up from the cavern floor.

Ted smiled, relieved. "You can feel the tension in that applause."

The PA system squawked. "Commencing one-minute countdown to Rho Gateway power ramp."

Ted turned back to face the camera. "I have to admit to a little dry mouth. Unlike the stasis field generator power-up, the gateway is going to be ramped to full power without a pause. The scientists will power it up, but they won't activate it until after the November Anomaly is isolated by the primary stasis field generator."

As the final countdown sounded, the camera shifted to a tight shot of the Gateway Device.

"Gateway device power ramp initiated."

Ted felt his hair stand on end, but he couldn't be sure if it was static electricity in the air or the tension in his body. In front of him, the producer and the camera people had a kind of tension, too, their bodies just going through the motions. They appeared to Ted like poorly designed computer simulations of the team he knew so well.

"Power at fifty percent…seventy-five…ninety…ninety-five…ninety-eight…"

There was a brief pause in the announcements.

"Gateway device power stabilized at ninety-nine point three percent of maximum."

Once again the sound of applause rang out from the scientists and technicians assembled below.

Ted exhaled. "I know you must be wondering why they're clapping, since we didn't get to one hundred percent power. I sure am. For an explanation, we go to Dr. Gerta Freiholt, a physicist from the matter disrupter team. Thank you for taking the time to help us understand what is happening."

The camera shifted to a white-coated woman with her gray hair pulled back in a severe bun. "My pleasure. As you can tell from the reaction from our ATACC crew, ninety-nine percent power is excellent. The system was designed with a certain amount of tolerance. While we would have loved to hit the one hundred percent target, anything over ninety-five percent is good."

"That's good to know. We have a couple of minutes until the next phase. Can you give us a quick overview of what scientists will be trying to do with the stasis field generators?"

"Well, first they are going to use the primary stasis field generator to capture and isolate the November Anomaly. Right now the anomaly is contained by powerful magnetic fields within a vacuum chamber."

The camera switched to a view of the steel ball suspended a few meters in front of the Gateway Device opening.

"When the stasis field is directed at the anomaly containment apparatus, it will instantaneously cut through all that steel, which will fall away onto the cavern floor. However, the stasis field will move at the speed of light, so before the pieces of the vacuum chamber have begun to move, the field will wrap itself around the anomaly, maintaining the vacuum and preventing any external matter from perturbing the anomaly."

"What about the metal casing? Isn't it going to fall right into the anomaly and won't all that metal knock it around?"

"No. It won't be able to touch it. Think of the stasis field as a force field that is so powerful that it can repel anything away from the anomaly. Even an explosion couldn't penetrate it."

"Sounds like the deflector shields on the starship *Enterprise*."

"That's one way to think about it."

"So what is the second stasis field generator for?"

"Good question. Once the primary stasis field generator has captured the anomaly, scientists will activate the Rho Gateway Device to create a wormhole into deep space. However, an opening into the vacuum of space would immediately depressurize the facility, sucking out the air and all of us with it. The secondary stasis field generator will form an invisible door sealing off the Gateway Device opening, before the gateway is activated. Once the wormhole has formed, scientists will confirm the far end coordinates to ensure it's not too close to Earth or within a star. Then they will use the primary stasis field generator to move the anomaly to the gateway, modulating the two stasis fields to allow the first to pass through the second and release the anomaly into the wormhole."

"And after that?"

"I would guess there's going to be a big party."

The camera shifted back to Ted's nervous smile. "Let's all hope and pray that happens."

"Approaching final countdown to anomaly capture." The last ten seconds of the countdown echoed through the cavern. "Initiating anomaly capture."

With a sound like thunder, the huge steel anomaly containment device came apart and crashed to the concrete floor. For several seconds, the only sound that could be heard was the reverberating echoes of its fall.

Then the alarm sounded.

"Warning…primary stasis field generator power at eighty-two percent and falling. Stasis field degradation detected."

At the ATACC, a bearded Scandinavian technician ran toward one of the large electronic racks, his long blond hair flowing out behind him as he leaped up onto the second level of equipment, ripped out a panel, rolled onto the floor, and slid his torso inside.

On his perch, high above the others, Dr. Stephenson shifted from one keyboard to the next, pounding his fist on the desktop in frustration. Suddenly his voice took over the PA system.

"Initiate procedure to swap primary and secondary stasis field generator controls. Dr. Trotsky, override the con from your position. Now!"

As the pulsing alarm blared, Ted stared in horror as the air surrounding the point where the anomaly containment device had previously been suspended acquired a pale-blue glow within what he could only imagine was the failing spherical stasis field.

A flurry of activity along the near side of the ATACC pulled his eyes away from the glowing sphere. Several people had moved to surround a gray-haired scientist at one of the ATACC workstations who had slumped forward over the controls.

Remembering who he was, Ted pulled himself together and pointed. "Get me a camera on that."

The video feed shifted, zooming in on the group of scientists gathered behind the workstation. A young woman in a white lab coat pushed her way through, physically lifting the scientist from the chair, handing his unconscious body to two men, then sliding into his chair. The woman's hands moved across multiple keyboards, her actions a blur, backdropped by a bank of flat-panel displays. The movements of her lithe body, the way her short, spiked, platinum-blonde hair framed her face, gave Ted a déjà vu moment, reminding him of a hot pop star rising up into the sky above her European concert audience.

"Warning…primary stasis field generator power at forty percent and falling. Stasis field failure imminent."

As he continued to watch the exotic young physicist work, Ted heard a low moan of dread rise up from the other scientists, a moan that entered the microphones and drifted out to a network audience of billions.

~ ~ ~

President Jackson stared at the CNN broadcast, surrounded by his national security team. General Smith's tense voice sounded through the encrypted satellite speakerphone.

"Mr. President. We are out of time."

Looking around the room, meeting the eyes of each member of his staff, each head nodding in affirmation, the president swallowed, then spoke with reluctant authority.

"General Smith, I authorize you to immediately implement Anomaly Fail-Safe Plan Bravo."

"Mr. President, I read back. *General Smith, I authorize you to immediately implement Anomaly Fail-Safe Plan Bravo.*"

"Confirmed."

"Roger, Mr. President. Smith out."

Raising his eyes once again to the television screen, President Jackson spoke again, his voice barely rising above a whisper.

"God help us all."

~ ~ ~

General Raymond Smith swiveled his chair and nodded to the only other person in the command and control bunker beneath Ramstein Air Base, just outside Kaiserslautern, Germany: Major Bob Glendale.

"You heard the president's authorization?"

"Yes, sir."

"Open your envelope."

As Bob reached for the envelope on the workstation in front of him, General Smith turned to face front, picked up a knife, and slit open his own brown manila envelope, spilling the contents onto his own workstation.

He glanced at the checklist, but he knew it by heart. This wasn't Anomaly Fail-Safe Plan Alpha. This was Bravo. That meant there would be no warning to the poor bastards inside the ATLAS cavern. The president had just given the nuke-it-now order.

Picking up the cylindrical red key with the #1 tag dangling from it, the general glanced over at Major Glendale, who had his own key in hand.

"Insert keys."

The major inserted his key in the console as General Smith mirrored his action.

"Activate on my mark. Mark."

As the keys turned in unison, a bright green LED lit up on the panel in front of General Smith. Flipping up the red trigger guard, General Smith took a single deep breath, pushing from his mind the thought of the innocents soon to die. Then he thumbed the toggle switch to DETONATE.

CHAPTER 120

Watching the imagery from a dozen separate worm fibers, Raul rubbed his hands in anticipation. Despite the heady stew of arrayed forces that had long been destined for this moment—an alien armada, Dr. Stephenson, three Altreian ship mutants, and the combined intellectual might of the Earth's best and brightest—only Raul had put it all together.

Here, floating in his own fortress of solitude, he could feel the power bubbling up through his neural net, the awesome force of God's will. Right now, at this singular moment, there was only one archangel, and Raul was it. Not God's son as he'd earlier believed, but his mighty right hand. His entire life had been in preparation for this.

Raul had checked and rechecked his preparations. After all, he'd only get one chance at this, and the tolerances were very tight. If he hadn't had complete access to the alien invasion plan right within his starship's archive, what he was going to do would have been impossible. But he had the gateway synchronization codes and the stasis field modulation codes from the original plan. And since Stephenson was intent on bringing the aliens through the gateway, he was going to have to match those codes.

The image of Dr. Stephenson calmly strolling through Raul's stasis field formed in his mind. Yeah, Raul had enjoyed a front-row seat at a demo of just what someone with knowledge of the stasis field modulation codes could accomplish. He just hoped Stephenson got to try that little number again.

It wasn't just Stephenson that was going to get a little surprise. The Kasari Collective had done this thousands of times on worlds across the galaxy. But they hadn't counted on their world ship being shot down on Earth, hadn't anticipated Dr. Stephenson's crazy plan to force world governments to build the gateway by creating a micro black hole.

That's what made the tolerances so tight. Stephenson was counting on a brief delay before he applied the gateway synchronization codes after creating the wormhole, just enough time to use a second stasis field to push the anomaly into deep space before locking down the other end of the gateway. It wouldn't do to have the alien *Wehrmacht* charge right into a blossoming black hole.

Raul didn't particularly want to be sitting on an ex-planet either. That meant he couldn't just sync the Rho Ship's own wormhole generation engine with Stephenson's gateway. So he had to let the initial stages of Dr. Stephenson's operation go as planned, before he made his play. And so did Heather and the Smythe twins. It was why they had to be on-site. Glorious.

Back when Raul had first gained complete access to the rebooted Rho Ship's computers and discovered that no living thing could survive a one-ended wormhole transit, he'd wondered why the Kasari hadn't just sent their robotic world ship through and then utilized it to form the far end of the gateway. After all, each ship had its own wormhole generation engines.

The problem was that, while the world ships could generate their own transit wormholes and could even establish a temporary link to a full-sized Kasari gateway, they couldn't produce one of the size and stability capable of transporting a Kasari invasion force and its equipment. And while their population seduction technique didn't always work, the Kasari had never experienced a failure, once a gateway had gone active. Until today.

As Raul watched the worm fiber imagery play out in his head, a slow grin crept across his face, his artificial eye firmly locked onto the feed of a black-garbed security guard.

"Hello, Heather."

CHAPTER 121

Weapons specialist Inga Hedstrom cradled the M25 counter-defilade target engagement rifle in the crook of her left arm as she scanned the ATLAS cavern. All the guards carried the M25, although they were only allowed to load the same goober non-lethal rounds that had been used to capture Heather and the Smythes in Bolivia. The thinking was that if anyone freaked out on G-Day, they could freeze him in place without running the possibility of damaging critical equipment. But today she had substituted high-explosive air burst rounds for the goobers.

Nodding to her Spanish teammate on the metal walkway twenty feet up and to her left, she let her visions take her.

Mark and Jennifer were in the cavern, going about their assigned duties, taking no notice of her. Today they all carried the Bandolier Ship headsets, wearing them around their necks, hers hidden beneath the black uniform's collar. Just one more precaution among the many they had taken. Heather just hoped they would be enough.

The countdown to anomaly capture was progressing normally, Dr. Stephenson on his perch at the primary command console, high above the rest of the scientists and technicians manning the ATACC workstations around the gateway's base.

"Approaching final countdown to anomaly capture." The announcement was replaced by the final countdown. "Initiating anomaly capture."

The anomaly containment device came apart, its parts crashing to the floor less than fifty meters from where she stood. Heather tensed. The culmination of all their planning was seconds away, and just like Mark and Jen, she was ready.

The blaring alarm gave way to an even louder PA announcement.

"Initiate procedure to swap primary and secondary stasis field generator controls. Dr. Trotsky, override the con from your position. Now!"

As Jennifer shoved the unconscious Trotsky aside and took over at the secondary control console, Heather saw Mark rip away the metal panel covering the electronics powering the primary stasis field. Mark had less than a minute to restore power to the primary field generator in order for it to pick up the secondary stasis field generator's initial mission, which was as important as Jennifer's taking control of the anomaly with the secondary stasis field.

As she watched the anomaly pulse energy into the containment field, equations cascaded through Heather's mind. The handoff from the primary to the secondary field generator had been expertly handled, but matter had leaked in, sending the anomaly into a death spiral. Until the primary stasis field regained power to seal the portal, Stephenson couldn't activate the wormhole device. If Mark was late by even a few seconds, none of this was going to matter.

"Primary stasis field power back online!"

A cheer went up from the ATACC as Dr. Stephenson shifted at his console.

"Immediate wormhole generation commencing."

No time for a countdown. Just enough to create the wormhole and validate the far end's space-time coordinates; then Jennifer would modulate the secondary stasis field to allow it to pass the anomaly through the primary and out into deep space. Then Jen would use the secondary field to destroy the gateway before Stephenson could open it up to the invaders.

Heather refined her calculations. Five minutes and seventeen seconds until the growing event horizon spilled out of the containment field and swept everyone to his or her ultimate destiny. If everything went according to plan, they should have two minutes to spare.

If everything went according to plan.

CHAPTER 122

"Why don't we have detonation?"

General Smith's voice over the secure telephone unit carried a tension that Captain Everett could feel like static electricity.

"Sir, we've lost comms to the nukes."

"Captain, I don't care if you have to manually initiate, I need that detonation. Whatever it takes."

"Wilco."

"Captain. Your country is counting on you."

Captain Everett set the handset back in its cradle, then began running toward the doorway that led to the ATLAS cavern. He was going to die today anyway. But maybe, just maybe, he could pull the plug on the thing that was about to eat his wife, his baby girl, and the whole damn planet.

~ ~ ~

"Far-gate active!"

The notification entered Commander Ketaan-Ra's mind through the nano-bot communication swarm distributed throughout his brain.

"Synchronization?"

"Not yet initiated from the far end."

"Why not?"

"It appears the wormhole is directed at a point in galactic zone 3AF2344XZ."

Ketaan-Ra hissed. He'd waited too long to have something go wrong now.

"Override from this end. Lock it down now."

"Dangerous."

"Do it."

"As you command."

As power was diverted to the activating gateway, Ketaan-Ra's detachment came to the ready. When the synchronization reached its final stage, Ketaan-Ra braced himself as the millions of nano-bots throughout his body compensated for the new world's atmosphere, gravity, and pressure differential. The process was straightforward. Start the change as the gateway went final, charge through the opening as the change progressed, arrive in the new world ready to breathe its air and function in its environment. It always hurt and this time was no different.

Unable to remember the atmosphere he'd been born breathing, Ketaan-Ra exhaled his final lungful of the ammonia-methane mixture he'd come to regard as normal, and leaped through the portal into a nitrogen-oxygen world.

CHAPTER 123

Mark tossed the steel panel onto the floor behind him, flipped onto his back, and pulled his head and shoulders into the electrical access duct. To his neurally enhanced eyesight, the limited ambient lighting seeping into the electrical panel from the cavern was more than adequate.

Since he'd rigged the power circuits for the primary and secondary stasis control panels, he knew what he was looking for without need of the normal test and evaluation procedures. Snapping open the cover on the primary control circuit panel, he found the faulty circuit immediately, a bad amplifier module on the main circuit board. Funny, all that power controlled by a tiny transistor. It took only a trickle of current to the transistor to turn on the main power channel. Conversely, the denial of that trickle cut the main power in an instant. Mark had counted on that when he'd installed the module with the faulty resistor, one chosen to build up heat and burn out within a minute of primary stasis control power-up.

The pungent odor of burned insulation tickled his nostrils as he grabbed the correct screwdriver from his tool belt and spun the first of eight screws free, catching each in his palm as it fell. Snapping the module free of its mounts, Mark snapped the ribbon cable free and tossed the useless circuit card out onto the floor by his feet.

Grabbing his toolkit, he popped open the top, selected the replacement module, and began reinstallation. The kit contained replacements for several of the high-priority circuits, but it didn't hurt that Mark had known exactly which one would blow and when.

As badly as they'd needed the primary stasis control to fail, they needed it back online shortly thereafter. Just enough downtime for Jen to tranquilize Dr. Trotsky and take over operation of the secondary stasis controls. Dr. Stephenson already recognized that she had far more talent than the older man. If not for Russian political pressure, Trotsky's uncle being the president of the Russian Federation, Stephenson would have already replaced Trotsky with the postdoc she impersonated.

Snapping the new module in place, Mark tightened the last of the screws, and thrust himself out of the compartment and back into the cavern.

As he watched, twenty meters away the portal activated. The effect was instantaneous. One moment the black steel interior was empty, the next a star field replaced it, the view into space so spectacularly clear that Mark expected to be sucked out into the endless expanse. The fact that he wasn't confirmed not only that the primary stasis field was back online, but also that Dr. Stephenson had used it to seal the gateway. Nothing would be passing through that field without the correct modulation code, and even then, after passing through the film, the object would be subject to the instantaneous changes in pressure, gravity, temperature, and atmosphere that the far side had to offer.

All Stephenson needed to do was validate that the space-time coordinates of the far end were far enough from Earth that the anomaly would pose no further threat, a near-certainty given the vast expanse available; then Jennifer would use the secondary stasis field to thrust the forming black hole through the portal. Immediately after that she would use the stasis field generator to destroy the gateway. After that they'd have fifteen minutes to get to Jack's rendezvous point.

Then the wormhole shifted.

CHAPTER 124

Dr. Donald Stephenson clenched his jaw, lines of concentration burrowing fresh fissures in his forehead. He could be angry later. Right now he had to fix this giant mess they found themselves in.

The almost disastrous handoff of anomaly containment to Dr. Trotsky's station had shocked him. If not for the decisive actions of Trotsky's impressive postdoc, taking over the secondary controls when Trotsky fainted, they'd already be dead. She hadn't wasted a second checking on Trotsky's condition, practically throwing the unconscious man out of his chair as she slid in to replace him.

As he finished sealing the portal with the primary stasis field, Dr. Stephenson activated the gateway. A tremor shook the cavern floor, rattling the scaffolding, and producing a momentary fluctuation in the power grid. Stephenson adjusted the controls to compensate, allowing the wormhole to come into being at its own pace. A glance at the impedance and temperature measurements for the thick super-cooled power cables brought the barest hint of a smile to his lips. Superconductivity was holding, despite the awesome current flowing into his gateway.

From his perch he could see the entire ATACC, had a direct view down into the portal itself. The scientists looked frozen in time, eyes locked on the anomaly trapped within the secondary containment field, the glowing blue orb reminiscent of a giant fortune teller's crystal ball.

In front of Stephenson, beside the computer keyboard, the gateway controls looked like a concert equalizer, an assortment of sliders and knobs that could be adjusted manually or set automatically via the computer. Dr. Stephenson leaned forward and pushed the largest slider all the way to the top. Within the gateway a star-field appeared, wavered, stabilized.

As he prepared to validate the coordinates, they changed, an altogether different scene appearing within the portal. What the hell? This wasn't supposed to happen yet. As Donald Stephenson stared at the army assembled in the vaulted chamber on the other end of the gateway, three alien creatures leaped across the threshold.

Then the portal shifted again.

CHAPTER 125

"What the hell?"

The imagery unfolding in Raul's sensor array made no sense, momentarily freezing him into inaction. Despite the initial glitches, the gateway had gone active, the far end of the wormhole targeted into empty space. The anomaly should have already been shoved through the portal. Instead, the gateway had somehow synchronized with the Kasari gateway. And, much to his horror, the lead members of the assault cohort leaped through the portal.

The first one through, the apparent commander, never hesitated, grabbing the nearest scientist with two of his powerful arms, the third pistoning a jagged blade into the man's torso as the fourth arm pointed toward a nearby security guard. Two spider creatures lunged out of the portal, one of them launching itself toward the black-clad female soldier, the other racing up the scaffolding toward a second black-uniformed military man.

As he saw the first of the spiders close on Heather, Raul snapped out of his brain freeze. Although the timing was all wrong, he couldn't let the Kasari continue to pour into the ATLAS cavern. Activating his own wormhole engine, Raul applied the synchronization codes, locking onto the ATLAS gate to seal off the Kasari portal.

Raul adjusted his worm fiber feeds from the ATLAS cavern. Where seconds earlier the portal had opened into the Kasari staging area, Raul's legless body now hung in the air within his Rho Ship's command center. Above the ATACC, a startled exclamation escaped Dr. Stephenson's lips. Raul ignored him, shifting his attention to the nightmare leaping toward Heather.

As it reached her, she blurred into motion, rolling sideways, regaining her feet with a nine-millimeter Glock in her left hand and her heavy rifle cradled in her right, the Glock firing so fast it sounded like an automatic, each slug penetrating her alien opponent's misshapen body as it spun to face her, knocking it backward, but not down.

Raul's neural net supplied him the reason she wasn't firing the larger weapon. It was an M25, the programmable explosive shells designed to engage at distance, each one exploding with the force of a small grenade, allowing its wielder to destroy enemies hiding behind cover but almost useless at close range since the round didn't arm itself until it had traveled thirty meters downrange. It was still a big bullet at point-blank range, but not one you wanted to waste unless absolutely necessary.

Enough of this shit. Time to grab Heather and bring her home before she got herself killed. As he shifted part of his own stasis field to reach through the gateway and pluck her from the madness of the ATLAS chamber, his lock on the ATLAS gateway destabilized, then resynchronized, this time on the Kasari gateway. Immediately, nine Kasari warriors spilled into the Rho Ship.

CHAPTER 126

Dr. Stephenson hesitated, but only for a second. Three Kasari commandos had entered the cavern, but not the entire assault unit. There should have been at least a dozen to rapidly secure the Gateway Device. And now gunfire had broken out, as one of the two multi-legged Graath killers had failed to instantly terminate the female commando.

Worse, the not-so-dead Raul had somehow diverted the gateway, synching it to the Rho Ship's wormhole star-drive engines. Shifting his attention to the anomaly decay calculations, Stephenson grimaced. If he didn't get control of the gateway in the next minute and a half, everyone involved was about to have a very bad day.

A glance down at the secondary stasis field control station gave him a rush of relief. Dr. Nika Ivanovich, the postdoc who'd taken over for Trotsky, remained at her station, maintaining containment of the anomaly and ready to launch it through the gateway if he could get it pointed away from Earth and not at the Kasari staging base. Stephenson had no intention of shoving an emerging black hole up the ass of the collective.

Throwing the gateway controller into maintenance override while the wormhole was active was a crazy risk, purging the synchronization codes as it performed a controller reboot. The theoretical effect on the wormhole was indeterminate. It would certainly break Raul's connection to the gateway, but would also deny the Kasari an immediate reconnection. That meant that the three Kasari who had already come through would have to try to gain control in the cavern until reinforcements could arrive.

While there was a very heavy NATO, French, and Swiss security presence on-site, almost all of that force was outside the building, its mission to protect the project from any attack from outside the secure perimeter. That meant the small special ops team on duty within the cavern was on its own until the rapid response force could get here.

As he initiated the gateway's maintenance override, Stephenson glanced down at the portal. The image of Raul floating inside the Rho Ship winked out, replaced by dancing star-fields. Damn it. The uncontrolled wormhole was waggling through space-time like a dog's tail. If it leaped deep into a galactic core before the controls rebooted, the primary stasis field draping the portal couldn't protect them. Still, the odds of survival were in their favor. Big sky, little stars.

Ignoring the continuing rattle of gunfire, Dr. Stephenson focused his attention on preparing for the moment the reboot completed, when it would allow him to lock the wormhole to its original coordinates.

Thumbing the microphone, he spoke into the PA system.

"Dr. Ivanovich. Prepare for anomaly transport within twenty seconds. Initiate on my mark."

One minute fifty-seven seconds until the end of the world. And, at the moment, all he could do was sit there and twiddle his thumbs.

CHAPTER 127

Mark stared into the wormhole device in disbelief. A vast chamber yawned before him, most of its floor space filled with the vanguard of the alien army they were here to stop. Before he had finished digesting this new circumstance, three aliens plunged through the stasis field. The first, a bipedal, four-armed being, standing a full seven feet tall, leaped onto the first tier of the ATACC, grabbed the nearest scientist from his workstation, and impaled him on a two-foot jagged blade.

As the man opened his mouth to scream, the powerful arm stabbed him again, transforming the sound into a bubbling wail that followed the man into death.

Two other creatures skittered across the cavern floor toward the surrounding scaffolding draping the walls on either side of the ATACC. From Mark's viewpoint they loped along like eight-legged gorillas, thick bodies the size of sofas, open jowls screeching a keening yowl. If they had eyes, he couldn't see them.

Mark started moving, his hand suddenly filled with the heavy hammerhead lineman's pliers from his tool belt, his legs driving him toward the four-armed alien that had just tossed the dead man into the panicked scientists scrambling away from the assault. Mark reached the thing's back as gunfire erupted behind him.

Off to his left, the wormhole shifted again.

Adrenaline flooding his system, Mark swung the pliers with every ounce of strength he could generate, the force of the blow caving in a section of the thing's skull, sending it crashing into the next row of elevated workstations. It slipped, arms flailing, but somehow regained its balance, whirling to meet its attacker with a wide sweep of its knife hand.

Mark threw himself sideways, barely avoiding the weapon's jagged tip. The creature turned to fully face him, rising into a crouch as it assessed its opponent, its head wound repairing itself as Mark watched. The smell of the thing filled his nostrils, an ammonia–diesel fuel perfume that made his eyes water. Its orange-and-black-flecked eyes blinked twice, lids closing bottom-up.

Then it plunged toward him, a second blade filling another of its hands. Mark accepted the charge, dropping to his back as he struck out with both legs, propelling every bit of his power into the quick thrust. Based upon the shock of the impact, he judged the alien's weight to be better than six hundred pounds. It didn't matter. The being might be big and able to heal in a way that made Priest Williams look like a sickling, but compared to Mark it was moving in molasses. The blow landed directly on the groin area, redirecting the alien's charge into a flailing heels-over-head flight over Mark and back out onto the open cavern floor.

Whipping his legs around, Mark landed back on his feet before the alien stopped rolling, his breath puffing out of his mouth and nose in twin attempts to clear the stench that threatened his oxygen supply. As blood wept down his face from a fresh scalp wound, Mark hurled the pliers at the rising creature's lower left hand, the tool opening as it spun through the air, its momentum tearing the long blade from its grip and sending it spinning along the floor toward the portal opening.

The alien ignored it, moving toward Mark once again, this time in a controlled fighter's crouch instead of a charge, its remaining sword at the ready, its other three hands swaying in a wrestler's pose. Mark turned and ran. Behind him the alien followed, and although it wasn't nearly as quick, it was fast. Halfway to the scaffolding, Mark turned hard right, then again, allowing his larger opponent's momentum to carry it past him.

The maneuver gained him five meters. Focusing on achieving all the speed he could generate, Mark let his legs propel him toward the alien's dropped blade. The slap of heavy boots on concrete behind him told him the race was going to be close.

CHAPTER 128

Raul's moment of hesitation almost cost him his life. The first alien to spill through the portal into his command center hurled a spinning blade with such force it would have passed all the way through his torso if it had reached him. Instead it glanced harmlessly off the invisible stasis shield he erected in front of his body. Seeing eight additional Kasari jump through the portal into the Rho Ship, Raul sealed it behind them.

Despite their training, the Kasari assault team wasn't prepared for the legless apparition that hung suspended in the air before them, wielding a stasis field for which they lacked the modulation codes. Neither did they expect his mind to be seamlessly interconnected with their own world ship's neural network.

As Raul looked beyond the nine members of the trapped Kasari assault team and into the vast expanse of the invasion staging chamber, he knew he didn't have much time. While the assault team offered no threat to him, even the stasis field could not long defend him against the advanced heavy weaponry available to the army in that facility. Its commanders had been stunned into inaction by the gateway's unexpected shift, but unless he enhanced the impact, their lack of coordinated response wouldn't last long enough.

Manipulating his field with long-practiced expertise, he filled the surrounding chamber with a tight grid of microscopic force planes, dicing the nine Kasari so rapidly even their super nanobots had no chance at compensating. Collapsing the force grid, he packed the orange-green Kasari soup into a ball and shot it back through the portal, where it exploded into the midst of the assembled troops like a giant paintball.

Raul didn't wait to watch it, turning his full attention to the worm fibers inside the ATLAS cavern. He couldn't just terminate his end of the gateway. The modifications he'd made to the Rho Ship's wormhole drive consumed so much power on initiation it would take weeks to recharge the reserves for another attempt. Disconnecting from the far end would shift his wormhole engines to some random point in space, throwing the starship's drive into its primary mode of operation, transporting it through the wormhole, a trip no one could hope to survive.

No. He had to stay linked to a far gateway until he brought the system down in a controlled fashion. That meant that if he wanted to get Heather, he had to stay linked to the Kasari gateway until he could reacquire the one in the ATLAS cavern.

Stephenson had done something to regain control of his portal, something that Raul needed to counter. And he needed to make it happen right now.

CHAPTER 129

Ketaan-Ra hurtled through the gateway, landing in the dimly lit cavern, accompanied by two Graath shock troopers just to his right. His shared nano-bot tactical display showed only two armed humans, one at floor level, another high up along the metal latticework that draped the walls.

He wasn't surprised by the lack of human military at the gateway. Of all the worlds they'd assimilated, most had had no armed presence at the portal. The whole point of building a Kasari-inspired gateway was to welcome the benevolent species that offered a world so much astounding technology. It made no sense to open the gateway and present a threatening presence to one's benefactors.

Motioning with an arm, Ketaan-Ra issued a mental command, sending the two Graath scurrying to eliminate the soldiers as he focused on understanding every aspect of his tactical display. Something was wrong with the portal behind him. He didn't need to look to confirm that it had lost the link with the Kasari staging planet. Only he and the two Graath had made it into the cavern. By now he should have had his entire dozen-member team already moving through the coordinated dance they'd rehearsed hundreds of times.

Worse, a bright red rotating threat matrix highlighted something he'd already seen with his own eyes, a glowing orb contained within a stasis field a handful of strides in front of him. The energy readings showed the field contained an asymptotic gravitational event with a rapidly expanding event horizon.

A bomb.

As hard as it was to believe what he was seeing, he couldn't deny what the data was telling him. Somehow this species had rejected the beneficial concept of assimilation and responded by using the Kasari technologies to construct a gravity bomb with a growing singularity at its core.

As the scanner displays flashed through his mind, instantly identifying each piece of equipment in the cavern along with its probable purpose, his initial assessment was confirmed. The stasis field containing the singularity was programmed to thrust it through the gateway upon a command from its operator. And if he didn't get control of that station very quickly, the humans might just succeed in destroying a Kasari staging planet, along with multiple gateways and millions of highly trained warriors.

A scowl spread across Ketaan-Ra's face. Not happening. Not through his gateway.

Turning to the left, Ketaan-Ra identified the human female operating the workstation on the third stair-stepped platform that wrapped behind the gateway. With a red numeric countdown in the corner of his sensory display, he leaped onto the first platform and grabbed the human male who had just begun to rise from his seat, impaling him on the dual-edged *kedra* and tossing the body aside as he prepared to leap to the next level.

A tactical alert triggered his attention, a human moving up behind him, fast. Very fast. The force of the blow staggered him, caving in the right rear section of his skull as he started to turn toward his attacker. For a matter of seconds Ketaan-Ra lost all tactical, while the nano-bots swarmed to repair the brain injury. Ignoring the loss of awareness, he whirled toward the human, pulling the second *kedra* from his equipment belt and driving his bulk forward with all the power his legs could deliver.

As his upper two arms reached to embrace his opponent and pull him into the sweeping blades, the human dropped to his back, his feet catching Ketaan-Ra in the junction between his legs with surprising force, adding a vertical component to his forward momentum, launching him over his target, one blade barely nicking the human's head. He hit the ground and rolled to his feet as tactical came back online. Ketaan-Ra knew he'd failed to compensate for this planet's lower gravity. Compounding that error, the human showed startling dexterity, far greater than anything he'd seen from the world ship's periodic reports on this planet.

One of the Graath had taken out a guard, but the other was having its own problems, taking fire from a human female who displayed traits similar to the one he was fighting. The tactical network incorporated this new data, adjusting the team's tactics as they moved.

A projectile flew from his opponent's hand so fast that it hit his lower left hand before he could move it out of its path, breaking the bone just below his wrist and sending the *kedra* skidding across the floor toward the portal. Again his tactical display shifted dramatically, showing a gateway connection to another point on this planet, a connection to the Kasari's own world ship.

Shrugging off this distraction, he prepared himself for the human male's charge. It never came. As Ketaan-Ra's wrist knitted itself back together, the human broke into panicked retreat. With his legs providing more controlled explosions, Ketaan-Ra gave chase, smiling at the cascading displays in his head. The chase wasn't going to be a long one.

The human cut to the right and, once again, the absence of sufficient gravity betrayed Ketaan-Ra, robbing him of the friction necessary to match the human's two tight turns. At least now the other's plan was clear. Get to the dropped *kedra*. He planned to stop and fight. Ketaan-Ra relaxed, letting his pace slow just enough to make sure the human got there first. It was the kind of fight he wanted, *kedra* to *kedra*, his four hands and superior strength and healing against this human's quickness. A truly worthy opponent.

~ ~ ~

Mark's finger closed around the alien sword's haft, feeling the grip adapt to his hand. As he whirled to face his pursuer, he measured the weapon's weight and balance, his eyes caressing the black sword's three-foot blade. Two razor-sharp edges swept to a Roman point, practically screaming for blood. He liked it.

The big alien came to a controlled stop three paces from where Mark waited, its own sword gripped in its lower right fist, the other three arms reaching toward him like a wrestler's. Like a couple of wrestlers'.

So it had learned Mark's momentum tricks. No more bull rushes. Just good old-fashioned man-versus-giant-four-armed-alien combat. A mental image from the classic B movie *Clash of the Titans* brought a grin to his face.

Amazing. The alien warrior appeared to be waiting for him to make the first move. As Mark raised the sword in front of him, another thought filled his mind.

Hail Caesar! We who are about to die salute you.

Then Mark's body blurred into motion.

CHAPTER 130

Heather tossed the M25 rifle up onto the third level of scaffolding, swinging herself up along the rifle's arc, ejecting one magazine and slapping another into the Glock as she landed. Fifteen feet below, the ugly beastie righted itself from the impact of fifteen nine-millimeter Parabellums, the holes in its body healing as it moved to follow her.

With visions filling Heather's mind, rearranging themselves as she and the alien creature danced their deadly waltz, she emptied the fresh magazine into the gorilla-spider, each round striking a different body part as she sought lethality data. The bullets tore the alien from its hold on the railing, sending it sprawling onto the floor below. And once again, Heather grabbed the M25 and tossed it to a higher level, following it up along the metal latticework with all the speed her body and training could provide.

Her vision shifted and Heather leaped to her left as a long blade flashed through the space she'd just occupied, clanged off the wall, and rattled down through the spaces between the steel walkways. Then, with a thin, mewling squall, the alien propelled itself up after her.

Click. Clack.

Another magazine replaced its predecessor. Once more the Glock spewed its lead saliva into her pursuer, this time targeting the small bulbous knobs Heather believed to be the thing's sensory organs. And although it continued its upward climb, it failed to follow her as she picked up the M25 and ran east along the north wall.

Realizing it had lost her, the creature paused, allowing the nano-bot healing process to restore its sensory array. It didn't take long. A mere eight seconds. But as it reacquired her, Heather finished lasing her target.

The projectile armed itself at thirty meters, tore into its target at thirty-two, and exploded with the force of a grenade. The Graath became a fine green-yellow mist, out of which writhing gelatinous blobs and twitching limbs whipped into the cavern below.

Before her exultant yell could make it from her lungs to her lips, one of Heather's visions stifled it in her throat. Leaning out over the railing, she looked up.

Less than ten meters up and to the right, a second gorilla-spider raced down the steel latticework toward her.

Heather spun left, running along the metal grating, her black boots making the flooring sing as she approached the near corner. Behind her she felt the gorilla-spider land on the walkway, the sound painting a clear image of its powerful eight-legged lope quickly closing the space between them.

The quick look she'd just gotten of this one had been enough. Unlike the four-armed alien fighting Mark on the cavern floor, the spider thing carried no weapons. Each of its eight legs ended in a hairy hand, each finger sporting raptor-like retractable claws. From the goo, blood, and intestinal splatter that covered its bulbous body, it must have torn apart her partner after wading through the goober munition's web. And if it got its hands on her, the result would be no different.

With each stride, Heather watched a hundred scenarios play out in her mind. Cradling the short rifle in the crook of her right arm, she hit the end of the walkway, spun and pulled the trigger. The explosive round had no time to arm, hammering into the alien body after travelling only 3.872 meters. And although it didn't explode, the impact lifted the black, hairy body, sending it rolling back along the walkway as if it had stepped in front of a speeding truck. Since she hadn't been braced, the recoil flung Heather backward, her left hand just catching the rail as she tumbled backward over it, her beret spinning away like a small black Frisbee.

Seeing the spider-thing right itself, Heather kicked outward, released her grip on the rail, and dropped the twenty-two feet to the concrete floor, transferring momentum into a forward roll as she landed. As she came back to her feet, she squeezed off another round into the alien as it scurried down the steel lattice after her. No time to lase the target or thumb in extra distance. It didn't matter. She hadn't gained the required arming distance, and her mind told her the alien had figured it out.

As the twenty-five-millimeter round knocked the alien from the scaffolding, Heather ran toward the Cage, a massive rack-support structure that housed all the heavy cables that carried power from the matter disruptor facility to the wormhole device and stasis field generators. The workmen who had built it, Mark included, all hated it with a passion that bespoke the claustrophobia the Cage generated in those who had experienced its interior.

As big as the thickly insulated cables were, most of the room was taken up with the pipes and cooling equipment required to keep them superconductive. Like everything else on this project, it had been designed with speed of construction and efficiency of operation in mind. Only enough crawl space had been left to allow workmen to wriggle along twisting paths and up narrow ladders. Mark had said there weren't many places inside the Cage where he didn't have surfaces pressed against both his front and back sides. And while that might have been an exaggeration, it wasn't much of one.

Add that to the wind that howled through these passageways from the powerful fans designed to clear the heat from the cooling machines and you had something Dante would have loved to include in his description of the lower pits of hell.

Pulling the Cage schematics to the front of her memory, Heather calculated how long it would take her to make the GF2 access door, the closest to her position. Overlaying time-sequenced imagery of her and her opponent's anticipated intercept paths, she managed to pull just a bit more speed from her adrenaline-fueled legs. She would beat spidey to the Cage, but getting the door open and getting inside before the alien ripped her apart was going to be close.

Her pursuer was adapting to each new twenty-five-millimeter impact, having compensated for the last hit in half the time the first recovery had taken. Without the explosive force provided by a fully armed round, another slug into its body wasn't going to do it. And having lost the Glock and her extra magazines in the fall over the railing, she was down to three rounds remaining in the M25's six-round mag.

She hit the steel gate with a downward swipe and pulled at the lever handle, sliding through and closing it behind her as the alien's bulk hit it, denting the metal frame inward and jamming the door latch. Heather turned sideways, sliding along the access way until she reached the first junction. Squeezing into the passage on her right, she heard the squeal of tearing metal as the alien ripped the gate from its hinges and flung it into the cavern.

At the first ladder, she began climbing.

A glance through a narrow gap between equipment and cables showed the alien squeeze into the narrow space, bones flexing and dislocating like a giant hamster's as it adapted to this new environment.

Heather climbed faster. Twenty meters up she shifted her body off the ladder and into an even tighter crawl space that forced her to lie on her back and wriggle her body forward along a shaft that scraped her back and sides. She knew what she was headed for, and although the alien had shown the capability to rapidly adapt, it was still quadruple her bulk, and the Cage would extract a price for that bulk.

Because the crawlways and chimneys between equipment were so tight that tool belts and hand-carried toolboxes were impractical, electrical tool cases had been bolted to the racks at strategic points throughout the Cage, providing engineers and technicians with an extensive set of test and repair equipment within ten meters of any point. Squeezing through a space not meant for passage, Heather took advantage of her small form to take a significant shortcut to one of these tool cases.

Popping open the latch, she found what she wanted. Ejecting the M25 rifle's magazine from the butt stock, she popped one of the high-explosive air burst rounds into her hand and set to work on it. Carefully cracking open the lower portion of the case, she gained access to the safe-and-arm circuit. Working with all the speed and dexterity her Bandolier Ship neural enhancements and

Jack's training had provided her, she made a simple logic circuit modification, bypassing the thirty-meter safety mechanism, setting the round to arm immediately upon firing.

A guttural roar of frustration three meters to her left alerted her to the alien's arrival at the point where she'd squeezed between equipment racks. Good. So there were limits to how much the creature could contort its body. It would have to find its way around. And unless it had a complete schematic of the Cage, as she did, that would take a while.

As she worked to put the round back together, Heather's mind tracked the alien's progress. Not good. If it didn't have the complete Cage schematic, it had a damn good approximation.

Rushing through her final task, Heather placed the modified round topmost in the magazine. Slapping it home, she chambered the new round, ejecting its predecessor from the right ejection port. The ejected round clipped the railing and spun away, the cling-clang of its passage sounding all the way down to the Cage floor, sixty-seven feet below.

Heather reached a new ladder and began climbing once again, the knowledge that she was now down to two rounds tugging at her mind. She shrugged it off. If the modified round didn't do the job, whether or not she had one or two additional shots wouldn't make a bit of difference.

CHAPTER 131

"Dr. Ivanovich. Prepare for anomaly transport within twenty seconds. Initiate on my mark."

Dr. Stephenson's voice nudged Jennifer into action. The data on the six flat-panel displays that wrapped halfway around her swivel chair felt like a demon, reaching out to grab her by the throat, nine-inch nails penetrating into her windpipe, shutting off both blood and oxygen flows to her brain. As fast as Stephenson had been in transferring stasis field control to her workstation, he'd taken longer than they'd projected, that delay funneling in extra feed matter to the anomaly, a creature that existed and changed on a femtosecond scale.

In a second light could race almost seven and a half times around the Earth. In a nanosecond light traveled almost a foot. In a femtosecond light barely got past one hundred thousandth of an inch, roughly three times the diameter of a human hair. In a femtosecond you could die before the electrochemical impulse traveled from one synapse to the next. All things considered, not a bad way to go. If you were dead set on dying.

The anomaly was on a decaying spiral with an acceleration curve that scared the shit out of Jennifer. And although they had very little time left, Mark and the alien were locked in a battle directly in front of the gateway. And as long as her brother was between the anomaly and the gateway, there was no way Jennifer was going to thrust the anomaly containment field through that portal.

If only the anomaly had been a bit more stable, she could have funneled off a little of the containment field and used it to pluck Mark out of the way before jamming the anomaly through the opening. But it was all she could do, using every bit of the energy available to the stasis field generator, to keep the micro black hole from becoming an instant big one.

Diverting just a touch of her concentration, Jennifer contacted Mark.

Can't hold it much longer. Get the hell out of the way.

CHAPTER 132

Operating in a maze of intertwined futures, Heather slithered through the tangle of pipes, cables, and machinery, steadily working her way up toward that point ninety meters above the ATLAS cavern floor where the Cage touched the ceiling, up on the sky-walk that ran from the Cage's highest gate to the cavern exit. That's where she wanted to be, but she wasn't going to make it.

Behind her, the gorilla-spider continued to adapt to the tight spaces, and as it did, its speed increased. Heather reached a turn and threw her body into the crawl space to her right, feeling a puff of air on her cheek as one of the clawed hands sliced the air where she had just been. The alien body hit the turn, all eight legs propelling it after her. From this angle Heather could see a toothy maw along the thing's underside. She assumed the horrible smell came from this orifice, although it wasn't helped by the human blood and excrement that still dripped from its body.

Grabbing a cable above her head, Heather swung herself up like a gymnast, twisting her body to miss protruding steel cable supports. The maneuver gained her three feet. The decision point was rapidly approaching, the moment she would be forced to fire the twenty-five-millimeter high-explosive round, danger close. And when she did, she wasn't the only thing likely to suffer collateral damage. The super-cooling system for the primary stasis field wrapped all the power cables in this section of the Cage, and that equipment wasn't exactly designed to withstand explosives. As she scrambled hand over hand up a two-inch vertical pipe, she looked up. Another twenty-five feet and she'd reach the ramp that would dump her onto the skywalk.

The claw speared her left calf, tearing an inch-deep gash in the muscle and almost tearing her loose from the pipe. Heather scissored her legs, the kick breaking the alien hand and ripping the claw free, sending the creature tumbling six feet down the shaft before it caught itself.

Heather focused on her leg, shunting away the pain and using her fine muscle control to constrict the torn veins, reducing the wound's blood flow to a trickle. But she was out of time. She would make her final stand right here and now. Swinging herself behind a metal panel, she swung the M25 back into the shaft, visualized the bullet trajectory, and pulled the trigger.

The concussive blast penetrated the thin steel plates, coating her body in alien slime as it lifted her from her perch and flung her against the outer railing, sending a tidal wave of pain through her right shoulder. Fighting to stay conscious, Heather saw that a foot-long sheet metal shard had speared her just below the right collarbone, a third of its length extending out her back. Her other symptoms pointed to severe concussion.

Struggling to a sitting position, she braced herself against the railing that had prevented her from falling 250 feet to the cavern floor below.

Shit. When does this get fun?

Then a new alarm Klaxon sounded, accompanied by a digitized voice over the PA system.

"WARNING. PRIMARY STASIS FIELD COOLING SYSTEM MALFUNCTION. PRIMARY STASIS FIELD POWER FAILURE IMMINENT."

As a new vision filled her mind, Heather wrapped her good arm and leg around the support strut.

Then, with a hurricane squall, the primary stasis field died, opening the portal to the vacuum of empty space.

CHAPTER 133

Mark was one with the dance. Once he'd thought he was meant for basketball, but he'd been born for this.

Adrenaline coursed through his system unchecked, fueling his attack. Dodging the alien's counterstroke, his black sword swept an arc that removed the alien's top left arm at the elbow, sending the clutching hand to the concrete floor between them.

The alien ignored the loss of a hand, lunging forward onto Mark's blade, its momentum aiding Mark in driving the full length through its thick torso. Only as one of its hands closed around his right wrist, preventing him from pulling the sword free, did Mark realize his mistake.

Twisting to the left, Mark grabbed the alien's sword arm with his left hand as the remaining alien hand grabbed his throat and squeezed. With electric sparks arcing across his dimming vision, Jennifer touched his mind.

Can't hold it much longer. Get the hell out of the way.

Bracing his arms like a gymnast performing the iron cross, Mark brought both knees up to his chest, leaned back, and hammered his heels into the alien's face, breaking what would have passed for a nose and rocking its head back. As the alien hammered at his ribs with its amputated stump, Mark scissored his legs around the thing's head, locked his heels, and squeezed.

Feeling the alien grip on his throat loosen slightly, Mark twisted his head to the side and bit into the alien fist, feeling bones snap between his teeth as the acrid alien blood filled his mouth, stinging his lips and gums. The alien's grip on his throat loosened another notch and Mark felt the blood flow return to his brain. Sucking in a rattling breath, he increased the pressure his legs were applying to the alien's head and neck.

He didn't have a lot of faith he could crush that skull or break its neck, but he could damn sure try. In the meantime he began flexing his pinned right wrist, making short sawing motions with the sword blade within the alien's torso.

Adopting Mark's tactic, the alien twisted its head and sank its teeth into the flesh of his thigh. Shrugging its shoulders up, it shoved hard with its three good arms, breaking Mark's grip and sending him tumbling across the cavern floor.

Ignoring the pain shooting through his leg, Mark rolled to his feet, prepared to meet the charge that didn't come. It didn't take a lot of imagination to figure out why. Watching the alien's fist and injured stomach knit themselves back together, he knew this was a battle of attrition he couldn't hope to win.

Mark spat the alien blood onto the floor, trying not to swallow any. Well, if killing the thing the old-fashioned way wasn't going to work, he'd just have to see how it got along without a head. As he readied himself for his next attack, high up, near the top of the massive power cage, a loud explosion sounded, its echoing report followed by the blare of a new alarm.

"WARNING. PRIMARY STASIS FIELD COOLING SYSTEM MALFUNCTION. PRIMARY STASIS FIELD POWER FAILURE IMMINENT."

Feeling his ears pop from the pressure change, Mark dropped the alien sword and lunged for the portal's titanium edge, his fingers closing on its lip as a blast of hurricane-force wind lifted his feet from the ground, trying to suck him into the wormhole behind him.

A quick glance over his shoulder made the situation clear. The alien had managed to grab the portal's far edge, but several of the scientists had been swept from their workstations as they and some of the monitors and keyboards tumbled into deep space. A glance up at Jennifer showed that she had managed to wrap her arms and legs around a steel rail, while, at his command perch, Dr. Stephenson clung to the elevated support structure.

Meanwhile, the November Anomaly sat unmoving, held in place by the stasis field containment bubble, glowing considerably brighter than the last time he'd looked at it. Now was the time to thrust it through the portal. Unfortunately, neither Jennifer nor Stephenson was able to let go to enter the required commands into a control station.

The howl of the wind nearly drowned out the screams of those swept from the scaffolding along the walls, but not the screech of tearing sheet metal and the crash of equipment flung against structural steel and concrete on its path into the wormhole. As Mark clung to his handhold he knew the wind wouldn't be stopping anytime soon, not with the LHC's twenty-seven-kilometer primary beam tunnel providing plenty of air, not with everything ventilated from the outside.

As a steel-case desk ricocheted off the portal five feet above him, Mark's thoughts turned to Heather.

Hey, babe. If you have any last save-the-day ideas, I'd appreciate them. Cause I'm fresh out.

CHAPTER 134

Donald Stephenson screamed into the microphone connected directly to the secondary stasis field control station. "Dr. Ivanovich. I told you to move the anomaly through the portal. Do it now!"

She didn't respond.

Glancing down at the containment bubble around the anomaly, he saw the problem. One of the technicians was fighting the Kasari in front of the gateway portal, blocking the anomaly's path.

He leaned closer to the mike. "Ivanovich. Move the anomaly now. We have less than a minute to get rid of it and redirect the gateway, or everyone on Earth dies."

No response.

Shit. The woman had frozen up.

To make matters worse, the sensor array had detected unusual gravitational variances moving around within the cavern, variances consistent with Rho Ship worm fiber technology. Raul.

For reasons beyond Stephenson's ken, the young idiot was trying to subvert the gateway for his own ends. So far he hadn't managed to grab gateway control again, but using the Rho Ship's neural net, he might manage it at any time. And if the anomaly was still sitting here in the ATLAS cavern when he did, everything Donald Stephenson had spent forty years working on would wink out in one sudden cosmic gulp.

Rising to his feet, Stephenson stepped toward the grated steel steps leading down to the third tier. If the Russian bitch couldn't do it, he'd take over her station himself.

The alarm sounded as he reached the bottom step, and if he hadn't braced himself against the structural support railing, he'd have been one of the first people sucked through the unprotected wormhole. Above his head, a large section of his primary control station tore free under the force of the explosive decompression, tumbled into the portal, and disappeared.

Death didn't scare him. Failure did. And as he clung to the railing, watching his staff and equipment being sucked out through the gateway, for the first time in his life, he found himself staring failure dead in the face.

CHAPTER 135

Multiple worm fiber views into the ATLAS cavern so horrified Raul that he began to shake. Not only had the Stephenson team lost the portal stasis field, they had failed to move the anomaly through the portal. With the damage being done to systems throughout the cavern, he couldn't project how long the gateway would remain functional. Worse, Heather was badly injured, barely clinging to a steel railing eighty meters above the cavern floor. If he wanted to get Heather, it had to be now.

As his neural net locked in the last of the gateway override codes, he restored his connection to the ATLAS portal, breaking away from the Kasari gateway. As the gateway connection synchronized, inside the ATLAS cavern it was as if a door had been slammed against a storm. Clinging to opposite edges of the portal, Mark and the Kasari he'd been fighting dropped to the floor. The Kasari recovered immediately, closing the gap and bringing his sword down in a sweeping blow Smythe barely managed to deflect. Then the Kasari closed with Mark, his momentum pushing Mark back against the portal's black wall.

Raul ignored them. Manipulating the stasis field, he reached out into the cavern, plucking Heather from her high perch, bringing her floating gently down to floor level as he pulled her toward the portal.

He was so focused on his task, he failed to notice a second young woman leap through the portal until she was already in the ship. With a shock of recognition, he released Heather, sending her tumbling onto the cavern floor, and shifted the stasis field to meet this new threat.

Then Jennifer Smythe was inside his head.

CHAPTER 136

Raul had been hard to miss as Jennifer had gotten up, her ears hissing and popping from yet another rapid change in atmospheric pressure. He'd been so obvious he'd even made her take her eyes off of Mark and the alien locked in close combat. That horribly misshapen figure, floating inside the open portal to the Rho Ship. He had been intent on Heather, who was floating through the air down toward the portal, trapped within a stasis bubble.

Jennifer's decision was instantaneous. She'd give him something to be intent about. Vaulting the two tiers of workstations that separated her from the cavern floor, Jennifer took three running strides and leaped through the portal, sliding to a stop in a clear area between a jumble of alien equipment. Ten feet in front of her, Raul locked his eyes with hers. Feeling a deadly intention replacing his initial surprise, Jennifer thrust herself into his mind.

For three seconds it seemed the shock of her mental assault would give her the upper hand. But now, as his alien neural net worked to eliminate her foothold, the balance of power was shifting. A thin smile spread across Raul's disfigured face, the appendage that had replaced his right eye shifting in anticipation.

Feeling her mental control slipping, Jennifer lifted the Bandolier Ship headband from its place around her neck, letting the buds settle over her temples. Whereas before she'd felt the power of Raul's neural net beginning to dominate her will, now Jennifer felt his mind recoil in surprise as he sought to understand what had just happened. Rather than try to take control of the Rho Ship's neural network, she focused on Raul, exposing the layers of desires, fears, and insecurities that made him who he was. And with every penetration, she released gentle waves of pleasure, a sense of her acceptance, even admiration.

And Raul reacted like a man dying of thirst who had just stumbled upon a stream of Rocky Mountain spring water. He drank her in.

So lonely. If she'd had more time, Jennifer would have pitied him. Instead, she ramped up her exploitation of his needs and weaknesses, encouraging him to show off his knowledge of the Rho Ship and its systems.

She concentrated on the Rho Ship's wormhole generation systems. As the knowledge of their design and function filled her mind, she saw what he'd done, reprogrammed the starship's wormhole drive to connect to the ATLAS gateway, bypassing its primary function of creating a wormhole and shoving the Rho Ship through it.

His will subject to Jennifer, Raul manipulated his neural net with a mastery that came with intimate familiarity, modifying the wormhole drive's programming with subtle elegance. The feeling of awe Jennifer fed him brought a smile to his lips, a smile that died as the realization struck him.

"My God! You've killed us both!"

As she turned her back on him, a barely audible whisper slipped from Jennifer's lips.

"I know."

~ ~ ~

Inside the Bandolier Cave, the coffee mug slipped from Dr. Hanz Jorgen's fingers to shatter on the stone floor, spewing its hot, black wetness up his pants leg. As a brilliant white glow replaced the Bandolier Ship's normal, soft magenta, he didn't even notice.

Hanz didn't know how he knew, but he did. Something powerful had just grabbed control of the Bandolier Ship's computers, drawing every cycle of their processing power. He could practically hear the alien circuits groan under the incredible demand being placed upon the system.

Staring at the glowing starship, he wondered what problem could tax it so intensely. Then, as a shudder traversed his body, Hanz decided he didn't really want to know.

CHAPTER 137

Heather tumbled across the concrete floor, coming to rest with her back against the first tier of workstations to the right of the portal, pain sending streaks of light lancing across her vision as the sheet metal spear twisted inside her shoulder. Fighting off a wave of dizziness, she struggled to her knees to see Jennifer standing inside the gateway device, a dozen feet separating her from where Raul's legless body floated in the air.

Jesus. What had Stephenson done to him?

Jennifer pushed her headset into place and a new vision filled Heather's mind. For several seconds Jennifer and Raul faced each other, frozen in place, a blitz of emotions playing across Raul's face.

Then Jennifer turned to face her, eyes as milky white as Heather's.

Take care of each other. I love you both.

Then the portal shifted back to empty space. As the decompression wind returned, Heather grabbed the workstation support, choking off the scream that rose in her throat. If she didn't do something in the next thirty-three seconds, the hungry anomaly behind her was going to eat them all.

Locking away the grief that threatened to incapacitate her, Heather channeled every ounce of adrenaline her body could produce, pulled herself up over the first row of workstations, reached out to grab the floor support for the next tier, and hauled herself up onto it. Once again, the spike in her shoulder twisted, leaving her gasping for breath as a red mist colored her vision.

Gritting her teeth, she lunged up onto the third tier and climbed up, anchoring herself onto the floor-bolted chair in front of the secondary stasis control panel. With her mental countdown ticking down, she grabbed the twin field positioning joysticks and thumbed the right throttle.

Eighteen seconds.

CHAPTER 138

Mark, adjusting to the jump in atmospheric pressure, was only halfway to his feet when the alien reached him, the blow staggering him. Still he managed to catch the alien's sword arm at the wrist as he was driven back against the portal wall.

Bracing his entire bulk behind the weapon's hilt, the alien forced the tip an inch closer to Mark's chest. The muscles in both his arms strained to the point that they threatened to pop through the skin; Mark hammered his right knee into the thing's groin. The tip of the black blade touched his chest, sending a warm wetness trickling down over his abdominals.

Mark twisted hard to the left, feeling the blade glance off his rib cage as the tip bit into the steel wall. Maintaining his momentum, Mark released his right hand, slamming the knife edge of his palm into the creature's throat, followed by a side kick that buckled its left leg.

Jennifer's voice entered his mind as he kicked the alien's damaged leg again.

Take care of each other. I love you both.

Before he could look up, another explosive decompression shoved him toward the wormhole. His left hand released its grip on the alien's sword arm and grabbed the portal's edge as the creature tumbled backward. He felt the alien grab his left leg as its sword spun away into the blackness beyond.

Mark twisted, managing to get a two-handed grip on the portal lip before the additional force of the alien body hanging on his leg sent them both on the same trip the sword had just taken. Raising his right knee, Mark sent his Red Wing boot crashing down into the creature's face, avoided the arm that swung out to capture it, and did it again. When that failed to have the desired effect, he began working on the hands clutching his left leg, breaking bones with every kick.

The creature healed fast. But not fast enough. The fifth kick broke its hold and, with a growl of anger, it fell into the portal and disappeared.

An instant later the brightly glowing anomaly bubble followed it through the portal.

CHAPTER 139

Holding on to the lower support railing on the stairs leading up to his primary gateway control station, and with less than thirty seconds remaining until the anomaly's event horizon breached its containment field, Dr. Stephenson had found himself mesmerized by the fight between the Kasari and the blond Swedish electrical technician. As hard as it was to believe, the big Swede had managed to survive the latest Kasari attack and was busy kicking its face in with his brown work boots. Then the Kasari's grip on the man's leg faltered and it slipped away, sucked across the pressure differential into the wormhole.

More importantly, one of the security guards, the team's lone female, had clawed her way up to a seated position at the secondary stasis field generator controls. And, although he could scarcely believe what he was seeing, she grabbed the secondary stasis field control joysticks, somehow managing to thrust the anomaly through the wormhole after the Kasari.

Despite the relief that coursed through his veins at the extinguishment of the current threat, he wasn't happy. The anomaly was gone, the Earth would survive, and he still had time to restore the gateway connection to the Kasari Collective, but something was still very wrong.

As he fought the wind on his way back up the steps to his control station, the image of the black-clad security dyke manning the secondary stasis controls replayed in his mind. No hesitation in her actions. She'd handled the controls as if she'd designed them, exactly as Dr. Ivanovich had handled them, far better than Dr. Trotsky, the scientist trained for that job.

Sliding into his chair and bracing his feet against the control station's steel framing, Stephenson pulled up the gateway diagnostics and confirmed the wormhole's remote location, deep in empty space. Even if the anomaly absorbed enough nearby matter to become a major black hole, it would take a very long time, and even then, there were no significant star systems near enough to worry about.

Shifting back to the gateway controls, as Stephenson prepared to enter the Kasari synchronization codes, he spared one last glance at the female security guard. She met his gaze, her eyes freezing him in place. As years of age melted from her face, the shock of recognition hit him. The McFarland girl!

Seeing her shove the stasis field control joysticks up and to her right, Stephenson dived off the rear side of the platform as it came apart all around him, heavy steel shrapnel ripping into his chest and neck as he tumbled the thirty feet to the concrete cavern floor, the impact breaking his right leg, sending the jagged edge of his splintered femur jutting out through his upper thigh.

He rolled right, grabbed a steel strut, and pulled himself under a piece of the damaged structure. Heather McFarland. The little bitch had tried to kill him.

It was no wonder he'd failed to recognize her. He'd watched ten years melt from her features in a second. Suddenly several pieces of the puzzle snapped into place. All this time he'd overlooked what was right in front of his face. Those three kids had been involved on the periphery of every key event for the last two years. The clues had been there all along.

Freaks of nature. No. Not nature. The Altreian starship!

They must have stumbled onto it long before the government found it inside that Bandolier cave. Only they'd done something to it, activated equipment that altered them, swallowed the Altreian anti-Kasari propaganda, become surrogate soldiers executing the Altreians' twisted agenda. And if Heather McFarland was here, the Smythe twins had probably penetrated the project as well. And they'd done a damned fine job of sabotaging his big day.

The depressurization wind had stopped. That meant they'd cut power to the gateway, most likely by physically damaging the cables with the secondary stasis field.

Bending at the waist, Donald Stephenson grabbed his right knee and shoved, forcing the splintered bone back inside the already healing wound. With a deep breath he checked the nanite repairs to his lungs and throat. Good.

As for McFarland and the Smythes, they were about to find out neither he nor his project was quite so easy to kill.

CHAPTER 140

Mark managed to hook his left elbow around the portal's super-structure, levering himself around the side and out of the brunt of the howling wind. The shriek of tearing steel brought his head around in time to see the primary control platform come apart like a sheep in a raptor's jaws. He didn't see Dr. Stephenson, but if he was inside that, he was dead.

Then the gateway died, the wormhole winking out, whipping Mark's body through another rapid pressure change that dropped him to his knees. Behind him, the crackle of electrical arcs and the smell of burning insulation told him all he needed to know. Restoring gateway power wasn't going to be a simple task.

Climbing back to his feet, Mark looked up at the secondary stasis field control station. Heather sat slumped forward over the controls, a jagged piece of steel sticking three inches out of her back.

WORMHOLE

Ignoring the blood leaking from his own side, Mark raced toward her and cleared the first row of workstations, his next jump landing him beside her chair.

Mark tilted her gently back, hearing his own breath hiss through his teeth. The sheet metal shard had penetrated just beneath her collarbone, high enough to miss her lung, but it was two inches wide. So much blood. Her uniform was soaked in it, and it had puddled in her chair, more dripping down through the steel grate below.

Mark tore off his shirt, ripped it in half, and knelt beside her.

Her brown eyes crinkled at the corners, a weak smile lifting the corners of her mouth.

"We did it."

"Yes we did. But we're not done yet." Mark squeezed her hand. "This is going to hurt."

Holding her shoulder back with his left hand, Mark squeezed the steel sliver with his right. He looked into Heather's beautiful face, saw no fear, and nodded.

Mark pulled. One swift, smooth pull. And although Heather made no sound, to his ears the passage of the metal shard out of her body sounded like a Civil War amputation saw. As the shard popped free, her blood splashed his on face, its metallic odor filling his nostrils.

Ripping off her shirt, Mark tore off the sleeves and used them to bind the balled-up halves of his own shirt into a tight pressure bandage. As he prepared to lift her from her chair, he saw the calf wound.

"Jesus Christ!"

Mark grabbed her ripped pant leg and tore it free. The wound was a jagged tear in the calf muscle, not arterial, but another bloody mess. Using the pant leg to bind the remains of her shirt to her calf, Mark tied it off, stood, and lifted Heather into his arms as rising despair threatened to overwhelm him. He'd already lost his sister today. He couldn't take losing Heather too.

"Hang on to my neck. I'll get you out of here."

When Heather didn't respond, he glanced down at her face. Her eyes were half closed, gone back to milky white. That was fine. Let her visions carry her away from the pain and sorrow of the present. In the meantime he'd get her the hell out of the death and destruction within the ATLAS cavern.

CHAPTER 141

The Swiss Air Force captain turned to see an American warrant officer approaching his chopper.

Annoyance tingeing his heavily accented English, he leaned sideways in the cockpit, his voice rising above the copter noise.

"I'm sorry, this is an emergency medevac flight. No passengers."

The American held out a sheaf of papers. The pages, buffeted by the rotor wash, revealed the noise suppressor screwed into the barrel of the Glock nine-millimeter pistol.

"Out of the chopper!"

As the captain hesitated, a small *spat*, like a sandal slapping the pavement, was the only sound that accompanied the slug through his thigh.

"Shit!"

Jack pointed the gun at the flight medic sitting next to the pilot.

"Last chance."

The man scrambled out of the cockpit, dragging the pilot out onto the tarmac with him as Jack stepped in and throttled the engine.

Just as at other area hospitals, the emergency staff at Meyrin's Hospital La Tour was overwhelmed. The panic that had spread at the televised reports from the ATLAS cavern had gotten worse after the loss of the live broadcast feed. So it didn't surprise him that there was no immediate reaction to his theft of the medevac helicopter.

As the EC635 lifted off from the hospital's improvised helipad, a security guard ran from the emergency entrance, fumbling with his holster strap. The spray of blood out the back of his head interrupted his attempt to draw his weapon.

Jack maneuvered the stick, waggling the chopper's enclosed tail rotor at the high window half a block away, and banked toward the LHC's ATLAS facility. Thumbing the TRANSMIT button on his QT-modified cell phone, he spoke loud enough to be heard above the cockpit noise.

"Nice shooting, babe. Pack it up."

Janet's voice came right back at him.

"OK, my lover. Go get our team."

CHAPTER 142

Heather opened her eyes as Mark climbed the stairs onto the third level of scaffolding that draped the ATLAS cavern's outer walls. Although the depressurization had pulled several of the scientists and technical crew from these walkways, many more, including a number of the scientists who had manned the ATACC workstations on the cavern floor, had managed to make their way to the exits during the fight that had raged through the cavern and the subsequent gateway malfunctions.

"We can't leave yet."

Her voice brought Mark to a stop. "What?"

"Stephenson's not dead."

Mark swung his gaze out onto the cavern floor, where Dr. Stephenson had just climbed out from beneath a rubble pile like some kind of giant cockroach.

"Doesn't matter. No way he can fix that," Mark said, nodding toward the Cage and its spark-spitting mess of cables.

"We have to make sure."

Understanding dawned on Mark's face.

"The nukes."

"We've got to set the timer."

Mark turned to look up at the high ramp that ran along the cavern ceiling and into the topmost part of the Cage. Back in that jumble of wires and cables was the spot where he'd bypassed the trigger line to the nukes.

"Might be hot."

"Let's hope not. The shorts in the power cables are low down in the Cage and each level is electrically isolated from the others."

Mark nodded. "OK, I'll do it."

"I should go with you."

"Not in your condition." Before she could object, he continued. "Your body stays here. Your mind can come along for the ride."

Both of them reached for their alien headsets, slipping them into place at the same time.

Nothing happened.

Heather couldn't understand it. No gentle tingling. Nothing. Her headset was just dead. She didn't need to look at Mark to know that his was dead too.

"Shit!"

Heather looked up at him. "We'll just have to do it the hard way then."

Mark set her down with her back against the steel wall. "Wait until I get up there and then you can try to make the mind link. If you can't manage it, don't push yourself. I don't need your help to set the timer."

As he turned away and vaulted up the stairs that would take him to the ladder that led to the high ramp, Heather fought off a fresh wave of dizziness. She had no doubts about Mark's capabilities. But what if stray voltage managed to travel through one of the nest of cables through which Mark would have to crawl to reach their splice? If she wasn't there with him, seeing what he saw, how could she sense what to touch and what to avoid?

Sitting up just a little straighter, Heather watched the muscles ripple across Mark's bare back as he moved up onto the ladder that would take him all the way to the top. She'd just have to make sure she stayed conscious long enough to make that happen.

CHAPTER 143

Mark knew the Cage inside and out. He'd installed a significant portion of the electronics, cables, and super-cooling equipment. The construction crew had been exceptional, but the workmanship was only average. The focus had been on making everything work and staying on schedule. That meant taking shortcuts here and there. It was one of the reasons Mark lacked complete faith in the electrical isolation between cage sections.

Although they'd thought it unlikely the military would actually remotely detonate the bombs, given the potential consequences, two weeks ago Heather had decided to have him disable the remote circuit, but leave the manual timer in place. The tricky part of creating the new circuit had been blocking remote detonation signals from reaching the bombs, while providing positive circuit test feedback to prevent anyone from detecting his splice.

As he reached the top rung of the ladder and stepped out onto the skywalk, he reached up and touched the concrete cavern ceiling, an old habit whenever he came up here. Not many people on the project had touched both ceiling and floor, and even though he was about to turn the whole thing into radioactive slag, he couldn't suppress the surge of pride in what he'd helped accomplish here.

Reaching the Cage, he pulled out his hot-circuit detector, checked around the entrance, and stepped inside. As his rubber-soled boots touched the steel grating, he felt Heather slide into his mind. She didn't try to communicate, but he felt her invade his senses, doing something he'd never experienced before. Heather wasn't sharing her visions, but manipulating the color of everything he saw. The effect was breathtaking. Greens and blues were good. The farther things got into the red end of the spectrum the greater the danger they presented.

Unfortunately, he wasn't seeing a lot of greens and blues.

Mark didn't know how long Heather could keep this up. He couldn't even imagine how deep she must have gone to make this happen, but it had to mean she'd totally abandoned trying to control the blood flow to her wounds. Mark just hoped his pressure bandages were good enough.

Moving as quickly as he dared along the narrow passage, Mark allowed his neuromuscular system to work its magic, sliding his body past dangerous wires, cables, and metal supports without accidentally touching any of them. He remembered how cool he'd once felt traversing the packed Los Alamos High hallway without brushing up against any of his classmates. That had been effortless; this was damned hard.

Reaching a point where a crawl space spilled off to his right, Mark opened one of the pre-positioned tool kits, extracted the tools he needed, slid them into his belt, and entered.

Damn. It looked like a red-and-yellow laser light show. For fifteen meters he worked harder than he'd ever worked in his life, contorting his body over, under, and around hot protrusions.

When Mark reached the panel that hid the nuclear timer device, he was relieved to find it a cool turquoise color. Unscrewing the panel from its supports, careful to avoid tipping the anti-tamper mercury switch, he set it aside. Then he inserted a tiny screwdriver, setting the timer for twenty minutes. Setting the tools on the floor, Mark didn't bother to replace the cover panel.

Unable to turn around within the crawlway, he prepared himself for the reverse passage. Then Heather's mind link went out.

Heather? You out there?

No response.

"Shit, shit, shit!"

Taking a deep, steadying breath, Mark forced his heart rate down to forty-six beats per minute. Time to find out just how perfect his memory really was.

CHAPTER 144

Jack flew over the top of the building that provided access to the ATLAS cavern, searching for the best place to put the chopper down. But he had no intention of landing until he got a call from Mark's, Heather's, or Jennifer's QT phone. It struck him that the *quantum twin* acronym was no longer adequate. Each of these devices had at its core one of five quantum-entangled particles, making each one operate as if it were part of a five-way conference call.

Of course they had to be turned on to work. He'd had no signal from Mark, Heather, or Jennifer yet and they were already five minutes behind schedule. As he hovered over the parking lot, he spotted people streaming out of the building, some climbing into vehicles, some lying on the ground as others sought to apply first aid. Some members of the crowd waved up at him, signaling for him to land.

Then Jack spotted Mark running toward an open space between buildings, Heather's limp body in his arms. He brought the chopper in for a hot LZ pickup, the skids never touching the ground as Mark lifted Heather inside and then swung up. Gaining speed and altitude, Jack banked away toward Lake Geneva.

Mark slammed the door shut, stretched Heather out, grabbed the medic bag, and began prepping a plasma IV.

"Jennifer?"

Mark's voice caught in his throat. "She didn't make it."

Jack reached back to place a hand on Mark's shoulder. "I'm sorry."

Mark nodded. "We're going to need some distance."

"How long?"

"Twelve minutes, eighteen seconds."

"OK. Got one more pickup on our way out."

Swabbing Heather's forearm with an alcohol swab, Mark slid the needle into her vein. "Good, maybe Janet can help me get the bleeding stopped."

Jack glanced back at Heather's bloody body, her pale face, and the purplish tint of her lips, then turned to face front, extracting every bit of speed the chopper could manage. He wanted to say he'd seen worse, that he'd been worse, something to assuage Mark's rising panic.

But no words would help Mark, so he kept his thoughts to himself.

Shut up and fly, Jack. Just shut up and fly.

CHAPTER 145

After Donald Stephenson had pulled himself out of the pile of rubble that was all that remained of his primary control station, a quick glance around the chamber had brought home the extent of the destruction inflicted by the McFarland girl. In addition to destroying the primary control station, she'd used the secondary stasis field to sever the main lines that supplied power to the gateway and to the stasis field generators.

But she'd overlooked one thing. The stasis field generators had a bank of emergency capacitors modeled on the advanced Rho Ship capacitor design. They couldn't store enough power to activate the gateway, but they had plenty of capacity to provide twenty minutes of secondary stasis field operation. And twenty minutes was all he needed.

Dr. Stephenson moved across the cavern floor, passing directly in front of the gateway device, its interior dimly lit by the red glow of emergency lighting and the reflected glitter of electrical lines arcing within the damaged power cage, where severed cables hissed and spat like angry cobras. Mounting the three tiers of steps that led to the secondary stasis field control station, he glanced at the blood pooled in and around the chair bolted to the steel grating. He dipped his fingers into it, raising them to his nose. Dr. Stephenson wasn't sure that it was enough to prove fatal to the McFarland girl, but it brightened his day.

Ignoring the blood, Dr. Stephenson seated himself in front of the terminal. The workstation was still powered on, drawing on its uninterruptable power supply's fifteen-minute backup battery. The battery indicator showed just over half of that charge remaining. Pulling up the emergency override panel, he switched power sources from primary to the emergency capacitor backup. As he tapped this new source, the battery warning indicator disappeared.

Dr. Stephenson's fingers danced across the keyboard, entering the commands that would bring the secondary stasis field generator back online. While he wasn't as quick as Raul's neural net, he was far from slow. An invisible bubble expanded across the cavern until it encompassed the area around his workstation, the stasis field generators, the gateway device, and, finally, the damaged portion of the power cage.

With that protective barrier in place there would be no further outside interference. Manipulating individual stasis field tendrils, he began repairing damaged power cables, making use of the network of cameras and instrumentation available to him. And without his having to worry about killing the power in the hot lines, his repairs proceeded far faster than any team of electrical engineers could have made them.

His first priority was to restore power from the matter ingester. That would allow him to dump a full charge back into the backup capacitors, as well as providing the power he needed to reopen the Kasari gateway.

Suddenly the outside of the stasis bubble went white. Despite the nearly perfect shielding, Dr. Stephenson felt his retinas burn out, momentarily blinding him before the nanites in his bloodstream could repair the damage. Only one thing could account for that flash, a nuclear detonation. And while the stasis field had protected him from the initial radiation and blast effects, all hope of restoring power had just evaporated, along with the unprotected parts of the ATLAS cavern and all the surrounding facilities.

Without being able to see it, Dr. Stephenson knew that only the stasis field kept him safe from the intense radiation and the super-hurricane force shock wave that hurled debris outward from the blast. In a few minutes those same winds would rush back to fill the void they had left behind. And although the emergency capacitor power would probably last long enough to protect him from that, no amount of nanites could save him from the hell that awaited when the stasis field began to die.

As his vision slowly returned, Dr. Stephenson rose to his feet to stare at the surreal scene. Like a child's snow globe, a dome of protection surrounded the undamaged section of the cavern while a roiling inferno altered the surrounding landscape. The ATLAS cavern was gone, the walls vaporized for hundreds of meters in all directions, the rock beyond that reshaped into a bowl of glowing molten glass.

With the scope of his failure burning his brain like a hot tong shoved up his nose, Dr. Stephenson turned in a full circle. In a handful of minutes, the secondary stasis field would slowly begin to fail, bathing him in a radioactive dose equivalent to that of a bad sunburn, painful but nothing his nanites couldn't repair. Then, in a decaying exponential, the radiation would keep rising, and, as when an egg was boiled in a microwave, there would come a point when fluids burst through the skin as his juices boiled away.

How long would it take him to die?

Not liking the result of his mental calculations, Dr. Donald Stephenson turned back to the secondary stasis field control station. For two and a half seconds, his finger hovered over the KILL POWER button. Then, as his finger descended, the protective stasis field winked out.

CHAPTER 146

President Jackson and his national security staff stared at the televisions, all tuned to CNN. At first the reporter had seemed to experience a kind of meltdown, but had regained her calm.

"For those of you who may have just joined us, we continue to follow our top story, the international effort to prevent the November Anomaly from becoming a black hole that threatens to destroy our planet. As we have been reporting, within the last few minutes we've received reports of a nuclear detonation centered at the ATLAS cavern. We go now to our White House correspondent Rolf Larson.

"Rolf. This has been just another in a sequence of what can only be described as disastrous events. Has there been any official White House response?"

"Karen, we've been awaiting an official statement on what has transpired within the ATLAS facility, beginning with what appeared to be an attempted alien invasion through the Rho Gateway, followed by a series of explosions and the loss of all broadcast feeds from within the cavern itself, culminating in a nuclear explosion at the site."

"Rolf, excuse me for interrupting, but we've just received confirmation that there has been a nuclear explosion at the ATLAS cavern. We are just getting the first video of the mushroom cloud as seen from Geneva. Oh my God. This is something we hoped never to see in our lifetimes."

"Karen, we're seeing it here on our monitors. This has to be heartbreaking for anyone with family members working at the site, for the military units that were positioned around the ATLAS site, and for the Swiss and French people. We here at CNN have also suffered the loss of Ted Cantrell and our entire crew reporting from the scene..."

From his position at the head of the table, the president muted the broadcast and turned toward Cory Mayfield, his director of national intelligence.

"Cory?"

"We've got General Smith holding on the line from Ramstein."

President Jackson pushed a button on his control console.

"General Smith. This is President Jackson here in the Situation Room with my entire national security staff. Give me a rundown of what you know."

"Mr. President, as you are aware, our attempts to remotely detonate the nuclear devices failed despite several attempts to correct the problem. Army Captain William Everett, our on-site nuclear weapons specialist, volunteered to manually detonate the nuclear warheads. From the fact that we're all still alive, it is clear that, despite the naysayers in the scientific community, the nuclear option destroyed the November Anomaly and the gateway."

"Casualties?"

"Only estimates so far, Mr. President. Each warhead had a twenty-kiloton yield. The blast occurred a hundred meters below ground. That's both good and bad. The ground helped limit the range of the immediate blast effects as well as the initial gamma pulse, but we'll see a lot of alpha and beta fallout due to the amount of dirt and debris sucked up into the mushroom cloud. Prevailing winds are westerly at ten knots. That's bad for Switzerland, Austria, and parts of Bavaria and Italy, but good news for most of the major European population centers.

"Our worst case estimate shows up to ten thousand killed in the initial blast, maybe ten times that over the coming weeks and months. I'll need data from our nuclear survey teams before I can be definitive."

"Thank you, General. That's all for now."

President Jackson disconnected the call as the door opened to admit Carol Owens, his chief of staff. Seeing the look on her face, President Jackson almost dreaded to ask.

"OK, Carol. What's happened now?"

"Mr. President, I just took a call from Dr. David Kronen at Los Alamos. The Rho Ship is gone."

The information failed to register. "Gone?"

"Yes, sir. Dr. Kronen says that one moment it was there and the next it disappeared and took half the building with it. Fifteen people are missing and presumed dead. If it had occurred during the day, we would have lost hundreds."

"What time did this happen?"

Carol swallowed. "Shortly after we lost the television feed from the ATLAS cavern."

The president lowered his head, massaging his temples with his hands. When he raised his face again, he looked directly into Carol's eyes.

"I want to keep this away from the public for three days. Tell Dr. Kronen he has that long to get me some answers. For now, we have to stay focused on the events in Switzerland."

Turning his gaze to the others at the table, he continued.

"Well, folks, we've got a bunch of frightened and angry people out there, all of them wanting to know what the hell just happened and what comes next. We can't deny being behind the nuclear detonation, nor do I intend to. So an hour from now I'm going to walk out into the White House Briefing Room and lay it all on the line. You've got until then to come up with the best way to spin it."

A sudden, unseemly surge of joy spread through the president. Yes, he'd been responsible for the killing of tens of thousands of innocent people, but he'd saved the planet. All things considered, not a bad day's work.

CHAPTER 147

Freddy Hagerman eased up the steps, trying to avoid busting his ass on the ice. Eight days after the almost-end of the earth, his fake leg wasn't doing him any favors. At the front door he paused, his finger hovering an inch from the doorbell. His timing was unusual, to say the least. Six thirty on a Monday morning wasn't the time he usually called on people. It wasn't a time people expected strangers to come calling. Or friends either, for that matter. But at this hour he knew the McFarlands would be home and so would their next-door neighbors, and he didn't want to have to do this more than once.

He pressed the button, hearing the chime echo through the house. Thirty seconds later a tall, slender man opened the door, a questioning look in his brown eyes.

"May I help you?"

"Mr. McFarland, my name is Freddy Hagerman."

The kindly look departed as if Freddy had slapped him. As the door began to close, Freddy stopped it with his left hand. "I'm sorry, but I really have to speak with you."

"I don't talk to reporters. Can't you people leave us alone?"

"This concerns your daughter and her friends."

If anything, McFarland's face grew colder. "It always does. Now get out of my doorway and off my steps before I call the police."

As the man reached out to shove him out of the way, Freddy held out a DVD case. "They sent you a video message."

Mr. McFarland froze, confusion clouding his features.

"If you'll let me in, I'll explain everything."

For several seconds nothing happened. Then McFarland blinked twice and stepped back to allow Freddy entrance. Stepping inside before he could reconsider, Freddy pulled off his brown leather driving gloves and stuffed them into his coat pocket.

"Who is it, Gil?"

Freddy turned to see a comely woman step into the living room, her right hand pushing a strand of gray-streaked brown hair behind her right ear.

"OK, you're in," Mr. McFarland said, his voice suddenly husky. "Say what you came to say."

Glancing back and forth between the two McFarlands, Freddy unbuttoned his coat.

"I'm here because last night I met with the president of the United States and agreed to hold off on publication of my story for one more day. For his part, he agreed to allow me to meet with you and the Smythes before he takes action based upon my story."

Holding up the DVD case, Freddy focused on Mrs. McFarland. "Heather and Mark recorded this video message and had it delivered to me two days ago, along with instructions that I first watch it with you and the Smythes. So here I am."

As his wife's knees buckled, Mr. McFarland grabbed her, supporting her to a seat on the couch.

"I'm OK, Gil. I'm not a child." As she turned to look at Freddy, Mrs. McFarland's damp eyes held his, her face regaining its composure. "I'm sorry, I didn't catch your name."

"Freddy. Freddy Hagerman."

"Mr. Hagerman, please take off your coat. I'll get some coffee started while Gil goes over to get Fred and Linda."

"Anna…"

"Gil, I told you, I'm fine. Now hurry over and get our friends. As for the coffee, I think we're going to need it."

By the time they'd watched Mark and Heather's video and Freddy had finished his story, Freddy felt as if every emotion had been physically wrung from his body, leaving behind an empty husk.

Gil and Fred had both called in sick, and Freddy knew that wasn't far from the truth. Despite the happiness that came from discovering that Mark and Heather were alive and well, the shock of Jennifer's heroic sacrifice had clearly left both families feeling as if they'd lost her a second time.

Against that backdrop, Freddy told his tale of government deceit, beginning with the murder of Jonathan Riles, the betrayal of Jack's team, and the sequence of murders and criminal actions that had eventually led to Mark, Heather, and Jennifer's flight to Bolivia, and their subsequent capture, torture, and escape.

The lead story in tomorrow's *New York Post* would carry Freddy's byline. But tonight the president would hold a nationally televised, prime-time press conference, informing the nation of the actions he would be taking to ensure the abuses detailed in Freddy's investigative report were properly dealt with and appropriate measures put in place to ensure that they could never happen again.

Now, as Freddy slid into his coat, said his good-byes, and trudged through the cold wind toward the rental car that would take him back to Albuquerque, he realized just how hungry he was. That was OK. He'd wait until he got to the airport to down a burger and a beer while he watched the president cover his ass.

In the meantime he'd savor the knowledge that the McFarlands and Smythes knew far more of the story than the president or public ever would. As far as the US government knew, Heather McFarland and the Smythe twins had perished in the nuclear explosion that killed so many at the ATLAS site. And Freddy intended to leave it that way.

CHAPTER 148

It had been almost a month since that fateful day in the ATLAS cavern. Seven kilometers southeast of Mesão Frio, Portugal, a cold breeze swept the vineyards that fell away toward the River Douro. Beautiful in spring, summer, and fall, the harsh specter of winter held the wine region in its deathly grasp, stripping the vines, leaving them as barren as this winter night. Though she felt the ghosts of all the innocents she'd killed reach out through those twisted vines, it was another ghost that brought Heather to her knees.

Aided by her augmented neural system's control over her human growth hormone production, her physical injuries had healed. The same couldn't be said of her mental wounds. Heather knelt beside Mark, tears leaking from her eyes to drip from nose and chin into the rich soil. And as Mark wept unashamedly beside her, Jack and Janet stood watch a short distance up the hill.

It was an odd place for a memorial service, no pastor or priest, only Mark and Heather kneeling together in the barren vineyard, crying and laughing, as a lifetime of Jennifer memories played through their shared minds. And though they had nothing of Jennifer left to hold in their hands, she would live forever inside them.

Their last sight of her standing beside Raul in the Rho Ship was almost too painful to bear, but they replayed it, sending out the good-byes they'd never had a chance to voice. Jennifer had launched the Rho Ship into its own wormhole, leaving nothing of herself for them to bury. Heather raised her face to the heavens. Somewhere in that vast emptiness between the stars, Jennifer's body floated, entombed with Raul inside the Rho Ship. The loneliness of the vision loosed a new round of sobs that left Heather shaking so hard that, had not Mark swept her into his powerful arms, she would have sunk to the ground.

When the sobs died away, she leaned back, wiped the tears from her face and then from Mark's, kissed him full upon the lips, and rose to her feet. Holding tight to his hand, she led him back through the vines to where Jack and Janet waited. Then, without a word being spoken, they began the half-kilometer walk back to their rented farmhouse.

E P I L O G U E

The panelists on *This Week with Carl Langford* included Missouri Senator Fred Charles, Ohio Congresswoman Beverly Francis, and Pulitzer Prize–winning investigative journalist Freddy Hagerman.

Senator Charles interrupted Congresswoman Francis. "Of course you're going to support the president. That's what you do. But there are a growing number of people who aren't toeing the official line, including many in the scientific community. You and those of your political persuasion have convinced yourselves that we narrowly averted an alien invasion facilitated by the Rho Project Gateway Device. Isn't it possible, even likely, that what we witnessed on the video feed from the ATLAS cavern was first contact with an alien race that has done nothing but provide us with highly beneficial technologies, a badly botched first contact?"

The congresswoman snorted. "Did you miss the way your 'friendly' aliens attacked our people?"

"Their first sight, upon stepping through the portal, was of a device that they would have identified as a bomb, along with security people who began shooting at them. Why wouldn't they defend themselves?"

"And what would you have us do? Rebuild the device?"

"I think we need to give the matter careful consideration. Clearly this alien race has benign intentions. Look at all the good that has come from our Rho Project research. Perhaps we can improve upon Dr. Stephenson's gateway design, send through a message expressing our deep regret at what happened in that first encounter, explain what we were trying to do with the anomaly."

"Senator." Freddy Hagerman practically spit the word onto the table. "Let's look at all the good that has come from your beneficial alien technologies. We have wars breaking out across the Middle East because of cold fusion. The Russians and Chinese have begun widespread distribution of their own versions of the nanite formula to their populations, starting with their military personnel. Blood-worshiping gangs of virtual zombies are draining nanited people in parts of Africa and South America. We're on the verge of the most catastrophic population explosion in history."

"All the more reason to seek a guiding hand."

As the argument escalated to the point that the host had to go to commercial, Janet called out from the kitchen.

"Jack. Turn that thing off and come to dinner. I think I liked it better before we installed the satellite dish and generator."

Pressing the OFF button on the remote, Jack walked into the kitchen.

"Perhaps you could provide a little distraction."

"Ha. That'll have to wait." She handed Jack the spoon. "Here, stir this for me."

Walking across the room, Janet stepped out onto the raised platform, her voice breaking the rain forest's late-afternoon silence.

"Robby. Come inside."

"But Momma …"

"No buts. You can play with your imaginary friend after dinner."

~ ~ ~

As the metallic tan Camry cruised along the rural New Zealand highway, Lilly Cravits adjusted the picnic basket on her knees and turned to look at Caroline and Wanda in the backseat.

"It'll be so fun to see their faces. Such a nice young couple. They've been working so hard to fix up the old Wagner farm."

To her right, James Cravits glanced up from his driving and harrumphed. "How do you know they're nice? You've barely met them. They could be on the run from the law for all you know."

"James! Really! Where do you come up with this stuff? They're nice."

"I don't know. They can't be older than twenty-five. How'd they get the money to buy the Wagner place? Why would young people want to move to rural New Zealand if not to get away?"

Turning her attention to her two friends in the back, Lilly rolled her eyes. "Well, I had a very nice talk when Amanda and Robert stopped by the store yesterday. They were software developers and made a lot of money off a cell phone app they created."

"So they moved to New Zealand?"

"They wanted to get closer to the earth."

James laughed. "Well, they'll get their wish, if I know the Wagner farm. I give them three months."

James slowed, turning off State Highway 6 onto a dirt road that led to the Wagner farmhouse. Sitting on four hundred acres of good farmland that stretched along the south side of the Pelorus River, the two-story timber house stood near an ancient-looking wooden barn, both badly in need of repair.

They'd just gotten out of the car when Amanda Blake stepped out onto the front porch and waved. James had to admit that she was a real looker, even in her dirty jeans and T-shirt, her face smudged with dirt.

"Excuse my looks. I'd have cleaned up if I'd known company was coming."

"Nonsense," Lilly said. "I knew you'd be in fix-up mode after all the hardware you two bought down in Havelock yesterday. The ladies and I thought you and Robert could use a couple of good meals that you didn't have to prepare."

Amanda's smile lit her face. "Oh, that's so nice. Here, let me help you with one of those baskets. Wow, these pies smell wonderful. And baked ham? Robert's going to think you're his fairy godmothers."

Following Amanda into the kitchen, they had just set the baskets on the counter when Robert Blake walked through the door. Also in jeans and a T-shirt, he was even dirtier than his wife. But as James shook Robert's hand, feeling the strength in the young man's iron grip, seeing his easy grin, he decided his Lilly was right after all.

Throughout the introductions and the shared lunch, he found himself genuinely enjoying their company. When the meal finally ended and they stepped out on the porch to say their good-byes, James actually regretted that the visit had come to an end.

As he slid into the driver's seat, he felt Lilly nudge his arm with her elbow.

"Well, James, you've met the Blakes. What do you think now?"

Starting the engine, he stuck his right arm out the window and waved.

"A vigorous young couple."

Lilly's laughter trailed behind them as they turned out of the driveway and onto State Highway 6 for the short drive back to Canvastown.

~ ~ ~

On the old farmhouse porch, Mark's arms encircled Heather's waist from behind, his lips softly brushing her neck.

"You know, after all that eating, I'm feeling a bit tired."

Heather turned to face him, her arms tracing a path up around his neck. "Tired, huh?"

A wicked grin spread across Mark's face.

"Nothing a little roll in the hay couldn't cure."

She raised her lips to his, then pulled back.

"What do you say we skip the hay?"

Sweeping her up in his arms, Mark carried his dangerous little wife across the threshold into their new home.

The farm work would wait for the morrow.

ACKNOWLEDGMENTS

I want to thank Alan Werner for brainstorming this story with me, putting in many long hours as we explored the twists and turns that brought it to this conclusion. I also want to express my thanks to my agent, Paul Lucas, and to the 47North Author Team who worked hard to help me bring this work to a broader audience. My fabulous editor, the talented Jeff VanderMeer, helped me put the finishing touches on all three of the Rho Agenda novels and his expert touch is evident throughout. Finally, I want to thank my wife, Carol, whose love, support, and encouragement make life worth living.

ABOUT THE AUTHOR

Richard Phillips was born in Roswell, New Mexico, in 1956. He graduated from the United States Military Academy at West Point in 1979 and qualified as an Army Ranger, going on to serve as an officer in the US Army. He earned a master's degree in physics from Naval Postgraduate School, completing his thesis work at Los Alamos National Laboratory. After working for three years as a research associate at Lawrence Livermore National Laboratory, he returned to the army to complete his tour of duty. Today he lives in Phoenix, Arizona, with his wife, Carol, dividing his time between developing simulation software for the US military and writing science fiction.